MY HERO

"Good God! I should've known it was you!"

I started at the familiar and unwelcome tones of a certain fish-and-fowl officer. You know. The one who was placed on this earth to be a major irritant to me. My very own life-sized hemorrhoid that no amount of cooling gel or soothing pads could shrink.

I pulled myself to a sitting position, wincing at the pain in my shoulder and the sogginess on my butt. "You almost ran me over, you—you speed freak!" I lashed out, the terror of the evening fueling my response. That and my wet hiney and lovely new water moccasins. I felt myself being hauled up out of the ditch with a sincere lack of gentleness.

"Run you over? Run you over? Hell, you were in the middle of the gawd-damned road in the middle of the gawd-damned night!" Far from the soothing, sympathetic, reassuring tones I needed, my rescuer's voice was harsh and accusatory. "Tressa Jayne Turner, you could be the poster child for the slogan *Shit Happens*."

Humpf. Clearly, this big, dumb oaf had missed Oprah's series on Sensitive Men and the Women Who Love Them.

KATHLEEN BACUS

CALAMITY JAYNE

LOVE SPELL

NEW YORK CITY

LOVE SPELL®

January 2006

Published by

Dorchester Publishing Co., Inc.
200 Madison Avenue
New York, NY 10016

ISBN 0-505-52665-4

Printed in the United States of America.

Visit us on the web at www.dorchesterpub.com.

To my mother, Betty,
for passing along the newspaper clipping
that started it all. Thanks, Mom!

To my eldest son, Nick,
and the triplets, Katie, Erick and Ashley,
for enduring way too many soup and salad nights
and micro-meals, and where the Chinese Buffet
became "home-cooked." Thanks for hanging in
there with me, guys. You're the greatest!

And finally, to Glynna,
who never let me give up.
You're next, woman!

CALAMITY JAYNE

Chapter 1

"Know what you call five blondes at the bottom of the ocean? An air pocket."

My lip curled. Despite the distorted cutting in and out of the Dairee Freeze intercom, I'd know that voice anywhere. "You know why Indians didn't scalp brunettes? The hair from a buffalo's butt was more manageable. May I take your order, please?"

"I was going to order some buffalo wings, but you've spoiled the moment. How about a chicken basket with onion rings?"

"With mouthwash on the side, I hope. Anything to drink?"

"A strawberry shake sounds good."

"That'll be five seventy-four. Please pull ahead."

I waited for the vehicle to move up, annoyed that this particular customer always seemed to know when I was working the drive-through. He pulled his candy apple red, four-by-four Chevy pickup truck alongside the narrow window.

"You still workin' here, Calamity?" he asked. "Gotta

be a record." He did an exaggerated head slap. "Oh, that's right. Your uncle owns the place. You have job security." He shoved a five and a one in my direction. "Keep the change," he said with a grin.

"Gee, thanks, Mr. Ranger, sir," I remarked. "Not working today? No reports of rabid skunks in the yard, snakes in the birdhouse, or bats in the bedroom? No varmints to relocate? No mating pelicans to spy on? Hey, somebody nailed a squirrel over at Second and Arthur. The tail was still moving. You might check that out."

Rick Townsend worked for the state Division of Natural Resources, enforcing fish and game laws. Three years ahead of me in school, "Ranger Rick" as I liked to call him, was, and still is, best buddy to my brother, Craig. And he was, and still is, a mega-irritant to me. Good-looking enough to be on magazine covers—and we're not talking *Field and Stream* here, ladies—Rick Townsend was still single and always looking. He had been known to step out with my archrival from my high school days, Annette Felders, a snobby brunette with drill team thighs and perfect hair, hence my brunette joke.

"No roadkill for me today, brat, but thanks for the tip. I plan to do some water-skiing later on. I'd ask you to join us, but, well, with you working two jobs . . ." He stuck his hands out, palms up, in a what-can-you-do? pose.

I grabbed his shake and passed it out the window to him, my fingers tightening around the cup, much as they ached to stiffen around his big, tanned, arrogant neck. The plastic lid popped off and the contents of the cup erupted over the sides and down my hand.

I thrust the mess at him. "Now see what you've done!"

"Me? What did I do?"

"You provoked me, that's what." I grabbed his chicken basket and dumped it in a sack. "You always provoke me."

"That's 'cause you're so much fun to watch get all riled up, Tressa," he had the audacity to admit.

I shoved his sack of food at him. "Will there be anything else, *sir?*" I asked, ticked at him but furious with myself for rising to his bait.

"Some ketchup would be nice. Oh, and one more thing. Did you hear about the blonde who sold her car so she would have gas money?"

I grabbed a handful of ketchup packets and baseballed them out the drive-up window. Unfortunately, Ranger Rick had moved on.

"One of these days I'm going to get the best of that Neanderthal," I said to no one in particular. I was going to have to spend yet another day slaving away at two jobs in order to pay the bills, while Joe Cool would be spending the afternoon on the lake, enjoying early June's unseasonably warm weather. "He's been a thorn in my side for more years than I care to count. A burr under my saddle. A pain in the—"

"Tressa, please, we have customers," Aunt Regina shushed me.

"Neck. I was going to say *neck*, Aunt Reggie."

She nodded. "Of course you were, Tressa. Of course you were. Don't you think you'd better get going? What time do you have to be at Bargain City?"

"My shift starts at two today," I answered, taking off my navy blue apron and handing it over to my aunt. "I'll have to go home and shower the deep fat fry smell off me, or Toby in sporting goods will be tailing me all night."

I work at a discount chain store in the electronics department. No, I didn't volunteer for electronics; it was the only opening available when I was looking for a job. As I frequently was. I figured I could bluff my way through, although I still have difficulty programming my VCR, don't know hip-hop from bebop, and am clueless when it comes to the latest popular video game systems. Still, with all those TVs in my department, I kept current on all the soaps, solved society's problems with *Montel* and *Maury*, and applauded Judge Judy's kick-butt justice. I could then receive free therapy with Dr. Phil after watching the aforementioned shows. Oh, and I got paid for it in the bargain. I'd say here my momma didn't raise no dummies, but the jury's still out on that one, I guess.

I jumped into my car, a 1987 white Plymouth Reliant four-door. Hey, it's all I can afford! I started it up, and cursed when I saw the gas gauge. The needle was below a quarter of a tank, and I put ten bucks worth in the other day. My little beater was going through petrol like my grandma went through Poligrip. I sniffed and frowned when I caught a whiff of gas (the car kind, not the onion ring kind). Just what I needed: a repair bill for a car that was on its last tires anyway. I wheeled out of the parking lot and checked my watch. Just enough time to run home, feed the critters, shower and change before heading back out for another exciting eight-hour shift at Bargain City.

I thought about Ranger Rick and the latest in his never-ending repertoire of dumb blonde jokes. I'd heard 'em all. "Hey, Calamity, didja hear about the blonde who took her new scarf back to the store because it was too tight?" Or, "She was so blonde that she got excited because she finished a jigsaw puzzle in six months and the box said 'two to four years.'" And, "Did you hear about the blonde who called to report a fire at her home? 'Just tell us how to get there, ma'am,' the dispatcher said. 'Duh,' replied the blonde. 'Big red truck.'" Ha, ha, ha.

Hey. My name is Tressa Jayne Turner, but in the small, rural Iowa hamlet I call home, I'm more often referred to as Calamity Jayne. Nice, huh? Okay. Level with me. You've already made some assumptions about me based solely on that rather unflattering nickname alone, haven't you? It's all right. Lots of folks who know me (all right, all right, and maybe some who don't) call me Calamity. I first started hearing that particular pet name when I was a wee, not-so-bonny lass with chronic skinned knees and chipped teeth. Since we're being honest with each other here, I must also confess I did my part to reinforce the undignified label, if not to earn it outright. It likely saw its beginnings way back in kindergarten when I took a bite out of my teacher's fake apple. Or possibly when I ran off and left my five-year-old sister in the restroom at the neighborhood park while chasing down "Little Peter" Patterson when he copped onto my baseball glove. Now that I think about it, poor "Little Peter" was never able to shake his nickname either. Hmm. Oh, in case you're wondering, my sister wasn't traumatized or anything. She was able to speak quite normally again in a month's time and had kicked that bed-wetting habit altogether by the next summer.

As an adolescent, and later, as a teenager, I learned to use my notoriety to achieve maximum favorable results. Translated, that meant minimum parental expectations. Which suited me just dandy at the time. Sandwiched between an all-state athlete big brother and a younger sister who really could be a rocket scientist (and look like a super-model doing it), mediocrity seemed the perfect place to hide.

Having a regularly assigned place at the low end of the curve is no big deal to a young girl whose only interest in school is the extracurricular activities it presents and where academics are just a minor inconvenience. However, as a grown woman nearing four-and-twenty, bearing the stigma of the "Calamity" label had become rather tiresome. So what if I've had more jobs since high school graduation than Bill Clinton has had lady friends, or Oprah has different-sized wardrobes? So what if I occasionally drive away from the service station with the gas pump nozzle still in my car and my giant sipper cup on the roof? "So what if I still haven't decided what I want to be when I grow up?"

I didn't realize I'd spoken out loud until I heard snickers from the car in the lane next to me and caught the amused looks of its two pimply-faced occupants. I resisted the urge to flip them the bird, made a right hand turn and headed north out of town.

I pushed my blonde, in need of fresh highlighting, hair away from my face and sighed. What was wrong with me? Why couldn't I find my—what was the word? *Niche*. Why did I move from one job to the next with no direction, no goals, no clue? My folks had insisted I take college courses at the area community college upon graduation. Two years and five changes in my course of study later, they threw up their hands and declared I was on my own until I knew what the devil I wanted to do with my life. At twenty, that didn't seem like such a big deal. Take a year off, find yourself, *then,* as the military slogan went: Be all that you can be. A stint in the military occurred to me until I saw the shoes they had to wear.

As the years went by and I was no closer to my destiny (the *Oprah* show topic two weeks ago), desperation set in. I lost more jobs than Jim Carrey did baby teeth; due, I know, to my dissatisfaction with the life I wasn't carving out for myself. With each job lost, the hated "Calamity" label was reinforced.

At Pammy's Pet Parlour I was let go after I released the sheriff's prized Doberman, Deputy Dawg, to his soon-to-be-ex-wife, Debbie. How was I to know they were embroiled in a bitter custody battle over an ill-mannered mutt with a skin condition and dog-breath?

Then there was the unpleasant incident at the tape factory. Let me tell you, Triple-M makes top-of-the-line adhesive. They were peeling me off that wall for hours.

The job at the local newspaper, now that was my absolute, all-time favorite. I was the crime beat reporter. My finger was on the pulse of the community, and I loved it. Okay, so I really picked up traffic court depositions and wrote obituaries. To this day I don't see how I could be faulted for switching those obit photos. I still maintain Miss Deanie Duncan looked a lot more like a Theodore (Stubby) P. Burkholder than Stubby P. Burkholder did.

I pulled into the gravel driveway of my humble abode. Okay, here's the really sad part. No, I don't still live with my parents. Give me a break. I live *next* to them. In a mobile home. My grandmother lived there until her health mandated she move in with her son and daughter-in-law, my pa and ma. Two years ago we swapped, her two bedroom double-wide for my room.

I pay rent. Almost every month, real regular-like.

I grew up on a modest acreage in a three-bedroom, split-level house. My father has worked at the same phone company for almost thirty years, although his employer has changed names five times in the last ten. My mother is a certified public accountant and does bookkeeping and taxes for a living. And no sirree, I *never* thought of following in their career footsteps—although I did think it would be cool to climb telephone poles with those spiky boots. However, since they use cherry pickers exclusively now, or so my father advises, I say where's the fun in that?

My golden retrievers, Butch and Sundance, were on me before I took two steps out of the car, one of the hazards of working at a fast food joint. They sniffed me and I ruffled their coats, wishing I had some fries to toss at them.

"How're you boys doin'? You been chasin' Gramma's cat again?" Butch and Sundance detested my grandmother's cat, Hermione. I know. Gag me. Gramma's as stubborn as they come. It took three falls and several broken bones before she finally admitted she needed someone close by all the time. My mother has a home-based office, so it works out well for both of them. I admire my mother. It takes a very disciplined person to conduct business under her own roof, especially with a cranky old lady around. I'd probably spend way too much time with my head in the fridge. Or the oven.

Butch and Sundance shadowed me down to the feed lot. I unlocked the gate and tromped to the small barn where I feed my brood. I have three horses. Okay, so one of them belongs to my mother. My mother rode horses before she could walk. She ran the barrels in her youth and was pretty darned good at it. Well, actually her horse did most of the running. I inherited Mom's love of horses, if not her math aptitude. My mother owns Queen of Hearts, a leggy sorrel quarter horse with a nifty white blaze. Mom's first horse was Royal Flush. I held to family tradition. My horses are Black Jack, or Jack for short, a stocky, black, half-quarter and half-Morgan; and Joker, a goofy, but lovable Appaloosa-quarter.

I filled the feed boxes with grain and whistled through my fingers. Within seconds, the thud of hooves against solid earth was definitive proof that my little herd was hankering for grub. I stepped back and held the barn door open. The horses moved to their stalls and began to eat. I often wonder if my offspring will be this easy to train.

I moseyed from stall to stall and gave each of the horses a bit of individual attention. Generally, I leave them alone when they are eating. Horses are like people in that respect—they don't like to be bothered when they are dining (please take note if your vocation happens to be telemarketing). I was running late, so I cut my fawning short and, instead, grabbed the pitchfork and filled the wheelbarrow with manure, vowing to load the wheelbarrow contents into the spreader the next day. Once the grain was gobbled, I shooed my beasties out of the barn, shut the door, and made my way to the trailer, my optimistic hounds still on my tail. Once at the front porch, I dumped some Mighty Mutt in their bowls, refilled their water and hurried to the shower. Fifteen minutes later, dressed in the requisite khaki slacks and white tee, and couldn't-resist white wedgie heels, I headed next door.

"You wearing that same outfit again?" My grandmother acknowledged me with her customary greeting.

"It's my work uniform," I told her, knowing full well she knew it anyway.

"You can't be seen wearing the same outfit day in, day out, kiddo. People will think you're hard-up."

"I *am* hard-up, Gramma," I said, and gave her a peck on a dry, rouged cheek. "I have a dead-end job—no, make that *two* dead-end jobs. I live next door to my folks. I eat practically every meal here with the exception of the ones I snitch at Uncle Frank's. I *am* hard-up, Gram."

She chuckled. "Naw, you're just a late bloomer, sweetie. That's all. Just like your Grandpa Will, bless his heart. He did things in his own good time. Eventually, he found his way in the world."

"He took over your uncle's hardware business, Gram."

"He knew a good opportunity when he saw it."

"Great Aunt Eunice says you threatened to divorce him and marry Old Man Townsend at the lumber yard if Grandpa didn't join the business."

"I did no such thing. The very idea. And he wasn't Old Man Townsend back then, my dear. He was quite a strapping—I did no such thing!"

I picked up the newspaper and glanced at it. Our state used to have two daily metro papers, one morning and one evening. Now we just have the morning paper. I like to think that means there's less bad news to report.

"We made the front page today," Gramma announced. "All about that dreadful lawyer passing drugs to his client right there in the county jail! Can you imagine?"

"Some attorney-client privilege," I snorted, not that

interested in the penny-ante dealings of a lowlife lawyer and his lowlife client.

"I hope they nail him," Gram said. "I've never liked Peyton Palmer. His hair looks like a toupee and he has nostrils the size of olives—those big, black ones, not the pimento-stuffed kind. I never trust a man whose hair looks like a wig. And you know what they say about oversized nostrils."

"The better to pick with, my dear?" I teased.

"Secrets," Gramma said. "It means a person has secrets."

"Not anymore," I said, and waved the paper at her before tossing it aside. "Where's Mom?"

"In her office, I expect. Why ask me? I rarely see her except when she needs to fill one end or empty the other."

"She's working, Gram. Besides, you have the intercom if you need anything."

"I'm not complaining, you know. No, not me. Why should I complain? I'm just a virtual prisoner here. But I've been thinking about getting online. You know. Surf the web. Go into one of those chat rooms. What do you think of that?"

I hoped the tremor in my right eye didn't show. "Any good leftovers, Gram?" I asked, hoping to derail what was sure to be a major pileup on the information superhighway.

"Here, let me make you a roast beef sandwich, dear. I put a roast in the Crock-Pot the other day and it was so tender you could cut it with a fork. I just love the meat at the Meat Market."

I helped Gram to her feet and let her fix me a roast beef on wheat with lettuce and mayo and a glass of milk. I persuaded her to join me, and we both wiped off milk mustaches with a satisfied "ahhh" once we'd finished our meal. I scooped the evidence of our refrigerator raid into the garbage, rinsed the glasses, and stuck them in the dishwasher.

"That was awesome, Gramma. Thanks." I gave her a quick hug. "I've got to hit the trail or I'll be late for work. They're letting people vote online for next season's lucky *Survivor* contestants, and I want to see their videos before I cast my vote. See you later, Gram."

I jogged to my dirty white Plymouth. It coughed and sputtered a bit before starting, and I found myself thinking about those *Survivor* castaways. Lounging about on the beach getting a to-die-for tan, looking buffer and leaner than if they'd spent a fortune at the finest fat farm. No rigid, structured schedule to conform to—except for those tedious little challenges and tribal councils, of course. No customers to wear that phony, the-customer-is-always-right smile for. No cones to dip. No curly-Q's to construct. I let out a long, frustrated sigh. Bush-squatting and worm-eating in the middle of nowhere with a bunch of masochistic strangers was looking better all the time; hairy armpits, sand up the butt crack and all.

I wheeled into the employee parking area of Bargain City five minutes before my shift began. I have a regular assigned parking space. Don't get the idea that this is some kind of a perk. My space is out back near the Dumpster. The manager "requested" I park in the same spot all the time so I won't leave ugly oil stains all over his parking lot.

I resisted the urge to cuss when my customary parking space was blocked by a garbage truck—I'm trying real hard to watch my language (after catching *Oprah*'s two-part show, *Personality Makeovers: Breaking Those Bad Habits*). I pulled my car into a space back behind the seasonally constructed greenhouse, shoved my key ring into my pants pocket, and trotted into Bargain City with a full sixty seconds to spare.

"Cuttin' it kinda close, aren't you, Turner?" Landon, the customer service dude on duty greeted me with a smirk. "Good news. You're gonna have to cover sporting goods, too. Peterson called in sick."

I groaned. Terrific. That meant hoofing it from one counter to the other all night. No *Oprah*. No *Wheel of Fortune*. No run to the Sonic for a chili cheese dog and tots. And precious few potty breaks.

"Maybe it will be a slow night," Landon tried to console me.

"It's Friday," I pointed out. "When's the last time we had a slow Friday night?"

"From what I hear, most of your Friday nights are slow," was his response. He didn't sound like he was joking.

"Who told you that?" I demanded, irritated to learn that how I spent my weekend nights, or didn't spend them, was the topic of conversation among my coworkers. Working two jobs had a tendency to put the kibosh on any social life. Once I actually found both the time and the energy to date, there was always the pesky little matter of locating the guy. I'm not that picky, but I do have some standards. Only unmarried men with full-time employment (I can't afford to support anybody else), a terrific sense of humor, and a full set of pearly whites that don't require removal at bedtime need apply. And believe me, folks, in my little one-horse town, said applicant line ain't snaking around the corner and down the block.

Landon scratched his head. "That little gem was courtesy of your brother Craig. I think it was Townsend who said to cut you some slack, that you were busy embarking on a new career, and with a few more months' practice, you'd have those little curly-Q's at the top of the ice cream cones down pat."

I wrinkled my face. Ranger Rick again. One of these days Rick Townsend would go too far and I wouldn't be responsible for the consequences. "I lead a very satisfying social life, contrary to what my brother and his absurd friend say."

"Yeah, right," the smirking customer service clerk responded. "And I have Jennifer Lopez waiting for me at home wearin' nothing but my Old Navy T-shirt and a smile."

"More like *George* Lopez," I muttered. "Say, don't you have refunds to quibble over? Customers to service? Something?" I headed to the employee area and grabbed my red Bargain City vest and prepared to begin a shift already guaranteed to last longer than an Academy Awards show. Or a pair of shoes you hate.

Two hours into my shift, I was cursing my cutesy new footwear. Running shoes would have been a much better choice, white ones with red shoestrings and bright red oblique stripes down the sides. I jogged from the electronics section to the sporting goods section like a shopper during the four hour only sale on the morning after Thanksgiving. By the time ten-thirty rolled around, my tail was dragging lower than the rusty tailpipe on my Plymouth.

"I should get double pay for working two counters," I pointed out to the assistant night manager as I prepared to leave.

"As I recall, we never docked you for that snack cake display incident," he had the gall to remind me.

"And I still say that was a stupid place to put a giant creme-filled sponge cake," I argued.

"Hit the road, Turner. You're scheduled back at eight A.M. tomorrow, aren't you?"

I nodded, bummed by the thought that I would go home and fall into bed, only to awaken and return to the exciting world of Bargain City at first light.

"At least you'll have a free Saturday night to enjoy your satisfying social life," Mr. Customer Service interjected, pulling off his vest as he prepared to end his shift.

"Oh? You get fired from the Dairee Freeze, Turner?" the night manager asked.

"No, I didn't get fired from the Dairee Freeze," I responded.

"Her uncle owns the joint," Customer Service explained.

I glared at them both. "See if I throw in any extra toppings on your next Dairee Freeze visit, gentlemen." I stomped to the exit before it dawned on me that I'd neglected to remove my own Bargain City vest. The heck with it. I'd taken enough abuse for one night. My feet were killing me, and my ears were still ringing with: *Customer assistance in sporting goods. Customer assistance in electronics.* I closed my eyes against the throbbing of my temples. First thing when I got home, I was going to pop a couple of headache tablets, wash 'em down with a light beer (or two), and fall into bed. I sighed. The only male companions I had waiting at home for me were two hairy gents badly in need of new flea and tick collars, toenail clippers, and some tartar-control mouthwash.

I plodded to my car near the back of the darkened lot. I opened the door, jumped in, and winced when the maracas joined the drumbeat in my head. I turned the key and prayed. Yes! Whitie started without a whimper, sputter, cough, or belch. I eased out of the parking space, hit the headlights, and headed out of town. We live around seven miles from Grandville, the county seat, on a curvy, dead-end gravel road off an old county blacktop.

Once I left the lights of town and turned onto County Road G-14, I glanced down to check my speed. Sometimes I get a little heavy on the accelerator. The dashboard was dark as my mood. What now? I tapped the dash with a knuckle. Nothing. I checked to make sure I still had working headlights. I fumbled around in the dark and finally found the radio, then pulled a face when a voice boomed out of the speakers discussing campaign finance and soft money. As opposed to hard, I suppose. Hey, as if it really makes a difference to politicians what their campaign money feels like, as long as it's green and negotiable.

I punched the buttons to switch the radio to one of my country channels. Instead, a noisy rap erupted, followed by an investment chit-chat (like I want to hear how well others are doing) and finally, golden oldies from my parents' heydays. I hit all the buttons again. Where was SheDaisy? Tim and Faith? Shania?

I twisted the dial. Probably the same snafu that robbed me of dash lights had erased all my radio station settings. I finally located my favorite station broadcasting the top-of-the-hour weather forecast. A chance of thunderstorms Saturday afternoon and evening. Figured. The last time I had a weekend night off, gas was below two bucks a gallon and the only Hilton that mattered had room service and pay-per-view.

I hummed along with the radio, keeping time on the steering wheel with my fingers, when I became aware of a thumping very much out of sync with the music. I shut the radio off and listened, grimacing when the car began to wander not-so-subtly to the right. Flip-flop. Flip-flop. Flip-flop. Ka-thunk. Ka-thunk. Ka-thunk. I pulled a face. This couldn't be good.

"Well, hell!" I slapped a palm over my mouth. "I mean heck!" I steered the leaning vehicle to the roadside, and cursed my lack of luck, lack of cell phone, and lack of knowledge concerning the location of the four-way directional hazard flashers of my own vehicle. I stopped the car and opened the door, trying to calculate the odds of there being a flashlight in my vehicle, then recalculating the odds of it being one that actually worked. I leaned down and stuck a hand under my seat, probing for a light. To my amazement, I pulled out a neon, glow-in-the dark, plastic flashlight. Cocky, I enjoyed the rare moment of personal triumph a bit before remembering to try the switch. I held my breath. I pushed the switch and wanted to crow with self-satisfaction when the light actually cast a respectable beam (after I gave it a couple light raps on the steering wheel). Ditz, huh?

I moved roadside to survey the tire, casting the flashlight beam first toward the grassy roadside ditch, praying there were no creepy-crawlies or leaves-of-three lurking in the darkness for an unsuspecting khaki-trouser leg. I turned the beam on a tire as flat as my chest in high school. I groaned, then groaned louder when the flashlight flickered once and went out. I gave it a good, hard shake and it came back on, albeit dimmer than it had been earlier.

I muttered a few choice naughty words I couldn't say out loud due to my self-improvement pledge, and chewed my lip. This was great. Just great. Alone on a dark country road, a good two to three miles from home with a flat tire, no cell phone, no AAA, and no one to come looking for me when I didn't get home. Wasn't this when the dude wearing black coveralls and a Captain Kirk mask usually showed up?

I narrowed my eyes at the darkness around me, then shook my head. Get real. I lived in rural Iowa. The most serious crime I could recall was when Rodney Kirkwood got arrested six years ago for wearing a dress to the senior prom. An off-the-shoulder, burgundy strapless. The color didn't suit him. And he hadn't waxed. A real crime.

I trudged around to the driver's side, pulled the keys out of the ignition and went back to the trunk. I stuck the key into the lock, but it refused to turn. I tried again. It wouldn't budge. I put the key up to the fading flashlight and squinted at it. Right key. I tried again. No luck. I yanked it back out, and tried to remember the last time I'd opened my trunk. I frowned. Had I ever opened my trunk?

I returned to the car and opened the glove box to check for a trunk switch. I shined the flashlight in the glove compartment, shoved aside a thick, oversized manila envelope and located the trunk-release button, and popped the trunk. I fingered the manila envelope and tried to remember what I had stashed in the glove box. I picked it up and looked at it. Tampons? Nah. Parking tickets? Nah. I'd had to pay all those when I renewed my registration back in March. I opened the envelope and peeked inside. My eyes crossed. My breathing grew shallow. In my very own grubby little mitts, I held a wad of greenbacks the likes of which this poor working girl had never seen before. I blinked. Oh, working in retail, I'd seen hundred dollar bills before, just not this many. Not all at one time. And never in the glove box of my '87 white Plymouth Reliant.

My heart began to pound. Perspiration pooled above my upper lip. There had to be ten grand here, easy. Mentally, I calculated how many curly-Q's on cone tops that would figure out to. How many, "May I take your order"s? How many double-dips and maraschino cherries? My mind reeled at the implications.

An owl hooted nearby, pulling me out of my money-induced catatonia. Ten grand or not, I was still afoot until I changed the tire. I shut the glove box, put my car key in my vest pocket, and returned to the rear of the vehicle, figuring if I couldn't manage to change the flat, what the hey? I'd buy four new tires in the morning. New tires? Heck, I'd buy a brand new car. One of those radical red jobs with the spoiler in the back, wire wheel covers, and real leather seats. I inhaled deeply. I could almost smell that new car aroma already.

I smiled and threw open the trunk just as the flashlight conked again. I grunted, thinking a trunk light would be a nice luxury. Not that I would have to worry about flat tires—not with my new shiny red sports car.

I pounded the flashlight with my palm. No luck. I hit it on the back of my car and it came on. I shined the waning beam into the trunk interior, puzzled to find a large, bulky gray canvas where my spare tire should be.

"What the—?" I grabbed hold of the tarp and pulled it back. Two large, buggy, surprised eyes stared back at me. "Holy Mother! Sweet Jesus!" I scrambled away from the car and into the grassy ditch, fighting the strong urge to pee in my pants. "Son of a bitch! What the hell?" I rasped, all past pledges concerning my language overhaul forgotten. I ran a shaking hand across my eyes and focused on corralling my heart rate and breathing back into healthy parameters.

I gathered what wits I had left and reflected on this latest complication. I let out a long, noisy breath. Okay. Okay. It was starting to make sense now. I took another deep breath in and blew it out. Okay. I had it. This was someone's idea of a sick joke. One of the wise-asses at work had copped onto an old mannequin from apparel and stuck it in my trunk in a juvenile attempt to scare the wits out of me. Okay, okay, so it was a successful attempt.

Who knew how long the sick little perp had been waiting for his moronic joke to unfold? As often as I opened my trunk, I could've been carting Mr. Mannequin around since Christmas. My lip curled. There was only one individual I knew who had the kahunies to mastermind such a despicable trick and the patience to sit back and wait for results. Ranger Rick.

I crawled up out of the thigh-high grass and retrieved the flashlight I'd dropped. The dumb jerk. I'd probably end up with chigger bites up the wazoo thanks to his latest stunt. I stomped to the trunk with only one thing on my mind: payback.

I shined the flashlight at the dummy for a closer look. *Whoa.* I'd never realized the male mannequins at BC looked so much like Grandville's own newsmaking, drug-smuggling attorney, Peyton Palmer, right down to the stiff-looking hairpiece and quarter-sized nose holes.

I grabbed hold of the dummy's chin to turn the head and flinched. The dummy's face felt cold and leathery against my suddenly tap-dancing fingertips. I moved the flashlight for a closer inspection. Everything went dark. "Dammit!" I pounded the flashlight on the open trunk lid. "Come on, you piece of crap!" I gave it another hard thunk and the light popped back on. I followed the path of the beam into my trunk and right into a big, dark, bloody hole on the right temple of the poorly treated mannequin.

I stared at the seeping hole and, for a few moments, applauded the lengths to which Ranger Rick would go in order to play this macabre joke, complete with bloody head wounds. As the seconds passed and I stared at that half-dollar sized hole, I began to process the grizzly scene. The blood and matter oozing from the deep headwound. The lifelike skin and eyes framed by thick eyelashes. The not-so-lifelike hair. I put my hand out and took hold of the dummy's toupee and gave a hard pull. I tried again, this time tugging the rug for all I was worth. I gasped and yanked my hand away.

Well, damn. Looked like I owed Ranger Rick an apology. He hadn't played a nasty practical joke on me, after all. There wasn't a mannequin in my trunk. There was a dead body in my trunk. And he used to be Peyton Palmer.

My flashlight went out. I let loose with a scream that would have put those horror movie queens of scream to shame. I dropped the flashlight and ran like you-know-what.

CHAPTER 2

I hadn't run since the girls' state track meet my senior year when I ran the third leg of the thousand meter medley. We came in sixth. Okay. Dead last. But we would've won if Callie Carter hadn't botched the handoff and made me drop the baton. Coach Willetts would have choked on his whistle at the pace I set on that dark, rock-riddled dirt road. I sucked air into underused lungs and sounded a lot like a lifelong asthmatic during a full-blown attack.

A stitch appeared in my left side, but trooper that I am, I ignored it. The vivid mental image of the stiff in my trunk loomed rather large in the motivation department, and provided more than sufficient incentive for me to keep motoring down that country road; shin splints, blisters and hyperventilation notwithstanding.

"Why me? *Why me?*" was the litany that kept me company as I plodded along in those had-to-have sandals, each pebble and stone underfoot a painful reminder of my unwise investment. (Hey, a girl can go without eating, but she must have a new pair of shoes at least monthly.) I hit the lighted intersection that heralded the state highway and headed for the nearest farmhouse, still about three-quarters of a mile and a good half-dozen blisters away.

I started across the highway when lights topped the hill and bore down on me. I'm almost certain I had that deer-in-the-headlights look before I screamed and dove for the ditch to the sound of screeching brakes and rubber being transferred from tire to pavement. The shock of a sudden cold-water dousing generated a body-length shiver. The only consolation I could muster was the hope that the low water temperature would kill off any disease-carrying mosquitoes that happened to dip their wick in my fair skin. I would not permit myself to contemplate the reptilian factor.

A car door slammed. The beam of a flashlight—a powerful one, not a wimpy one—flickered from side to side as the occupant of the vehicle made his way back to my not-so-scenic locale among the tall grass and foul water. I was appalled when my teeth began to chatter louder than those fake wind-up ones you bring out when you're bored. Undecided as to whether I should come out, come out, wherever I was, or stay put, the decision was taken out of my hands when a beam of light struck me full in the face, blinding me. I raised a shaking hand to block it.

"Good God! I should've known it was you!"

I started at the familiar and unwelcome tones of a certain fish-and-fowl officer. You know. The one who was placed on this earth to be a major irritant to me. My very own life-sized hemorrhoid that no amount of cooling gel or soothing pads could shrink.

I pulled myself to a sitting position, wincing at the pain in my shoulder and the sogginess on my butt.

"You almost ran me over, you—you speed freak!" I lashed out, the terror of the evening fueling my response. That and my wet hiney and lovely new water moccasins. I felt myself being hauled up out of the ditch with a sincere lack of gentleness.

"Run you over? Run you over? Hell, you were in the middle of the gawd-damned road in the middle of the gawd-damned night!" Far from the soothing, sympathetic, reassuring tones I needed, my rescuer's voice was harsh and accusatory. "Tressa Jayne Turner, you could be the poster child for the slogan *shit happens,*" Ranger Rick continued, his own anger evident by the erratic shaking of the flashlight in his hand.

Humpf. Clearly, this big, dumb oaf had missed Oprah's series on "Sensitive Men and the Women Who Love Them." I yanked my arm out of his grasp and slapped at the hand that held the flashlight. "And you could be the pin-up boy for Habitat for Inhumanity," I snarled back.

Rick shined the flashlight on me, from the top of my dirty, straggly, sweaty head, to the tips of my grungy little piggies encased in water-logged, now putrid-white, no-sling-back sandal. I'd lost one in the murky depths of the ditch, but I wasn't about to go fishing for it in front of Rick Townsend. Instead, I stuck my nose in the air, hoping to salvage a bit of dignity.

"What the hell are you doing out here?" Ranger Rick took my arm and steered me toward his pickup, which was up the road a piece. "That old Plymouth poop out on you again?"

I stopped. I clamped a hand to my mouth. My Plymouth! I gasped and grabbed Rick's arm. The body in the trunk! I gasped louder and clamped my hand back over my mouth. The money!

"What the hell is wrong with you?" Ranger Rick asked, no doubt in response to my weird contortions.

I grabbed his arm again. "My car!"

"Yes?"

"Flat tire," I managed to get out past those again chattering teeth.

"Okay. Where?"

I pointed a quivering finger in the general direction of home. "Farley Road, before you get to 120th."

"Let me guess. Your spare tire was flat. Or nonexistent," my knight in rapidly tarnishing armor remarked. "You do know how to change a tire, don't you?" I could sense that *whatta-ditz* tone in his voice.

"I most certainly do know how to change a tire," I replied. "I'm a farm girl, remember? Besides, my dad made me pass his change-a-tire-in-seven-minutes-or you-don't-get-your-driver's-license drill. I just couldn't *get* to the spare tire." My voice began to crack again, recalling the reason I couldn't get to the spare.

"Full of empty pop and beer cans?"

My limited supply of patience with this khaki-clad cad barely registered on my tolerance dipstick and my temper gauge was in the red.

"Actually, no." I chose my words with care, delivering them through clenched teeth, anticipating a certain grim satisfaction by the huge helping of crow the ranger would have to chow down on when I presented him with the cadaver in my car. "I couldn't get to the tire due to the corpse in my trunk. You know. The one with a hole in his head big enough to be a cup-holder."

Even with the limited light of the flashlight, I could

imagine the rapid blinks in succession, the rolling of his eyes, the curled lip, the . . .

"Are you nuts? Or drunk? On something?"

"Maybe. Definitely not. Probably should be," I said in answer to his predictable response.

"What in God's name are you talking about? Corpses and cup-holders? Of all the ridiculous—"

"It's true!" I grabbed hold of his arm and started pulling him toward his pickup. "Swear to God, there *is* a dead body in my trunk! He was all covered up with a tarp or something and when I lifted the plastic, *ugh,* there he was. Of course, at first I thought it was some asinine practical joke you—some asinine practical joker played. But the closer I looked, the more I realized it wasn't a dummy at all. It was Peyton Palmer! Of course, Gramma would say it was still a dummy, but that's beside the point." Once I began to verbalize my ordeal, I couldn't seem to stop. The words tumbled off me like the four-pack towers of toilet paper I bowled over at the store last week. "So, I dropped the flashlight and ran. I was so scared I left the money behind. I did consider going back for it at one point, but decided against it. I mean, like it's not as if the cops are gonna let me keep it or anything. They won't, will they?" I squinted at my brother's pal. "Hello! Are you getting any of this?"

"You're telling me that you found a dead body in your trunk, that the body had a hole in his head, and that the body just happened to be that of Peyton Palmer, local attorney, Kiwanis president, sports booster, and ex-city councilman?"

"You forgot accused drug smuggler," I said, then nodded. "Yes, *yes!* That's exactly what I'm telling you." I shoved him toward his blinking four-by-four (he knew right where his hazard lights were located, Mr. Smartypants) and opened the driver's door. "Now get in there and get help," I yelled. "This is an emergency!" I ran around to the passenger side door. Okay, so I couldn't actually run due to my flapping footwear, but I moved as fast as I could. I hauled myself up into his monstrosity of a truck, expecting to see Ranger Rick dialing 911 on his cell phone to call in the cavalry. Instead, he flipped the dome light on and turned to stare at me, a look of this-takes-the-cake on his too-handsome face.

"Well?" I asked. "Why aren't you calling the police? Don't you have your cell phone?"

"Take it easy, Tressa," he said, and grabbed for the cell phone in the console at the same time I did.

"Aren't you going to call the cops? Don't you think they might be a tad-bit interested in checking out a report of a body in a trunk? A dead body with a big, oozing, black hole in the side of its head? The dead body of a well-known local attorney with a big, oozing, black hole in the side of his head? Or are you afraid you might interrupt a donut break?"

"Listen, Tressa." Townsend ran a hand through his hair. "I can't call the sheriff's office with an unconfirmed report like that."

I stared at him. "What do you mean unconfirmed? I saw it with my own two eyes. I'm an eyewitness!"

Townsend shook his head. "I need more, Tressa. You're not all that . . . uh . . . reliable," he faltered. "Oh, I think you think you saw something in the trunk, but I don't think you saw what *you* think you saw."

"Huh?" I said. Ranger Rick was beginning to sound a lot like me.

He wiped a hand over his eyes. "Look, Tressa.

Think about it. There you are. All alone. Dark country road. Car breaks down. Naturally, you're uneasy. Things have a way of seeming more dramatic than they really are. Characteristics are tainted by dread and fear. It's natural, really." He patted my shoulder again. "It's not uncommon."

I shrugged his hand off my shoulder. "Cut the psychobabble, Townsend. You're no Dr. Phil. You want confirmation, Mr. Ranger, sir?" I snapped. "You'll have your confirmation. But you better step on it. It's a warm night, and Mr. Palmer is decomposing as we speak."

Townsend gave me another shake of his head, put the pickup in drive and pulled out. My spit began to dry up at the thought of seeing the body again. But, hey, why would I have to see it again? I could just point Townsend in the direction of the trunk and stay a safe distance away—like, the next area code. Much as I wanted to be a part of the moment when Ranger Rick gazed down on poor Peyton Palmer all twisted up like a Mr. Salty in my trunk, and was forced to acknowledge I was right, I didn't think I could handle another peek, especially under the super-high intensity beam of Townsend's state-issued flashlight. No, I'd keep a safe distance away. Like, inside the pickup. With the doors locked. And the windows rolled up.

"How much further?" Townsend asked, and I jumped.

"Should be just ahead," I said, as our headlights revealed the outline of a white car with the trunk open.

"You didn't use your four-way flashers?" Townsend asked.

"They weren't working," I snapped.

"You need a new car, Tressa." Ranger Rick shook his head.

"Of course I need a new car. Someone dumped a dead body in my trunk. I could never drive a car that had a body dumped in it." I shuddered. "It wouldn't be . . . right."

He expelled a noisy breath and pulled up behind the abandoned car. I shut my eyes so I couldn't see the outline of Palmer Peyton sardined in my trunk.

Townsend grabbed his flashlight. "Stay here," he ordered.

Like I wanted to get out and have another look-see.

He exited the truck and walked to the rear of my vehicle. He raised his flashlight and aimed it at the contents of the trunk. I closed my eyes again and held my breath, waiting for Townsend to beat a path back to the truck and, of course, apologize profusely, then get on the phone and call out the county mounties. I waited. And waited. I opened one eye just a bit, then opened both eyes wide when I saw Townsend had disappeared. Where the devil was he? My heart was just beginning to make little *rat-a-tat-tats* in my chest when I caught sight of his silhouette near the front of my car. Why wasn't he phoning the proper authorities? Townsend wasn't trained for crime scene investigation. I'd seen enough crime shows to know that. This was a matter for the sheriff's office. The state police. Those state DCI technicians who wore the ugly blue jumpsuits with "Crime Lab" on the back and drove the big, honking crime scene van chock-full of evidence bags, yellow crime scene tape and latex gloves.

I watched as Townsend pulled his six-foot-three-inch frame out of the driver's compartment of my car. He walked toward me, his slow pace at odds with the urgency of the situation. He stood at the hood of his truck. "Tressa." He motioned to me.

I cracked the window an inch. "What do you want?"

"Could you step out of the truck for a moment and come here?" he asked.

"Why?" I queried, a sense of unease building that I couldn't explain.

"I have something to show you," he said. "Come here."

I shook my head. "I've seen it. I'll have the picture branded in my subconscious for years to come as it is. I don't care to reinforce the image by catching something I might've missed the first time around."

"Tressa."

"Oh, all right," I said, knowing that my stubborn streak was equaled only by Rick Townsend's own pigheadedness. "I'm coming. But don't blame me if I puke all over and destroy all kinds of forensic evidence."

I opened the truck door and scooted to the ground, losing my other sandal in the process. I took teensy-weensy baby steps until I reached the right front quarter-panel of the truck. "Okay, I'm here. What do you want?" I asked Townsend, who was now at the open trunk of my car.

"Come here, Tressa." He held out a hand.

"I can't," I told him. "I think I'm in shock."

"Tressa."

"Okay, okay, I'm coming," I said. "Just don't be surprised when I sue you for the cost of my therapy." I inched closer to the trunk.

"Sometime tonight would be nice," Townsend remarked.

"What's the hurry?" I asked. "*He's* not going anywhere." I motioned toward the trunk, expecting to see poor Peyton Palmer's sightless, staring eyes, and blood-matted, lacquered hair. What I saw was a set of jumper cables, a fishing pole, and, from a cursory look, a couple of really raunchy magazines. My mouth flew open.

"Where is he?" I shouted, almost an accusation. "Where's Peyton Palmer?"

"Probably at home in bed, asleep like most normal folks," Townsend replied.

I stared at the trunk of the car. "I don't understand. He was there. All twisted up and grotesque-looking, just staring at me." I grabbed Townsend's flashlight and examined every nook and cranny of the trunk. "This can't be. He was right here. Under a gray tarp. And he was dead as a doornail. I know dead when I see it. And he was most definitely DOA."

Townsend took the flashlight from me. "I'm sorry, Tressa, but as you can see, there's nothing there."

"The money!" I grabbed the flashlight again and hurried to the front seat. "There was a ton of money in an envelope in the glove box, Townsend. Ten grand, easy." I opened the glove box. "It was right here in a manila envelope." I put a hand in the glove compartment and pulled it back out. I pointed the flashlight at the palm of my hand, illuminating a handful of Trojans. I stared at the little squares trying to make sense of the incomprehensible. What were prophylactics doing in my glove box?

Above me Townsend coughed, and I closed my fist.

"It's nice to see in some areas of your life, you come prepared," he remarked, a grin in his voice.

"Those are not mine! I've never seen them before!"

Townsend clicked his teeth. "Obviously, I was wrong about your Saturday nights, Calamity," he said.

"Go to the devil, Townsend!" I yelled, frustrated that nothing was going the way it was supposed to. First, a dead body gets up and walks away when nobody is looking. Then I lose about a zillion dollars in cash, and in its place I find rubbers for a partner I don't even have.

I waited for the ridicule to begin, the laughter, the "*dur*, *dur*, *dur*ring" to start, but to my utter amazement, Townsend never said a word. Instead, he pulled me into his arms and whispered reassuring little nonsense words that meant nothing and everything.

I tried to process the radical change. This was a side of Rick Townsend I'd never seen. A soft, vulnerable side. A sensitive, caring side. A sexy as all-get-out side. I sniffled against his shirt. He smelled good—a rugged combination of fresh country air and man. My heart began to make those little pitter-patter beats against my rib cage again, but this time the fear I felt was very different from my fright of earlier. Confusion cluttered my thought processes. This was my childhood nemesis. The big H. The man who had made my adolescence intolerable. The boy who repeatedly asked me when I was going to grow boobs, once over the public address system at homecoming festivities. This was the man who had set me up to meet my high school heartthrob, Tommy Dawson, only to present me with Louie "the Stick" Parker. The man who coined the nickname "Calamity" for general use. No.

No, I couldn't have any tender feelings for the man who stole my bathing suit top at the church youth mixer. None. Zip. Zilch. Zero.

Shock, I reminded myself. Just shock. I moved away from Townsend.

His big hands cupped my shoulders and his thumbs made a circular motion that eased none of the stiffness out of my cardboard cutout stance. "You've had a helluva night, Calamity," he said, still close enough for me to feel his warm breath on my face.

"I don't understand any of this. I'm not crazy. I saw what I saw. I'm not crazy." I repeated that part just in case he'd missed it the first time around.

"The mind can play tricks on us, Tressa," Rick said, a tender edge to his voice that was so out of character that it was hard to believe it was coming from him, and even more unlikely, directed at me. "It could happen to anyone."

Yeah, right. Well, then, why didn't it? Ever?

"I think I should know what I saw in my own trunk, for crying out loud. Give me a break."

Townsend sighed. A real loud sigh. A sigh that said, *What am I gonna do with you?* That kind of sigh. He put a hand to the side of my face and stroked my cheek, his touch ever so soft and gentle. My lips quivered. I looked up at him, but couldn't see his face, which was probably a good thing considering he thought I was a craven little coward who had dark, deserted road-induced hallucinations.

"Listen, Tressa, I have something to tell you," Townsend said. "It's very important and you really need to hear it. This can't wait."

My breath caught at the serious tone of his voice.

What could he have to tell me that was so vital, so crucial, that I had to hear it now, in the middle of this personal crisis? I bit my lip and held my breath.

"Tressa?" Townsend now had both paws on either side of my face. I could feel my heart putt-putt-puttering like Uncle Frank's ancient outboard. I ran my tongue over lips as dry as our farm pond had been during the drought of '97.

"Yes?" I squeaked.

"This is not your car."

Chapter 3

It took a while for Townsend's words to sink in. I admit it; I can be rather dense at times. Especially when those *times* include a disappearing corpse, a mysterious envelope full of cash (also, sadly, among the missing) and a cross-country trek on shoes that have about as much support as odor eaters. I stared at Townsend. "Huh?'

"Come with me, Tressa." Townsend walked me to the back of the vehicle again. I dragged my feet, not trusting that Counselor Palmer hadn't done a Houdini and was just waiting to scare the crap out of me again.

"Come on," Townsend urged.

I found myself back at the trunk once more. It was still empty. I wasn't sure whether to be relieved or frustrated.

"You own a Plymouth, right? A piece of crap, white Plymouth Reliant?" Townsend asked.

I nodded. "I'll resent that remark later, at a more appropriate time. And are you blind or something? There it is." I pointed to the car.

"Ah, but there it isn't," Townsend replied.

Before I could respond, Ranger Rick illuminated the back end of the vehicle with his trusty flashlight. Standing out like a beacon to my disbelieving eyes was the silver *Chrysler* emblem scrolled across the back.

"Chrysler?" I looked over at Townsend. "*Chrysler?*" I repeated.

"Chrysler." Townsend echoed. "Not Plymouth. Not Reliant. Not yours."

I gulped. "You mean—"

"Calamity Jayne Turner, at this point I should probably advise you that you have the right to remain silent."

"You mean—?"

"Auto theft, ma'am."

I grabbed the ridiculous man's flashlight and shined it at the rear license plate. "Oh, my," I murmured in amazement. I limped to the driver's door and slid behind the wheel, running the beam along the inside of the vehicle. Now that I could actually see the car's interior, I saw the subtle differences. The varied instrumentation. The wood grain trim. The koochie, koochie, hula girl stuck on the dashboard.

Townsend opened the passenger side door and sat down. I barely gave him a thought. My eyes could not leave the hula girl. "Tressa?" he murmured, but for the life of me I couldn't respond. Instead, I poked the Hawaiian dancer and she sprang to life. I watched her wiggle and contort in ways that, no doubt, figure prominently in men's fantasies.

"How could something like this happen?" I whispered. "I mean, how could I just get in and drive away in somebody else's car?"

When Townsend didn't answer right away, I could almost imagine what was going through his mind. On an off day, Calamity Jayne could manage something like that rather easily.

"But this car was parked where I park." I initiated a preemptive defense of my actions. "It's the same color. It looks a lot like my car, and the lighting is so poor in that back lot they ought to issue white canes. I was so tired after working all day and half the night, and I just jumped in and turned the key and—" I stopped. "Hey, hold on a second. My key! I used my own car key, Townsend. How could that be? How could my car key work in somebody else's car?"

Townsend let his breath out in a long, drawn-out, noisy exhalation of air. "Actually, although this kind of thing is rare, it's not unheard of with these K-car models. I remember several years ago reading a report of a similar incident occurring. This guy thought he was hopping into his in-laws' car. It wasn't until days later when he returned it, that he found out he had taken the wrong car and the one he'd been driving was reported as stolen. His mother-in-law's car had been impounded and towed. Betcha he never hears the end of that at family reunions." He chuckled.

I tried to make sense of what I was hearing. "You're telling me I stole a car? I *stole* a car?"

"Uh-huh. As we speak, chances are your old clunker is leaking oil into interesting Rorschach grease blots on the parking lot at Bargain City," he said.

I acknowledged the evidence before my eyes. "I'm a car thief. A criminal. A felon. A two-bit thug."

"An accident looking for a place to happen."

I glared at Townsend. "This is no joke. I've committed a crime here. I've been driving around in someone else's car." I slapped my hand to my forehead. "Townsend, do you know what that means?"

"That you broke down in somebody else's car for a change?" he suggested.

"No! It means that nobody dumped a dead body in my trunk, after all."

Townsend let out another long, deep breath. "Thank God, you've finally come to your senses. I have to admit, you had me worried there for a while."

"What it means," I went on, "is that someone stashed Peyton Palmer's body in this car for safe-keeping."

"What!"

"Okay, so maybe 'safe-keeping' is the wrong word. Don't you see? The killer never expected to have someone jump in and drive away with his stiff. He probably planned to dispose of the body later, in the dead of night." I winced. "No pun intended," I apologized, then grabbed Townsend's arm again. "That's it! The body. He came looking for the body." I looked out at the darkness around us. "He came looking for the body, and he found it."

"Are we back to that again?" Townsend's disgust was evident in his voice.

I was saved composing an appropriate reply by the short, loud bursts of a police siren and the appearance of flashing red lights.

"Geez, it's the cops!" I announced with conflicting emotions. My first impulse was to beg Townsend to hide me, but I managed to hang on to a measure of composure. Instead, I grabbed the collar of his shirt. "I can count on you, right? To, uh, help, uh, explain about my little mix-up with the cars?" I asked.

Townsend laughed. "Oh, yeah. Absolutely. You can count on me."

I frowned. Yeah, right. I could count on him to broadcast this night's activities via the mutual aid frequency in his state vehicle. By the time the old timers gathered at Hazel's Hometown Café at first light, I would be the clown of the county. Again.

The car with the revolving bright lights pulled up behind Townsend's truck, spotlighted it for a moment, then pulled alongside it. I waited for the officer to announce over his speaker, "Come out with your hands in the air." The wait was worse than lying naked under a sheet in the exam room waiting for a pelvic exam from Dr. Coldfingers.

"What's the hold-up?" I asked Townsend when the deputy made no move to exit his vehicle.

"Hold-up? As an admitted felon, I'd probably use a different choice of words." I caught the grin in his voice. "And he's probably running the plate number through the computer to check for hits." Townsend interpreted the delay, as unconcerned as a retiring schoolteacher on his last day of teaching.

"Hits?"

"Wants or warrants. Ten-ninety-nines."

I gulped and checked the rearview mirror again. "What if someone has already reported the car stolen? What if that deputy comes up here with guns drawn?"

"In that case, I suggest you give up."

Sweat pooled on my upper lip, and my underarms began to drip like a Dairee Freeze dip cone in midsummer. "Shouldn't we get out?" I suggested. "Go back and explain?"

"What if he thinks you're making a run for it?" Townsend replied. "Some of these small town officers tend to be a little trigger-happy. You know—shoot first, ask questions later."

I kept my eyes fixed on the squad car in the rearview mirror. Just when I was about ready to jump out of the car and scream, "Okay, okay, I did it. Arrest me. Haul me in," the driver's door of the cop car opened and, for the second time that night, a flashlight beam headed in my direction. "He's coming!" I whispered.

"Whatever you do, don't make any sudden moves," Townsend advised, suppressed laughter turning his voice husky. The beast.

I watched the deputy approach until he directed his flashlight right into the rearview mirror. Then, instant blindness. Neat trick.

The deputy stopped beside the driver's door and rapped on the window. I didn't move. He rapped again, harder this time, with his flashlight. I held my breath and stared straight ahead.

"What the hell are you doing?" Townsend asked. "Open the window."

"You told me not to make any sudden moves." I reminded him.

"Oh, for God's sake, Tressa, open the damned window."

"All right. All right. Just make up your mind." I turned the window handle. "It won't open!" I hissed.

"Then open the door!"

I yanked the door handle hard and shoved, praying my earlier failure to follow the lawful order of a police officer hadn't tainted the officer's ability to be fair and impartial. And serve and protect. The door flew open. It impacted with the knuckles of the officer's right hand and his shin. The collection of curses that followed left me in little doubt what the term "swore like a trooper" meant. Suffice it to say, the good officer's choice of words had very little in common with fellow men in uniform Andy Taylor, Sgt. Joe Friday, or Dudley Do-right.

I bent over and retrieved the flashlight the deputy had dropped, getting an up-close and personal look at the accoutrements on his gun belt. The handcuffs. The mace or pepper spray. I didn't get close enough to distinguish which, and didn't ever plan to. And last, but not least, the holstered (thank goodness) firearm that looked like it could inflict some serious bodily damage. "Here you go." I wedged the flashlight into the crook of his arm. "Everything good as new. A place for everything and everything in its place," I babbled.

"Hope you're not expecting a thank-you." The deputy took his flashlight and directed its beam across the top of the car. "Evening, Rick." He nodded to Townsend, whose head appeared above the car's roof.

"Doug," Townsend greeted him. "Nice evening."

"It was," the deputy replied. "Seems we got a bit of a problem here. I ran the plate on this vehicle and got a hit. Car was reported stolen out of Des Moines a week ago."

I swallowed. Real loud. Like if-I'd-had-an-Adam's-apple-that-sucker-would-be-bobbing-up-and-down-like-a-yo-yo loud. "Wait. Hold on." I heard my own voice rise to just below the shattering fine crystal stage. "A week ago? That can't be right. I just took the car two hours ago."

"You recall me advising you earlier that you had the right to remain silent, Calamity?" Townsend asked. "Now might be a good time to take that to heart."

"Sounds like good advice, Miss Turner," the officer agreed. "Real good advice."

"How—how did you know my name?" I stammered.

"Hell, everybody knows the story about the pooch parlour and Deputy Dawg. Made the sheriff mad as hell, havin' his wife hold his pup as ransom for a bigger settlement."

I shook my head. "But how did you know it was me, here, now?"

"Would you believe your coworkers were, uh, concerned when they left work after you and found your car still in the parking lot? There was some speculation that your vehicle had broken down and you'd called someone for a lift, but no one saw you come back into the store to use the phone or hitch a ride."

"And they were so concerned about me, they called the police?" Nice, warm fuzzy feelings swept over me.

"*Well,* not exactly. See, the night manager, he wanted to tow your car. Says it makes a helluva mess in the parking lot, but—"

"Tow my car? The worm!"

"But when the city went by for the impound—"

"Impound!"

"—it was decided we'd better conduct a welfare check first just to be sure you hadn't been abducted or anything. I was heading out to check your residence. It might comfort you to know that the odds were heavily in your favor over any possible abductor. As a matter of fact, several folks expressed sympathy for the unsuspecting soul who chose to snatch you."

"Of all the—"

"I imagine you have an interesting explanation for being out here in a stolen automobile, don't you, Miss Turner?"

"As a matter of fact, I do, officer," I said, still piqued by my coworkers' insensitive remarks.

"I was sure you would," he said. "Let's all have a seat in my patrol car. Shall we?"

Once in the squad car, which by the way smelled of stale cigarettes, dirty socks, and Altoids, I related my story of the confused car caper to Deputy Doug, highlighting important facts such as my long work hours, the dark parking lot, and the fact that my own car key fit the ignition of the vehicle in question. You know. The hot one. To his credit, Officer Samuels didn't bust out laughing or act like I was one banana short of a split. Still, I hadn't gotten to the good stuff yet—the part about Peyton Palmer's dead body and the wad of hundreds.

"As Officer Townsend here may have told you, Miss Turner, this kind of incident is isolated, but it does happen on occasion, especially with the K-car series. It really doesn't surprise me in the least that it happened to you."

Townsend coughed in the back seat, and I wanted to slug him, which was unfortunate, because an admitted car thief has to show some restraint in front of an officer of the law.

"Seems like unusual things have a way of happening to you," the deputy went on, "or those individuals in close proximity to you. I'm recalling the time you kidnapped that young fellow from the Dee-lux car wash in the capital city. That had everyone talking for weeks."

"I did not kidnap that man." I protested my innocence. "How was I to know he was still wiping down the back seat, hit his head, and blacked out?"

"Or when you got banned from the local car wash for leaving all that horse shit in the self-wash bay."

"I was hosing out a horse trailer, for crying out loud."

"Sounds like a car wash issue," Townsend commented from the back seat.

"And how about the time you went skinny-dipping at the church youth mixer?"

"I was not skinny-dipping. The lunatic in the back seat stole my suit."

"You gonna believe me or an admitted car thief?" Townsend piped in.

"When did you realize this car didn't belong to you?" the deputy asked, ignoring him. I frowned as he began to scribble notes on a yellow legal pad. Notes on a legal pad couldn't mean anything good.

"Well, I uh—actually, I didn't realize I was, uh, driving the wrong vehicle until, uh—" I hesitated, not wanting to admit even the body in the trunk and the fistful of Ben Franklins hadn't tipped me off, and that if Townsend hadn't pointed it out to me, I might never have noticed. "Uh, Townsend pointed it out," I mumbled real low and fast through my fingers, hoping neither man caught the admission.

"Townsend pointed it out? When?"

Nice. "When he brought me back to get my car."

"Your car is in town."

"Well, yes, I know that now, but I didn't then."

"And you abandoned this car because?"

"Because of the flat tire, for starters."

"Flat tire?"

"Front passenger side. But I don't have to worry about that now, do I? You can't say that was my fault. How can someone be blamed for a flat tire? It's like an act of nature or God or something, isn't it? So I don't have to worry about the flat tire. Do I? I mean, it isn't even my car. Therefore, it isn't my tire. Right?"

The deputy gave me a strange look and appeared to have difficulty getting his train of thought back on the rail. "And you couldn't change the flat?"

I shook my head, feeling I was inching closer and closer to a very deep, dark precipice.

"Why not?"

Townsend cleared his throat several times. I winced, knowing that once I forced the words forming in my brain out through my tight lips, things would never, ever be the same. Being involved in a murder, however slightly, had a way of changing things. Lots of things.

"I couldn't get to the spare tire," I said.

"Why not?" the deputy repeated.

I hesitated.

"Why couldn't you get to the spare, Ms. Turner?"

"Tressa." Townsend's terse warning didn't elude me.

I scrunched my face up, struggling to find the right words. Tell me, what is the correct way to inform a police officer that you found the body of a prominent attorney stuffed in the trunk of a vehicle you'd just stolen? See my dilemma?

I unscrunched my face, opened my mouth, and recited the words that seemed to have become my mantra of late. "Well, you see, deputy, I couldn't get to the spare tire because Peyton Palmer's cold, dead body was obstructing my access."

"Shit," Townsend offered from the back seat.

"Holy shit," echoed Deputy Doug.

"No shit, Sherlocks," I said.

Ooops. Sorry, Oprah.

CHAPTER 4

You've seen it in the movies, especially those oldies but goodies, that not-so-subtle psychology of the interrogation room, an old standard in on-screen and literary police procedurals. You know what I'm talking about. The heavy cigarette smoke blown to best advantage. The strategically placed, high-intensity lighting. The two-way mirror the "suspect" is not supposed to suspect is there. The offer of a cup of coffee or can of soda accompanied by an I'm-your-pal-now-spill-your-guts smile. The good cop/bad cop scenario played out with flawless precision and painstaking attention to roles.

Not! At least, not Knox County's production. The only resemblance to silver screen interrogation scenes was the foam cup filled with a beverage the color and consistency of tar clutched in each of the officer's mitts. I politely declined. Okay, so first I pointed out the results of recent studies relating to caffeine and increased impotence rates, then declined.

By the time I got around to reciting my tale of terror

in the tall grass to the threesome in the sheriff's office conference room at the ancient courthouse, the terrible trio almost had me convinced I imagined the whole thing.

"Let me get this straight. What you're telling us, Miss Turner, is that you *see dead people?*" Deputy Doug Samuels—or Deputy Dickhead, as I'd come to refer to him—said with a smile that wasn't a smile at all. You know the one. The smile that makes you want to stick a Post-it note on that says: *Insert knuckles here.*

"Not people, deputy. Person. As in the singular noun." I wished my high school English teacher could have heard me. *See?* I'd crow. *I did learn something, after all.*

Knox County Sheriff Steve Thomason cleared his throat. Tall and long-limbed, with a shortly cropped, standard police haircut, a nicely trimmed black mustache, and spit-shined leather shoes, so far he'd contributed little. And Townsend? Townsend had spent the better part of the last two hours shaking his head.

"Ms. Turner," Deputy Samuels continued, "I don't know if you're aware of it or not, but Peyton Palmer, the individual you claim to have seen deceased in the trunk of a vehicle, is the target of a county investigation into the smuggling of narcotics into the county jail facility."

"I had heard something to that effect," I sniffed, wondering if they thought I was illiterate as well as delusional.

"While I'm not at liberty to discuss certain details of the investigation, let me just say that we have reason to believe Mr. Palmer may be involved in other questionable activities. As our investigation is active and ongoing, we would not like to see it jeopardized in any fashion by wild, uh, unsubstantiated claims of bodies in trunks and holes in heads."

I couldn't believe what I was hearing. Hadn't the nitwits listened to a thing I'd spent the better part of my night, thus forfeiting the better part of my limited amount of REM sleep, explaining? "Investigation? What investigation? The target of your investigation is at this moment probably in the early stages of post-mortem lividity." I struck a particularly gruesome pose complete with hands posed like stiff claws, tongue hanging out and my eyes rolled back in my head. The three mouseketeers exchanged dumfounded looks, probably wondering where the ditzy blonde had picked up such command of the pathology of the dead. I just love those medical examiner thrillers, don't you? The ones that make you leave the lights on long after you go to bed and compel you to get back up to check out the closet and under your bed, "just in case."

Sheriff Thomason drained his cup of tar, crushed the biodegradable-in-about-a-zillion-years cup and tossed it in a nearby trash can. He folded his arms, crossed his long legs, and leaned on an adjacent table. At well over six feet tall, in his late thirties to early forties, the sheriff appeared to me to be one of those just-the-facts-ma'am types. No frills. No finesse. No sense of humor. But maybe that was just with me.

"Listen, Ms. Turner," the sheriff began, his body language sending a silent but discernible message that the psycho who'd handed his beloved pet over to the enemy had a credibility problem to hurdle the size of China's Great Wall. "You've told us a rather unlikely tale here. And say, for the moment I'm prepared to believe you. Tell me, where's the physical evidence to support your story? Where's this suspicious envelope of money? Where's the blood? For that matter, where's the body? We've done a cursory search of the trunk, and I promise we'll do a top-notch forensic examination, but so far we haven't turned up one iota of physical evidence to corroborate your story. Nothing."

"Maybe it's the remake of *Invasion of the Body Snatchers*, Sheriff," Deputy Dickless, or was that Dickhead, said with another stupid grin.

"You ever actually do any police work between movies, Deputy?" I asked. "You know. Solve crime? Catch the bad guys? That sort of thing." Out of the corner of my eye I saw Townsend put his head in his hands. "What? What did I say?" I batted my eyes. "What?"

"About that evidence," Sheriff Thomason prodded.

I shook my head. "I don't know. I don't know where the body or the money went. I don't know why there weren't any bloody guts in the trunk. You guys are the pros here. You figure it out. I told you he was wrapped up in a big, gray tarp of some kind, so maybe there wouldn't be any seepage."

"Seepage?" Townsend lifted an eyebrow. "Seepage?"

"Shut up, Townsend!" I snarled. "Listen, Sheriff, I don't have all the answers you're looking for, but I do know this. Someone took that body from the trunk while I was going for help. It was there when I left, and gone when I came back, and as dead men tell no tales, I am relatively sure they can't haul ass either."

A loud, long-suffering sigh, attributable to almost anyone in the general vicinity, including me, echoed off the walls of the conference room.

"If what you say is true, Ms. Turner," the sheriff continued, "how would these—"

"Body snatchers?" Townsend offered.

"—individuals know you were there at that exact location at that exact time of night?"

The little hairs on the back of my neck began to get that creepy, don't-look-in-the-basement sensation. A chill I hadn't experienced the likes of since I bit into a giant Chilly Willy dill pickle with my two front teeth, sent a quiver through me. My tongue took on the texture of the extra coarse sandpaper we sell in the hardware section of Bargain City. "They followed me," I whispered. "They must have followed me. From the time I left work 'til the time I discovered the body in the trunk and hit the gravel running. That means they saw me. They might even know who I am. My name. Where I live." I slammed my hands down on the table and jumped to my feet. "Protective custody! I demand protective custody. Twenty-four hour guard! The federal witness protection program! Something!"

"Now who's been seeing too many movies?" Deputy Doug quipped.

I looked from man to man, waiting to see who could hold out the longest without laughing. It was a three-way tie. The fiends!

"I fail to see the humor in the situation, gentlemen," I said. "I've just informed you that a homicide has occurred within your jurisdiction. Now, are you going to investigate or not?"

"Sure, sure, we intend to investigate your report, Ms. Turner." Sheriff Steve pushed away from his perch. "But I'm going to tell you up front here that I think we'll find this has all been a mistake, much like the mistake you made taking the wrong automobile earlier this evening. Like Townsend here said, circumstances played a role in convincing you that you saw something that you didn't. Woman on her own. Stranded on a dark country road. Insufficient lighting. The imagination has a way of playing ugly tricks on a person. How many hours did you work today, Ms. Turner?"

I was taken aback by the abrupt subject change. I resisted the urge to tick off my work hours on my fingers. "Let's see, I opened up the Dairee Freeze at nine or so and worked 'til almost one, then pulled an eight-hour shift at BC. Why?"

"And the day before?"

"Pretty much the same, except I didn't get out of BC until after midnight because we had to unload a truck."

"So, you've been working two jobs on a pretty regular basis?"

"When she's not between jobs." Townsend apparently thought he'd gone long enough without hearing the sound of his own voice.

"I'd say drop dead, Townsend, but I've seen enough corpses for one day," I snapped, and turned back to the sheriff, not liking where this line of questioning was going. "I suppose next you'll be asking me if I'm taking any prescription or illegal drugs, whether I'm under the care of a physician for any psychological problems, if I hate my mother, suffer from acute PMS, or if I'm currently menstruating." I straightened my work vest and fished my keys out of my pocket. "You have my statement, officers," I said with as much dignity as someone who was padding around in dirty, bare feet could. "What you do with it is up to you. If there's nothing further?"

An uneasy silence followed. Sheriff Thomason finally shook his head and crossed the room to open the door for me. "We'll be in touch," he promised.

Yeah, right, if they wanted to sell raffle tickets so they could buy new reserve uniforms, they'd be in touch. Or, if I had a delinquent parking ticket, I'd hear from them. Or the next time they needed a good guffaw, they'd look me up.

"We'll get someone to drive you back to your vehicle," the sheriff said with special emphasis on *your*. He looked at Deputy Doug, who shook his head so violently I thought he'd give himself a case of whiplash.

"That isn't necessary," I said. "I'll walk."

All eyes in the room dropped to my feet. Townsend, who'd had a ringside seat in the corner, stretched and rotated his shoulders. "I'll see she gets home."

I placed my hand against my chest. "Be still, my heart," I muttered, and grudgingly accepted the ride. I'd need skin grafts on my feet if I walked much more.

As we wheeled into the Bargain City lot, depression settled over me like a heavy shroud. Where before my it-could-have-happened-to-anybody defense seemed plausible, seeing my jalopy parked right where I'd left it back by the greenhouse gave me second thoughts. Townsend was right. Stuff *did* happen to me. All the time. Like the time I worked as a delivery person at Town Square Florists. Somehow I got the cards switched on the floral bouquets and ended up taking the "*Long Distance Best Wishes to the Happy Couple: Today is the first day of the rest of your life*" arrangement to the double funeral of an elderly couple killed in an auto mishap, and delivered the "*With Deepest Sympathy at this Tragic Time*" plant to the newlyweds.

Or the time I was looking at bubble gum machines, couldn't find where the balls went, and happened to look up and see another customer who appeared to be having the same problem. "I see you're having the same difficulty I am," I said to the other prospective gumball purchaser, only to find out I was speaking to my own reflection on the mirrored wall. Or the time I shut the light out on my mother in the windowless restroom of a Chinese restaurant, leaving her to grope for the toilet paper and perform her ablutions in the dark. To this day my mother will not visit a Chinese restaurant with me. Of course, that may be because of the time I stuck bean sprouts up my nose to entertain the grandson of one of mother's friends. Several days later he was rushed to the hospital for extraction of a lima bean. That's one way to get out of eating those nasty vegetables, I suppose.

The inevitable consequence, however, of my Murphy's Law lifestyle was the acquisition of a rather unpleasant reputation. My mere presence was enough to guarantee one of three reactions from local residents. One, they'd snicker. Two, they'd tease me mercilessly. Or, three, they'd run for cover. It was almost as if they thought if they got too close to me, a little white farmhouse might come tumbling down out of the heavens and fall on them. Ding-dong. I hadn't decided yet which reaction hurt the most.

"I'll follow you—see that you get home all right." Ranger Rick pulled up to my car. I took a real close look this time just to make sure it *was* my car.

"No thanks." I mustered as much spunk as I could, considering I felt weak as a newborn filly. "I can manage on my own, Ranger Townsend." I hoped the chill in my voice gave him a case of frostbite.

"Be reasonable, Tressa," he said.

After the night I'd had, I was as likely to attain reasonable as I was to land a job as a foot model for corn-remover pads. I opened his truck door and stepped down, wincing as my tootsies made contact with the pavement. "Good night, Townsend. I won't forget how wonderfully supportive and helpful you've been this evening."

Townsend shoved a hand through his hair. "Come on, Tressa, cut me some slack here. What do you want from me?" he asked.

"Respect," I said. "Just simple respect. It's all I've ever wanted." I paused, wondering why I'd never demanded it before. "I'm right about Peyton Palmer, you know. Dead right. And once that is shown beyond a reasonable doubt, I'll expect a heck of a lot more from you than a simple apology, bucko. Let's see, maybe something along the lines of a full-page ad in the *Gazette*. Or perhaps you could wear a T-shirt that says 'Tressa Turner is not a ditz.' Because, whether or not you and those small-town, small-minded rumdums believe me or not, there's trouble here in good ole Grandville. Trouble with a capital 'M' as in murder."

Townsend rubbed a hand over his eyes. "Tressa, if your tale of murder and mayhem turns out to be true, I'll have your initials tattooed on my butt."

"Your bum's mine, Townsend," I vowed, then felt my cheeks grow warm when his eyes widened and I caught a glimpse of something there I hadn't seen before. "Uh, that didn't exactly come out the way I meant it to, but you get the drift. And no welshing."

"You know, to make this a fair bet, Turner, if Peyton Palmer turns up alive and well, you're gonna have to promise to desecrate your flesh, too." He tapped his chin. "Hmmm. Maybe a tiny raccoon on your tushie? How about it?"

"Sure," I said, thinking this bet was way out there. Still it was a slam dunk for me. I knew poor Peyton Palmer was a goner. "I have nothing to lose. I know what I saw." I held out a hand to formalize our bet. "A raccoon tattoo to the loser it is. But you better get those buns of steel prepped, Ranger Rick. I hear the procedure is rather painful."

"Buns of steel?" Townsend laughed. "I'm flattered, Turner." His grip on my hand tightened. "I never knew you noticed."

"Oooh!" My romanticized version of Townsend dissipated like steam on a mirror. I tried to stomp to the driver's side door of my vehicle, but only managed to look like I'd had a few too many. I got in and shut my door. Men.

For about half a second, I contemplated hopping in the back seat and sleeping in my car since I had to be back at work in four hours, but the lure of a light beer was one I couldn't resist. I turned the key and was comforted by the traditional belches, sputters and coughs of my Plymouth. Honest to goodness, guys, I almost teared up.

I pulled into my driveway with a huge sigh of relief, accompanied, of course, by several loud backfires. In my rearview mirror I saw Townsend drive by slowly. I didn't know whether to be touched or ticked. I put my head in my hands, trying to make sense of what made no sense at all.

Murder had come to our sleepy little farming community. But I was the only one who knew it.

My breath caught somewhere between my uvula

and lungs. Correction. Two people knew about the murder: me and the killer. I mean the killer and I. Grammatically correct or not, that knowledge scared the h-e-double-hockeysticks out of me!

Chapter 5

Saturday dawned gray and gloomy, which made it a heck of a lot harder to haul my kiester from my nice, soft bed. The two light beers I'd consumed to celebrate reaching home safe and sound didn't help matters, either. I gave quite a bit of thought to calling in sick to Bargain City. I wasn't certain I was up to being the butt of more dumb blonde jokes. Eventually, however, economics won out. I needed the moola.

Besides, at this very moment I might already be vindicated. The police would have had ample time to run all their little chemical tests on the trunk to check for bodily fluids. Ick. They were certain to know by now that Peyton Palmer had not been home blissfully slumbering, but, indeed, had been doing a rather crude impression of a spare tire.

I felt bad for his family. I supposed he had a wife. Kids, even. I'd have to find out. Under the circumstances, a condolence call was probably in order. The widow would probably want to know all the gory details concerning my grizzly discovery. Bummer.

I eased out of bed and made my way to the shower. I was ready to head out the door by seven-thirty. I grabbed my red, refillable coffee mug, hesitated, then popped the lid off, peered at the bottom of the cup, and cringed. Yuck. I gave the cup a good wash with antibacterial soap and hot water, while dismally wondering what critters were multiplying on the bottom. I brightened. Wasn't penicillin discovered in the same way? Maybe there was a cure for the common cold growing on my coffee mug. Or a cure for zits. Toenail fungus, maybe? I could be rich. Famous. Somebody important. I stared at my reflection in the compact window over my compact sink in my compact kitchen. *Somebody.*

I stuck my tongue out at myself, checked the counter for my car keys, then remembered I'd dropped them in my vest pocket. I grabbed the vest from the back of a dining room chair, and scooted out the door. The pooches greeted me as they always did, with drool dripping from way too much tongue and the whacking of happy tails against my legs. I filled their water bowls and dumped out more chow, then jumped in my car—emphasis on *my* car—and blew my mongrels a kiss before backing out.

On the way to Bargain City, I stopped for a fill-up. A cappuccino fill-up, that is. I always just buy ten dollars worth of gas when I need to put fuel in my car. Old whitie wouldn't know how to run on a full tank. Besides, I figure when he conks for the last time, why waste an entire tank of gas? Of course, ten bucks doesn't get me very far, especially when my mode of transportation gets less miles per gallon than a cement mixer. Still, I was glad to be back behind the wheel of my car. No bodies. No blood. No rubbers (sigh). Just pop cans, Snapple bottles, a tennis racket that hadn't seen a whole lot of use, and several tennis balls that routinely rolled from the back to the front depending on my driving habits. I stood in line at the counter to pay for my drink.

"Did ya hear about the excitement last night?" Harve Dawson, a skinny, bowlegged little wrangler who used to do all our horseshoeing and hoof-trimming until a back injury robbed him of that avocation, took a bite of a blueberry donut, and directed his question to the middle-aged clerk, Mary, behind the counter.

My ears perked up, and I scooted closer to old Harve. I held my breath. Ready or not, here it came. In a few short seconds, I would be thrown into the limelight, a local celebrity, the hometown girl who had exposed murder in the heartland. *Murder in the heartland.* Now, that had a certain ring to it. Maybe there was a book in this somewhere. Even a miniseries. Who would play me, I wondered, and raised my cup to my lips to appear casual, unaffected.

"*Ouch!*" Cappuccino scalded my upper lip. So much for casual.

"Excitement? I sure did." Mary, never one to turn down a good gossip, leaned across the counter. "It is shocking, isn't it? I mean, how humiliating to be found like that!"

Behind Harve, I nodded. Being stuffed in the trunk of a 1985 Chrysler Le Baron was not the most dignified way to be remembered.

"I would be mortified," Mary went on, "just mortified, if that was one of my family members. Pillars of the community? Ha. Snooty well-to-do's, is more like it. Kind of makes you glad it happened. It's about time, I say."

I frowned. This class warfare was getting out of hand if working-class folk were expressing glad tidings due to the fact one of the country club set had bought the farm in a particularly gruesome and violent manner. What was next? La guillotine?

"Who called in the report?" Harve asked.

I took a deep breath. This was it. Showtime.

"Someone fed up with some people getting away with murder around here. I guess Townsend was out there, so maybe he called it in." Mary smiled. "He was with a lady friend, naturally. I guess they were getting very touchy-feelie. I heard she was all over him like cling wrap on a sticky roll."

All over him like cling wrap! Oh, I knew I should never have let my guard down with that weasel.

"I don't know where you're getting your information," I spoke up, "but for the record, I have never played touchy-feelie with Rick Townsend, or anything else for that matter. He gave me a brotherly hug, that's all. A strictly platonic, no hanky-panky, no cling-wrappy hug. Got it?"

Harve and Mary exchanged surprised looks.

"You were there?" the convenience store clerk asked.

"Yes, of course."

"With Townsend?"

"Well, yes, but you see, I was shaken, vulnerable. I needed comfort. Reassurance. That was all."

"Huh?" Harve contributed.

"You were there? You saw everything?" Mary queried.

I nodded, directing my eyes downward.

"I bet that was a sight!" Mary continued. "Lord, I wish I could have been there to see it all in living color. Makes you wish you had a video camera handy.

That would be a sure grand prize winner on *X-rated Home Videos*!"

I jerked my head up. Yuck. What kind of sicko actually wanted to witness such a gruesome, ghastly sight, let alone tape it for Nielsen ratings?

"Describe everything to me." Mary leaned further across the counter with a feral gleam in her eye. "Every last detail."

I looked over at Harve the Horseman. His tongue darted out and retrieved donut crumbs from his lip, his eyes wide with anticipation. What was wrong with these people?

"I'm sorry, I really can't discuss the details of this since there is an ongoing investigation." I hedged, not willing to share my celebrity with Damian and his evil twin sister here.

"Investigation?" Harve took his green CO-OP cap off his head, smoothed his thinning hair, and put the hat back in place. "What investigation? They know who did it. They've already made arrests."

I put a hand on the counter to steady myself. Talk about your brilliant police work! I'd been convinced when I left the sheriff's office last night that the authorities hadn't believed a word I said. Now here, the next morning, they'd already made an arrest. "That's fantastic!" I gushed. "Utterly fantastic. What awesome police work."

"Say what?" Harve snorted. "Barney Fife could've solved this crime. They were caught red-handed."

Caught red-handed? How? Where?

"Something was red, but I guarantee you it wasn't hands," Mary snickered.

Harve hooted. I blinked. How could these people be so callous and unfeeling?

"How could you?" I asked, at my wits' end with Thelma and Louis here. "How could you?"

"What's got you all bent out of shape?" Harve asked.

"You *are* discussing last night's criminal activity, aren't you?" I said.

"What the hell do you think we're discussing?"

"I'm missing something here," I said.

"How can that be?" Mary turned disbelieving eyes on me. "You said you were there. You should know all about it."

"I do. I do. At least, I think I do." I took a gulp of my cappuccino to jumpstart my brain function.

"Well, then," Mary gave me an exaggerated wink. "You must have seen 'em all *au naturelle*. Tell me. Who's the best hung?"

"What? *What?* What was that?" I sputtered and began to cough. The contents of my mouth spewed out right onto Harve the Horseman's eyeglasses, down his cheeks, and onto the collar of his white shirt. "I'm sorry! I'm sorry!" I grabbed a napkin and began to wipe his glasses.

"What in the hell is wrong with you, sister?" Harve gave me a whack on the shoulder. "You okay?"

Was I? I had my doubts. Supersized ones.

The door chimed. A mailman with ugly, knobby knees came in.

"You hear about the ruckus last night?"

I picked up a nearby local newspaper and stuck it in front of my face.

"The boys' baseball team was caught skinny-dipping out at the lake on the New Holland side last evening," the bony-legged mailman went on. "They've all been charged with possession of alcohol by a minor. There go the play-offs."

I brought the paper down to nose level. Underaged drinking? Skinny-dipping? Since when did that qualify as a crime spree? Why were these people obsessing over teenaged partying when they had a murderer in their midst?

"We got an eyewitness here." Mary motioned at me. "As a matter of fact, I was just getting the straight skinny from her when you came in," Mary said with an obscene wink.

"You were at the scene of the crime?" the mailman asked, with a perverted wink of his own.

"No? Yes?" My head was spinning. I tossed the paper down, stuffed the damp napkin behind Harve's eyeglasses, and threw my money on the counter. "Late. Gotta go," I managed. I hit the door on a run, dribbling French vanilla cappuccino down my front.

"That's our Calamity," I heard Harve the Horseman chuckle.

I pulled away from the convenience store in a hurry, my tailpipe scraping loud and long on the inclined drive. I tossed my hair away from my face and sneered. The good people of Grandville would be laughing out of the other side of their mouths when news of the real crime and my personal involvement hit the streets. Then I would have the last laugh and a brand-new, respectable reputation. Romeo Rick Townsend would have a cute little tattoo on his behind, and all would be right with the world.

I worked my shift at Bargain City in a funk. For all I know, someone could have said, "hand over all the money in the register," and I would have asked "paper or plastic," dumped it in a bag, thanked them, and urged them to have a nice day.

The law enforcement community, it seemed, was keeping a lid on this investigation tighter than my Uncle Frank's grip on his wallet. We're talking pickle jar lid tight here, folks.

I supposed the secrecy was appropriate. Given the nature of the crime and the circumstances relating to it, it was wise to avoid the media circus that would erupt once word was out. Still, in a community where your neighbor clocked in what time you took your nightly whiz, the brake man at Barney's Brakes and Exhaust knew you'd been through two bad relationships and were just getting back out there socially again, and where the meter reader knew your Great Aunt Eunice was a lesbian, keeping this story under wraps for this long qualified for miracle status.

Had the cops found the body? Were the forensic tests completed? Did the police have any suspects? Had the next of kin been notified? Had Townsend given any more thought to his tushie tattoo?

The afternoon crawled by slower than it takes a cold sore to heal. I was daydreaming about a gorgeous cowboy with a great smile running his fingers through my hair and looking deep into my eyes. Of course, in my fantasy, I had someone else's hair—someone for whom the term "the frizzies" is a mystery. I had earphones on, listening to sample CD tracks, imagining myself anywhere but where I was, when it dawned on me there was a customer to my right, almost rubbing elbows with me. I pulled my headphones off and turned. A long set of ugly fangs greeted me. I gasped, and then recognized the fangs as belonging to a rather frightening cobra tattoo coiling around a rather large arm.

"Sorry," I gulped. "Did you find everything you needed, sir?" I watched, intrigued, as the cobra seemed to wriggle when its owner's muscles tensed.

"As a matter of fact, no, I haven't found everything I need." Cobra Man moved closer, his brewery breath hot on my face. "But I'm guessin' you'll be able to help me out. You are the helpful type, aren't you?" He tapped my Bargain City name tag. "Tressa?"

"That depends on what you want," I replied, my eyes drawn to the silver stud pierced through his left nostril, and the collection of them in his left eyebrow, before returning to the serpent decorating his arm.

"I want my property," the snake charmer said, and wound a lock of my blonde hair around a dirty-nailed finger. "I want my property," he repeated, "and I want it now."

"P-p-p-roperty?" I stammered. "Did you check the lost and found at customer service?"

The serpent performed another recoil. "What I want was never lost, but it sure as hell was found. And you, blondie, found it. Now, I want it back. Simple as that. So hand it over."

"If you could be more specific, sir—"

"I ain't got the patience for game playing, bitch. Just hand over the green and everything will be cool."

"Green?" My god, I thought, a robbery! "Is this a robbery?" I asked, with a pathetic tremor to my voice.

Tattoo Ted's eyes shot open, and he looked around. "Just calm down, you stupid bitch. I didn't say nothing about no robbery. I'm here to retrieve my personal property, that's all. I happen to know it came into your possession last night. You got it. I want it back. End of discussion."

Up until this point I was pretty much playing a guessing game on how to serve this particular customer. His references to *green*, *property*, and *the other night* finally got the old cognitive abilities firing, and it became clear as the slithering serpent on the bulging biceps. Since I was fairly certain my visitor didn't want Peyton Palmer's body back, even though it might well be green by now, I concluded he was inquiring about the envelope of Bennies that had almost made me wet my drawers.

"I'm sorry, sir, but I don't have the particular item you're interested in." I hardly recognized my own voice. In my dreams I'd wished for a voice this husky.

The finger tangled in my hair yanked hard on the twisted lock. My eyes began to tear, and I knew how the early settlers must have felt before they said goodbye to their scalps. "This ain't no goddamned raincheck I'm asking for, girlie. You got something belongs to me and I aim to get it back."

"But I can't—" I started to explain I couldn't give him what I didn't have when he clamped another dirty hand over my mouth.

"I hate the word 'can't.' Implies a lack of effort. I hate it almost as much as I hate Buttinsky blondes who can't keep their goddamned nose out of things that don't concern them. But believe me when I say, I know how to motivate reluctant women." He sneered, and I almost gagged at his brown, putrid teeth. "I've had lots of experience."

I was about ready to promise my firstborn just to get the guy off me, when one of my regulars arrived to play the demo video games for an hour or so. I could have kissed the little brat.

"You still have the same, dumb old game previews?" He came up to Tattoo Ted and me. "Hey, are you supposed to be making out in here?" the freckled lad asked, staring at the motley character's hand in my hair and fingers on my mouth. I took advantage of my pint-sized savior's arrival and freed myself from the repulsive grasp of my supposed admirer. I hustled to the boy and put a shaking arm over his shoulders.

"I'm so glad you came in today," I said, steering the boy to a more populated area of the store. "You can't imagine how glad I am you came in today."

"Huh?" The little twerp I'd kicked out a record number of times looked up at me. I cast a backward glance. Cobra Man had disappeared.

"Your boyfriend is over there," the red-headed youngster pointed toward the garden center. "I think he's trying to get your attention."

I spotted my beau. He tapped his watch, then made a disturbing slashing gesture across his throat, turned, and walked out.

I proceeded to grab my carrot-topped rescuer in a giant bear hug and planted a wet, slobbery kiss on him. He ran from the store screaming.

By five o'clock, I was feeling uneasy, both from the previous night's excitement and my more recent encounter with Tattoo Ted. I was now convinced I was in very real danger. I was being stalked at my workplace by a probable killer who thought I had his stash of cash, and he was bent on getting it back or taking it out of my cowgirl hide.

I threw my vest in my locker, clocked out, and hurried to my car. I needed answers to the questions that had been cycling through what was left of my mind. The cops would have no reason to keep their progress from me. After all, I was the one who brought the report to them in the first place.

I stopped for a chili dog and soda, and managed to leak chili sauce on my white shirt. My earlier fright did not seem to diminish my appetite. I have yet to find something that will. Sigh.

I parked my car on the square outside the courthouse and tried the door. It was locked. Well, duh. Of course. This was Saturday. The courthouse was closed. I walked around to the south side of the building where the sheriff's office was housed. This door was locked, as well, but there was an intercom button, which I pushed.

"Yes, may I help you?" A woman's voice came out of the box. At least, I thought it was a woman; the sound quality was as bad as the Dairee Freeze drive-up.

"Uh, yeah. I need to speak with Deputy Di . . . uh Doug, Doug Samuels. This is Tressa Turner. I spoke with him last night concerning a . . . a . . . a tire problem."

"Ooo-kay." There was a long pause. Then, a buzz and the lock was released. I grabbed the door and stepped into the cool interior of the courthouse. I was met by Deputy Samuels.

"Afternoon, Ms. Turner." The deputy folded his arms across his meaty chest. "What can I do you for?"

I think my mouth flew open. I'm not sure. "Do? I'm here for an update, of course. Oh, and to crack your case for you. You know. Last night's top-secret case. The one with all the elements of a Grisham novel."

"Uh-huh. I was thinking more along the lines of

Grimm's fairy tales," he said with a smirk. He looked at my soiled shirt. "I suppose you're gonna tell me that's blood," he added.

"Would you believe me if I said yes?" I asked, returning the comment with a sneer of my own.

"What do you think?" he remarked.

I took a deep breath. "Listen, Deputy, I know who killed Peyton Palmer."

I watched the good deputy's jaw drop like the first hill on the Twister at Adventureland.

"Say what?" he managed.

"I know who murdered Palmer! Well, I don't actually know his name because he didn't actually introduce himself, but I could pick him out of a line-up or from a mug shot book in a heartbeat. He has some rather ornate piercings and a rather interesting tattoo. The sooner he is in custody, the better. For me. You see, he seems to be under the false impression that I have that thick envelope of money I told you all about. You remember. The one that disappeared with Peyton Palmer's body." I stopped to wait for the deputy's reaction. None was forthcoming. "I've just cracked your murder case, Officer. What do you have to say to that?" I pressed.

Deputy Samuels took hold of my elbow and steered me toward an alcove right outside the men's john. Bad lighting. Dubious ambiance.

"Listen, Ms. Turner, Tressa, I think it would be advisable if you kept low-key about that police report you made last night. The less said, the better."

I nodded. "I get it. You don't want to jeopardize the investigation. I understand. I haven't said a word to anyone. But some progress is being made on the investigation. Right? What have you learned so far? Have the tests on the trunk been completed? How is Palmer's family holding up? Can I start looking through mug shots now?"

The deputy ran a hand through his hair. "There isn't that much to tell."

"What do you mean?" I was getting a weird feeling about this investigation. Like, *was* there an investigation? "Just what has the investigation established so far?" I asked.

Deputy Doug shook his head. "I don't know how to tell you this. Of course, this is preliminary, but . . ." He stopped.

"Yes?"

"I probably shouldn't say anything. It isn't my place."

"Why? Isn't this within your jurisdiction?"

"Technically, yes, if a crime was committed, it would be within county jurisdiction."

"Well then?" I said. Then, "Wait. Did you say *if* a crime has been committed? If? I don't know about you, but last I knew killing someone and stuffing their lifeless body in a trunk was considered a crime."

The deputy's nose wrinkled like he smelled something foul, something other than the unpleasant odor coming from the men's john. "It's like this, Ms. Turner—Tressa. We checked out your story and, so far, we've found nothing to substantiate your claims. The car was clean. Trunk. Interior. We turned up squat."

This was surprising, though not outside the realm of possibility. There was that danged tarp to consider. "What about Peyton Palmer's wife? His family? What do they have to say? Did they even realize he was missing?" I wasn't sure how long Peyton Palmer had been dead, but from the looks of him, not long.

"I don't know about that, Ms. Turner. The local PD handled that part of the inquiry."

"What are they saying?"

"I can't really comment on that, Ms. Turner."

"But they do know about last night, don't they? About the car and the trunk and the money?"

Deputy Doug shuffled his feet. "Ms. Turner, I really can't say more—"

"More? You haven't said anything yet."

"Ms. Turner, listen . . ."

"Deputy Samuels, have the authorities or have they not notified Peyton Palmer's family that he is dead?"

"But he isn't, Ms. Turner." A footstep caught my attention as Sheriff Thomason emerged from the shadows. He nodded to Deputy Samuels, then directed a pained look at me.

I tried to remember what I'd said before the sheriff entered, stage left. "Isn't what?" I finally thought to ask.

"Isn't dead, of course."

"Excuse me?"

"Peyton Palmer isn't dead."

CHAPTER 6

Peyton Palmer isn't dead. Peyton Palmer isn't dead.

As often as those words cycled through my head, I found myself wishing they were set to music. Something really punk. Or maybe a rap.

Yo, Peyton Palmer isn't dead.
That wasn't no hole in his head.
He ain't a swimmin' with no fishes.
That's what you get, you listen to ditzes.

But although it had a certain ring to it, it wasn't the ring of truth. I'd seen the contents of that trunk with my own two eyes, and if other things about me are a bit cockeyed, my vision is twenty/twenty.

What about Palmer's wife and family? I'd asked the sheriff.

The missus Palmer, Sheila, apparently an artsy-fartsy sort who was into all things crafty, had checked into a hotel for a stamping conference around three Friday afternoon. According to the cops, Sheila last spoke with her husband Friday morning before I, uh, stumbled across him later that night. He'd planned an all-dayer on the pontoon Saturday, if nothing came up at the office, Sheila advised.

How convenient, I thought, already pointing the finger of suspicion at the Martha Stewart wannabe—well, apart from Martha's little stint upstate, that is. Conveniently out of town. Trying to establish an alibi, maybe? Still, Omaha was just a two-hour drive.

I asked when Palmer had last been seen. Thomason's eyebrows went toward his hairline. My guess is, he was surprised I'd asked two intelligent questions in a row.

Dennis Hamilton, Peyton Palmer's law partner, told the local police that, as far as he knew, Palmer had put in a full day's work on Friday. He'd seen him there. But Hamilton had been in court all afternoon and hadn't returned to the office afterwards. He assumed Palmer had been in the office Saturday as well, as the attorneys took turns working Saturday mornings and it had been Palmer's turn. Hamilton couldn't say for sure, though, as he hadn't dropped in, and the secretary had weekends off. Sometimes, he admitted, they would check the offices for messages, then lock up and leave if things were slow.

Local police checked the Palmer residence. There was no answer when they knocked, the machine picked up when they called, and there was no sign of Palmer's silver SUV.

Not knowing much—okay, anything—about such things as decomposition rates, rigor mortis, livor mortis (or is that liver mortis?) my abbreviated examination of the corpus delicti yielded few clues. I recalled reaching out and touching skin that seemed so cold I felt a chill up to my armpit. But that may have had more to do with my realization that I was touching a dead guy rather than an accurate assessment of his body temperature.

What about a search warrant for his house? I'd pressed. What about his boat? Had they checked his boat? Inquired at local restaurants? Local watering holes? Maybe someone saw Palmer earlier in the evening. What about the threat I received at Bargain City from Tattoo Ted wanting his wad of hundreds back, I continued, sensing the law enforcement-types bristling at my tenacity. Fine for them to drag their feet; they weren't the ones with a self-mutilating, possibly murderous, psychopath making disturbing throat-slashing gestures at them in their workplace.

The officers humored me by permitting me to file a report, and promised to permit me to look through the mug shot books the next day, then hustled me to the door with the assurance that the case was being handled with the degree of attention it warranted. That was not a comforting thought.

I sulked all the way home. If the local butcher, baker, or candlestick maker had reported this incident to the police, they would have called in the National Guard. Even the drunks that closed the local taverns each weeknight by puking in the bushes would have elicited more action on the part of law enforcement.

I pulled into the driveway and spotted a dark blue Buick in my folks' drive. Oh, crap. Taylor was home for the weekend. I'd forgotten all about her Royal Highness coming home. Taylor is my sister. Don't get me wrong. I love my baby sister. I do. It's just that I don't fare well by comparison. You be the judge. Homecoming Queen vs. Detention Queen. 4.0 GPA vs. trade school recommendation. Honor Society vs. Humane Society. Miss Iowa contestant to Miss Rodeo Queen runner-up. You get my drift.

I surveyed the Buick with a wrinkled nose. When my grandmother could no longer safely operate a motor vehicle, the little princess inherited my grampa's like-new, full-sized Buick for college purposes. As usual, it was spotless. Trust Taylor to cover all her bases. Before the end of the weekend, my father would be sure to point out once or twice how immaculate sister-dearest kept the car, and how she made sure the oil was changed every two thousand miles. My father does it with the best intentions, of course. He's thinking that eventually I'll sit up and take notice. But I figure, hey, why change the oil at all? As much as my car leaks, I'm putting in a quart of fresh, clean oil once a week, easy.

I survived the attack of my dogs, carnivorous creatures, Butch and Sundance, and played with the hairy varmints a bit before I filled their bowls and went in. I wasn't in the trailer more than forty-five seconds before the phone rang. I was tempted to let the machine get it, but didn't want to miss a call from the police if, by some freak miracle, they actually got off their donut duffs and decided to do some police work.

"Tressa, honey, you remembered about tonight, didn't you?" My mother tends to get right to the point. I think it's an accountant thing. Time is money and all that.

"Tonight?"

"Taylor's birthday."

I hesitated.

"We're going out. To celebrate. As a family."

I scratched my head and tried to act dumb. (Hey,

stop that. I know what you're thinking.) "Gee, Mom, I don't recall—"

"I told you myself, Tressa." My mother cut me off like the big hook that drags people off stage at the comedy clubs.

"I don't think—"

"I wrote it in big, red letters on the dry erase calendar I bought you."

"I must have—"

"I left a message on your machine every night this week."

"I really can't remem—"

"Tressa Jayne Turner."

"Taylor's birthday supper. Family dinner. Gotcha."

"We're meeting your brother and Kimberly at Calhoun's around seven. Do you want to ride with us?"

Right, and give Dad the ideal opportunity to praise Taylor's automobile maintenance? No way. I declined gracefully, citing animals to be fed, thinking if I hustled my buns, I could run *my* car through the car wash and do an end run around little sister. Of course, there was still that little nuisance of being banned from the car wash.

I jogged to the horse barn and did the chores in record time. I felt guilty because I'd had so little time to spend with my tiny herd, and made a vow to devote Sunday afternoon to getting reacquainted.

Lathering down in the shower later, I contemplated how to break the news to my family that I had discovered a dead body in the trunk of a car I'd taken by mistake, and now there was a very good chance the killer was after me. I hesitated to go public with the information. Truth be told, once my grandma hears something, well, it's like telephone—telegraph—tell-an-old-lady. It would be all over town quicker than the flu after Christmas vacation. And since the police were moving slower than the line at the drive-up bank on a sweltering Friday afternoon at quitting time, having the particulars of my discovery hit the streets too soon could jeopardize the outcome of the investigation when it finally kicked into high gear. About the time I applied for Medicare at the rate it was currently going.

Besides, Taylor, Craig and Kimmie would be there. Craig is three years older than me. His best friend, you recall, is Ranger Rick, the beastie I plan to put out of my misery someday. Craig and Kimmie have been married for three years. Kimmie works in the county clerk's office. Craig is the sales manager for a car dealership. He cringes every time he sees me drive up in my reject from the auto salvage yard. If he's heard it once, he's heard it a thousand times, "You sell Calamity a decent set of wheels yet?" I'm sure this figures prominently in his tendency to needle me. That and the fact that he thinks I'm wasting my life.

I shook my head. No. Better to wait until I could speak with Mom and Dad privately about my little car predicament. Spring it on them when they were alone, and after Dad had relaxed with a beer or two. I twisted a towel around my head, another around my body, and padded to my bedroom. I dug through my underwear drawer, trying to find a pair of hipsters that weren't "religious." You know. Holey. I finally found a red thong that looked like it was purchased at Hookers-R-Us. I threw it aside and settled for a pair of white old-lady undies Gramma had given me several years ago when I went into the hospital for minor knee surgery so I would have "proper" underclothes. One of these days, I needed to do laundry.

I stood outside my closet trying to decide what to wear. It's a challenge to glamorize a body that is most at home in tank tops, cut-offs and cowboy boots. I usually end up looking like I'm playing dress-up. It just isn't a natural look for me. I'm more the Meg Ryan does Dallas type. Comfy. Informal. Rumpled, yet cute.

For the most part, I suppose you could say I'm average. I've always been comfortable being average. It's a low-risk place to be. I'm average height: five-foot-seven. I'm average weight. (Okay, so I could lose a few pounds and not miss them. But, who couldn't?) I am admittedly a bit cleavage-challenged, having inherited my modest bosom size from my beanpole mother. Still, those Wonder Bras work wonders, don't they, ladies? Thanks to three years of orthodontic treatment, I lost my what's-up,-doc? overbite, and ended up with a rather nice smile if I do say so myself. Usually by this time of year I have a terrific tan started; however, two indoor jobs and zero time and money for the tanning salon had left me looking like a wraith.

I have your basic blue eyes, nothing fancy, and, as we've already established, blonde hair. My naturally curly locks have always been the bane of my existence. I always envied girls with straight, silky blonde hair. I look like a peroxide Shirley Temple, without the cute dimples, talent, or fame. Left to dry naturally, my hair spirals into perfect corkscrew curls, all around my face. You can imagine how thrilled a devout tomboy was with a head of curls. Once, when I was twelve, I tried to straighten my lion's mane with my mother's steam iron and scorched my hair so badly, I had to have it cut even with my jawline. Even when I pull my hair back into a ponytail, those danged curls escape and frame my face with frizz. I go through a bottle of gel a week easy, plastering my hair to my head.

I finally decided on an olive-and-white floral print sundress, mainly because it was clean and not wrinkled. I gelled my hair, slapped on some foundation and blush, brushed mascara over my lashes, and doused myself with Bargain City clearance body splash. Although I'm not gorgeous by any stretch of the imagination (even mine), I don't clean up half-bad. And if I really gave a you-know-what, I could probably turn a few heads. Some of them even male. Up to now, I hadn't found the guy worth the effort.

My sister can turn heads without trying. Not that she's any more beautiful than the next supermodel centerfold. She just has more—what should I call it? Charisma. The truly incredible thing about Taylor is she's genuinely oblivious to the fact that she is the cause of rampant spousal abuse. When she walks by, women frequently hit, poke, or jab their husbands or boyfriends.

It was nearly eight when I left the trailer. I jumped in my car and started it, then noticed the gas gauge was how-low-can-you-go low. I should've put ten bucks worth in, after all. I checked my watch again. I considered snitching some gas from the tank Dad kept for his farm toys, but decided that would take way too long and I would end up smelling like Eau de Petrol. I tossed my key in the ashtray, and my eyes drifted to the blue Buick. I hesitated a good thirty seconds before I hoofed it to the Buick, and slid behind the wheel. The key was in the ashtray and there was a full tank of gas. It was a sign. All I had to do was make certain I left the restaurant first, and no one would be the wiser.

My folks had reserved the big party room in the back. I arrived just as the waitress was taking drink orders.

"Oh, here she is." I waved to Aunt Reggie, who'd noticed my arrival. I smiled at Uncle Frank, and my eyes drifted down the full tables toward the end. The smile froze on my face. Since when did "just family" include Don and Charlotte Townsend and Don's father, Joe?

"So, here you are." I didn't need to turn around to figure out who'd sneaked up behind and almost scared the old lady panties right off me.

"You! What are *you* doing here, Ranger Rick?"

"I was invited. At least, I think I was. From your reaction, I can't be all that sure."

"Who invited you?"

"Your folks. Actually, I think it was your grandma's doing. You know, I believe she has the hots for Granddad."

I took another look at the shriveled old man next to Gram, the guy who had been such a strapping young businessman in the olden days, and focused my attention back on his annoying grandson. "You're nuts," I hissed.

Townsend gave me one of his crooked smiles. I'd seen him use that smile on others, and I'd sneered at the phoney baloneyness of it. Now, being the sole recipient of its splendor—well, even I had to admit it had its charm.

"I'm not the one who played hide and seek with a

dead guy," he remarked, and took a lock of my hair and tucked it behind my ear.

"Stop that! And lower your voice, you moron. I don't want everyone in the restaurant to know about all that. At least not yet. Not until the cops get their heads out of their rear ends and take this seriously."

"We need to talk about the other night, Tressa. I'm worried about you."

I thought about my snake charmer pal and made a noisy swallow. "I'm worried about me, too. But we can't talk here. Please, Townsend. Promise me you won't say a thing about the other night." My voice raised in the heat of the moment, catching the table occupants at a lull in their conversations.

"What was that about the other night?" My brother, Craig, has the biggest ears in the family. And the biggest mouth next to yours truly. "You two got something you want to tell us?"

"Uh, no, not at all. We were just, uh, discussing the baseball team's arrest and suspension," I explained.

"Oh, you're good," Townsend whispered in my right ear. I elbowed him and made my way to an empty seat by Gram. Townsend proceeded to greet Taylor with a kiss on the cheek and took the seat beside the birthday girl, opposite me.

"Real tragedy," Rick's father commented. "We had a decent shot to take States this year. I'd say they were pretty harsh with the boys. After all, it was just alcohol."

"You wouldn't say that if your son or daughter became a human hood ornament for one of those boys-will-be-boys driving drunk, though, would you, Mr. Townsend?" I said, grabbing an onion ring from the appetizer platter closest to me. Hey, I like my beer as well as the next cowgirl, but I draw the line at drunk driving.

Don Townsend gave me a look that I interpreted as, Stick to your dip cones, dippy. "Interesting insight," was all he said.

"I'm with Tressa on this one, Mr. Townsend," Taylor interjected. "Rules are rules. And, like laws, if they are to work, they must be enforced fairly and impartially, without special consideration for Jeff the Jock, Debbie Drill Team, or other members of the upper socio-economic segments of society. In other words, you do the crime, you do the time."

"Yes, I can see that you're probably right on this one, Taylor," Don Townsend conceded. "And splendidly articulated, as usual." He lifted his glass of wine in her direction. "To the brilliant birthday girl."

Everything went red in my head. An oozing, gushing, crimson red. I had a hard time focusing. Oh, so *Taylor* was right. What was I then? Too damned dumb to take part in a grown-up conversation?

Perhaps I should have been grateful for Taylor's defense of me. I am not the most tactful of individuals. Over the years, my family has often felt the need to explain my actions, smooth things over for me, excuse me.

Grateful? Yeah, right. More like fed-up. I was sick and tired of being the object of ridicule, head-shaking and knee-slapping. I'd had it up to here with opening my mouth and having no one listen, *really* listen, to what I had to say. My folks did it. My grandparents did it. My brother and sister. My friends. Townsend. Now, even the police were doing it. Have a good ole laugh at the ditz's expense, give her a cookie and a pat on the head, and send her on her way. "*You be a good girl and go on home, now, ya hear? We'll take care of everything.*" Snicker, snicker, snicker.

A wave of sadness swept over me. I took a long swallow of my wine, then raised my glass in a solemn toast to myself. "To Tressa Jayne Turner," I murmured. "A woman with a story to tell."

I looked over and caught Townsend staring at me. I blinked away each and every betraying tear that dared to consider rolling down my cheeks.

I've had a lot of experience hiding my feelings. Used to be I'd laugh right along with the crowd when they were having a chuckle at my expense, and take their all-in-good-fun teasing in stride. At the time, I thought I was the clever one, dumbing myself down sufficiently to avoid catching parental heat for my lackluster performance in academia, and a *que sera, sera* approach to life. But as it turned out, I didn't get the last laugh at all. Now, at twenty-three, I inwardly grieved for what I'd lost as a result of my foolish insecurities.

The truth was, I was as about as credible as the boy who cried wolf. Or maybe Teddy Kennedy on water safety.

But I truly *did* have a story to tell. And it was an A number one murder-mystery with enough gory stuff to satisfy even my grandmother. The trouble was, no one would listen.

I sat there for a moment, mulling over the sad state of my life, when goosebumps began to pop up all over my arms. My heart rate increased and my breath caught. Why hadn't I thought of this before? I'd just been handed the mother of all opportunities to change the course of my destiny, to right the wrongs of the past, to obtain a measure of justice, and to finally, finally, get my due. My very own murder-mystery just waiting to be solved!

The possibilities tumbled about in my head like the clothes in the super-giant capacity clothes dryer at the U-B-Clean Laundromat. It was brilliant. No, *I* was brilliant.

I filled my wine glass and brought it to my lips again. I, Tressa Jayne Turner, was about to embark on a quest to expose a killer, rescue the citizenry, redeem my honor, and banish the specter of Calamity Jayne once and for all to the pages of folklore.

I lifted my glass in Townsend's direction. His eyes narrowed. I gave him a toothy smile. Brace those buns, Mr. Ranger, sir, I toasted. Brace those buns.

The meal was tedious, as expected. I wanted to numb the effects with another glass of white wine, but decided I needed a clear head for sleuthing purposes. Besides, there was Taylor's car to consider. Instead, I concentrated my efforts on my thick, pink rib eye (remember, I live in cow country), cottage fries, and Texas toast. Oh, and a nice, healthy green salad for roughage. By the time I'd consumed my meal, I was glad I hadn't worn a garment with a waistband. I shoved my chair back and rubbed my tummy. When they brought the cake out, however, I had my second wind and, to be polite, ate a small sliver.

Throughout the evening, I'd kept my eye on Ranger Rick. It was clear to me, and therefore to others more astute than me, that there was a concerted effort underway to promote the idea of a Taylor Turner/Ranger Rick romance. The chair reserved for Rick. (*I wonder if someone would have pulled it out from under me if*

I'd chosen to sit there first?) The conversation clearly chosen to point out all the things the two had in common. Like post-high school education. Setting professional goals and achieving them. Vehicle maintenance. Even being drop-dead gorgeous.

"Look at those two. Don't Rick and Taylor make a striking couple, Jean?" Charlotte asked my mother.

"They do both have that lovely dark hair, don't they? What do you think, Don?"

I resisted the temptation to stick my finger in my mouth and make a gagging sound. Instead, I did what I was famous for.

"Oh, by the way, Rick," I batted my eyes. "How is Annette? From what I hear, you two are rather close." I batted my eyes again. "Can we expect an announcement soon?"

Ranger Rick slid an arm around the back of my sister's chair, leaned back in a casual manner, shook his head, and cast his eyes downward. "I didn't want to put a damper on the celebration here, but," he looked up at me, "Annette and I parted company quite a while back. For good, this time. It's been coming, and it's for the best."

"Oh, Rick, I'm so sorry!" My mother suddenly needed a drool bib. She was positively salivating. "I know that can't be easy. You two have been seeing each other off and on for some time."

Taylor reached over and patted Rick's free hand. "I'm sure this is a difficult time for you," she said. "If there's anything I can do, let me know."

From my perspective, the ranger didn't look all that shook-up. Of course, I'm a cynic. And Taylor is the sensitive, giving daughter.

"That's strange." I wasn't ready to let Ranger

Romeo off that easy. "Several folks who were at the lake the night the baseball team went au naturelle said your lady friend was on you like—what was it? Oh yes, cling wrap on a sticky bun. Or something to that effect. If it wasn't dear Annette you were with, who was it?"

Townsend put a hand to his chest. "I'm touched, Tressa," he said. "I didn't know you cared."

"You're right, Townsend." I tossed back the last swallow of my wine. "You are touched. I was just making polite conversation. That's all."

Townsend smiled. "You, being polite to me? Now, that's a first, isn't it? What's the occasion?"

"Why, it's Taylor's birthday, of course," I replied. "I have to be good on my little sis's birthday, don't I? What kind of big sister would I be if I was rude to one of her birthday guests? You did say you were invited, didn't you?"

"Of course, he was invited, Tressa," my father spoke up.

"Well then, there you go," I said, noting that Townsend hadn't answered my question about the lady at the lake. I didn't like the glint in his eye when he turned to Taylor.

"Taylor, I saw the Buick in the parking lot. How do you keep it looking showroom quality while you're working and going to school?" he asked. I jabbed him in the shin with a sandaled foot.

"You must be mistaken, Rick," my father said. "Taylor rode with us."

"I don't know, Phil. I could have sworn it was the Buick. So shiny you need sunglasses to cut the glare. And that cute little black-and-gold smiley face on the top of the antenna."

I tried to kick Townsend again, but he blocked my kick. All eyes turned to me with varying measures of dismay—or perhaps horror.

"You drove my car?" A quaver was noticeable in Taylor's usually well-modulated voice.

"Tressa?" My dad queried.

"Yeah?"

"The Le Sabre?"

"All right, all right. I drove it. So what? It's fine. Not a scratch on it. I swear. I was low on gas and running short on time, so I drove it. What's the big deal? It's just a car, after all."

My grandmother reached over and rapped me on the knuckles with a teaspoon. "Just a car? I'll have you know your grandfather loved that car. He washed it three times a week, whether it needed it or not. Parked it out in the boonies whenever we went to the store, so no one would open their door and put a ding in it. I had to hoof it half a mile to protect that chassis, little missy. Just a car? I can't believe you said that!"

I patted her arm. "It's okay, Gramma. I'm sorry. And the car is fine. Just fine." I pulled the car key out of my purse and handed it to Taylor. "There. Take it. I'll ride home with Mom and Dad."

Taylor gave me a stiff nod. I gave Townsend a nasty glare. The jerk. He knew there was a hands-off sign when it came to the Buick. I made another jab at his shin with my foot, but found my ankle caught in a very firm grip. My foot was yanked up, and my butt started slipping forward off my chair. I reached out to grab hold of the table to prevent myself from sliding off onto the floor and under the table, but succeeded only in clutching a section of the tablecloth. In my descent to the ground, I brought the table linen, silverware, cutlery, plates, cups, glasses, and an assortment of condiments with me. Screams and gasps erupted around the table.

I got even, though. While I was under the table, I bit Townsend's ankle.

It was way after eleven when we were finally ready to leave the restaurant. The mothers felt duty-bound to clean up the mess one of their party had caused. Personally, I thought Townsend should have cleaned up, but judging from my parents' expressions, I kept that opinion to myself. Taylor was stoic, as always. Her birthday supper was ruined. She would bear her indignity nobly. While Rick Townsend consoled the birthday girl, his gramps played patty-cake in a dark corner with my grandma over a margarita. And me? I was drafted for under-the-tables clean-up duty. I'm sure the restaurant staff breathed a collective sigh of relief as we headed out the door, thinking no tip was sufficient to cover this party from hell. They certainly lost no time locking the door behind us as we left.

Muted good-byes were exchanged all round. Gramma wanted to ride with Taylor in the Buick. She tried to talk Taylor into letting her drive "for old time's sake" without success. I was opening the door to my folks' car when I heard the first scream.

"Oh my God! My car!" I tried to tell myself that wasn't Taylor's voice shrieking like the lead female in our local amateur operatic, but Gramma's "What the hell has she done to Papa's car?" pretty much cinched it. In the tradition of my Grandpa Will, I'd parked in the space furthest from the restaurant behind a storage shed. I ran with the others over to the Le Sabre. Mint condition no longer described the automobile. Totaled was more like it.

I took it all in. The flattened tires. The smashed headlights and taillights. The busted windshields and windows. The bent antenna with the sad little yellow face hanging unhappily upside down. The dents on the hood, trunk, roof, doors and fenders reminiscent of shoe or boot impressions.

Rick and my brother opened the driver's side door. I held my breath, praying the interior, at least, had been spared.

"Geezus!" I heard Craig say. "Talk about overkill."

I bravely stepped forward to take a firsthand look.

A big mistake. The dome light amply lit up the interior in all its glory. Red paint was sprayed across the dash and along the seats. Knobs, do-hickeys and doodads were missing from a battered dashboard. Seats and upholstery were slashed. My mind reeled at the senseless carnage.

All eyes turned to me.

A snapshot of Peyton Palmer's ghostly white face freeze-framed in my mind, followed closely by the tattoo of a large, venomous snake. Despite the sultry heat of the humid June night, I shivered.

Overkill.

Chapter 7

The police were called to take a report. When the responding officers asked who had driven the object of the police report to the restaurant, I could swear I saw money pass between the two cops.

"Was that a pay-off I just witnessed?" I asked Townsend, who'd been drafted to stay with me until the paperwork was concluded and the flatbed arrived.

"More likely winnings," he said, from the tailgate of his truck.

"Winnings? What kind of winnings?"

"I don't think it would improve your disposition if you knew."

"Oh." I said. "Oh!" I scribbled my signature on the tow slip and thrust the clipboard back at the officers. "I thought gambling was illegal or against police regulations or something," I commented.

"It isn't gambling if it's a sure thing." The officer who had pocketed the money smiled and passed me my copy of the tow receipt. "The car will be at Peters's Garage. The insurance agent can look at it there." He looked over at Townsend. "You'll make sure Miss Turner here gets home safe and sound, right, Rick?"

Townsend mumbled something the officer must have taken as affirmation. I marched to Townsend's truck and climbed in the cab. Through the open sliding windows to the bed, I heard one of the officers suggest it would be safer for Townsend if he made me ride in the back of the pickup. I slammed the window shut so they would know I'd heard them and their idiotic joking.

When Townsend got in the pickup, I gave him the cold shoulder. Well, at least for as long as I could hold out. I'm not one of those women who can sustain the silent treatment for very long. I like to talk way too much.

"I suppose you think all that was pretty funny," I said, staring straight ahead. "Another laugh on the dumb blonde who burnt her nose bobbing for french fries last Halloween. Hardy, har, har."

Townsend took a deep breath. I'd have bet the farm his jaw was making funny little spasms and his brow was crinkling.

"I find nothing funny about the destruction of another person's property, Tressa," he finally replied. "Nothing at all."

"You can't think I had anything to do with Taylor's car being trashed." The idea that he could even entertain that notion hurt me more than I cared to acknowledge.

"Cut the drama queen routine, Tressa. It doesn't become you. And, for the record, no, I don't think you had anything to do with the vandalism. But I do think you're a frigging walking, talking Stephen King novel. Forget that crap about an accident looking for a place to happen. There's no looking. You just happen wherever the hell you are at the time."

Townsend took a corner too fast, and I went careening across the seat. I hauled myself back to my own corner.

"Well, excuse this imperfect soul for inhabiting Jellystone Park, too, Mr. Ranger, sir. And, frankly, I don't see how I can be blamed for tonight's crime spree, any more than I can be at fault for simply opening a trunk and finding a corpse. It's not as if I asked for something like that to happen. 'Please, please, let me! Let me find a dead body on a dark road in the middle of the night.' Hello. Does that make any sense at all?"

Townsend shook his head. "No, but I'm used to that when you're around, Calamity."

"Stop calling me that!" I pounded on the dashboard. "I am not a calamity. I'm just . . . unusually unlucky."

"Right."

My folks' house was dark when Townsend pulled into my drive. Not surprising, considering it was well after two A.M. I yawned. Thank heaven tomorrow was Sunday. I didn't have to go in to work 'til noon, and I had the perfect excuse for begging off church. Our minister is not the most dynamic of speakers, and with a full night's rest I still have trouble keeping awake.

The minute I stepped out of Townsend's truck, I knew something was very wrong. Butch and Sundance were nowhere to be seen. No drool. No dirty paws. No dog breath.

"No way," I said, and put my fingers in my mouth

and gave a shrill whistle. "Here, boys. C'mon, boys." I whistled again.

"Jeez, you'll be calling the pooches in from the next county with that whistle," Townsend said, and handed me my purse.

"Something's wrong," I said, hurrying toward the trailer.

Townsend followed me up the narrow sidewalk. "What are you talking about?"

"Butch and Sundance."

"The mutts?"

"They always come greet me. No matter what time I get home." I called and whistled again, picking up the sounds of muffled barks from the direction of the barn.

"That's strange," I said, and opened the gate and took off in that direction. The barks grew louder.

I ran to the barn and unlocked the door. My pups bounded out the door like bargain hunters at first light at Crazee Dayz on the town square. "How did you guys get locked in the barn?" I bent down and gave them each a big hug. "I don't get it," I said to Townsend, who'd followed me. "Why would they be in the barn?"

"Maybe your dad put them there," Townsend suggested. "Or Taylor."

"But why?" The sick feeling I experienced earlier when I saw the demolished Buick made an encore performance.

"C'mon, boys." I walked toward the trailer, the red meat I'd consumed earlier in the evening a heavy wad in my gut. I reached in my bag for the key, then recalled I'd left my keys in my car before I'd switched to the Buick. I ran to the Plymouth, retrieved the key from the ashtray, and hurried to the front door. Townsend took the key ring from me.

"I have to whiz," he said.

"Didn't anyone ever tell you to do that before you leave?" I teased, then stepped in and turned the light switch on.

"Hell's bells," Townsend said.

I looked at him, then at my dining room and kitchen, or what purported to be my dining room and kitchen. Frankly, it was hard to tell what I was looking at. The place looked like it had been used for a WWF free-for-all. My table and chairs were overturned. The refrigerator was standing open, its contents spilling onto the floor. The kitchen faucet was running and the sink was overflowing. Dishes and plates were busted. In the living room, sofa cushions were slashed, flower pots upended, and my quaint little knickknacks were now pea-sized gravel.

My bedroom was just as bad. My mattress had been violated and my drawers emptied, leaving my holier-than-thou underwear in plain view. I was shaking so much I had to sit down, so I chose to join my intimate apparel on the floor. I couldn't decide if I was shaking because I was so afraid, or because I was so friggin' angry. How dare someone break into my home? Destroy the property I worked—Gramma worked so hard to acquire!

"You okay, Tressa?" Townsend asked from above me.

"No, I am not okay," I said, trying to keep my lips from shaking along with the rest of my body. "Some scum-sucking, deadbeat, no-good bastard broke into my home. I am definitely not okay!"

Townsend bent over and grabbed the red thong panties from the floor and used them to pick up the phone. Seconds later I heard him recite my address. Then he cradled the phone.

"Don't know if they will dust for prints, but, just in case, we better not touch anything."

I nodded, so weary that Townsend could have made a lewd suggestion and I would have yawned in response.

"I'm gonna have to use the john," he said. "It can't wait."

Any other night, the idea of Rick Townsend in my trailer with his pants unzipped would have left me short of breath and low on spit. But this night, I couldn't manage even the teensiest naughty thought. That injustice, if anything, deserved retribution. Big time.

Once Townsend was finished, I excused myself, leaving him to greet the police (I was up to here with coppers), and headed to the bathroom. Good lord, even my john hadn't been spared. They'd dumped my toiletries all over the place and done something quite obscene with my curling iron and the bathtub faucet.

I went to pull the electrical appliance out and drew back the maroon shower curtain. In big, block letters reminiscent of my Mystical Mauve shade of lipstick, were four words: *"PAY UP OR ELSE!"* My throat tightened. My chest hurt worse than when I'd taken my first spill from a horse, and unwisely tried to inhale. A cold sweat began to form on my goose-pimply skin.

I sank down on the toilet seat and stared at the words. This was not the act of some bill collector gone postal. Nor was it my mother reminding me I owed her seventeen dollars and some odd cents for groceries. No, this little greeting card had nothing to do with financial insolvency, and everything to do with corpses, cash and cobras. I noticed my light brown

Perfect Blend eye pencil sitting near the sink. I picked it up, pulled out a length of two-ply toilet paper, and started writing.

1. Left work
2. Took the wrong car
3. Flat tire
4. Body in trunk
5. Cash in glove box
6. Body not in trunk
7. Cash not in glove box
8. A visit from Cobra Man
9. Buick vandalized
10. House destroyed
11. Lipstick threat

I looked at my list trying to do a dot-to-dot. You know, make some connections. Nothing jumped out at me. Usually that's what it takes for me to have a clue. Obviously, cobra guy thought I had the money. I *had* returned the money to the glove compartment, hadn't I? What if I'd dropped it? What if, when the killer returned for the body, he couldn't find the money? It was hardly a stretch to believe a hard-up blonde who was chronically out of work had pocketed the green.

A short rap sounded at the bathroom door. "You fall in or something?" Townsend asked.

I quickly wadded up my toilet paper notepad and flushed it. I opened the door. "Townsend, you gotta see this!"

"See what?" The look on his face suggested he did not think there was anything in the can he cared to see. I grabbed his arm and hauled him to the bathtub.

"Look." I pointed at the Mystical Mauve message. "What do you make of that?" I asked. "Doesn't that prove something to you? Well, doesn't it?"

Townsend took so long to reply I wondered if he was having difficulty reading the four words.

" 'Pay up or else.' Do you see that? Or else? Now I don't know about you, but generally when I hear the words *or else* I'm thinking major threat. As in 'or else, you're history.' 'Or else, you're dead meat.' 'Or else, you join the spare tire club.' Or else. Get it?"

A deep crease marred Townsend's brow. I considered telling him that frowning like that would produce wrinkles, but suspected I would hear something like, "I only get crinkles when you're around," or something like that, so I kept it to myself.

"You're not telling me you think there is a connection between the Peyton Palmer piece of fiction and this?" Townsend said.

"It's as clear as the lipstick on the wall," I asserted. Actually, it wasn't all that clear to me, but Townsend didn't have to know that.

"So you think . . . what, exactly?"

"Do I have to draw a picture?" I asked, hoping that Townsend would complete his own dot-to-dot in his head and, perhaps, fill in the some of the blank spaces in my own mental picture of how and why this was all unfolding.

"That would be helpful," Townsend said.

"It's all about the money, man," I proclaimed. "The green. The moola. The Mr. Franklins."

"Money?"

Clearly Townsend wasn't drawing any mental pictures or conclusions in his head. And they called me a ditz.

"The envelope with the hundred dollar bills. The one that was in the car, then wasn't in the car. The one the killer thinks I have. The money he wants back *or else*. That money!"

"You're telling me that your trailer was broken into by Peyton Palmer's killer because he was looking for the money he was paid for a hit on Palmer? Is that what you're saying?"

I stared at Townsend. *Was* that what I was saying? What was that about a hit? I blinked. A hit! A hit on Palmer? Of course. That would account for the money in the glove box. Payment for services rendered. All that was left was disposal of the body. It made perfect, if chilling, sense. I thought about my silver-studded snake charmer. If ever a person looked like a hit man . . .

"A hit man! A hit man is after me! A hit man who wants payment for professional services rendered, and if he doesn't get it, he'll provide his services to me free of charge! God, what do I do, Townsend? What do I do?" I grabbed his shirt. "You don't have a spare ten grand just lying around, do you?" I asked.

"Get a hold of yourself, Tressa. You're making some awful big leaps here. After all, the cops don't think there has even been a crime committed. Other than vehicle theft, of course. They're convinced this was all just a big misunderstanding. Now you've got hired killers stalking you."

"But don't you see, Townsend, it makes perfect sense. Why trash my house? Because the killer was searching for his pay. Why strip Taylor's car? Because the killer saw me driving it and thought the money might be in there. Why does he think I have his blood money? Because I was in the getaway car and found the money, and now he can't find it and thinks I have it. He even came to Bargain City threatening me today. If it wasn't for that twerpy little video game freak, I could be in someone's trunk myself."

Townsend ran a hand through his hair. I couldn't read his expression. Maybe that was a good thing.

"This is all connected to Peyton Palmer's death, Townsend," I insisted. "I know it."

"Hello. Anybody here? Hello?"

"Back here," Townsend yelled in response to the calls from the other room. He turned to greet the officers. I grabbed his arm and stopped him.

"You *do* believe me, don't you, Townsend?" I asked.

Rick gave me another inscrutable look. "One thing I can say about you, Tressa, is that you're definitely not a dull date." He turned and left.

"Date?" I said. "Who said anything about a date? Townsend? Townsend!"

By the time the authorities left my humble abode, the place had gone to the dogs and I was in the dog house. As soon as the officers were done with their crime scene analysis (What a joke! The *CSI* guys would kick their butts), I herded the dogs indoors. Not that they were such brilliant watchdogs. They'd proven that. It just made me feel better knowing they were around. Besides, they gave me somebody to vent with. I could rant, rave, stomp and spit for all I was worth and they would listen. Well, actually they were doing more foraging in the kitchen for goodies on the floor than listening, but occasionally they took time out from their garbage-disposal impressions to give me a lick and a leg rub to let me know they were with me.

The police had rejected my theory faster than

Darva Conger rejected her who-wants-to-marry-a-millionaire. They were convinced this was just a random break-in, just like the random vandalism of the Buick. And the lipstick love note? Didn't that provide the officers with proof that this was not a random act, but rather a calculated threat against the person of Tressa Jayne Turner? Not if they thought Tressa Turner wrote it herself.

Although they didn't come out and say it directly, I could tell that was the absurd theory being floated about by the county sheriff's office. In an out-of-control bid for attention, beginning with the Peyton Palmer story, and culminating with the menacing Tattoo Ted, Buick vandalism, and the house break-in, the cops were trying to pin this all on me.

"Stupid hillbillies." I picked up a sofa cushion from the floor. "Fools. Dickheads." I shoved the cushion back on the sofa, sat down and looked at the carnage that was mi casa. I suddenly felt like the unappreciated little runt in the movie who had to single-handedly defend his home against dangerous criminals. Unfortunately, I wasn't going up against a couple of morons in a carefully choreographed movie production. This was real life. Real death. I was on a hit man's potential hit list, but nobody believed me and time was running out. While my future might not seem as rosy as some, I was determined to hang on to it at all costs.

I gathered my pooches, checked the doors and windows, grabbed a butcher knife from my kitchen drawer, and padded down the hallway toward my bedroom, shutting and locking the door behind me. I crawled into my bed, man's best friend on either side of me, and lay awake, watching and waiting for things that went bump in the night.

CHAPTER 8

"*Ouch!*" I rubbed the back of my head where I'd whacked it on a shelf in my dad's garage. I found what I was searching for and tossed it into an old backpack from my community college days. I took another quick look at my father's tool bench to see if there was anything else that might come in handy, and grabbed a pair of brown jersey gloves. That should just about do it. I didn't have much time. I wanted to be well away from the homestead before the household began to rouse for church.

I'd done a lot of thinking while I'd shoveled up the mess in my trailer earlier that morning and wished for a skid loader. After agonizing for what seemed like hours, I came to the conclusion that, for now at least, the less said to my folks about the whole Peyton Palmer mess and my theory connecting the Buick's battering and mobile home melee to his murder, the better. I wanted to protect my family. I just wasn't sure how.

"Tressa?" I jumped a good two feet.

"Dad! You startled me. What are you doing out here?"

My dad's brow began to furrow. Why did foreheads always do that when I was around?

"I was wondering the same thing about you, Tressa. What are you doing out here? You're not planning on taking *my* vehicle now, are you?" His forehead furrows were plowed-quality now.

"No, of course not. I was just looking around."

"What have you got there?" he asked, and motioned to my backpack.

"Oh, I just grabbed a few, uh, tools. For some minor home maintenance. Repairs. That sort of thing." I sidestepped toward the door.

"What repairs?" my dad hollered to me as I scurried off. "And what the devil do you need gloves for?"

"In case I hammer my thumb," I yelled back, thinking that was about the dumbest reason I could give. Still, I could hardly say, "So I don't leave fingerprints," now, could I?

I jumped into the Plymouth. Confession time. I snitched gasoline from my dad's farm tank. I keep a running tab, though. I figure I owe him, what, close to a grand by now?

It was half-past six in the A.M. when I parked my car down the street a discreet distance from Peyton Palmer's house. He lives—or rather lived—in an affluent section of town, in a wooded area behind the Grandville Community Hospital and Clinic. This is the area that all the kids hit big time on trick or treat night. You can get your Halloween bag filled with top-of-the-line goodies in record time. We're not talking fun-size bars here, folks.

I'd phoned the Palmer residence from the Get 'n Go

earlier. It creeped me out to listen to a dead guy tell me he was unable to come to the phone. Talk about your understatements.

I pulled my visor on. Then my three-dollar shades. I zipped up the front of my navy blue nylon jogging suit and stepped out of the car. I slipped the backpack over my shoulders, then began a slow trot toward the Palmer house. I'd seen this in a movie once. To the casual observer, I looked like any other jogger. The key was to look like you belonged and, if challenged, BS your way through.

I hoofed it down the street in front of the house in question, a gray three-story with a partially bricked front and a three-car garage. Keeping my speed steady, I made a sudden, sharp left and headed right down Peyton Palmer's driveway toward his garage and backyard. I moved to the south side of the garage where I noticed a window. It was too high for me to see into, so I looked around for something to stand on. The bird bath caught my eye. It was one of those heavy-duty numbers with the look of carved stone. The top comes off so you can dump the water and clean out the scum. I started to grab hold of the bird bath, then jumped back as if I'd walked into an electric fence. Gloves, I reminded myself. I rummaged through the backpack for the ugly brown work gloves and slipped them on, then dragged the pedestal of the bird bath over to below the garage window. I climbed up to take a look. The nearest two bays were empty. Along the far bay sat a John Deere lawn tractor, and a trailer loaded with a golf cart and what looked like his-and-hers golf bags propped in the back.

Disappointed, I returned the bird bath to its proper place, then proceeded to climb the stairs to a two-level, sprawling rear deck, hoping the window treatments would afford me some prime snooping opportunities.

I peered through the French doors into a dining area or breakfast nook. It was bigger than my kitchen and dining room put together. The window fogged up so I swiped a hand across the pane. Sudden movement in the reflection to my right whirled me around. I pivoted, performing a somewhat spastic kung fu move, accompanied by a guttural, "Hee-yaw!"

The tiny furball poo-pooing in the yard a few feet away was not the least bit impressed by my aggressive attack mode. I wondered if his owner, on the other hand, would be chagrined at being caught in the act without a pooper scooper and paper bag.

I transferred my attention from the pooping pup to its leash holder, momentarily blinded by the neon orange of his blast jacket and the glare from white, bony knees.

"Oh, no," I mumbled, recognizing the senior citizen. "I mean, hello." I greeted Ranger Rick's grandfather, Joe Townsend, hoping he didn't recognize me in my workout get-up. "Going to be another hot one," I said. I suck at small talk. Can you tell?

"Especially when you're wearin' gloves," he said. "Don't I know you from somewhere? You looking for the Palmers?"

"Uh, as a matter of fact, uh, yes." My brain struggled to come up with a plausible reason I would be peeking in the Palmers' back window on a Sunday morning wearing work gloves and a running suit. I shook my head. There was never a good reason for wearing work gloves with a running suit. "You see, I, uh . . . was hoping to get a, uh, comment from Mr. Palmer on an, uh, article I'm writing for the local paper." I tried to remember where my faded press pass from my days at the *Gazette* was. My billfold, maybe? I pulled my gloves off, grabbed my wallet from the backpack, and flipped through the video rental cards, the Subway club coupons, and the ATM card that was a joke. You had to have something in the bank before those things spat money out at you, right? Bummer.

"Aren't you one of the Turner girls? Not the bright one. The other one. What's this about a newspaper article?"

It took restraint, but I ignored the insult. "About Palmer's arrest. I wanted to get his perspective, his point of view. You know, tell his side of the story. I haven't been able to hook up with him."

"Oh, really? Did you try the front door?"

My eyes narrowed. So the old fart *had* been spying.

"Well, you see, I did call, but I got the machine," I admitted, "and I confess. I decided to do some snooping." I shrugged. "You know how we newspaper folks are." It occurred to me that perhaps old Joe here was the self-appointed neighborhood watchdog. If so, maybe he could prove useful. "Do you know the Palmers well, Mr. Townsend?"

"I've lived in this neighborhood for almost thirty years. Peyton Palmer moved across the street from me, oh, I'd say around ten years ago or so. He's compulsive about his lawn. One of those fellows who mows when the yard don't need it, just to show off. Makes the rest of us look like deadbeats. He got married, oh, two or three years back. Married a gal young enough to be his daughter, or close to it."

"Do you know the Palmers well?" I repeated my earlier question.

"They keep to themselves for the most part," he

said. "It's not like it used to be when neighbors were more like extended family. Now folks just come home from work, pull into their garages and disappear."

"Is that what the Palmers do?"

"He's gone a lot of the time."

"And Mrs. Palmer?"

He winked, and his thin lips made a lopsided grin. "She has her interests."

"Interests?"

"It's really none of my business. I don't know if I should say anything, you being the press and all."

I smiled. When someone says they probably shouldn't say something, you can be certain they are going to. Every time. Works for me.

"Mr. Palmer is going through a lot right now, the poor fellow," I said, trying to get over feeling like I was being disrespectful to the guy. He was dead, I told myself. He had no feelings to hurt anymore. Still, it felt . . . wrong. "At a time like this, he should be able to rely on his wife to be there, to support him."

Old Joe got a look in his eye like Gramma gets when she's been to the senior center and comes back home with a load of dirt on someone.

"He can rely on her to carry on when he's not at home," he said.

My ears began to burn. "You mean Mrs. Palmer is having an affair?"

"Affairs," he said. "One feller would park down the street. Like you did. And he'd wear a running suit like you did. And if someone saw him, he'd just keep on running. Funniest damn thing I ever saw. Come to think of it, I haven't seen him around in a while."

"Did you recognize the man?" I tried not to sound

too anxious. "Did he have a rather ghastly snake tattoo? Was his nose pierced? Did he have arms as big as tree trunks?"

He gave me a *huh?* look.

"I don't know if I really should say," he said.

I fought the urge to give him a good, hard shake and scream, "Tell me, old man! Tell me or else!" Having your life threatened tends to make you a bit cranky.

"I wouldn't want to see this in the newspaper, you know," he added. "Just in case you really are a newspaper reporter."

I made a crossing gesture over my heart, followed by a totally perverted version of the Girl Scout hand sign. "This is strictly off the record, Mr. Townsend. Girl Scout promise." Okay, so I was never a Girl Scout. But how was gramps here to know? "I give you my word. I won't print anything you tell me in the paper." True enough.

"Well, in that case." He leaned close to my ear. I could smell the Polident. "It was his partner."

I gave him a blank look. "Partner?"

"His law partner. Dennis Hamilton, as in Peyton and Hamilton, attorneys-at-law. That partner."

"Partner?"

He nodded.

"Peyton Palmer's partner?" I sounded like I was performing a tongue twister.

He nodded again. His lips puckered so much, his mouth resembled a chicken's rear end.

"Sheila Palmer is having an affair with her husband's law partner?"

"Was having," he said. "Now"—he raised his hands—"who knows?"

"Hot dang!" I said. "Did you tell the police any of this?" I asked.

His brows came together. "Police? Why would the police be interested in any of that?"

I did a mental head slap. Why, indeed? The police weren't trying to locate Peyton Palmer. They didn't believe he was dead. But, say I was to present a compelling case to them that clearly showed Peyton Palmer was, in fact, deceased, they would have to take me seriously then, wouldn't they? I chewed my lip. Where did I begin? What did the dicks on *Law & Order* do once they had their first lead? Motive, I decided. Nail down the motive first and then see where that takes you.

I grabbed my pen and notepad out of my bag and hurried toward the senior citizen. "Mr. Townsend, if you could just spare me a few more minutes of your time, I have a couple more questions."

Joe Townsend gave me a strange look. I hoped it was because I looked like an ace reporter. "You've stepped in it now, girlie," he said, and at my puzzled look continued. "Poop. You've stepped in Kojak's poop."

"Kojak? I looked down at the dog near my feet and the doo doo on my shoe, and sighed. "Story of my life," I muttered. "Story of my life."

"You know, you kinda remind me of your grandma." Old Man Townsend took my arm.

"Oh, did she often step in it, too?" I asked, curious as to just how he felt about my grandmother.

"Only all the time, girlie. Only all the time." He pulled on my arm. "Come on home with me. I've got some buttermilk brownies waiting. Old lady Winegardner baked them. That woman wants me bad.

She's always bringing me goodies to eat. They'll go good with a fresh pot of coffee. Then, you can ask me anything you want. Of course, you'll have to remove your shoes."

I allowed myself to be led away. Hold chocolate out in front of me and I'll follow you anywhere.

Two hours, a half-dozen buttermilk brownies and a probable case of acute abdominal distress later, I knew more about the corpse in the trunk than I'd cared to. Several times during my little chit-chat with Joe (we were now comfortably on first-name terms), I almost let it slip that Peyton Palmer was, well, wherever it was attorneys went after they'd put in their final court appearance, so to speak. The tablespoon of booze in the coffee didn't help. By the time I left Joe's, my lips were looser than those baggy drawers the high school guys wear. But it was worth it. My little steno book was chock full of dates and times, vehicle descriptions, and license plate numbers, and Joe's observation that the founder of the brownie feast was as hot for his bod as both major political parties are for the White House.

What I found out from Watchdog Joe convinced me more than ever that I had found at least one *pow! bam! socko!* motive for Peyton Palmer's murder. Sex, lies and a sizable inheritance. Passion and greed. Had to be the top two answers to the *Family Feud* question: Name a motive for murder. And who better to benefit from Peyton Palmer's untimely demise than a widow doing the nasty with his law partner? All the gruesome twosome had to do was find someone willing to off poor Peyton (I was beginning to think of him as "Poor Peyton"), for, say, ten grand or so. And let's face it. What attorney doesn't know some lowlife like my Bargain City buddy willing to do someone in for a wad of green? Now, if I could just tie my pierced friend to Sheila Palmer or Dennis Hamilton, I could present my murder-for-hire theory to the police—and demand my due.

I scribbled in my steno book again, recapping what I knew, or thought I knew so far, and what I just made up as I went along. My working theory was that Sheila Palmer and Dennis Hamilton had, either independently or in collusion with each other, conspired to kill Peyton Palmer. According to the cops, Sheila Palmer had been out of town when Peyton was killed. If true, it appeared she had no hands-on role in his murder. Still, Dennis Hamilton could easily have put a slug in Palmer's head before he left the office Friday afternoon or later that same night. Still, I thought it more likely a contract job. Attorneys don't like to get their hands dirty. Besides, there was the envelope of money to consider. Payment in full for one dead husband.

That was my current working theory. But just how did I go about proving it? I thought for a moment. Weren't criminals supposed to return to the scene of their crimes? Maybe one of my suspects would inadvertently lead me to Peyton Palmer's body. After all, who would ever expect some ditzy blonde airhead might actually set up surveillance on two murder suspects in order to prove a murder took place? I frowned. Not a soul. That's who.

I looked down at the notepad I held in my lap. *Where are you, Peyton Palmer?* I'd written. "Where are you?"

CHAPTER 9

Okay, at this point I started getting second thoughts about the amateur private eye business I'd started. You know the feeling. The one you get when you promise to be a bridesmaid in your friend's wedding and then get a look at the bridesmaid dresses. Or, in a moment of extreme weakness, you agree to a blind date set up by a senior citizen who still has the hots for Guy Lombardo.

What made me think I, of all people, could solve a murder-mystery? I was the intellectual lightweight of the family. The space cadet. Jerry Lewis to everyone else's Dean Martin. Did I really think I could do the cops' work for them with any level of competency at all?

Remembering the lipstick greeting on my bathroom wall, and the dangerous character who'd delivered it in person, dispensed any lingering doubts. You betcha I could do the cops' work for them. You bet I could. Funny how fear of bodily injury and painful death works wonders on the old self-esteem. I consulted my steno pad again. Since it was Sunday, I would have to put off any interrogation of Palmer's staff until the following morning. I wanted to see if my snake charmer had ever visited the offices of Palmer and Hamilton, attorneys-at-law.

Meanwhile, I had about two hours before I had to be back at Bargain City for a six-hour shift. Used to be, stores didn't open up on a Sunday in Grandville so folks could spend the day at church and with their families. Unfortunately, or fortunately if you're like me and need a paycheck, small-town retailers realized they were missing out on lots of business, so they began to open on Sundays, with shorter hours. Our Dutch neighbors to the west still observe that closed-on-Sunday tradition. You need something on a Sunday in New Holland, you either do without, or get in the car and drive twelve miles to the county seat.

I looked back through my notes to a boat I'd drawn during my visit with Joe. He'd confirmed Peyton Palmer was an avid boater and rarely missed an opportunity to get out on the lake. It was his passion, Joe said. Hmmm. No wonder Mrs. Palmer diddled his law partner. Palmer's passion meant I needed to do a little nosing around at the marina, take a look at his boat, and see if anyone could recall seeing Palmer or Hamilton at the lake Friday afternoon or early evening.

Unfortunately, I knew even less about boats than I did about how e-mail works. Which meant I needed someone who was familiar with things nautical, someone who routinely visited the marina, who knew the regulars and who could chew the fat with them and not draw undue suspicion. My belly made a gimme-antacid-now sound. I groaned.

Townsend. It would have to be Townsend. He had a

boat at the marina and almost lived there himself. And I'd take bets he was on a first-name basis with the Devil himself. I'd have to recruit Townsend to help me check out the marina. Convincing him would be the sticky part.

I decided to conduct a quick drive-by of Dennis Hamilton's home, which was located on a quiet little cul-de-sac in an older part of town. A long, elegant white brick ranch-style home, its garage door was open and a classy silver Lincoln sat inside.

I drew a quick sketch of the home and neighboring houses, in case I had to come back after dark. Just the thought gave me corn-starch mouth.

I was putting the final touches on my masterpiece when my passenger side door was flung open. I gave an abbreviated yelp before I recognized the long legs folding into my car as belonging to Townsend, the younger. He was gorgeous, as usual, sporting black bike shorts, a nylon black and gold V-neck, and a tan that made you itch to see if there was any white anywhere.

"What the h—what are you doing here?" I demanded, quickly covering my notebook. "You could give a person a heart attack sneaking up on them like that," I complained.

"I'm riding my bike. The question I have for you is, why are you sitting at Dennis Hamilton's house looking like a bad impression of a stakeout?"

"Oh, is this Dennis Hamilton's house?" I asked. "I didn't know." My eyes caught sight of a for-sale sign in the yard next to Hamilton's. "I was just checking out the house with the for-sale sign. I might be interested."

"In what? Cutting the grass for the realtor?"

I wrinkled my nose. "No. As a matter of fact, I was

thinking about purchasing a home. I hear they have some super deals for first-time home buyers."

Townsend pulled his sunglasses off. "If you're really interested in this piece of property," he said, "I think I can help you out. I know the listing agent personally. I'll just give her a call and see if she can come out and get you in to take a look at it." He pulled his cell phone out of his shorts pocket.

"That is so nice of you," I said, in a voice that conveyed just the opposite. "But I'm just in the very preliminary stages of my search. These things take time. Careful consideration."

"And money, which you must be making more of at Bargain City and the Dairee Freeze than I suspected if you can afford a house worth nearly a quarter of a million."

I began to perspire as if I really were considering a purchase of that magnitude. "A person can dream, can't they?" I squeaked.

"Fess up, Tressa." Townsend put his phone away. "You're spying on Dennis Hamilton. Why?"

"I'm not spying," I said. "I'm just admiring his landscaping. I thought I would make a few sketches to take back and incorporate at my own humble abode."

Before I could stop him, Townsend swiped my notebook and had it open.

"Give that back to me!" I made a lunge for it. "Give it back!" Yeesh. I sounded just like an elementary school sissy asking the school bully for my sack lunch back.

"What the hell is all this?" Townsend shook his head. "Good lord, Tressa, are you nuts? You can't be serious. You're butting into an official police investigation here. That's serious shit!"

I snatched my pad from him. "There is no police investigation, Ranger Townsend, and you know it," I snapped. "The cops think I'm a raving lunatic. They don't take me seriously. They never have. And neither do you."

"That's not true, Tressa." Rick took hold of my chin and turned my head to meet his gaze. I had to give him credit. His expression looked serious enough. But he had donned a similar sober countenance when he'd offered me a lift to the State Fair one day but failed to mention he was also transporting snakes for a display at the Division of Natural Resources building.

I am petrified of snakes. I think it goes back to my childhood hay-baling days. When you bale hay, it is inevitable that you will, from time to time, bale a snake or two. (PETA folks, please remember that this happens purely by accident.) Sometimes the snakes would die. Sometimes they wouldn't. Sometimes, they would come slithering out of the hay bales. Usually they would slither out of the hay bale I happened to be stacking. With the history I shared with Townsend, there was ample reason for me to be skeptical about anything he said.

I grabbed his hand. "It *is* true, and you know it, Townsend. I admit I've had my meathead moments, but it doesn't help matters when you are always front and center ready to spotlight them. Regardless of what you or anyone else thinks, I do have a brain and it is quite adequate for my needs, thank you very much. Now, if you'll excuse me, I have more house hunting to do."

"Tressa, you've got to let the police handle this."

"But they're not handling it, Townsend. You said it yourself. They think it's all a hoax. And while they are sitting around with their fingers up their . . . noses, I'm Bambi's mother trying to elude the great white hunter in a construction-paper forest. So you can do one of two things here. Either help me solve this mystery, or get the hell out of my way!" I was stunned by my kick-butt-and-take-names ultimatum. What do you know? I was a regular Dirty Harriet!

Townsend blew out a gale force blast of breath that sent my pine air freshener swinging. "All right, Tressa. Have it your way," he said.

I frowned. "What does that mean, exactly?" I asked.

"What the hell do you want me to do?"

I smiled at Townsend. "Oh, you're just gonna love this assignment. It's right up your alley."

"Hell," Townsend said.

I filled him in.

"Hell," he said again.

I didn't have time to go home and change before I went to work, but I figured: Who cares how a lowly electronics associate looks? As long as I wore my red vest and kept behind the counter, who was to know what I was wearing from the waist down?

I was flipping the TV channels between a WPCA golf tournament, to NASCAR, to one of those infomercials that promise a six-pack if you buy their workout video, when the clearing of a throat at my checkout alerted me to a waiting customer. I hurried over to my counter.

"Sorry," I apologized for keeping him waiting. "Did you find everything you needed?" He moved a stack of CDs towards me.

"This will be all, thank you," he said, and I scanned

the tunes—oldies, but goodies. Sinatra—Frank, not Nancy—Nat King Cole, Tony Bennett and some Yanni instrumentals. I raised my eyebrows. Music to get lucky by. I ran his total and he handed me his credit card. I blinked when I saw the name. Dennis Hamilton. Hello! The same Dennis Hamilton who, according to one nosy old goat, was showing more than his briefs to his murdered law partner's wife? The guy I'd staked out earlier in the day? The same fellow who figured prominently in my own little version of Murder in the Heartland? Talk about your opportunity knocking! I looked at the mood music and my customer with renewed interest.

In his mid-to-late thirties, Dennis Hamilton wore his light brown hair wavy on top and closely-cropped on the sides. Sharp, angular features partnered with a weak chin kept him from being handsome. Several inches taller than me, he was of medium build. His pale blue eyes lacked color and warmth. Not exactly my idea of a hot, secret love, but then again, Peyton Palmer had been no pin-up.

"Nice selection of tunes," I said as I zipped Hamilton's card through the machine. "Very romantic." I batted my eyes at him. "I love Sinatra. Frank, not Nancy," I qualified, and performed a Marilyn Monroe pout. I must not have done it very well, because the only reaction I got was a vague look and an impatient tap on the counter. "Don't you?" I tried again, leaning toward him in what I hoped was a hi-there,-big-boy,-come-up-and-see-me-sometime come-on.

"Since I'm purchasing his CDs, I'd say that was evident." He checked his wristwatch, an expensive one from the look of it. Of course, anything that didn't come free with a backpack purchase qualified as expensive to me.

"Don't I know you?" I gave up my vamp persona. It rarely ever works for me, anyway—I always have trouble keeping a straight face. Instead, I opted for the more direct approach, keeping his credit card clutched tightly in my Manic Mauve nail-colored fingers. "Hey, aren't you that attorney I read about who got charged with smuggling drugs to his client right in the county jail? Something like that?" A deep red stain began to make its way from the collar of his tan three-button polo shirt, and infused his general neck area. Even his ears turned a bright crimson.

"You're mistaken. That was another local attorney. Peyton Palmer."

"Was," was right.

"Oh my gosh! I'm so sorry, Mr. Hamilton. But I was sure I saw your name mentioned in the article."

"Peyton Palmer is an associate of mine. We work in the same law firm. That is the only connection I have with his affairs." *Other than the little one with his wife—or rather, widow.*

"I'm curious. How does a person smuggle drugs into a jail, I wonder? Do they hide it in their shoe? Swallow it like those, what do they call them—camels—do with those heroin-filled balloons?"

"Mules!" he snapped, reaching for his credit card.

"What?" I asked.

"They're called mules, not camels."

"Mules. Right. Gotcha. Hey, maybe they call them camels in the Middle East?" I joked. "How would someone get drugs into a jail of all places?"

"I have no idea how the drugs were passed in the jail facility, or even if they were passed at all," Hamilton snapped, clearly unhappy with the topic and the person who had chosen it.

"The article didn't say. Who was the inmate he allegedly passed drugs to? Do you know? What was he in for? How is Mr. Palmer holding up?" *By now, not so good.* "What about his family? His wife? Is Sheila sticking by him?"

I'd gone too far. Crossed the line. Given a whole new face to nosiness.

"How do you know Sheila?" Hamilton asked.

"I do a little, uh, stamping," I threw out, hoping he would consider a mutual stamp junkie harmless.

"Sheila's very gifted," he said. "Very talented, indeed."

I fought the inclination to roll my eyes. How hard could stamp-collecting be?

"I have rather a nice collection of stamps myself," I said. "Some of them haven't even been canceled."

Hamilton gave me a strange look. "Sheila Palmer doesn't collect stamps. She designs stamps for ink pad stamping," he said. "What's going on here? Why are you so interested in Peyton Palmer and his legal troubles, anyway? Why are you asking all these questions? I came in here to buy CDs, not be hassled by a minimum wage sales clerk." He grabbed his credit card out of my hand, and scribbled his signature on the credit card receipt. "What the hell is wrong with you?"

I stapled his receipt to his bag. "Just friendly conversation, sir. That's all." I handed him his CDs. "I hope your lady friend enjoys the tunes."

He snatched the bag from me and stomped away. Another satisfied customer.

I sighed, totally bummed out because I hadn't

learned a thing from Hamilton other than he was hoping to get lucky. And where did that leave me? With a big-time headache, a lot of questions, and a feeling that time was running short.

I finally clocked out at six-fifteen. I had arranged to meet my reluctant comrade at the marina around seven-thirty. That should give me enough time to run home, change my clothes, and throw a meal in my face.

I stopped by Uncle Frank's and finagled a tenderloin, fries, and a diet drink by promising to close up for him the following weekend, so he could attend some classic car show in Des Moines.

I winced when I walked into my house. There had been no visit from the little cleaning elves in my absence. I wasted little time in the shower. It crossed my mind that I really should shave my legs, but decided what for? I was on a fact-finding mission, not a man-finding one. It was business. Strictly business. Besides, Townsend wouldn't notice my legs if I had a peg at the end of one and a Barney slipper at the end of the other.

I threw on a black T-shirt with the word *Diva* scrawled in gold across it and a pair of black jeans at least one size too small. I swore off tenderloins and fries as I inhaled and struggled with the zipper. I stuck my feet into a pair of old, black tennis shoes that I used for mucking out the stalls, grabbed a black and gold baseball cap from my softball days, and headed out, looking like Buffy the Vampire Slayer goes Goth.

By the time I reached the marina, I was cursing the jeans, which kept giving me a big-time wedgie. My luck, I'd probably get a hemorrhoid. I found a parking place not far from Townsend's pickup truck, and made my way toward the marina office, trying to look inconspicuous, which was proving rather difficult considering I had to pull my jeans out of my butt crack with every other step.

I was about to enter the office when Townsend hailed me, shook his head, and motioned for me to join him.

I took small steps, hoping my pants would cooperate. Ha. Fat chance. I made a face and pulled at my rear end.

"What are you dressed for? A Marilyn Manson concert? You forgot the black lipstick, black fingernails, and body piercings." Townsend greeted me in his usual cavalier manner. "You don't have any body piercings, do you?"

"For your information, I'm blending in so I won't be noticed."

"You don't think anyone is going to notice someone grabbing their own ass?" Townsend's eyes crinkled with amusement.

"I'm not grabbing my ass. I'm grabbing my jeans. And could we please change the subject to something more urgent?"

"I don't know. Ass-grabbing seems pretty high-priority to me." He grinned.

"It would," I said. "Why did you stop me from going in the office?" I extricated a tiny notebook from my back pocket—no small feat, I can tell you. "I jotted down some questions off the top of my head I thought we might want to ask."

Townsend closed my notebook with tanned fingers. "I think I can save you some time by telling you what I've learned." He took my arm. "Let's talk on my boat."

I followed Townsend to his water craft, a gorgeous silver and metallic blue something-or-other. He helped me negotiate the crossing from dock to vessel. I had difficulty spreading my legs far enough apart to bridge the gulf. When I was comfortably ensconced on a rather nice padded seat, and my pants were slackened around my nether regions, Townsend offered me a diet soda, which I politely declined. No way was I going to squeeze more into the jeans from hell.

"So, what have you learned?" I took out my pen and notebook. "When was Peyton Palmer last out on the lake? Does anyone recall?"

Townsend looked at his hands, then fiddled with his can of pop.

"Well?"

"You're probably not going to like this much," Townsend said. "In fact, I can guarantee you're going to have a hissy fit when you hear what I have to tell you. So, before I say a word, I want to remind you that I am only the messenger, so don't shoot the messenger. Okay, Tressa? Messenger. Got it?"

"Oh, for heaven's sake, Townsend, I can assure you no matter what you have to tell me, you're safe from attack. Feel better?"

Townsend shook his head. "We have a history, remember, Calamity."

"*Ancient* history, Ranger Rick," I assured him. "Now get on with it."

He took a very, very deep breath, like a man preparing to dive off a very high cliff. Or propose.

"Okay, here goes nothing." He wiped a palm on his navy shirt. He took another breath. "All right. According to several boaters, Peyton Palmer did, indeed, take his boat out this weekend."

I started scribbling in my notebook. This was good stuff.

"What time did they say he headed out Friday evening?" I inquired, my pen poised to jot down the times. "What time did he come in?"

Townsend shook his head, then took a long, hard swallow of his drink. "Well, you see, Tressa, the thing is . . ."

"Yes?"

"Nobody saw Peyton go out on Friday night."

I gave him my best dumb blonde look. Okay, so in this case it was the real thing. "Huh? But you just said—"

"I said he took the boat out this weekend. The thing is, Tressa . . . What I'm trying to tell you, is that . . ."

"Oh, for crying out loud, just spit it out, Townsend! What are you trying so hard not to tell me?"

"Peyton Palmer didn't go out on his boat Friday night, Tressa."

"But you just said . . ."

"He went out *Saturday*. Saturday morning."

I fielded Townsend's information with my usual aplomb. My jaw just totally relaxed. My mouth flew open. I may have even drooled a tad bit, but I was wearing black, so who can be sure. I jumped to my feet and sent the boat wildly rocking.

"What do you mean, Saturday?" I'm pretty sure I was yelling at this point. Or maybe I just sounded that way to myself because my ears are so close to my mouth. "Peyton Palmer couldn't have been out to sea on Saturday, because he was already swimming with the fishes Friday night!"

The next thing I knew I had Townsend by the shirt and was shaking him (or maybe it was just the rocking of the boat), and we both went ass-over-appetite over the side.

CHAPTER 10

There's one thing worse than in-your-butt-jeans, and that is wet, in-your-butt-jeans. Townsend was the first one back in the boat. I was beginning to prune by the time he bothered to offer me a hand. For a while there, it seemed to me he had every intention of leaving me in the water.

He threw me a towel. "You better get out of those wet grab-ass jeans," he said. "I think I have an extra pair of sweatpants around here somewhere."

"Is this your amateurish attempt to get me out of my pants?" I eyed him through a jungle of wet hair. "Because if it is, it won't work. Besides, I couldn't pry myself out of these jeans with a crowbar."

Townsend laughed, grabbed another towel, and began to dry off his dark hair. I was envious of the way his fell right into place, except for one dark, dramatic lock perfectly poised over his forehead. By contrast, I probably resembled Medusa, or the goddess of the deep.

"If I put that kind of move on you, C.J.—how did

you put it before? Oh, yes, your 'bum would be mine.' "

"Oh, puh-lease!" I twisted the towel around my head. "I've known you way too long to fall for any of your lines, Ranger Rick. You forget. I've seen you and my brother's Macho, Macho Man routine from the get-go. Corny and cornier. Thank God, Craig has married and settled down. Well, semi-settled down."

"Craig says you have a hard time with men," Townsend said. "Fear of intimacy, I think he said."

I scowled. "More like fear of being stuck with some knuckle-dragger with delusions of godhood," I snapped. "And for the record, my brother is insane. I'm just very selective, that's all," I said—probably more to convince myself than him. "I'm like Everest. It's a long, hard climb, bucko, but once you've made it to the top, man, is it worth it!"

"Sounds like a challenge." Townsend pulled the towel off my head and wrapped it around my neck, keeping hold of both ends. "I never could resist a challenge," he said, and I could feel his warm breath on my cheeks. My vision blurred. I shook my head.

"Uh, something else about Everest you should probably remember." My voice suddenly went Darth Vader on me, complete with heavy breathing.

"What's that, Tressa?" Townsend pulled on the ends of the towels and propelled me toward him.

"Many climbers find Everest unattainable. Only those with the utmost stamina, unflagging endurance, immeasurable intestinal fortitude, and death-defying determination make the summit."

Townsend smiled, then put his lips on mine for a mere moment. "Thanks for the warning, Kilamanjaro," he teased. "I'll proceed with caution." He gave me another light peck, one way too short for me to ascertain how he rated as a kisser. And, of course, that was the only interest I had in his kiss. Purely clinical. Curiosity only. Nothing more. Pinky swear.

Yeah right. I could tell myself that 'til the cows came home, so how did I account for the furious pounding of my heart and my sudden breathlessness?

The drubbing in the lake, I told myself. That was the reason. Not Townsend. Not his kisses. Never, ever.

Liar, liar, pants on fire. The childhood rhyme ran through my head. I winced. That *pants on fire* part was way too close for comfort. It was a wonder steam wasn't billowing out in all directions from my wet trousers.

"Do you suppose we could get back to the reason we're here?" I was proud I sounded so convincing. In reality, I probably wouldn't have complained all that much if Townsend had insisted on another quick peck—or a bushel, for that matter—but he didn't. "Your sources are mistaken. About Peyton Palmer, I mean. He couldn't have been up to an early morning outing on the lake Saturday because his dinghy had already set sail for the last time the night before."

Townsend motioned to a seat. "You better sit down, Tressa," he said.

"You gotta be kidding." I slapped a hand to my soggy butt. "I can't even bend at the waist here. Why? What's going on?"

Townsend pulled a hand through his hair, then turned away from me. I saw his shoulders lift and his spine straighten—like a soldier marching off to battle. Or a taxpayer walking into the IRS office for his first audit.

I waited, thinking Townsend was not usually so reticent about sharing information.

"Tressa." Townsend turned slightly. "They towed Peyton Palmer's pontoon earlier. It was found abandoned and floating in the middle of the lake. There was no sign of anyone on board." He turned away again to stare down into the murky water.

My heart gave a flip. "What?"

"The police also found Palmer's SUV parked in the marina lot. They speculate Palmer took the boat out early Saturday morning, then, at some point, either fell overboard or jumped. No suicide note was found, so authorities are leaning toward the accidental drowning theory. They found empty booze bottles on board. I guess Palmer liked his liquor. They figure Palmer was drowning his sorrow. Sorry. Bad choice of words there. One wrong step. Overboard. Too drunk to swim, the guy didn't stand a chance. Tressa?" He stopped, probably to assess my reaction—and any threat to his well-being.

I managed to sink into a seat despite my crotch-constricting garment. "Tell me you're joking," I said. "Please, tell me this is all a joke."

Townsend took the seat across from me. "No joke, Tressa. I wouldn't joke about something like this."

I was silent for a moment, trying to process this unbelievable turn of events. "Slap me. Pinch me. Shake me. Just wake me up and tell me this is all a bad dream," I pleaded.

Townsend took my cold hands between his two warm ones, rubbing them vigorously. "I'm sorry, Tressa," he said. "I don't know what to say."

For once in my life, I couldn't think of anything to say either. Nothing made sense. If one was to believe what Townsend and the police were saying, no way could I have seen Peyton Palmer in the trunk of a car

Friday night. But, I knew I had seen Palmer. Had even touched him. And this little rendition of *Showboat*? Pure illusion created by a killer who was determined to end a murder investigation before it got started and, in the process, brand this cowgirl loco.

"Palmer's boat may have been out on the lake, Townsend," I finally said, "but Palmer? Well, he may have been along for ballast, but he was definitely not swatting mosquitoes and chugalugging brewskies. Unless, of course, you believe in ghosts. Or zombies. Because, I'm telling you, Townsend, Peyton Palmer was already dead Friday night."

Townsend sighed. "You're sticking to that story?"

"Like the superglue between my fingers when I worked on the Dairee Freeze homecoming float last year."

"Do you know how crazy this sounds, Tressa? What you're suggesting?"

"I'm not crazy, Ranger Townsend," I told him. "But someone would sure like to have people think that I am. You said the cops searched Palmer's boat. Right?"

Townsend hesitated. "Yeah."

"Are they still there? Searching, I mean?"

Another hesitation. "No. They packed up some time ago. But you can't go snooping around that boat. It's part of an official investigation," Townsend pointed out.

"Did they leave someone guarding it?" I asked. "Wind crime scene tape around it? What?"

Townsend shook his head. "I told you, they already searched the damned thing."

I stood.

"Tell me you're not thinking of doing what I think you're thinking of doing," he said. "That's nuts!"

"You don't have to come with me. I wouldn't think of making you an accessory after the fact. Just have the decency to bail me out if I get arrested so my poor, old grandma won't stroke out. Okay?"

I moved stiffly off the boat—not all due to my offending apparel—and managed to traverse the gulf and reach the dock. I started down the wood planking, when I was grabbed from behind and spun around.

"You're going the wrong way, Calamity. Palmer's boat is this way."

"You believe me?" A warm, gooey, chocolatey-chip feeling poured over me.

"Let's just say I'm keeping an open mind—and keeping you out of further trouble."

"That's an improvement over your body snatcher remark the other night. I owe you for that one, you dog."

"Yeah, well, I reckon I'm paying for that now," he said.

I had to hand it to Townsend. Despite his earlier hesitancy, he took to snooping, I mean sleuthing, like a Labrador takes to water. Once we crept onto the boat—I mean, boarded the vessel—Townsend was Mr. Cool, Calm and Collected, methodical and efficient in his search.

"Palmer runs a tight ship," I said, when nothing of interest came to light. "Neat as a pin. Too neat, if you ask me," I added, taking in the positively sparkling pontoon. "What's he got, a pontoon cleaning lady?"

Townsend shrugged. "I told you, the cops took some evidence."

"That's right. Evidence of overindulgence. What was Palmer supposedly drinking? Beer? Wine? Whiskey? Vodka?"

"I think it was whiskey," he replied. "Why? What does it matter?"

I shrugged. "Just curious."

"Are you about finished here, Miss Drew?" Townsend asked. "That is what you're doing, isn't it, Nancy? Amateur sleuthing?"

I ignored him and continued my search, careful to use a hankie to raise the seats when I looked beneath them. "Hey, what's this?" I pulled a leopard-spotted thong swimsuit bottom out of the crease in one of the chairs, and swung them from the end of my pen. "You wouldn't happen to have one of those bags like CSI uses?" I asked Townsend. "For evidence."

Townsend's white teeth shone in the dimming evening light. "What do you suppose that is evidence of?" he asked. "Indecent exposure?"

"More like poor taste. No wonder the owner discarded them. Do you know how uncomfortable these things are?"

"Can't say that I do," Townsend replied. "But apparently you do."

My face flushed. "I bought some as a joke for my grandmother after she gave me old lady underwear. Grandma ended up giving them back to me on my birthday."

"And you tried them on."

"Only out of curiosity, I assure you. They're not my style."

"Which is?"

"Something between granny bloomers and a pipe cleaner."

"What a shame."

"Can we please drop the subject of my underwear?"

"You brought it up," Townsend pointed out.

I mumbled something about men and breech cloths, spotted an empty Taco Juan's sack on the dock, snared it, and dropped the spotted underwear in the sack.

Townsend stared at me. "You're actually going to take that?"

"It's evidence. DNA and all that. Besides, these swim thongs tell me at one time Peyton Palmer had a lady friend on this boat."

"How do you know they don't belong to Sheila?"

I gave Townsend a get-real look. Sometimes men can be so dense.

Then, "Sheila? You know Sheila Palmer, Townsend?"

"I knew her as Sheila Davis, from junior high," was all the response I got.

"Were you friends?"

"Sheila was two years ahead of me."

Clearly nonresponsive. The fact that he hadn't said anything up to now about being on a first-name basis with Palmer's spouse made me wonder what else Townsend was keeping from me. Like maybe it wasn't Annette Felders doing the cling wrap imitation the other night. Gee, where had this come from?

"Can we go now?" Townsend added, climbing off the boat, leaving me no choice but to follow. We headed back to the marina parking lot. I looked at my watch. Ten P.M. Still early enough to do some damage.

"Well, uh, thanks for the help, Townsend." I suddenly felt nervous. And this around a fellow who'd been a fixture at our house since he was ten. "I've got to head home and finish cleaning up before Gram gets a look at the trailer and has the big one."

"You know something, Tressa?" Townsend grabbed my hand and pulled me to a stop. "Do you realize you've never once called me 'Rick?' You've called me

Ranger Rick, Carp Cop, Bassbuster, Squirrel Security, and a whole helluva lot worse, but you've never called me just plain Rick. Why is that?"

First, kisses. Now, personal questions. What was going on?

"Uh, why do you ask?" I said, not about to admit that maintaining an adversarial attitude had always been standard operating procedure where Rick Townsend was concerned. I'd kept my brother's handsome devil-of-a-friend (emphasis on the devil) at arm's length through the years by fueling a mutual, initial hostility. I can't even recall when I started seeing Rick Townsend as something more than a sub-creature. It was probably about the time I began to realize that boys weren't so icky, after all. Townsend did come in a nice package (even if the contents might be a disappointment), and I wouldn't be human if I hadn't noticed the way his jeans hugged his football player thighs, and how his muscle shirts showed off all those, well, muscles. And since he was at our house so often he had his own Christmas stocking, well, a girl in the throes of puberty is going to take advantage of the opportunity to gawk. Of course, I was way too clever to let Townsend think I had thoughts about him other than dark, destructive ones. If he had even an inkling that he made an impression on me other than a negative one, I was pretty sure he'd use that information to his advantage. Besides, it's what's inside that counts, right? Okay, ladies, you can quit laughing now.

"I probably spent as many hours at your house growing up as I did at home," Townsend went on. "I sure as heck ate as many meals there. And not once do I recall you calling me Rick. Seems kind of odd to me, that's all."

I tried to read his expression, to figure out what he was up to now. I felt off-balance, on a slippery slope. Why the devil did he want to psychoanalyze a perfectly good feud at a time like this? I fell back into the safety net of my porcupine defense mode.

"Oh, so in addition to being a ditz, I'm also odd. An oddball. A curiosity. How lovely."

"Good God, Tressa, why do you always do that?"

"What? Do what? What am I doing?"

"Wage war. Make assumptions. Jump to conclusions. See things that aren't there."

"Oh, so we're back to *that* again."

"What again?"

"The body in the trunk, of course. The one that is all in my head. To think I was just starting to harbor the hope that you actually believed me. I should have known better. What is this—humor a ditz day? Keep your best bud's sister out of Bedlam week? Adopt a delusional dweeb month? What?"

Townsend pulled me to him, and I could feel my nipples harden, and it had nothing to do with my cold, wet T-shirt.

"It's National Kiss-a-Clueless-Woman Day," he announced, and laid one on me that had nothing in common at all with the teasing, totally-too-brief touches of earlier. This one was a tongue on the tonsils, forget about the wedgie, shut up and kiss me kiss. By the time he was finished, if I hadn't been clueless before, I was after.

I struggled to appear angry and offended, and to regain the ability to speak.

"Wh-wh-what do you mean 'clueless'—?"

Townsend placed a palm over my hot, swollen lips.

"Shhhhh. You don't want to spoil the magic of the moment, Tressa." He walked me to my car, opened the front door, and, like a zombie, I got in. He closed the door and leaned in the open window. "You're going straight home, right, C.J.?" he asked.

I nodded.

"Good. We'll talk soon."

I nodded again.

"Say good night, Tressa," he said.

"Good night, Tressa," I said.

Townsend grinned. "Say, good night, Rick."

I hesitated.

"You can do it. Go on. Say it."

I closed my eyes and shook my head. Why did I feel if I called him by his first name all my carefully crafted defense mechanisms would blow apart like Wile E. Coyote's crazy Road Runner traps?

"Come on, T. Do it."

I clenched my teeth and shut my eyes even tighter.

"Tressa."

"Good night, Range—"

"Tressa."

"Good night, R-R-Ri-Rick," I finally got out.

Townsend gave me a pat on the cheek. "Good girl, Tressa. Good girl. Next time we get together, we'll work on the stuttering."

My eyes flew open, but Townsend was already walking off toward his boat, whistling as he went.

I gave my own cheek a slap. Wake up, girlfriend. What was I thinking? The guy was trouble with a capital -T. He was the Don Juan of the DNR. A ranger Romeo. A lake Lothario.

Nah-uh. No way.

I started the car and threw it into reverse. One couldn't become addicted on just three kisses, could they?

Uber-uncomfortable in the tight, sodden togs that were probably impacting my ability to conceive sometime down the road, I drove home slightly above the speed limit. I pulled into my drive and hurried to the trailer, anxious to rid myself of the need to hold my gut in any longer.

I unlocked the door, switched the lights on, and was unsnapping my pants when the phone rang. I glanced at my watch. It was half-past ten, too late for the folks to be calling unless it was an emergency. I hurried to pick up the phone.

"Hello?"

"Pay up."

"What? What was that? Speak up."

"Pay up."

I proceeded to bite clean through my lip.

"Listen. I told you I don't have the item you're inquiring about. I left it where it was. Please, just leave me alone. Okay?"

"Check out the barn. Next time it won't be your granny's cat."

The phone went dead. I dropped the phone and flew out the door, the dogs on my tail. I sprinted across the barn lot, stopped, and stood just outside the barn door. Inside the barn was silent and menacing. I swallowed my misgivings, stepped in, and flipped the light on. The dogs raced past me, directly to the back stall, and began to bark. I grabbed a pitchfork near the door and pointed it, prongs out, as I made my way through the barn. I stepped around a pile of horse manure. Butch and Sundance were barking up a storm. I reached the stall and saw the dogs jumping up to get at something hanging from a rope in the middle of the stall door. I looked up. Gramma's gray and white kitty was suspended from a nail by baling twine, its furry little neck stretched and extended, one kitty-cat eye open, one closed.

I tossed the pitchfork down, grabbed the rope above the cat's head, and, supporting the animal in my other hand, frantically tried to loosen the rope that encircled the stretched neck. To my immense elation, I detected movement from the cat. I continued to massage her distended body, and soon, Hermione was showing definite signs of life.

I sat on a bale of hay and stroked Hermione, giving her soft, reassuring words of encouragement and solace.

A hard knot of cold resolution settled in the very marrow of my bones. Steel determination reinforced my spine. The killer had crossed the line. Destroying my property—I mean Gramma's property—and dismantling Taylor's car was one thing. But leaving Gramma's beloved pet dangling from a nail in the barn was something else altogether. It was personal. He'd made it personal.

I gently set Hermione down, picked up the pitchfork, and jabbed a nearby bale. It was personal now. And I was personally going to nail this bastard. Whatever it took.

All I needed now was for someone to talk me out of it.

I jumped in my Plymouth and pointed the car back toward town, fear and anger continuing to wage a battle for supremacy. I drove by Peyton Palmer's house, surprised to see lights on in the home. I drove by again just to make sure I was looking at the right house. Townsend Sr.'s bug light was on, and I took a chance he wouldn't mind a surprise visitor. He was sitting on the porch in a wicker loveseat as I approached the stairs. He peered at me through binoculars.

"I was just thinking about you," he said. "I tried your number several times, but kept getting your machine. Sheila Palmer is home." He set the binoculars down with a Cheshire cat smile, and consulted a pad on the small wicker table beside him. "It was six-fifty-six when she drove in."

"She drove in? Was she alone?"

"Yep. Is something wrong? You smell like a wet dog."

I sniffed an armpit and shrugged. Body odor was the least of my worries. "I had a bit of trouble at the lake. Nothing to worry about." If you called tampering with evidence and obsessing over a few little kisses nothing to worry about.

Old Man Townsend raised one eyebrow like I'd seen his grandson do countless times. How do people do that, anyway? He put the pad down with a flourish. "Old Mrs. Winegardner brought over some cinnamon rolls this morning. I'm thinking they would be awful good if they were nuked in the microwave for thirty seconds or so. You interested?"

"Do bears cr—uh, eat in the woods?" I corrected myself before I offended the old fellow. I licked my lips. "You wouldn't happen to have a cup of coffee to wash those rolls down, would you, Joe?"

"Do bears shit in the woods?" He winked and rose from his seat. "I'll be back in a jiff."

I stared after the old gent, wondering if I would be as feisty as he was when I was his age. I thought of my gramma. What was I thinking? Chances were excellent I'd be a heck of a lot worse. Or better, depending on your point of view.

I sat and chatted with Joe while I consumed several (okay, four) wonderfully gooey, sinfully rich, jumbo-sized cinnamon rolls. I decided Mrs. Winegardner was a keeper, if only for her cinnamon rolls and buttermilk brownies. I was on my final roll when the garage door across the street suddenly opened and a silver Honda sedan backed out.

"There she goes," Joe said. "Come on. Hurry." He picked up his notepad, grabbed my arm, and pulled me toward my car.

"Where are we going?" I stuffed the remainder of the fourth roll in my mouth.

"To tail her, of course. You want your story, don't you?"

I slapped a hand to my mouth. "Tail her? Of course! But you can't come along." I came to a sudden stop. "This could get dicey. Maybe even dangerous. There's more going on here than you know, and I don't have time to get into it." I did not want to have to explain to Townsend what his dear, old granddad was doing in the middle of a meddling murder investigation. I already had one tough guy ready to inflict serious pain on me.

Joe patted the pocket of his putrid-green wind suit. "No sweat, I'm packing heat. Besides, I knew there was more to this than that human interest story you tried to snow me with. Now come on, girlie, or we'll lose her!"

I followed the wrinkled, shriveled Rambo-wannabe to my car, feeling that too-familiar sensation of things whirling out of control. I cast a sideways glance at Townsend, Sr. "Are you sure, Joe?" I asked.

"Let's roll, Kato," he said with a grin.

I pulled out of his drive and followed the silver sedan turning left a block down the street. "Who the heck is Kato?" I asked.

"Kato. You know, The Green Hornet's sidekick. Bruce Lee. Kung fu."

I stared at him. "The Green Hornet? What is that?"

"A crime-fighter, girl. In the sixties, I think. My wife loved that Green Hornet. She used to like me to wear a black mask to bed, and she would peel that baby off—"

"I don't want to hear this!" I yelled.

"An excellent crime-fighting vehicle, the Black Beauty," Joe continued. "This here jalopy leaves a lot to be desired. Hey, pick up the pace, gal, we're losing her."

I blinked. How on earth did I get stuck in a comic book crime story with my gramma's main squeeze and my archenemy's pistol-packin' grandpappy?

"Step on it, sister!" Joe urged.

I sighed, shrugged, and put the pedal to the metal. "The Green Hornet at your service, sir," I said.

"Don't be ridiculous, girl. You're Kato. Kato always drove."

"I don't want to be Kato," I said.

"You could be Batgirl," Joe suggested.

I gave him another look. "I'd rather be Catwoman," I said. "She's hot."

"She was also a villain."

"A reformed Catwoman, then. She's seen the error of her ways and is trying to give back to the community."

"Reeeowr!" Joe made a growling sound and I drove on, thinking sooner or later, I had to wake up. Please, God.

CHAPTER 11

"Where do you suppose she's going?" Joe asked.

"How should I know?" I mumbled, frustrated because I was forced to acknowledge that, in all likelihood, I was never going to wake from this dream. God help me. This was my life.

"What's that?" He raised a hand to his ear.

"I said, how should I know?"

"Don't snap at me, she-cat."

We followed our target into a fast-food restaurant at the corner of highways eighteen and six and watched her pull up to the drive-through. "Oh, for heaven's sake," I grumbled, "she just had a Big Mac-attack is all."

"You can't know that for sure. She may be checking to see if anyone is following her."

I started to park the car, but Joe grabbed my arm. "No, don't! Get behind her in the drive-up."

"Won't that be just a little bit too close for comfort?" I asked, acceding to his wishes, figuring we'd just find Mrs. Peyton Palmer heading for home after her fast-food run.

"It's bound to be a lot less conspicuous than parking in the lot and not going in," was the reply. Then, "I'll take a quarter-pounder with cheese, fries, and a cola."

I turned to my companion. "What?"

"Now who's hard of hearing? We have to order something. If we just drive past the window without ordering, we might as well hold up a sign that says, 'Object in rearview mirror is tailing you.' "

I hesitated only briefly. "I suppose you're right. I'll have the same."

We pulled up at the pay window, and I suddenly realized I was dead broke. As in I had nooooo money, honey. I gave a frantic look at my unwanted sidekick.

"What's wrong?"

I rifled through my purse.

"Don't tell me. You don't have any money? You don't have any money at all?"

I held up a dollar bill with a grimace. "It's all I've got."

"Well, that's just rich. What do we do now?"

I slammed a hand on the steering wheel. "Don't blame me. I wasn't the one who suggested we order something in the first place."

"Well, why didn't you tell me you were broke?"

"I'm always broke. It's my SOP."

The Honda in front of us pulled away from the pick-up window.

"There she goes," Columbo observed. "She's getting away!"

I waved my puny dollar bill at the student in the pay

window. "I'm sorry, I left my wallet at home. I'm really sorry. I don't know how it happened—"

"Oh, for pity's sake, quit obsessing and step on it!" Starsky put a white orthopedic tenny on top of mine, and we peeled away from the window and out into traffic.

"Stop that!" I poked the old man's skinny leg "You want to get us killed? Anyway, she's probably going home," I said, annoyed that I wasn't going to get my quarter-pounder after Maniac Magoo next to me raised my hopes and aroused my tastebuds.

We followed Sheila Palmer to her husband's law office, which was located in a brick building on town square at the corner of Third and Main.

"I really wanted that burger, too, you know," my passenger grumbled, echoing my own thoughts, as we watched the office lights come on. "No money. What do you do for a living, anyway, girl? Flip burgers somewhere? Work at the five and dime?" He picked up the taco bag and pulled out the leopard thong and held it up.

"Whoo-doggy!" he said. "You don't find these at most Taco Joints."

I snatched the spotted atrocity out of his hands and felt my cheeks burn. "Anyone ever tell you not to mess with things that don't belong to you? This is evidence."

"Of course, it is," he said. "Of course, it is."

I lowered myself in my seat doing a slow burn. Why was it whenever I was around Townsend men my blood pressure soared?

"So is it burger flipping or five 'n diming?" he asked again.

"Both," I mumbled.

"Speak up, young lady. And sit up. Young folks slouch too much. You'll end up with a curvy spine and a butt flat as a silver dollar, and men like to see some curves. You know. 'So round, so firm, so fully packed,'" Townsend's grandad began to croon.

"For your information, gramps, most women do not care to be built like the Pillsbury Doughboy," I said, still grumpy about the burger thing.

"Here she comes!"

"I see her. I see her," I said, following at a discreet distance. At least, it seemed discreet to me, but how would I know?

"She made another right."

"I thought you senior citizens were supposed to have trouble with night vision." I was beginning to see just where Ranger Rick got his annoying tendencies.

"There. She's heading out of town."

"I can see that."

"Don't lose her. Where do you suppose she's heading?" he asked again.

"Do I look like Psychic Sylvia?" I asked.

"You know, you're about as feisty as that grandmother of yours," he muttered.

"And you're about as big a pain in the derrière as that grandson of yours," I countered.

He fell silent, then chuckled. "That boy can sure get you all riled up, can't he? I never saw the like, except for maybe me, and Hannah the Hellion. Every time we were within spittin' distance, sparks flew hotter than Fourth of July fireworks!" He chuckled again. "Old Hannah. She was always brewin' for a good fight."

"Hannah? Hannah? Are we talking—is Hellion

Hannah my grandmother?" I asked, keeping my eyes on the taillights a quarter of a mile ahead of us.

"One and the same."

"She threatened to marry you if my grandpa didn't go into the family business."

"That brought old Will Turner up to scratch in a New York minute."

"You mean, he really thought Gramma would leave him?" I'd never thought of Papa Will and Grammie Hannah as a Bogie/Bacall kind of match, but they seemed content with their life together. Still, the idea of Gramma lusting in her heart for another man had never occurred to me.

"Your grandma and I fought like cats and dogs from the first moment we met," Joe explained. "My father was the mayor. Her father was the chief of police. And they hated each other. They were constantly at war, so I guess it was inevitable battle lines would be drawn, and we would be on opposing sides. By the time our folks weren't at each other's throats anymore, the feelings of anger and hurt went too deep to heal overnight. We made some inroads when my hitch in the service came up, but by the time I got home, your gramma was engaged to Will. Will was a good man. He gave Hannah a good life. I married Ruthie and we had thirty-nine wonderful years together."

Tears stung the corners of my eyes. "Darned allergies," I said, a hoarse tone to my voice.

"You know, you and my grandson remind me of Hannah and me," Joe said. "It's almost like looking into the past. You two faunch and fight like crazy, but I get the feeling there's something smoldering just below the surface ready to ignite into a raging inferno one of these days." He sighed. "Ah, memories."

I rolled my eyes, more for the appearance of sloughing off his words than anything else. I did not want any association with Rick Townsend to be remotely related to such concepts as burning desires and a consuming passion kept banked for years. No way.

I tapped my head. "What's the name of that old-timer's disease again?" I joked.

Joe laughed. "You're a ornery one, aren't you? And not too hard on the eyes, either. You and your gramma got that in common."

I gave the shadow in the passenger seat a hard look. "You put your hand on my knee, gramps, and you pull back a stub," I warned.

The old man laughed so hard his upper plate fell out.

"Holy crap!" I said.

"Not to worry, I just snap 'em back in place."

"I'm not talking about your falsies, Joe. I'm talking about Sheila Palmer's destination. She's turning off to go to the marina."

"So?"

"Do you know who is at the marina?"

"No, not off the top of my head."

"Your grandson," I yelled. "That's who. And if he sees you with me, he'll freak. He'll probably throw me into the lake again!"

"Again? When did he throw you in the first time?"

"Earlier this evening." I chewed my lip and tried to decide what to do. I wanted to see who Peyton Palmer's widow was meeting, but I did not want to do so at my own peril, which would be the case if Rick Townsend found his dearly beloved grandfather riding shotgun with yours truly.

"Why'd he do that?"

"Do what?" I asked, pulling slowly onto the road that led to the marina.

"Rick. Why'd he toss you in the drink?"

I shrugged, and watched brakelights appear on the car ahead. "I don't know. Maybe I tossed him in."

"You tossed Rick in the lake?"

I slowed the car down to a crawl. "Maybe we fell in. The point is, if your grandson sees you here with me, he'll fit me with cement overshoes, and toss me over the side for real. I'll be guppy food by morning."

"You aren't really afraid of my grandson, are you?" Joe leaned across and I could smell coffee on his breath. "He's really just a pussycat at heart."

"Yeah, a pussycat with great big, sharp Cujo teeth, and claws the size of Edward Scissorhands."

"Edward who?"

"Never mind. Sh. . . . shh. What was that? Did you hear that?"

"Hear what? You sniveling about my grandson? Hell, yes, I heard it. And it's downright pathetic."

"No! I thought I heard something. Never mind. Be quiet now. Let me think. Okay. I've got it." I pulled off the road and into a clearing surrounded by trees. "You stay here in the car and be the lookout while I go up on foot and check out Palmer's old lady. Got it?"

"What the devil am I supposed to look out for clear back here? There isn't a confounded thing to see. I want to be in on the action. Kick butt. Take names."

"If we're discovered by your grandson, you'll think kick butt. If I get my hind-end chewed, I'll kick your nosy behind back to Dakota Drive and leave you on old lady Winegardner's doorstep!"

"Hey, I'm the Green Hornet, remember. You take orders from me."

"Oh, for crying out loud. Okay, you can come. On one condition. You leave your piece in the car. Do you even have a permit for it?"

"I'm almost certain I do," he said. "But I really don't think it's smart to be working undercover without a sidearm."

I counted to ten. Okay, so I only made it to five before I took possession of Grampa Townsend's gun. I stared at the heavy metal firearm, which more closely resembled a cannon. I looked over at Joe. "What is this?" I asked. "Did you mug Dirty Harry or something?"

"It's a Colt Pyton," Joe enlightened me. "A superb firearm."

I grunted and shipped the weapon into the glove box.

"Here's the deal," I explained, as we headed toward the marina a few minutes later. "I know where Palmer's boat is docked. I was on it earlier."

"You were on his boat? What did you find?"

"Evidence," I said.

"Ah! The exotic underwear." He rolled his tongue and made another growling sound.

"I told you they weren't mine."

"No, I imagined not. You probably go for more conservative undergarments."

"Gee whiz. What is it with you Townsend men and underwear?"

"Just making polite conversation."

"Discussing a woman's choice of underpanties is not polite. Just kinky."

"Really? Kinky, huh? Does that turn women on?"

I was having a hard time walking and talking at the same time. The hot, humid night air was making me huff and puff like the big, bad wolf, when the real wolf striding next to me was showing relatively little exertion.

"Kinky is not synonymous with romantic, Joe. Sorry."

"What do women like? I mean, the women of today?"

"Why ask me?" I wheezed. "Anyway, ask a dozen women what they think is truly romantic, Joe, and you're bound to get a dozen different answers."

"What do *you* find irresistible in a man?" Joe persisted.

"What are you doing, writing a book?" I stopped to catch my breath. I really needed a good exercise program. "For the record, Joe, I don't think the man exists who can fulfill my qualifications. I want a guy who is strong but also gentle, who can be both serious and funny at the appropriate times, someone who is comfortable leading and equally comfortable following. He must be secure enough with who he is to allow his mate the freedom to be who she is, but who is savvy enough to know when his lady needs his undivided attention and gives it unconditionally, who loves no matter what, in spite of human foibles and failings. I want a mate who is best friend, confidant, lover, teacher, student, nursemaid and therapist all rolled into one. Oh, and he has to adore dogs, horses and children, not necessarily in that order."

"Now who's writing a book?" Joe said.

My cheeks grew warm again. I'd never confided that much about Mr. Right to anyone before. What was wrong with me?

"I suppose your idea of a dream date is being picked up in a fancy, schmancy car and being wined and dined in a gourmet restaurant. Women like that sort of thing."

"Ugh, not this woman." I stopped to catch my breath and wipe the perspiration from my brow. "I'm more a light beer and hot dog kind of girl. You doing okay, Joe? Need to sit down for a minute? Take a break?"

"Naw. I'm top-notch," he replied.

Goody-goody for you, I thought, and smacked at a mosquito the size of a dragonfly before pulling my pants away from my rear.

"What are we waiting for?" he asked.

"I'm formulating a plan of action."

"How to do away with a senior citizen by allowing swarms of mosquitoes to suck the blood from his body?"

"Why would they want your iron-poor stuff when they can feast on my cholesterol-saturated plasma?" I swatted at the buzzing in the general direction of my left ear.

"I've got an idea."

"Well?"

"I could make like a drunken sailor, lurch up to Palmer's boat, and act real obnoxious . . ."

"Yeah, like that would be hard."

"That way I could find out who Sheila Palmer was meeting."

"And she would say, 'Oh look, it's my nosy neighbor, Joseph Townsend, retired businessman, Jaycee member, and snoop extraordinaire. Hello, Joe, what do you know?' Yeah, that'll work, all right."

"Okay, Miss Leopard pants. What's your take?"

"I say we just mosey by, take a look-see, and if anyone asks, we're on our way to your grandson's boat.

Of course, we're really not on our way to your grandson's boat. We'll take a gander at Palmer's boat, see who she's with, and make a U-turn back to the car. That's my plan."

"Sounds dull as dirt, if you ask me," Joe whined.

"I didn't ask. Now, let's go. And act casual."

Right. An old duffer in a godawful neon wind suit, and a hat that said Jackie Chan Fan Club, and a blonde with fly-away hair dressed in damp black and pulling at her crotch. Nothing there to draw anyone's attention.

We struck out in the direction of Palmer's craft. My insides were churning worse than when I'd ridden that mechanical bull at the state fair two summers back.

"Lookin' good," Joe said. "Looking good. Almost there. Just a few more steps."

"Would you pipe down?" I hissed. "I don't need a play-by-play."

We made our way toward the boat, and with each step I was more certain of discovery or worse. Something didn't feel right. The boat appeared deserted.

"I was sure this was where she was headed," I whispered. "Where else could she be?"

"Beats me," Grampa Townsend said.

We stood at the bow—or is that stern—of the top-of-the-line pontoon.

"Well?"

"Well, what?" I asked.

"What do we do now?"

"I'm thinking. I'm thinking."

"Someone's coming!" Joe whispered. "What do we do, or are you still thinking?" The wiry, little leprechaun reached out and grabbed my hand and hauled me aboard the pontoon. "Come on."

"What the hell are you doing?" I asked, keeping my voice low.

"Hiding."

"From what?"

"My grandson."

"Oh." I crouched along with Joe, feeling absolutely no shame for cowering in the shadows, my hand in the death grip of a cantankerous old man.

"So, where is he?" I whispered.

"I could have been mistaken," he said. "But since we're already on Palmer's boat, we might as well have a look around."

"Why, you old—"

"Watch it now. You ever heard of elder-abuse?"

"You did that on purpose!" I hissed. "You never heard a danged thing. I should have known better than to trust a Townsend."

"Now hold on just a minute."

An abbreviated yelp, cut off by a slamming door, quieted the whispered objections of the old man whose fingernails were biting into my hand.

"Well?" Gramps said. "What do we do now?"

"Get the heck out of Dodge," I decided.

"You first." Joe motioned toward the dark path we'd just taken.

"Age before beauty."

"Ladies first."

"Ah, hell." I took his hand and we matched arm-in-arm toward the car. "Come on, Inspector Clouseau."

"You know, you really should clean up your language if you want to find a young man. Lots of fellows won't get serious about a woman who talks like a truck driver. *Oprah* did a show a while back on bad habits. I stopped leaving toenail clippings in the living room. Ruthie would have been so proud."

"Let's go, Gramps."

"Would this be a good time to remind you it was you who insisted I leave my revolver in the car?"

I stopped and gave him the evil eye.

"You will let me know when it would be a good time," he said.

I began to growl.

"Do you suppose there are cougars hereabouts? There's been several sightings of big cats reported in Iowa, you know."

I squinted at the dark line of timber. "Of course not," I asserted.

"Good thing, because you made me leave my gun in the car."

"Joe."

"Do you know what this reminds me of?" he asked.

"No, what?"

"*The Wizard of Oz*. That 'lions and tigers and bears, oh my' part."

"Joe?"

"Yes?"

"Shaddup."

"Young people these days."

CHAPTER 12

Hand in hand we made our way back to my car. By this time, according to my Bargain City, cheapo, glow-in-the-dark watch, it was just after one. I muffled a yawn, thinking even a lonely bed would be welcome this night—or, rather, morning.

"See anything?" I asked.

"Oh, so now you're asking the senior citizen who is supposed to have trouble with night vision if he sees anything? Before, all you could do was criticize. A person can't please you."

"Remind me, Joe. Why did I bring you along again?"

"Because of my Colt Python. Oh, and for my ability to remain calm in an emergency."

Calm? I'd probably need sutures from the fingernail marks the old goat had left on my arm. I muttered a few naughty words under my breath—I didn't want another language lecture from Gramps. I really began to feel for Rick Townsend. I knew what it was like to have a grandparent who made pit bulls run off with their tails between their legs, who thought they were the Jay Lenos of the geriatric set, and who, bless their heart, still believed a condom meant something you put on a wiener. Which, in a way, it is, I guess.

"Here we are," I announced, immeasurably relieved to make it back to my vehicle without stumbling over a snake, tripping over a corpse, or running into a ranger. I opened my car door and sank to the seat. "C'mon, grandpappy, let's split this pop shack."

Joe settled into the seat beside me. "I should have stayed home. I would have had more fun clipping my toenails."

"Well, why didn't you? Nobody invited you along to begin with." I gave an exaggerated, long-suffering sigh. "A person just can't please you," I remarked, throwing his earlier criticism back in his face.

He chuckled and shut his door. I reached for my keys tucked into my back pocket. I checked the other pocket. I got out of the car and tried to check my front pockets. I couldn't even get my pinky finger into either one, so I figured it was a safe bet my keys were not there.

"Okay, so where are they?" I said aloud.

"Where are what?"

I summoned my courage, then answered. "Uh, my keys. I seem to have misplaced my keys."

"You've lost your keys?"

"I didn't say lost. I said misplaced. As in placing them somewhere I've missed. Let me think a second."

"Uh-oh. She's thinking again. This can't be good."

"Joe, please."

"You need one of those fanny packs. If you wore one of those, you wouldn't lose anything. Mrs. Winegardner always wears a fanny pack when she power walks. You can't tell whether she's coming or going, but she never loses a thing."

"That's enough, Joseph."

"Why don't you just use your spare? You do have a spare key, don't you? Everybody has a spare key."

"Take a look around you. I drive a beat-up Plymouth Reliant that doesn't even start half the time. What do I need with an extra key?"

"This is great. Just great. Here we are stranded in the middle of nowhere, without a flashlight, and no food."

"Food? You just ate a bunch of cinnamon rolls."

"I have rapid-fire metabolism. I burn calories faster than Jackie Chan can lay out a dozen bad guys. Ooo-ah!" He made a goofy, Chinese kung-fooey move. At least that's what it looked like. Then again, he could have been praying.

"You're sure you don't have an extra set? How about in the glove box? Could there be a spare key in there?"

I flipped on the dome light. "Elvis could be in there as far as I know," I said. "But knock yourself out. Just be careful with that stupid gun."

"A Colt Python is not a stupid gun," Joe snarled. Then, a second later. "It's also not in the glove box."

"What?"

"My Colt. It's gone! You lost my Python!"

I slid across the seat and stared into the glove compartment. It was empty, relatively speaking. There was a handful of super-absorbency tampons, a bottle of pills to combat cramps, and a mini-pad with wings wrapped up in plastic. This mini-pad, however, was unique. It was decorated with a crudely drawn red bow and looked like a tiny present. Curious, I pulled the pad out and held it up. "To Tressa" was crudely written on the mini-pad, accompanied by four words, also written in a blood red color. I hoped it was just blood red, not real blood. It said:

PAY UP OR ELSE!

Despite the muggy night and high humidity that was wreaking havoc with my hair, I began to shake. Icy cold tendrils of terror crept ever so closer to vocal cords that were working overtime trying to vibrate a warning to my comrade.

"Lock your door." I sounded like one of those computer-generated voices devoid of feeling or emotion. I slid to my side of the car, shut my door, and pushed the lock button down, then reached in the back and locked the back door.

"What?"

"Door. Lock," I managed.

"What's that, again?"

I lunged across the seat, reached around Joe, and locked us in.

"I could have done that if you'd just asked," Joe said. "Why are we locking ourselves in?"

I showed him the mini-pad present. It seemed to take an eternity for him to read it.

" 'Pay up or else?' What's up with that? You got the bill collectors on your tail, little lady?"

"Yes, but that's beside the point."

"You're holding out on old Joe, here, aren't you?" He gave me back my gift. "What's the deal, Lucille?"

I debated how much to tell the old guy. Truth be told, I didn't want anything to happen to him, no matter how irritating he was. The more I was around him, the more he reminded me of my own grandma.

"I'm being threatened," I said, and told him about my little trunk discovery, the trashing of the Buick and my trailer, my visit from Cobra Man, and ended with the abandoned pontoon. I left out the part about Gramma's pussycat, Hermione. I wasn't ready to verbalize that heinous act yet. "The only thing I can figure is the killer thinks I have the money, and he wants it back."

"Don't you think you could have mentioned this a little sooner? Like before I volunteered to go on this little ride-along program?"

"Nobody twisted your arm, old man."

"Doesn't it seem strange to you that a killer would risk being exposed just for a wad of dough?"

"Yeah, maybe. So?"

"Seems to me there has to be more to it than that. But what?"

"I don't know and right now, I don't care. All I want is to get us out of here. Someone out there has your gun, Joe. Someone who already popped Peyton Palmer. Someone who thinks I have their paycheck. And we're stranded here like two sitting ducks." I reached up and shut the dome light off.

The sudden, muffled report of what sounded like a gunshot drowned out the whispered observations of the old man.

I squeezed Joe's hand. "My god! Did you hear that?"

"I'm hard of hearing," he insisted.

"Joe!"

"Oh, you mean that gunshot? No, I didn't hear it!"

"Joe!"

"Okay, okay, so I heard it. What do we do about it?"

"Why do you keep asking me what do to do? You're

the elder here. You have years of life experiences. And years. You were in the service. Surely you've had incidents similar to this. What did you do then?"

"I usually waited for orders," he admitted.

I tried to think.

"Maybe someone will come along and we can hitch a ride?" Joe suggested.

"Okay. So how do we know it isn't the same person who pinched your Python and left me that little love note? Personally, I don't think I want to take that chance. Do you?"

I put my head on the steering wheel. Where could I have dropped my keys? I snapped my fingers. "The boat!" I screamed. "Palmer's boat. When you hauled me onto the boat, I bent down. I bet you anything my key ring popped out. It's on Peyton Palmer's boat!"

I could hear my companion swallow in the dark. Or it could have been me.

"You mean we have to go back out there and walk to that blasted boat?"

"I don't see what choice there is. But, Joe, there's no reason for you to go. You stay here, and I'll go look for the key. Lock yourself in. No one will bother you. Probably."

"Oh, I get it. Convince me to lock myself in your car and become human bait for some pistol-stealing mass murderer. Well, it's not going to work. I'm going with you."

I breathed a sigh of relief and said a little thank-you to my Fundamentals of Psych professor. He'd lectured on reverse psychology before I dropped the class. This was back when I thought I might like to be a therapist like Dr. Phil, just before I made the switch to animal husbandry, and just after I'd dropped public relations.

I did not plan on making that trek back to the boat alone. No way. No how. Uh-uh.

"Joe, I really think it would be better if you stayed here. It's a long, hot hike, and you never know what or who we might encounter. Besides, you're probably getting faint from no food and that high metabolism and all." I cinched the deal by adding, "You know, you're not as young as you used to be."

"I'm going with you and that's final," Joe announced, pounding the dash with a bony hand. "Besides, what kind of Jackie Chan man would I be if I left a puny young thing like you to face unknown danger alone?" He opened the door. "All for one and one for all!" he said, then added, "You know, I could use a Three Musketeers bar about now."

"I could use a musketeer," I said. "One who looks good in tights."

"Who loves dogs, horses and children, but not necessarily in that order," Joe added.

"You remembered!" I said, touched that the old guy had actually absorbed my wistful wish list for the perfect mate.

"I never said I had trouble listening, kiddo. Just hearing."

"Know something? You're a pill, Joseph Townsend. A real pill."

We joined hands again as he came around the front of the car. "It runs in the family."

I smiled. "Don't I know it?"

It took us much longer the second time to make our way to Peyton Palmer's boat than it did the first. That's because we kept stopping to listen for anything unusual. You know, like Michael Myers breathing, stealthy footsteps, or the cocking of a Colt Python.

We reached the boat still in one piece. I had even come to terms with my wedgie. Hey, what's a little discomfort compared to loss of life? The marina lighting left much to be desired. I would have lodged a complaint. That is, if I'd had a boat stored here. Or is that moored?

"Do you remember where we were cowering?" I asked as we approached the Palmer boat a second time.

"Cowering is a pretty strong word."

"Resting, then."

"We were standing about here, so that would mean we were resting right about there." He pointed to the corner of the boat.

I nodded, climbed into the boat, and proceeded to slip and slide across the deck. I put a hand down to keep from falling. "Be careful," I warned Joe. "It's wet here. And very slippery." Funny. I didn't remember it being wet when I'd done my yellow-belly coward routine earlier.

My eyes scanned the deck of the boat. The light reflected off something shiny. I took a step closer. It looked like . . . it was. A key ring. My key ring!

"Stay where you are, Joe," I called. "I think I've found my key."

I skated toward the object that promised escape from Marina Macabre. I reached out to take my keys. It was at that point, I realized they were clutched in a hand. A human hand. My horrified gaze traveled upward from the hand to rest on two, wide-open, heavy-lidded, hooded eyes, and long, hideous fangs. I gasped. I'd seen fangs like that before. Recently, as a matter of fact. On a particularly gruesome tattoo on an equally gruesome character. The snake charmer!

I snatched my keys and drew back a hand covered in blood. I looked down and suddenly realized just what I'd been slip-sliding around in. I scrambled across the deck on all fours, and reached the edge of the boat just in time to lose the cinnamon rolls I'd enjoyed earlier to the sea. Or lake. Or whatever.

"You sick?"

My head draped over the side of the boat, I tried to stop Joe. "Stay back!"

Of course, it was too much to ask that a Townsend male follow a lowly woman's advice. Thirty seconds later, I was joined at the rail by Ranger Rick's granddad where, our heads stretched over the side, we puked and retched in stereo.

"I thought you said you had rapid-fire metabolism." I wiped a shaky hand across my mouth when I was relatively sure I had finished regurgitating. "You shouldn't have anything to toss up, then."

"Stomach juices." Joe's voice was weak.

"I'm sure I saw some chunks."

"Prove it!"

"Hold it right there! Don't move!" A powerful beam of light hit us, or rather our tail ends, as we were still on all fours with our necks resting on the side of the boat. "Hands in the air! Nice and slow!"

"Hell!" Old Joe and I chorused in complete synchronization.

"I bet now you wished you'd stayed home and cut your toenails," I commented. "What would Jackie Chan do in a situation like this?"

"He'd cuss. In Chinese, of course," came Joe's reply.

"Do you know any Chinese phrases that are right for this occasion?" I asked.

"I sure do."

"Well?"

"We deep dung."

CHAPTER 13

"Son of a bitch! I'd know that tight-ass anywhere. Good god, Turner, what the hell are you doing back here?" Rick Townsend thundered.

I was feeling pukie again. The man was going ballistic, and he hadn't even ID'd my cohort in crime yet.

"Hands up! Turn around slowly!"

Oh, terrific, he'd called in the cavalry. Deputy Dickhead to the rescue! I pulled myself off the side of the boat and turned very, very slowly around.

"Don't shoot!" I raised my hands. "I'm unarmed."

"You again!" Deputy Doug Samuels's eyes were almost as big as the corpse's.

I made a feeble attempt at a smile. "Yeah. Me again. But this time there really *is* a dead body. One you can see, touch, and"—I shuddered—"step in."

"Body? That it next to you?" Deputy Doug asked. "What's it doing hanging over the edge of the boat like that?"

"Uh, no." I looked back at Joe, who I guessed was long over his vomiting, but was now in hiding from his grandson. "That isn't the body. Not the dead one, anyway. At least, he wasn't a few minutes ago."

"Who the hell is it, then?" Deputy Samuels asked.

Townsend holstered his weapon and stepped forward. "That skinny ass in the neon green would be Joseph Townsend."

"Your grandfather? *That* Joseph Townsend?"

"The Joseph Townsend who has a hell of a lot of explaining to do."

"Forget Joe, he's fine. Maybe his electrolytes are out of kilter." I turned to Deputy Samuels. "He has a really rocking metabolism. It's the body over there that needs your attention." I pointed in the direction of the not-yet-stiff stiff.

"Nice. Real nice." Mr. T decided it was time to come up for air. "You know, I could have had a massive coronary which required lifesaving measures and what do you do? You tell them 'forget Joe, he's fine.' Forget him? You're more concerned with the dead than the living!"

"Oh, poor baby. Maybe later Mrs. Winegardner can kiss your boo-boos and make them all better."

"Would you two just be quiet!" Rick Townsend helped his granddad to his feet, leaving me to fend for myself. "Careful, Pops. It's slippery."

"Oh, gee, thanks for the newsflash, ace reporter." I hauled myself to my feet and did a Michelle Kwan move across the deck, careful to avoid looking in the direction of the body slumped against the side of the boat. Deputy Doug moved gingerly toward the corpse, and crouched in front of it.

"You recognize him?" Townsend asked.

"Of course I recognize him. That's Tattoo Ted. He's the guy I told you about yesterday. That's the same guy who threatened me at Bargain City yesterday and, no, I don't need to take a closer look to make a positive identification."

"I was addressing Deputy Samuels," Townsend snarled, helping his grandfather off the boat and onto the dock. "Are you warm enough, Pops?" he asked in a tone far removed from the one he'd just used with me.

"I *am* a bit chilled," Joe whined. He caught my eye and winked.

"I have a blanket in my truck. I'll be right back."

I hauled myself over the boat and onto the dock. "Why you old . . . phony baloney! You've been sweating up a storm all night. I'll need to put a new pine air freshener in my car to cover up your body odor."

"Ha! That's a laugh. Your car smelled like rotting hamburger before I ever stepped foot in it. It ought to be confiscated by the EPA and crushed!"

"Here, Gramps." Townsend draped a gray blanket over his grandfather's shoulders. "Now, do you two mind telling me what the hell is going on? What are you doing out here in the middle of the night?"

I stared at my toes. I wasn't accountable to Rick Townsend. He could grill me 'til dawn and I wouldn't tell him a thing. Not one danged thing.

I pointed at his grandfather. His grandfather pointed at me.

"—He made me do it!"

"—She made me do it!"

I stared, openmouthed, at Joe. "What?"

"Townsend!" Deputy Doug called.

"Yes?" piped up Joe.

"He's talking to me, Gramps." Townsend patted his grandfather on the shoulder, gave me a stare that would freeze the devil's underwear—if he has any, that is—and moved to converse with the deputy sheriff.

Joe jabbed me in the ribs. "Okay, let's get our stories straight."

"What do you mean, get our stories straight? We have to tell the truth, Joe."

"All of it?"

"Yes, all of it."

"Even the part about carrying an unregistered, loaded handgun?"

"You can't mean . . ."

"The Constitution guarantees us the right to keep and bear arms under the Second Amendment!"

"This is not the time for a history lesson, pops!" I hissed.

"What are you two whispering about?" Deputy Samuels called out. "You wouldn't be trying to get your stories worked out, now would you?"

"See!" I pinched Joe, but got only blanket. "Now he's suspicious."

Townsend disembarked and waited for Deputy Samuels. I could tell from their approach that I was not going to like what they had to say.

"Either of you recognize this?" The deputy dangled a familiar-looking sidearm in front of us.

"My Python! You found my Python!"

I stepped on Gramps's toe. "You can't be sure that's your Python, Mr. Townsend. Why there must be hundreds of them out there."

"What do you mean? Of course it's my gun. I'd know my Colt anywhere." He reached out to take the weapon, but the deputy pulled it out of his reach.

"I'm afraid I can't let you touch it, Mr. Townsend,"

he said, with no real regret. "You see, sir, this revolver appears to have been the murder weapon."

"Murder weapon?"

"That's right."

"He's dead, then?"

"As a doornail," Townsend, Jr. elaborated.

The deputy nodded. "Body's still warm, though."

"We heard a gunshot. Didn't we, Joe?" I swallowed and looked around. "That means the killer could still be close by." I shivered, and Joe put his blanket around both of us.

"I would say it is a very good possibility that the killer is close by." Deputy Doug gave me a look I didn't much care for. "A good possibility."

"What does that mean?" I asked.

"Didn't you say the victim was the same guy who threatened you yesterday? The one you made the report on?"

"Yes, but—"

"And you had the apparent murder weapon in your possession at one time?"

"Well, yes, but—"

"And you were found at the murder scene. Sounds like motive, opportunity and means to me," Deputy Doug said.

My teeth began to chatter at what he was suggesting. "You're forgetting, Deputy. I also have one very upstanding, very pillar-of-the-community type as my airtight alibi."

"An upstanding pillar that likes to carry large caliber revolvers," the deputy pointed out.

"There is another suspect, you know. And she had means and opportunity, and motive." I glanced at

Ranger Rick. "I'm still working on that one. But, you should talk to her. You should talk to Sheila Palmer."

"Sheila Palmer? What does she have to do with this?" the deputy asked. I realized in all the excitement I had forgotten all about the target of our rather ill-advised tail.

"We followed her. From town. That's why we're here."

"Followed her? Why the hell would you follow Sheila Palmer?"

"To find out what she knew about her husband's disappearance and murder, of course," I explained, exasperated that they just didn't seem to get it. "Listen, I was being treated like a joke by the same people who were sworn to protect me. I was being threatened by some guy who'd make Vin Diesel think twice. I got a tip that Mrs. Palmer was at her residence." Joe elbowed me. I winced, but ignored him. "I followed up on what I thought could be a lead, and here we are. By the way, where is Sheila? Shouldn't you be questioning her about her whereabouts, why she is here, why there's a dead body on her boat, why her husband was stuffed in the trunk of a car with a hole in his head? Things like that?"

"Sheila Palmer could not have shot your tattooed admirer." Rick Townsend took a step toward me. I was suddenly uneasy.

"Oh yeah? Why couldn't she have been the shooter?" I asked, fairly certain I probably wasn't going to care much for his answer.

"She couldn't have been the shooter because she was with me," Townsend said. "She's been with me since she arrived."

All kinds of emotions bombarded me upon processing his words. Shock, disillusionment, anger, fear, and, yes, okay, even pain. It didn't take a Bill Gates to figure out what the two had been doing, and I didn't think it was the dispensing of sympathy to the newly grieving widow.

I tried to appear unaffected by his words. Who Townsend spent his time with had nothing to do with me. Or did it? Suddenly, I thought about my earlier murder-for-hire scenario. I'd cast Dennis Hamilton, philanderer-at-large, as the other man, who was therefore implicated in the knock-Peyton-off scheme. It appeared that I might now have to recast that role. Rick Townsend had joined the cast of characters in my little whodunit.

As a suspect.

A chill rippled over me. Suddenly I was as cold as a Dairee Freeze Arctic Blast. Townsend, Sr. took my hand and we huddled together.

The sheriff was called out, the state called in. Joe and I sat in his grandson's pickup and watched the activity increase, waiting for further instructions.

"Our fingerprints are on the murder weapon, you know," Joe finally said.

"You don't have to remind me."

"If you had let me bring the gun along in the first place, this never would have happened."

"If you'd left it at home, this never would have happened," I pointed out. "Or if you had butted out instead of playing some ridiculous Dirty Harry fantasy."

The driver's door was suddenly yanked open and I almost fell out.

"Move over, Turner." Townsend's clipped order compelled me to obey without a word. Well, almost without a word.

"Where are we going?" I asked, still reeling from his alibi defense of Sheila Palmer.

"I'm going to take you back to your car. From there, I will follow you into town to the sheriff's office where the sheriff would like to have a nice, long chat with you both."

"Couldn't it wait until morning?" I am not above whining on occasion, and this occasion called for it. Besides, things always looked better in the light of day. Though I wasn't sure if that went for murders, too.

"No, Turner, it can't wait. Don't you realize you are now involved in a murder investigation?"

"Hello! That's what I've been trying to tell everyone since I found the surprise stiff in my trunk Friday night. No one took me seriously. Now another person is dead, I'm being threatened, and my pants are so far up my wazoo, they may require surgical extraction!"

"Why the hell did you get my seventy-five-year-old grandfather—"

"Seventy-four," Joe interjected.

"—involved in your hare-brained, in-over-your-head, reckless, amateur crime-fighting? How could you be so irresponsible? Oh, sorry. I lost my head there. I forgot who I was talking to. Irresponsible is your middle name!"

"For your information, Mr. Ranger, sir, your seventy-*four*-year-old grandfather wouldn't take 'no' for an answer. As a matter of fact, up until we ran across the body, he was complaining about being bored. Besides, we had no way of knowing what we were getting into. How could we? I thought we'd just take a nice, little drive and be home in bed by midnight."

"There is no such thing as a nice little anything

where you and that wreck of a car are concerned. And you should have been home in bed."

With me.

Hold it. Had he said that last part, or had I just imagined it? I stared at him.

His eyes held my gaze. "When you were threatened again, why the hell didn't you call me?"

Probably because I would have ended up home in bed. With him. And I wasn't about to make that leap of faith. Not yet. Probably not ever. It was funny. Not funny, ha ha. Funny, weird. In all the years I'd known and fought with Rick Townsend, I always knew deep down that I didn't want to be his enemy, but I always felt it was the safest place to be. Safest in terms of heart-health, I mean. I knew from day one that if I let this gorgeous man be anything more to me than my brother's best friend, and mean anything more to me than a nuisance, I would end up with a mortal chest wound. A cracked aorta. All right, all right, I'll say it: *A broken heart.* I may not be the smartest gal in the heartland, but I know trouble looking for a place to happen, and Rick Townsend had TRESSA'S HEARTACHE written all over him.

"I couldn't call," I said, truthfully. "I was afraid you wouldn't believe me again."

"You have to learn to trust me, Tressa, but you have to do that on your own."

This from a guy who'd just admitted he was playing the Skipper to our first murder victim's wife's Ginger. I wondered if he was aware of how fast my heart was beating, how shallow my breathing had become, how much I longed to reach over and push that dark, errant lock back and plant a lip-lock on him that would erase all my doubts and fears, and dare me to dream.

But, of course, I didn't touch his hair or kiss his mouth. Real life wasn't a romance novel where the characters took chances on love and were always rewarded in the end for their heart-of-a-gambler ways. I feared I was like those swans—or is it pelicans—who mate for life. Yes, I know, in today's disposable world where folks take new lovers as often as I buy a pair of shoes, and discard them just as quickly, and prenuptial agreements are drafted more often than wills, that sounds really corny. But I really think, for me at least, life in the fast lane of love would result in a crash-and-burn extravaganza worthy of those TV shows featuring death and destruction.

"How come it's grown so quiet over there?" I'd forgotten Joe was even in the truck cab. "A bit ago you were ripping into each other. What happened?"

A long pause. Rick Townsend's gaze moved to my lips. I could see little knots of tension rise in his jaw. "Nothing, Pops." He met my eyes again. "Nothing at all."

He stopped his truck across from the Plymouth and got out. I turned to Joe. "I guess I'll see you downtown," I said. "But don't expect the interrogation room you've seen in the movies. You'll be disappointed."

"No bright lights?"

I shook my head.

"No two-way mirror?"

"Not that I could see."

"Did they offer you a smoke?"

I shook my head. "But the coffee definitely was cop quality. You could float a coin on that stuff."

"At least that's something."

I jumped down from the truck and winced. Once I

finally made it home, and managed to remove a certain offending garment (probably with wire cutters), I was going to toss it in the incinerator, squirt it with lighter fluid, light it and have a weenie roast.

"I'm following you, remember," Rick Townsend advised.

"I'll try to keep it under fifty-five," I snipped.

"Just keep it between the lines."

"Yes, sir."

If my first experience with police interviews had not lived up to my expectations in terms of drama, the second more than made up for it. As I suspected, they interviewed us separately. All the credible cop shows separate witnesses . . . and suspects, too, I realize now. I was a little uneasy not knowing what wild stories Joe was telling. Now that the shock of finding a murder victim and having the wits scared out of him had worn off, no telling how Mr. Super Hero was embellishing the story. No doubt he was putting himself in a good light and casting me in the role of—you guessed it—the helpless, or I suppose hapless, female.

Tell the truth, I'd told Joe, *and nothing but the truth. Everything will be fine if you tell the truth.* Only, I'd told the truth and everything wasn't fine. It wasn't fine at all.

"I've explained why you'll find my fingerprints on the gun. I was saving an old man from shooting himself in the foot, or worse. I've told you why I was following Sheila Palmer. Someone around here has to solve this murder—Peyton's, not Tattoo Ted's. He wasn't dead at the time. It's not as if I had a choice here. No one believed me about the body. Peyton's, not Tattoo Ted's. And the killer was trying to discredit me big time."

Then, "I don't know why the maxi-pad with the blood red message wasn't in my car. I left it there. On the front seat. Before we left to find the body, the tattooed one. Maybe Joe picked it up. Ask him. He saw it. He can verify it was there."

I was lucky. Rick Townsend chose to sit in on his grandfather's interview. I was grilled by a grumpy state agent, the local DARE officer, and a sheriff who clearly was not impartial. Hey, how long can you hold a grudge over a canine custody dispute?

"Miss Turner, let me give it to you straight," Deputy Dawg's owner said. "We've got your fingerprints on the murder weapon. You were at the scene of the crime. You have the victim's blood all over you."

"Ditto for Joseph Townsend," I reminded him. "And as far as opportunity, Joe and I were with each other from the moment we left town until you split us up. Joe did tell you that we were together the entire time, didn't he? Didn't he?"

I hate it when cops put on their cop faces.

"Do I need an attorney?" I used the standard witness-turned-suspect line.

"Let's just say I wouldn't plan any out-of-town trips," the sheriff replied.

I swallowed. Finally. An honest-to-goodness hall-of-fame cop line. Addressed to me. Gulp.

I was allowed to leave just as the sun was coming up, but I had to promise to return at ten to give a formal statement. I kicked around the idea of getting an attorney to go with me, but didn't have the money for a retainer, and didn't want to hit my folks up for it. Besides, I had an airtight alibi. Or as airtight as one could have depending on a cranky old fart to vouch for your whereabouts.

Experience had taught me not to wait for the cops to get off their duffs and do their jobs. Besides, this had turned into something way beyond a personal safety issue, although that angle was still the most compelling. I was on a crusade here for ditzy blondes everywhere, those women unfairly labeled "dumb" for their unique, eccentric personalities, who were given a wink, a pinch, and a leer, rather than credibility, who were taken about as seriously as stop signs are by bicyclists.

I'd had it up to here with being talked down to. I was over being overlooked and underestimated. I'd had my fill of being patronized and pointed at. I wanted to be laughed with, not at. Consulted, not advised. Considered, not left off the list altogether. I wanted respect. Simple R-E-S-P-E-C-T. And by, golly, I was going to get it. Or die trying.

(Yikes! Strike that last part, okay?)

CHAPTER 14

The eastern sky was just beginning to lighten when I left the county courthouse, bleary-eyed, and loopy from the amount of a legal, addictive stimulant I'd consumed (i.e. caffeine) at the sheriff's office. I crawled into bed, promising myself I'd only sack out for a couple hours, then head next door to brief the family on the rising body count witnessed by their loved one. Four hours later, I was awakened by the persistent barking of two hungry dogs, and an annoying beam of sunlight that slapped me in the face. I pulled myself from the bed, did the zombie shuffle to the bathroom, and turned on the shower, letting the hot water cascade over my tense neck and shoulder muscles.

I rehearsed what I was going to say to my folks. "Mom. Dad. I have good news and bad news. The bad news is I found a body in the trunk of a car. The good news? It wasn't my car." Or: "The bad news? I was the target of a hit man. The good news? I found the hit man's body at the marina last night." Or: "You know how you all are always worrying about me being such an underachiever? Well, guess what? I found not one dead body, but *two!*"

I could hear them now. "What were you thinking?" "How could you take the wrong car?" "Why didn't you tell us before?" Yadda, yadda, yadda. Except for Gramma. She'd go ballistic over her mobile home, and Grampa's car, and want to kick some serious booty.

I frowned. Face it. There just wasn't a positive way to spin the events of the previous forty-eight hours. Unless I engaged the services of the Democratic National Committee.

I fed Butch and Sundance, picked up Hermione from a pillow in my living room where she'd been recovering, and trudged next door.

"Can you call Dad and ask him to come home, Mom?" I caught my mother on one of her potty/check-on-an-old-lady breaks. "I have to talk to the entire family. There's something really important I have to tell you."

"You're not pregnant, are you?" my gramma chimed in from the living room.

I shook my head furiously at my mother's raised eyebrows. "I'm not pregnant!" I yelled. "I'm just involved in something with personal safety ramifications."

Seeing my mother's face turn white, I added, "I think I should be safe now that the hit man who was threatening me is dead."

My mother blanched, grabbed the cell phone, and speed-dialed my dad.

"Phillip. Get home now." Pause. "Tressa Jayne," was all she said next, then she disconnected.

"Your father will be here shortly," she said.

I followed her into the living room to wait.

"Better make this snappy," my grandma spoke up. "My show starts at eleven, and today we find out who the real father of Reeyanda's baby is. Frank, Caleb, Terrence or Cappy."

I sat down on the ottoman next to Grandma and waited for the DNA test results.

My family reacted to my news pretty much as I predicted. Taylor grew rather fond of the phrase, "I don't believe this." My father paced the rug repeating, "My daughter found two bodies. Not one, but two!" My mother sat ramrod straight in her chair and wanted to know why my car key worked in another automobile, and if there was, perhaps, a cause of action there. And Gram? Bless her heart, when I put Hermione in her lap and explained the kitty's heroic role, (leaving out the exact manner of torture), Gram responded by inquiring if one could acquire the services of a merc over the Internet. Atta girl, Hellion Hannah!

Gramma was also surprisingly interested in hearing all about my partner in crime-fighting, Joltin' Joe Townsend.

"Did he, or did he not talk about me?" My grandma took on the qualities of a seasoned prosecutor cross-examining a reluctant witness.

"Who?"

"Joseph Townsend, of course. Did he talk about me?"

"Well, yes, in passing. We talked about a lot of things."

"Did he tell you I was in love with him, the old liar?"

"No, Gramma, I don't believe he mentioned love. He said you two fought like cats and dogs."

"And I usually won." She sat back in her rocker with a half-smile on her face. "What else did he say about me?" she asked.

I got up and gave her a kiss on the cheek. "He said you were a real pip, Gramma. A real pip."

"A pip, indeed," she said, but I could tell she was tickled. "Did he tell you about the time I stole his skivvies when he was swimming in the old strip pit? I don't think he ever knew I hid and watched him walk out, naked as the day he was born. I couldn't leave without knowing he was okay, now could I? And it wasn't like I left him there with no clothes at all. I'd left behind one of my favorite sundresses. It was bright yellow and aqua with thin, delicate little straps—you call them spaghetti straps now—and the cutest row of ruffles with elastic tucks across the bust. Very chic."

I giggled. "Did you, by any chance, leave him coordinated footwear?" I teased.

"Heavens no! With his big feet, he'd have ruined them. As it was, I never got my dress back."

"Oh, why not?"

"To tell you the truth, I think he took a liking to it. He wasn't wearing it the other night, was he?"

I gave a loud laugh. "No, Gramma, but it was close." I hugged her tight. "Real close."

I left my family still trying to come to terms with the latest calamity I'd stumbled into, citing another police interview scheduled for that afternoon. My parents wanted to go with me, but I refused; I didn't want them any more involved in my murder mess than necessary. And once the identity of Tattoo Ted was known, perhaps the pieces of this whodunit would fall into place.

The more I got to thinking about Tattoo Ted's threats, the more convinced I was that Joe was probably right. There had to be more to it than just cold hard cash. What killer risks all for a measly (well, not so measly to me) ten grand or so? So, maybe there was more in the envelope than just money, like something the killer wanted so desperately he was willing to kill yet again to get back. Maybe that explained why I hadn't been killed. Maybe as long as the killer thought I had it, I was safe from harm. Maybe he couldn't take a chance of the envelope falling into the wrong hands once I was dead. I shook my head. Too many maybes. I needed facts.

Like, why would a highly respected attorney like Peyton Palmer risk his good name, law license, livelihood, even his freedom, to play mule for a jailed client? (Some service. I can't even get a pizza delivered out where I live.) And what connection, if any, was there between Peyton Palmer's alleged drug-smuggling, his subsequent arrest for same, and his recent murder?

These questions and a gazillion others were foremost in my mind as I made my way back to town. Who better to get those elusive answers, I decided, than a nosy newshound? I took a deep breath. It was time for this ace cub reporter to resurrect her sorry career.

The editor of the *Grandville Gazette* (I know, P.U.), is Stanley Rodgers. Stan reminds me of that guy on NYPD Blue. No, not Jimmy Smits, unfortunately. No, not Ricky Schroeder, either. The older guy. The pudgy one. Only Stan doesn't have as much hair. And he has a bigger gut.

Stan was always willing to give a person a second

chance—or, in my case, a good half-dozen chances. I just know he felt bad about letting me go the last time. He was in tears, the poor man. And seeing as how I had just happened onto the biggest story this neck of the woods had seen since the high school band performed in the Tournament of Roses Parade, I felt I owed it to my former employer to let him have first chance at the scoop. Providing, of course, he'd find it in his heart to provide me with gainful employment again—or cover, at the very least. The bell on the door tinkled as I walked into the newspaper office.

"Is Stan in?" I asked Joan, the receptionist secretary proofreader photograph developer advertising assistant.

She did a double take when she saw me. "You want to see Stan?"

I nodded. "I'm almost certain."

"I don't know. He's not in very good humor this morning. Another time might be better. Like when hell freezes over."

"This can't wait, Joan," I said. "And surely he's not still ticked about that obituary thing."

"It was his wife's Aunt Deanie you identified as Stubby Burkholder."

"That's water under the bridge." I brushed her misgivings aside. "I've got a blockbuster, headline-grabbing, breaking news story that I'm working and, well, I felt a certain loyalty to Stan to bring it to him first. Professional courtesy and all."

"What kind of news story?" Joan's extension began to ring, and I took advantage of the opportunity.

"That's okay, I know the way. You just go ahead and answer your phone there." I hurried down the hallway to Stan's office, a place I seemed to have spent an inordinate amount of time given the relatively short period I was actually employed by the man. His office door was open, and he was at his desk reading advertising copy. I rushed in and shut the door behind me.

"You'd think with Spell-Check we'd get the damned things spelled correctly," he was saying. "Carrots has two r's last I knew."

"Only the orange kind, not the 'dahlang, it's simply divine' kind!" I suggested.

"What?" Stan looked up over his half-glasses at me. You know, I've never understood the half-glasses thing. Either you need eyeglasses or you don't. He jerked the black frames off and stood. "What the devil are you doing here?" he asked.

I took a seat in front of his desk and crossed my legs. "I'm here to give you every newspaperman's dearest wish."

"Employees who can spell?" he asked, and sat down again.

"No. I'm here to offer you the biggest scoop since you broke the bus barn scandal five years back. They were talking about that for months."

Stan sighed, grabbed a starlight mint from a dish on his desk, and stuck his glasses back on the end of his nose. "The good ole days."

"Not necessarily," I told him.

"What do you mean?"

I leaned forward in my seat. "Stan, you're a good newspaperman. Naw, you're a great newspaperman. You have the vision, the instinct, and, uh, tenacity, yes, that's right, tenacity, to go after a story no matter where it may lead. You have the reputation of being a hard-nosed journalist, someone not afraid to take on the big boys, the establishment, to get at the truth.

When you exposed those school employees working on automobiles for profit using school district facilities, tools, parts and school time, you took on the superintendent, the school board, and the bus drivers union, and didn't even blink an eye, because your cause was righteous and just and because the public had a right to know. You believed so strongly in their right to know, you didn't back down. That was your shining moment, Stan. Your glory days. When was the last time you felt that rush of adrenaline that comes from chasing that elusive story, sniffing out that next piece in the puzzle, loosening the lips of that next informant?" (Okay, so I was getting a bit melodramatic, but I was on a lifesaving mission here. *My* life.)

"Did you feel that energy when you printed those letters to Santa last year from selfish, money-grubbing, greedy little grade-schoolers whose every sentence to dear old Ho Ho began with 'I want,' 'I want,' 'I want'? Not a 'how are you, Santa,' 'how are Mrs. Claus and Rudolph,' or 'thank you for the Playstation II you brought me last Christmas' to be found. Just more gimme, gimme, gimme.

"Did you feel that surge of euphoria when you reported on Jim Bob Billy Bob receiving a ribbon for showing his prize goat at the county fair? Well, if you're tired of reporting tea times at the nursing facilities, and the pee-wee kickboxing finals, have I got a deal for you. I've got a story that will make you a king among newsmen." I swept my hand across the air in front of me. "I can see the headlines now: 'Murder Comes to Grandville. Prominent Attorney Missing and Presumed Dead. Unidentified Victim Found Shot to Death on Boat.' "

Stan's attention was directed from his ad copy to

me. He leaned back in his chair. "What the hell are you talking about, Turner?"

"I'm talking about headlines, Stan. Banner headlines! Award-winning headlines!" I eased back in my chair. "How does that grab you, Mr. Editor-in-Chief?" I wondered how long it would be before Stan ordered me the hell out of his office, or, conversely, fell to the floor in uncontrollable laughter.

"Like I'm gonna take it in the shorts again if I listen to you," Stan responded. "But go on. I'm feeling in need of a good laugh today. So, fire away, Calamity."

Half-an-hour later, I still expected Stan the Man to give me a good swift kick in the pants and out the door. For a while during my rendering of Tressa & Townsend's Trip to Marina Macabre, Stan performed more facial contortions than Jim Carrey does in a two-hour motion picture. To my immense shock, however, my ex-boss now simply frowned at me over the top of his butt-ugly spectacles. Geez, had I put him into a catatonic state? I waved my hand in front of his face. "Stan? Hello, Stan! Earth to Stan! You don't believe me, do you? That's why you're sitting there in La-La Land like my gramma during Sunday sermons. You think I'm a fake, a fraud, a phoney baloney, full of something other than hot air. You think I'm just jerking your chain, pulling your leg, feeding you a crock." I stood up, ready to haul my own ass out of the newspaper office, rather than suffer the indignity of someone else doing it for me. "You think I'm having a breakdown, trying to scam you . . ."

"I think you're telling the truth. Or some cockeyed version of it," the newspaperman inserted. "Sit down, Turner."

"Wh-what?" I managed.

"I said 'sit.' "

I felt my knees make like Jello jigglers, and I sank back into my chair. First, I'd managed to convince Rick Townsend to keep an open mind about disappearing corpses, now I had a very cynical journalist believing a tale that, even for me, had to be harder to swallow than Gramma's dumplings.

"Are you serious?" I asked. "You believe what I've told you?"

Stan doodled with his pencil. "Nobody could concoct such an outrageous, incredible, logic-defying series of events, and have them all be perfectly in character—for you, that is—without there being an element of truth in there somewhere. I heard about an incident at the marina last evening."

"If a slug through the head from a Colt Python qualifies as an 'incident,' " I pointed out.

He sat forward. "We'll need more information before going public. Verification from a competent . . . I mean credible . . . uh, independent corroboration on some of the facts relating to the investigation. I'll get Smitty on it right away."

I stood ever so slowly. "Smitty? Smitty? I thought you understood the conditions on my giving this scoop to the *Gazette*," I said. "I'm working this story up solo, pal—solo as in if you don't see fit to give me carte blanche with this exclusive, you know, an insider's perspective and all—I'll be forced to peddle the biggest local news story of the century to your competitor." I hesitated, savoring the next moment: "*The New Holland News*."

Stan gasped. His face took on the color of the salsa I drizzle over the belly burners at Dairee Freeze. He grabbed his chest as if suffering an onset of heartburn from eating said belly burner. He stood and put his hands palms down on his desk. "You wouldn't!" Stan and his competitor of Dutch descent were not on the best of terms.

"Oh, wouldn't I?" I picked up his office phone and buzzed Joan out front. "Get Paul Van Fleet over at *New Holland News* on the line!" I barked. "ASAP!"

Stan grabbed the phone from me. "Never mind, Joan," he said, and cradled the phone. "Christ, Turner, you got a problem, you know that?"

"Problem, Stan? Problem? I'm finding corpses in cars and on boats. What next? Greyhound? I have some sicko trashing my car—well, actually Taylor's car—the same sicko trashing my mobile home—well, actually Gramma's mobile home—using poor defenseless family pets as behavior modification props, and leaving not-so-nice greeting cards for me that imply great bodily harm. I'm stalked by a guy who'd make a carny worker look like Mother Teresa. The guy ends up dead, and my fingerprints are on the murder weapon. Yeah, I guess that qualifies as having a problem, Stan. But the big problem here is that the cops don't believe most of what I've told them and that leaves me where? Exposed, Stan. Exposed and vulnerable. If the cops aren't going to do their job, then someone has to get out, pound the pavement and build a case against this perp so the good people of Grandville can sleep peacefully in their beds again and I can get on with my life, or what purports to be a life."

"Geez, Turner." Stan ran a hand through what was left of his hair. "You've been watching too much *Cops*. Besides, the good people of Grandville are sleeping peacefully in their beds. They don't have a clue what the hell you're talking about."

"My point exactly. We've got to warn them there is a murderer in their midst."

"And start a public panic based on what? The cops haven't even acknowledged a crime has been committed."

I leaned across the desk and snagged a foil-wrapped chocolate kiss from his candy dish. "Doesn't that seem strange to you? What *is* law enforcement hiding? And why? I have the inside track here, Stan, but I need an 'in' that only press credentials can give me. I need access to information. Sources only you have. What do you say?" I stuck my hand out. "Partner?"

Stan looked at my hand, crossed himself, and stuck his hand in mine. "You report directly to me. No one else, hear? And the *Gazette* retains all rights to your stories and photographs. Exclusive rights. Got it? Oh, and one more thing." He squeezed my hand. "For Christ's sake, Turner, use Spell Check & Grammar Wizard."

"Yes, sir, boss man." I pumped his hand. "Now, about my salary."

An hour later, I had my new press pass, conditional part-time employment (conditional on my not screwing up), and a new respect for my boss. He'd outlined our article, highlighted what we knew, and how we knew it, and where we could obtain further confirmation or corroboration to tighten the story. He pointed out gaps and ways we could attempt to fill them. He promised me a photo and dossier on the inmate who'd fingered Palmer in the drugs-for-order charge. I had a to-do list that made a "honey-do" list look tame in comparison.

Be professional. Be discreet, Stan warned me. Operate below the radar. In other words, don't open him up to public scorn or liability. Gotcha.

"And don't get shot," Stan called out to me as I left his office. That piece of advice I could've done without.

I left the newspaper office with a new sense of worth, a vastly improved outlook on my life, and every reason to want to hold on to it.

I walked to my car, spotted my Taco John's evidence bag, and, on impulse, entered the offices of Palmer & Hamilton, Attorneys-at-Law. The receptionist's desk was empty. When the boss was away . . .

I peeked down the hall toward the offices. If I could just get a look at Palmer's files. The low hum of voices came from behind a closed door past the reception area. I moseyed down the hall away from the hushed voices. The first office I came to was a conference room. Dennis Hamilton's office was next. It was dark and unoccupied at present. At the far end of the hall was a copy room, restroom, and Peyton Palmer's office. I stepped into that and quietly closed the door.

The armpits of my shirt were wet. I hurried to Palmer's desk and opened drawers. I wasn't sure what I was looking for, but the opportunity to nose around was too good to pass up. I was tempted to turn on the computer and access his files, but to be honest, I'm technologically challenged. I have trouble zapping customers' credit cards through the machine. I'm always happy when they choose to do it themselves and all I have to do is press the appropriate key when prompted.

A door opened out in the hallway. I froze. Then, "There's no one out here." A female voice. The click of a door shutting. Then giggling. Hello. I was intruding on a little bit of office nooky. I couldn't even get any on regular date nights. This gave a whole new meaning to "I gave at the office."

I continued my search of the office, stopping short of using the letter opener to pry open the locked desk drawer; I decided I'd pressed my luck enough. I cracked the door and peeked out. All clear. I crept down the hall toward the front door. I'd just made it to the reception area when the door opened. Rick Townsend walked in.

He seemed surprised (not pleasantly) to see me. The feeling was mutual.

"Tressa, what are you doing here? They're waiting for you over at the courthouse. I think they may be ready to send out the posse. You better get a move on."

"I'm going, I'm going. I just wanted to check something out." I gave him the once-over. "What are you doing here?"

"Rick! What a nice surprise! I didn't know you were going to stop by today!"

My olfactory senses came under assault from a potent whiff of cologne I was sure was way more expensive than the Bargain City Fresh Blossom Body Spray I had splashed on earlier. Annette Felders, legal sex-retary, attired in a white vest top trimmed in navy and a navy skirt, wiggled toward us. Her brunette hair was swept up on her head, with two perfectly matching tendrils falling in front of each delicate ear, just so. The delighted grin with which she greeted Townsend transformed into a just-sucked-a-lemon grimace when her eyes came to rest on me. "Tressa." She eyeballed me like I'd just let a particularly loud, offensive gasser.

"Annette," I responded, and gave her a sickeningly sweet smile.

"Is there something I can do for you? Point you to the nearest exit, maybe?"

I was just tired enough, and pissed enough, that I

was aching for a fight. "Why, yes, as a matter of fact, there is something you may be able to help me with, Annette. You see, I'm looking into the disappearance of one of this firm's partners, Mr. Peyton Palmer, and how it may tie in to a homicide at the lake last night."

Beside me, Townsend shifted his weight onto my powder blue-striped walking shoes. (Hey, the shoes were thirty percent off and I really was going to start walking every day. Honest.)

"Looking into? What do you mean?"

"For the *Gazette*," I said.

Her eyes narrowed. "I thought you got fired from the *Gazette*. That unfortunate obituary thing."

"Naw." I waved my hand. "That was the layout guy's fault. I still give the paper a hand now and then. So, what can you tell me about Peyton Palmer's disappearance?"

"What do you mean, disappearance?"

"Oh? Is he in then? Could you buzz him, please? I'd like to speak with him. Or is he indisposed at present?" *Disposed of was more like it.*

Townsend gave me a hard pinch on the elbow. Like grandfather, like grandson.

"I'm covering the whole drug-smuggling, abandoned pontoon, body-in-the-trunk angle. You know. For a human-interest piece."

"They have you covering the Palmer story?" Her brows indicated she was dubious.

"Oh, no. Stan is handling the law enforcement angle. I'm just supposed to get the background. By the way, where were you Friday night?"

Her mouth dropped open. She quickly closed it, then looked over at Townsend. "I was at home. Alone."

I tried to raise one eyebrow. It's harder than it looks. "Alone? On a Friday night?"

"That's right. Not that it's any of your business."

I shook my head. "I'd like to go back and tell my editor that you were cooperative," I said. "Tell me, Annette, when did Rick Townsend break off his relationship with you?" I ignored the ranger's quick intake of breath next to me.

"I don't see what that has to do—"

"Just answer the question, please."

"*I* broke it off with him. Months ago." Annette's chin lifted. "There's someone else." Oh, vanity, vanity.

"What about the drug charges against Peyton Palmer? Did he really pass drugs to a client in the jail? Who was the client? Why would Palmer take a chance like that?" I peppered her with questions.

"I don't know anything about that."

"Was Palmer's wife really having an affair with Dennis Hamilton? How did Hamilton and Palmer get along? Did you ever hear them argue?"

"You'll have to ask Dennis Hamilton about his relationship, if any, with Mrs. Palmer. And perhaps Dennis and Peyton didn't always see eye-to-eye. So what? Sometimes folks just don't gel with each other. Now, I've answered all the questions I plan to. I'm going to give the paper a call and see if they really sent you over here. I don't believe you're working for them at all. A total airhead like you? No way."

I wanted to leap across the desk and turn her nice little coiffure into a rat's nest. Or male pattern baldness. Instead, for some bizarre reason, I whipped the exotic jungle underwear from the taco bag. "Do these, by any chance, belong to you, Miss Felders? And remember, we have DNA."

"Where did you . . . ?"

"Geezus, Tressa," Townsend said. "Put those away!"

"Get out!" Annette screamed. "Get out before I call the cops!"

The door opened and Sheriff Thomason walked in. Boy, was I impressed. Telepathic 911!

"So here you are, Miss Turner. I saw your car. You're late for our appointment." He turned to Annette. "Anything wrong, young lady? You look upset."

"Get her out of here! She said she was working at the paper and was asking all kinds of questions, waving underwear around. Just get her out of here. This is a professional law office."

"Where is Counselor Hamilton, by the way?" I asked. "I was thinking of retaining his services. Is he by any chance in?"

"No!" The receptionist was losing it.

"Fine. No problem. I'll get Merle Hansen over on First. I hear he's had lots of experience. Oh, just one more question, Annette." I held up the thong. "Where'd you leave the matching top?"

"Get out!" she screamed. "Get that crazy bitch out of here!"

I shrugged and stuffed the undies back in the taco bag and turned to Townsend. "You never did say why you were here, Townsend. Did you?"

He gave me a hard look. "No comment, ace cub reporter," he said.

I sighed. So much for flying below the radar.

Chapter 15

I gave yet another formal statement to the police. I was becoming a pro at spilling my guts. I rehashed what I'd told them the night before, including my visit from the deceased—before he was deceased, that is—reminding them again that I had filed a report with their office. I covered the threatening phone call, but left out the particulars concerning Gramma's kitty cat. I couldn't quite shake the feeling that the authorities still believed I'd taken artistic license with the truth, seeking my fifteen minutes of fame, kinda like one of those nuts who made their own kids sick so they could be around doctors and hospitals, and I didn't want them thinking I could string up Garfield.

"We'll need to print you, for comparison purposes," Deputy Doug told me. "Then we can compare your known prints to the prints on the glove box and the murder weapon." The DARE officer was gone, but the deputy was joined by Sheriff Thomason, and the grumpy state agent.

"So the Colt was the murder weapon?" I gulped.

"The ballistics report isn't back, of course, but judging from the entrance wound, I'd say, yeah, it's a safe bet. Besides, it's been fired. Recently."

My stomach had a Maalox moment. "Well, you're bound to find my prints on the gun," I said. "I already told you, I took the gun from Joe. His prints will be on there, too. And the killer's, hopefully." I gave a crooked smile. "There are other prints on the gun. Right?"

"We're not at liberty to say at present, Miss Turner," the sheriff said.

I felt the noose tighten. "I see," I managed, wondering when the handcuffs would come out, before or after "you have the right to remain silent."

"Fortunately for you, Ms. Turner, so far Joe Townsend's story and yours check out. We'll know more after his formal statement, but it appears he backs up your account of the events of last night."

Yes! Joe hadn't blown it, after all. "Oh, that's good news. Very good news!" I blew out a lungful of air. "Then I don't need to get Merle Hansen to represent me?"

"Hasn't-got-a-clue Hansen?" Deputy Doug snorted "He's eighty if he's a day."

"Experience is the best teacher," I said.

"The last time he was in court he fell asleep during his own cross."

"Hmm. Sounds like a lawyer I can afford."

"What was that all about over at the law office earlier?" The sheriff poured himself a cup of coffee, his back to me. "Something about a leopard thong and a story for the *Gazette*?"

"I got my old job back. Actually, it's a way better job. I'm doing investigative reporting. Since I have information relating to the murder investigations at hand, who better to report than an eyewitness with, uh, hands-on knowledge?"

"Investigations?" the sheriff asked.

"Peyton Palmer and Tattoo Ted. By the way, do you have an ID on the deceased yet? Deceased number two, that is. What connection did he have with Peyton Palmer? Any known enemies? Criminal record? Any other interesting tattoos?"

"Stan gave you back your job?" Deputy Samuels asked.

I nodded. "On a trial basis. But I'm hoping for something more long-term." I took out my notebook, flipped back the cover, and picked up a pencil. "So, who's the vic?" I asked.

"You're free to go, Miss Turner," Sheriff Thomason growled. "Again, please don't leave town without notifying the sheriff's office. And don't print anything in that newspaper that could jeopardize this investigation."

"Don't you think people have the right to know what is going on in their own community?"

"I said you're free to go, Miss Turner," the sheriff reiterated.

I decided not to press my luck, and hustled my cookies out of the courthouse before they could change their minds.

It was two-thirty. Joe had given his statement at one. What I needed was to sit down and have a little tête-à-tête with Dennis Hamilton. And Sheila Palmer was on my to-do list. I sighed, thinking she was probably on Townsend's to-do list, too.

Then there was the doper inmate who'd snitched out Peyton Palmer. Once Stan tracked him down, I'd see what, if anything, I could learn from him.

I called in sick to Bargain City for the afternoon shift. (No sermons, please.) I didn't want to quit until I knew I wasn't going to have to go back and beg for the old job back at some point down the road. I put some gas in the Plymouth, courtesy of dear old dad again, then went next door to do the chores. It was approaching six when I finished up with the critters.

I showered the horsey smell off me and made a quick call to my best friend, Kari Carter. Kari's been my best friend since fourth grade, when her family moved to Grandville. Her father is a local optometrist, and her mother works in his office. Kari is nothing like me. Thank goodness, you're thinking, right?

Kari teaches middle school English to sixth graders. All throughout high school, Kari knew she wanted to be a teacher. She tutored students in reading after school. She was a cadet teacher for the middle school language arts department her senior year. That's when Kari decided teaching middle-level-aged students was her calling in life. I go back and remember what I was like in junior high, all those raging hormones, boy problems, and self-esteem issues, and I tell you, I have to admire anyone who faces a classroom of thirty adolescents at various stages of puberty all day long, day after day, and still retains an enthusiasm for their vocation. Oh, and their sanity, too. A couple hours of babysitting with the Parker twins and I was ready to hit the bottle, and I'm not talking baby formula here.

Kari is getting married during winter break to Brian, a physical education teacher at one of our elementary schools. She's all wrapped up in wedding and honeymoon plans. I'm her maid of honor. Like me, Kari is blonde and great-looking. (I just had to get that in somewhere.)

During the summer, Kari helps out at the Dairee Freeze sometimes. She accepts me for who I am. Well, most of the time, anyway. That doesn't mean she wouldn't like to see me married and settled down. Why is it when women become engaged, they think everyone around them has to be one-half of an adorable little whole in order to be truly happy? Before Kari met Brian, she was, as she liked to call it, footloose and fancy-free. Now a certain ball and chain has the romanticism of a glass slipper. Kari won't even consider the possibility that a woman can be single and happy.

"Now, remember, you have to get over and try the bridesmaid's dress on, ASAP," Kari said, when I met her for a bite at the local Subway. "I've got to have the dresses ordered by next Tuesday at the latest."

I tore into my meatball sandwich, belatedly wishing I'd gone on that diet like I was supposed to.

"Things have been a little bit hectic," I told Kari. "Lots going on."

Kari nodded, and slowly unwrapped her less-than-eight-grams-of-fat turkey sandwich. "Working two jobs will do that to a person. I still say you would make a super teacher! Why, we could teach at the same building. Wouldn't that be awesome?"

I made a face and took another bite of my sub. "I'm not the teacher type," I said.

Kari gave me a look I'd seen before and shook her head.

"Tressa, one of these days you're going to have to decide what you want to do with your life. You can't go on working two nowhere jobs, living a nowhere life. You need to find a decent career, a decent guy, and settle down in a decent life. You know. Get your act together."

The meatball I was chewing became wood shavings. I stopped eating.

"Where is this coming from?" I asked. "Have you been talking to someone about me?"

Kari buried her head in her meal. "People are just worried, Tressa. You always seem to be in the middle of some conflagration."

Since Kari had graduated from college, she'd grown fond of big words. I'd have to look "conflagration" up at a later time to be sure, but from the context of the sentence, I thought I could decipher the meaning.

"You've never had a problem with me before, Kari," I said, hurt that my best friend was dissing me now.

"I don't have a problem with you now," she replied. "It's just that some people seem to think your behavior is out there. You know. Beyond Thunderdome. And with the wedding coming up and all . . ."

Kari stopped. I wrapped up the remains of my supper and stood.

"Are you saying you don't want me in the wedding?" I asked, more hurt at the possibility than I could have imagined.

Kari stood and reached out for my shoulder. "No, no, not at all. I just want you to get your head screwed on straight. That's all. Rick—I mean, Brian just suggested I talk to you, that's all."

Too late, she realized she'd spilled the beans.

"Oh, so all this concern was generated by Townsend." It was becoming clear now. Townsend was a great pal of Brian's. He'd apparently gone running to enlist Kari's assistance in getting me to back off my crusade for justice. But was it out of concern for me, or in Townsend's own best interest if I ceased and desisted?

"I'll be in touch about the dresses," I said. "If I'm still a member of the wedding party, that is."

Kari nodded. "Of course you are, Tressa," she said. "Of course you are. I'm sorry."

I nodded. "Me, too," I said, dumped my sandwich in the garbage, and walked away.

I headed back to the newspaper office to check in with Stan. I hurried back to his office, but he was nowhere around. A photograph on his desk caught my eye. I walked around to get a better look and almost lost a meatball. There, in living color (okay, black and white), was every woman's answer to birth control: the Cobra King himself, Tattoo Ted. My nausea grew.

"Hey, Turner, I got that info you were requesting." Stan returned to his office with a coffee cup that said *Reporters kiss and tell.* "Oh, I see you've found it already."

I picked up the mug shot and pointed at the terrifying profile. "Who is this?" I asked.

"That's him. That's Mike Hill."

"Huh?"

"Palmer's client. Drugs. Jail. Criminal charges. That Mike Hill."

I shook my head to clear it.

"What's wrong, Turner? Think you can track him down?"

I slumped into Stan's chair. "I know right where he is, boss," I said.

The publisher's eyes grew wide, no doubt wondering how I'd come by such information. "You do?"

I nodded. "That's the good news."

His eye's narrowed. "And the bad news?"

"I don't think we'll be getting a quote."

* * *

I left the newspaper office around eight P.M., after I'd typed up a short narrative for Stan outlining my brief, albeit memorable, contact with Mike Hill, aka Tattoo Ted, aka The Snake Charmer, aka Cobra Man, the inmate who'd ratted out his lawyer. It was hard to put my brain around the concept of a killer at large in a town where folks rarely locked their doors, children were free to roam at will, and the local cops got a boner whenever they got to use their top lights and sirens.

I reviewed my list of suspects. First there was Sheila Palmer. According to Joe, she liked to indulge in extracurricular marital activities. Poor Joe. He probably hadn't anticipated his own grandson as a participant. Sheila's infidelities, if true, gave the wandering spouse a motive to rid herself of her present entanglement. I couldn't help but wonder what Joe Townsend was making of his grandson keeping company with a married woman. I knew I was surprised. And, yes, disappointed. I could only imagine what his family was thinking.

Next on the short list was Dennis Hamilton: Sheila Palmer's reputed ex-lover, and her husband's law partner. Was he so obsessed with Sheila that he'd offed her husband in order to clear the way for them to be together, or was there a legal issue pertaining to the law practice that came between the two partners?

I was also beginning to get a queasy feeling in my gut about our local men in blue—or khaki, as the case may be. Law enforcement was dragging their feet worse than kids heading back to school after summer vacation. I'd lay odds both Deputy Doug and his grudge-holding boss, Sheriff Thomason, probably needed their shoes resoled from all their heel-dragging. Just why were they so afraid to do their jobs? What were they afraid they might find out? Or I might find out?

It hadn't escaped me that both times I stumbled onto a corpse, Deputy Doug had been on the scene lickity split. First with Peyton Palmer, and then with Tattoo Ted—I mean Mike Hill. Coincidence? I had to wonder.

By that same reasoning, however, Rick Townsend also fell under the same umbrella of suspicion. He'd been at each of the crime scenes. When my mobile home had been redecorated, he'd used the john first. He had more than sufficient time to leave the lovely message for me in the shower. He'd been at the marina. It appeared he had a relationship of some sort with the wife of one victim, and a past relationship with the secretary of that same victim. It was time to ask myself, how well did I really know Rick Townsend?

Then there was the mysterious Mike Hill. In my nice, neat little murder whodunit, the who was Mr. Hill. I'd pegged him as Peyton Palmer's murderer. That could still be true, I supposed. The question was why? Why had he killed his own attorney?

I did a palm-to-my-forehead number. Well, duh, I was sure there were tons of people who dreamed of offing their lawyers—or the ex-wife's attorney, for sure. But who had killed Mike Hill, then? Was the same killer responsible for the deaths of both Peyton Palmer and Mike Hill, or were there multiple killers afoot in our fair city? And of most interest to me: Was there still someone out there who thought of me as a loose end that needed to be taken care off?

Minutes later, I found myself pulling into the

Palmer driveway. I cast a look across the street to see if Joe was on duty, but didn't spot him. Just as well. I didn't need his skinny butt nosing into my investigative reporting. Not to mention a guy was dead because Joe Townsend thought he was Dick Tracy, although I couldn't picture Dick wearing a neon green wind suit.

I went to the door, the front one this time, and rang the bell. I whistled while I waited, wondering if Sheila Palmer would check me out through the peephole first. You do realize what a peephole is really for, don't you? Security, you say? Come on. If someone comes to your front door to do you harm, they're too stupid to be much of a threat. Like, are they really going to let you get a look at them through the peephole first? Naw. They're gonna put their thumb over the hole. Or better yet, they'll go around to a back peepless door. No. Peepholes were invented so you could pretend not to be home if the Latter Day Saints are out door-to-door in your neighborhood with their pamphlets, or the kid down the street is selling ugly wrapping paper for a fundraiser. That, ladies and gentlemen, is what a peephole is really for.

After I'd been peeped at, the door opened.

"Yes?" A slim, young woman with shiny brown hair (yay, another brunette), and a tan that didn't come out of a can, looked up at me.

My mouth dropped open. I know it did. "You're Sheila Palmer?" I couldn't keep the surprise out of my voice. Here I'd been expecting Naomi Judd and gotten Ashley.

"Yes? May I help you?"

I fumbled with my press pass and stuck a toe in the door so she couldn't close it. I'd picked that up from the big screen; I just never thought I'd use it.

"Hi," I shoved my ID under her nose. "I'm Tressa Turner. I work for the *Gazette* and I'd like to ask you a few questions." Geez, I almost sounded like I knew what I was doing!

"You're Tressa Turner?" It was her turn to show surprise. "I've heard of you."

I nodded. "I have attained some notoriety," I admitted. "But don't believe everything you hear."

"I heard you got buried alive under a pile of pumpkins trying to find the perfect jack-o-lantern. Was that true?"

"Well, yes, but I was only ten at the time."

"I heard you collected horse manure and stuffed it in Annette Felders's gym bag. Was that true?"

"Well, yes, but she'd dyed Joker's tail orange."

"I also heard you found my husband in the trunk of a car. Was that true, too?"

I met her speculative gaze with a steady one of my own. "I'm sorry, Mrs. Palmer, but yes, that's true, too."

She hesitated for a moment, then opened the door. "Well, I guess you'd better come in."

I stepped into the Palmer foyer and looked around. Quality and style were apparent in the carefully chosen furnishings, wall coverings, draperies and accessories. "You have a lovely home," I told her in all honesty, and with just a touch of the little green-eyed monster.

She motioned for me to take a seat. "It's Peyton's home, really."

Correction. It was all hers now.

"I can't imagine what you thought when the police came to you with the story of what occurred Friday night," I began.

"Actually, the police didn't tell me about the events of that evening."

I paused in the process of opening my notebook to my list of prepared questions. "Oh? Who told you then?"

Her hands fluttered nervously in her lap. "Rick told me. Rick Townsend. You know Rick, of course."

I gave a quick nod, hoping my pencil wouldn't snap from the death grip I had on it. "And this was when?"

"It was sometime Saturday. I don't know. Midmorning, I guess. I can't recall."

"I thought you were out of town?"

Her hands fluttered again. "That's right. I was in Omaha."

"At a stamper convention. Right?"

She nodded. "I'm hoping to open a craft shop, and I wanted to learn all I could about stamping, so I could present workshops."

Workshops? On stamping? Didn't you just jam the stamp down on an ink pad and slam it on your paper?

"So, what did Ranger Ri . . . Townsend tell you?"

Sheila hesitated and looked down at the hands in her lap, as if she had the answers written there. Not that I'd know anything about that kind of activity, of course.

"He told me there had been a report filed with the sheriff's office that indicated Peyton had met with an accident, or foul play, and he was either injured or possibly even dead."

"Did he give you any specifics?"

Again the pause. "He said the information hadn't been verified and there was some reason to believe it was bogus because . . ." She stopped.

"Because?"

"Because the, uh, source of the information was . . . unreliable."

I began to draw little nooses in the margins of my paper. "Did he tell you who this unreliable source was?"

"No, not at that time."

"What *is* the nature of your relationship with Rick Townsend, Mrs. Palmer?"

She twisted the rather large diamond on her ring finger. "We're . . . friends. I've known Rick since grade school. I was two years ahead of him."

This sounded a lot like the story Ranger Rick had given me at the marina. I made a pretense of writing something on my notepad.

"Did the police ever contact you about your husband's disappearance, Mrs. Palmer?"

"Yes, a Deputy Samuels contacted me when they found Palmer's boat on the lake, and his vehicle at the marina."

"When was that?"

"Sunday afternoon."

"Were you still in Omaha at that time?"

She shook her head, and her silky brown hair fell neatly into place. "I was back. I got back in town around noon, I suppose."

I made another note, to check if this jibed with Joe's log.

"Did your husband ever take other people out on his boat? Ever lend it to anyone?"

Sheila smiled. "Peyton loves to show off his little toy. He'd entertain clients, friends—"

"Business associates?" I interrupted.

She shrugged. "My husband is a very generous person. He's lent the boat out a time or two. And, as I said, we do lots of entertaining on the boat, so everyone within our circle of friends and acquaintances is familiar with it."

"Speaking of business associates," I said, "there's talk that you and your husband's law partner, Dennis Hamilton, were, uh, keeping company? Any comment on that?"

She gave me a vague smile. "Don't believe everything you hear," she said.

I figured she wasn't going to say any more about her extramarital gymnastics, so I dropped that subject. "Can you think of anyone who might want to harm your husband? A client who threatened him, or was unhappy with his representation? What about Mike Hill? He was your husband's client, the one your husband smuggled drugs to in the county jail. Did he ever threaten your husband?"

"*Allegedly* smuggled," Sheila Palmer corrected, and I could tell from the set of her mouth I was on treacherous turf.

"You mean your husband was innocent?" I asked.

"Is innocent. I'm not sure of a lot of things, Ms. Turner, but I am sure of one thing. My husband would never give drugs to a client of his. Never."

"Then how do you explain the charges?" I asked. Then, "Wait! Are you saying he was set up? By who? Why?"

She looked me straight in the eye. "You're the hotshot investigative reporter," she said. "Investigate."

I gave her a long, assessing look. She had a lot to gain if Palmer was dead, yet here she was defending him, at least on the drug charges. That didn't square with me. I reckoned she knew much more than she let on, but was being very tightlipped. She was a suspect, I reminded myself. A prime suspect. I had to dissect each tidbit of information as closely as I did each selection at the China Wall buffet on a Friday night.

"What was your husband's reaction to the drug charges?" I asked.

"Initially, he was stunned. Later, the anger came."

"Who was he angry with?"

"My husband has been . . . preoccupied for some time. He seemed in a world of his own. Secretive. At first I suspected he was having an affair."

"Was he?"

"No."

"You're sure?"

"Yes. His preoccupation had to do with his law practice. His business. At least, that was my impression. He wouldn't discuss it. When I asked, he would just say it was a case he was working on. Once I learned Peyton had disappeared, I went to his office to see if I could find anything that would point to what he'd been struggling with the last few months."

"Were you successful?"

Another poignant pause. "No, not really."

"Let's get back to Mike Hill. What do you know about him?"

"Not much. He was charged with possession with intent," she said, and I raised my eyebrows. "I'm an attorney's wife. I'm familiar with legal terms."

"Had your husband represented him before?"

"I don't think so. I think he was referred to him or something."

"Referred? By who?" Or is that *whom?*

"I don't know. Maybe it wasn't a referral, per se. I remember Peyton was hesitant to take the case. He didn't normally represent drug dealers. He had a younger sister who was an addict. She died of an overdose. I don't think he ever got over that."

"So why did he take the case?"

"I believe Dennis convinced him he should. I think he waved the old every-person-deserves-a-defense banner in Peyton's face. Peyton takes his obligations as an attorney seriously. So, he took the job."

"Did your husband and Hamilton disagree over anything else?"

She pushed her dark hair away from her face. "There's tension. There usually is in any partnership. Dennis wants Peyton to be less selective about clientele, take on more criminal cases, and Peyton is reluctant to do so. It's basically just a difference in philosophies."

"So, there were problems between Hamilton and your husband."

"Certainly. But none that I think rise to the level of a motive for murder, Miss Turner."

"What about a crime of passion?" I threw it out there. What the heck? She could only show me out.

"Dennis is a very complex individual. I might see him killing for gain, but not to gain a wife."

"So, you do think he's capable of murder?"

She stood, signaling an end to our interview. "Under the right circumstances, Miss Turner, anyone is capable of murder."

Chapter 16

With that comforting thought in mind, I made my way back to my clunker. The heat had broken earlier and the evening had cooled off considerably. I slid into the front seat, and was just about to pull out when someone popped up in the back seat. I did a Pavoratti-pitched squeal and punched at the figure.

"Hey, stop hitting me!"

With a groan, I recognized the voice. I should have seen the glow-in-the-dark wind suit.

"Geez, Joe, you scared the living crap out of me. What are you doing back there?"

"So, what did you learn? What does she know about the vic from the other night? Does she believe her husband is dead? And which time, the first or the second? Did the leopard thong belong to her? Is she boinking my grandson?"

I gave a grunt of disgust, pulled out of the Palmer driveway, and into Joe's.

"I can't divulge what a confidential source tells me, Joe. I'm a reporter now. There are rules."

"Did she say she was telling you the stuff in confidence?" Joe asked.

"Well, no."

"Then you can tell me. I've shared with you. Surveillance information. License plate numbers. Vehicle descriptions. Brownies. Cinnamon rolls."

"Complaints. Ulcers. Colt Pythons. Colt Pythons that are used to kill people."

"Who else can you trust?" he pointed out. "I have cinnamon coffee cake drizzled with cream cheese frosting."

I was so hungry my belly button was touching my backbone. "You do have a point," I said. Joe was the one individual I could say for certain had not committed either murder. And it didn't hurt to have another perspective, an alternative point of view. And there was that coffee cake to consider.

"Can we nuke the coffee cake?" I asked.

"You can even do the honors," Joe said.

"I'm in."

Although the coffee cake took the edge off my hunger, when I left Joe's I was still hungry. Pizza, I thought—Thunder Rolls Bowling Alley's pizza. The bowling alley serves the best in town. In the small cozy lounge, you can get a cold draw and a small pizza (okay, in my case, medium), and be content as a new foal enjoying its first warm meal. I checked my billfold to make sure I had the moola to cover my order this time around.

I took a booth in the corner, my back to the wall, and facing the only entrance, and ordered a medium sausage and pepperoni with green peppers, mushrooms and onions, and a light beer. I leaned back against the wall and closed my eyes. I really needed to get some sleep; when I blinked, my eyes felt like sandpaper rubbing together. I yawned, thinking maybe I'd just curl up right here in the booth and sleep 'til they booted me out at two.

I was about to dig into a second slice of heaven when I heard the name Mike Hill. I looked up and saw two rather tough-looking, black-clad biker types at the bar nearby.

"I heard he got it with an effing cannon. Blood and guts all over the effing boat," said a thin guy with a pasty white complexion and greasy, long black hair, to his drinking partner who could've passed for a bald Scorpion King.

"Serves the bastard right," the companion, a very well-muscled specimen with a head as shiny as a bowling ball, replied. "News on the street is Mikey was a snitch. Nobody touched Mikey. Nobody."

"Well, somebody reached out and effing touched him, didn't they?"

The big guy laughed. "Guess it don't pay to be no snitch, huh?"

"You got that shit right," his comrade agreed, already ninety-proof.

I slipped out of my booth and sashayed up to the men. "I'm sorry. I was just over there eating my pizza, and I overheard you talking about Mike Hill. Are you friends of Mike's?"

"Who the eff wants to know?" the foul-mouthed biker slurred.

I pulled out my identification. I was doing that a lot. "I'm a reporter for the *Grandville Gazette*. I'm doing a story on Mike's death. What can you tell me about him?"

"He was a prick," biker number one said. "He was a piece of effing dung."

I winced. "I don't think I'm allowed to print that in the newspaper," I said. "Does he have family hereabouts? A mother, father? Wife? Siblings?"

"How the hell do I know? Do I look like a freakin' genie-logical expert? He was a traitorous prick. He'd prostitute his own mother for a dollar. The little worm got what he deserved."

"I heard you say a moment ago that he was a snitch. Does that mean he was working for the police as an informant? On drug cases, specifically?"

The straggly speci-man laughed. His teeth were the color of my motor oil. "He was an equal opportunity chickenshit. He'd screw a friggin' goat if there was money in it."

My legs shook. I was so, so thankful in that moment that Mikey hadn't had the opportunity to further our own acquaintance.

"Do you happen to know who he was working with? Which cop, or cops, I mean?"

Stocky-biker number two gave me an up-and-down look. "Cops keep their informants under wraps when they are alive. That's why they call 'em *undercover* informants. You think they gonna fess up if it's their snitch who dies? Hell, they'd never get another informant to work with 'em again. You better go on home and play with your Barbie dolls, blondie." He dismissed me and returned his attention to his drink.

I could feel the tips of my ears grow hot and my nostrils flare. This was way too close to the head-patting, cheek-pinching (face, not rear) patronizing I'd endured for way too long. I straightened my shoulders and thrust my chest out. "For your information, gentlemen, in the last seventy-two hours I have discovered one dead body in a trunk, another on a boat, found a wad of dough that would keep you in black leather for some time, had my sister's car trashed and my home destroyed. I've been harassed by a tattooed maniac, been thrown in the lake and questioned by the police not once, not twice, but three times! I've been assaulted, insulted, ignored, and followed. I've received death threats, prosecutorial threats, and blisters the size of half-dollars. Barbie dolls? Try freakin' Colt Pythons and crime scene tape, buckos!"

I guess maybe that lone beer had gone to my head. I waited, prepared to have to defend myself from the sharp edge of a broken beer bottle, but I held my ground. I expected vile language to spring forth, for hands to clamp around my throat and squeeze, to hear my last gasping breaths forced from my body.

Instead, what I got was laughter. A lot of it. I looked from biker number one to biker number two. Their shoulders were shaking with uncontrollable mirth. Biker number two grabbed a napkin and mopped his eyes. He patted the bar stool next to him.

"Have a seat, blondie. Now, tell Manny, whaddaya need to know?"

By the time I left the bar, I had some solid information, a new understanding of bikers in general, and had exchanged numbers with a giant named Manny. Call if I ever got in a jam, he said. Yeah. As if.

I checked my back seat for nosy old men, then decided to take another spin by Dennis Hamilton's house. No real reason. I just wanted to feel like I was doing something. Besides, if I wanted to make my part-time job at the *Gazette* a full-time gig, I'd have to produce more than the average bear cub reporter.

I circled Hamilton's cul-de-sac and parked illegally. The neighborhood was dark. Small-town folks are generally early-to-bedders. My folks usually make it through the weather on the ten o'clock newscast, but rarely to Leno. They're early risers, though. Sleeping in to them is anything past dawn. I, on the other hand, am a night person. I love to sleep in. We're talking noon here. Of course, the last time I was able to indulge myself in a sleep-in was around the last time I enjoyed a nice, leisurely bubble bath rather than a shower. Working two jobs and keeping a menagerie tends to cut into personal time.

I flipped on the interior light and pulled out my notes from my recent interview (if one could call it that) with Sheila Palmer. She didn't react the way I expected a widow to act, grieving or not. Frankly, I wasn't even sure she believed me about her husband being dead. She had that poker face down to an art. And I still couldn't get a handle on where she stood with Rick Townsend and Dennis Hamilton. Something told me Palmer's trophy wife was collecting some trophies of her own on the side, but I still had difficulty casting Rick Townsend in the role of gigolo. Maybe that was because I didn't want to believe it.

I did believe Joe, however, when he said Hamilton and Sheila Palmer got together when Peyton was out of town. Hamilton was certainly planning to entertain a lady friend Sunday evening when he'd bought the CDs. Had he and the widow lady planned a cozy little get-together to celebrate the removal of an inconvenient hubby? Sheila Palmer had said she returned early Sunday, but we only had her word on that. The neighborhood watch commander hadn't clocked her back in until Sunday evening at around seven.

I was most intrigued, however, by the information I'd elicited from my two inebriated friends at Thunder

Rolls. With a murdered snitch, the finger of suspicion usually pointed to those individuals being ratted out. Okay, so then where did the snitch's lawyer fit into the picture? So far, I had a jailed drug dealer-turned-snitch, a possible set-up of his attorney, the murder of his attorney, the murder of the snitch, and a payoff of some sort. Just what that added up to, I didn't know, but I was more determined than ever to find out.

I made a few more notes, and was just about ready to head for the barn when red lights filled the interior of my car. I flipped my interior light off and felt a moment of been-here-done-this as I tracked the progress of the officer by his flashlight beacon. I was smart enough to look away this time before the blinding beam hit me in the face.

"Good evening, Miss Turner. Or I guess I should say, good morning? What brings you out here at this time of night?"

I let out a long, loud breath. Great. Another installment of Calamity Jayne meets Deputy Dickhead.

I dropped my notepad to the floor and pushed it under the seat with my heel. "Oh, hello, Deputy. Nice night, huh?"

"It was," he said with a bit of a snarl. "The city got a call about a suspicious vehicle parked on the cul-de-sac here, so I offered to check it out."

"That was sweet of you," I said, "but isn't this city jurisdiction?" I was at once suspicious of this fellow who showed up more frequently than zits on a first date.

"They were tied up with a disturbance at the Thunder Rolls."

I thought of Manny and Carver, and was glad the deputy couldn't read my expression.

"So, what are you doing?"

I remembered Townsend asking a similar question, and the lame house-hunting excuse I'd given, but I didn't see any other semi-plausible reason for being here, so I used it again, with a few modifications. "The folks have been considering a move to town, and I saw this place—"

"Cut the crap, Turner. Your father would sooner sell his first-born daughter than get rid of his little hunk of the American dream. I know exactly what you're doing here."

I gulped. "You do?"

"Yep. And I don't like it."

"You don't?"

"Nope."

"And?" I was fairly certain there was more.

"And, you ever heard of interference with official acts?"

I hadn't really, but guessed it was just a judicial way of saying I was butting into an official investigation, and there were legal consequences under Iowa law for doing so. But that was just a guess. "How am I interfering with official acts by sitting in my car?"

"For starters, you're parked illegally."

I'd forgotten about that.

"Listen, Turner." He crouched by my window. "And listen real good."

"Listening good," I whispered.

"There is an ongoing criminal investigation. You could be considered a material witness in that investigation. As such, you could be detained and incarcerated for an unspecified period of time. Is that what you want?"

Was he kidding? Who wanted to be put in jail?

"No more bad impressions of Nancy Drew," he

continued. "Things could get real unpleasant if you continue to stick your nose into things that are better left to the professionals. Are we clear on this?"

Great. I was being threatened again. Not by a tattooed snake charmer with arms like logs, but by a no-necked officer of the law. I had to hand it to Deputy Doug. His threat was subtler than "Pay up or else." Loss of life as opposed to loss of freedom was still more compelling, but I had no desire to share a cell with a woman prisoner who could bench-press me, or one who might take a fancy to my gorgeous blue eyes along with everything else.

"Clear as the Dairee Freeze drive-up window," I said.

"Good." He then proceeded to ask for my driver's license, registration and proof of insurance, and scribbled out a ticket for illegal parking, and a warning for defective equipment. Dang. He'd noticed the droopy tailpipe.

I snatched the tickets from him, signed them, and thrust his metallic clipboard back at him. "I do have one question, Officer," I said, so angry with the deputy that the words rolled off my tongue faster than Joe Townsend snapped up the last piece of Mrs. Winegardner's coffee cake. "Which officer was working Mike Hill as a confidential informant? You, maybe?"

His quick intake of breath satisfied my thirst for payback. I pulled away to let him stew for a change. Butt out? Get real, Kojak.

I was feeling pissy after my encounter with Deputy Doug and decided, who better to share that pissy mood with than Ranger Rick. Besides, I had a few questions to ask the good ranger, not that I thought I had a Dairee Freeze dip cone's chance in Maui to get any answers. I also wanted to see if Sheila Palmer had run to Townsend for comfort and assurance after I'd grilled her. Okay, okay, so maybe "grilled" is a bit much when she kind of led the discussion. Still, it was safe to assume she'd want to talk things over with someone, and that led me to Rick Townsend's doorstep. Well, actually to his windows—initially.

Townsend lives in a small ranch home on the outskirts of Grandville. He shares the house with a brown and white pointer named Hunter (uninspired, I know), who lives in a very nice kennel in the backyard, and a snake or two, which was one reason I was not a frequent visitor to the Townsend home. That and the fact that I'd never received an invite.

I cut the headlights and left the car down the lane a safe distance, then crept up to the house on foot, hoping Hunter was either safely tucked away for the night or not in the mood to point me out. Townsend's red pickup was parked in the driveway, and the lights were on in the house. I moved up to the living room windows, but couldn't get an unobstructed look due to the bushes along the front. I figured Ranger Rick had planned it that way. Or should I say, *planted* it that way? A phone rang inside the home and was quickly picked up.

A small window was open, and the curtains were drawn back enough to allow adequate peeping. I looked around for another convenient marble birdbath to perch on. Instead, I spotted a quaint park bench placed under a huge old oak. Perfect. I slid the bench across the grass, making minimal noise (if a grunt here or there doesn't count), and finally maneuvered it at an angle between the stubborn bushes.

I stepped up on the bench. It tilted slightly. I put an eye up to the side of the screen and looked in. I frowned. The window I'd chosen was a bathroom window. About the only thing I'd find out here was whether Townsend rolled his toilet paper from the front of the roll or the back, and what his color scheme was. Dark green and maroon, I noted. Colorful, yet manly. About that time, Townsend strolled into the bathroom. I remained perfectly still, hoping to avoid drawing his attention to my head perfectly framed in the window. Townsend reached in and turned on the shower, then left the room.

I gulped. Townsend was going to take a shower. That meant Townsend would take his clothes off before he took a shower. I swallowed. That meant a naked Townsend would be stepping into the shower shortly. Perspiration beaded on my upper lip.

I did one of those internal dialogues. You know, the devil on one shoulder urging you to have fun, live a little, and the angel on the other beseeching you to resist temptation. What could it hurt? the little devil in me asked. The last time I'd seen a naked man was when some fat guy lost his bottoms at the wave pool last summer. On the other hand, would I want someone ogling me through my bathroom window? I thought about that a bit. Of course, I wouldn't. Would I?

I shrugged. Since I didn't have a bathroom window, the point was moot, anyway.

I had just decided to do the noble thing and reposition my park bench when the opposite end of it was suddenly lifted off the ground. I slid off, crashed into a rather large, sticky yew, and rolled down the length of the tree, landing in a heap beside a family of raccoon lawn ornaments.

I heard a deep chuckle, then, "Window peeking,

Calamity? I don't know if I should be flattered or call the cops."

I sprang up with righteous indignation, embarrassed by being caught in the act. Then I caught the sound of the shower still running. "You set me up, you pig!" I yelled.

Townsend chuckled again and replaced the bench. "How the hell do you figure that? What? I made you drive all the way out here, pull my bench to the bathroom window, and forced you to peek in at me? You're nuts. Maybe I'd better call the cops."

"Go ahead," I spat, brushing yew needles from my arms and legs. "Call Deputy Do-wrong. He's already written me two tickets this evening. I could help him make his quota for the night and he could go home."

"What the hell are you talking about now, Tressa?"

I suddenly felt very tired, and very sad. And, as always, very misunderstood.

"Just forget it," I said.

"Forget you were hanging outside my bathroom window waiting for a glimpse of my naked body? Not hardly." He took my arm. "You look like you could use something to drink. Besides, if that shower runs much longer, I'll run out of hot water."

I let myself be led to his front door, then inside. "You aren't entertaining anyone, are you?" I asked, remembering the reason I had come here in the first place.

"Just the dog and the snakes," he said with a grin. I was not happy to be reminded about his slithering housemates.

"Those reptiles—"

"Are all tucked in for the night. Hunter, too, or you wouldn't have made it down the driveway with all body parts present and accounted for. Where'd you park, by the way?" he asked, going into the bathroom.

"Up the lane," I admitted. "And I didn't come here to cop a look at your family jewels," I said. "I wanted to ask you some questions. I just wanted to make sure you weren't entertaining anyone."

"I see," Ranger Rick said, re-entering the room and sitting me down at his kitchen table. He handed me a caffeine-free soda.

"You got any of the hard stuff?" I asked.

"Hard stuff? As in alcohol?"

I shook my head. "Caffeine," I replied.

He laughed. "I'm decaffeinated."

I snapped the top, took a drink and pulled a face. "Bully for you."

"So, what did you want to see me about, Tressa? It's kind of late for social calls."

I snorted. "This isn't a social call, and you know it. I'm working the Peyton Palmer-Mike Hill thing for the *Gazette*. Since you are, shall we say, cozy with one of the chief suspects, naturally I have some questions."

He eyed me but said nothing.

"You *are* cozy with one of the chief suspects, aren't you?" I pressed.

"Chief suspects?" he said, lifting a brow.

"Sheila Palmer, of course. The vic's wife. The person who stands to inherit his money. The same person who was seeing his law partner not so awfully long ago. Ooops, I'm sorry, Townsend. Did you know there were other men?" I was being bitchy, but it had been one of those nights.

"I know where I stand with Sheila," Townsend replied.

"Oh, that's good," I said. "A person should always be secure in a relationship, especially when one party's spouse turns up dead." I took out my notepad. "Sheila Palmer told me you called her in Omaha and told her about my gruesome trunk discovery."

"Alleged gruesome trunk discovery," Townsend amended.

My lip curled. "When did you call her?"

"Saturday, somewhere around noon or thereafter."

"How did you know where to reach her?"

"I had her cell phone number."

I bit my tongue at this admission, but never missed a beat.

"How did she react to the news? Was she shocked? Dismayed? Hysterical? Giddy?"

Townsend's eyes narrowed. "I'd say she was surprised."

"Pleasantly?"

"Of course not. She was skeptical."

"What does that mean?"

"Skeptical. To doubt or question."

"I know what it means. Why was she doubting or questioning?"

"Well, it was unconfirmed at the time. Still is, I guess. Isn't it, Calamity?"

I ignored his implication that I was still wrong about Palmer-in-a-trunk.

"How come your grandfather didn't know you were seeing Sheila Palmer? He has his neighborhood covered better than the Secret Service covers the first family."

"Let's just say I was sensitive to his feelings."

I snorted. "Yeah, you're the sensitive type, all right, Townsend. Did you know Mike Hill was a confidential informant?" I watched his face for signs of surprise, but was disappointed.

"Yeah. So? Most cops have dirtbags they use as informants. That's how a lot of drug cases are made."

I leaned forward. "So this *is* all about drugs, then?"

"I didn't say that, Tressa. I was speaking in general terms. Besides, from what I hear, Hill's death could have been accidental."

I stared at him. "Accidental? How?"

"He took the Colt from the glove box. Most cons can't resist firearms, and Gramps's was a doozy. Hill messes around with it. It goes off. Bang. One dead guy."

"But why was he on the boat?"

"Who knows? Maybe he was there to rip somebody off. Maybe he was there looking for something. Maybe he planned to meet someone later. The point is, one theory the police are working is that the shooting was accidental. They'll know more once the autopsy results are available."

My stomach reacted to the autopsy reference. "How do you know so much about this investigation?" I asked, suspicious again.

"You have to ask? With my grandfather's handgun as the murder weapon, and him riding shotgun with Calamity Jayne herself? I sure as hell am going to make sure I find out as much as possible."

I nodded. It bit, but it made sense. "Then, why don't you understand why I have to pursue this investigation for reasons of my own? They're just as compelling," I said.

Townsend reached across the table and took my hand. Underneath the table, my legs were doing the jitterbug.

"I don't want to see you get hurt, Tressa, or get in more trouble."

I looked up from his hand on mine and looked into his eyes. "Why?" I asked. "Why do you care?"

For a moment his eyes seemed to lock on mine with fierce intensity. His thumb rubbed erotic little circles on my palm. I couldn't look away. I couldn't even blink. His voice, however, was teasing when he replied.

"Hell, Craig would kill me if I let anything happen to you," he remarked. "And Granddad has become rather attached to you, too."

I pulled my hand from his, disappointed but determined not to show it.

He reached for my hand again. He must have seen something in my face, after all. I wasn't as good at poker faces as Townsend and others.

"Your grandfather is a legend in his own mind," I said, to cover any tender feelings inclined to show themselves. "He thinks he's a crime-fighter. He'll give Jessica Fletcher a run for her money."

"Tressa, you've got to let this go," Townsend said. "For your own good. Let it go."

I released my hand from his and stood.

"*I*'d better be going," I said.

Townsend sighed, stood, and walked me to the door. "Tressa, listen. Let this go. Let the authorities figure it out. Take a vacation. Get away for awhile. You're encroaching on dangerous territory, invading rival turf. For your own safety, as well as for the safety of those you care about, just leave it alone. Go back to your job at Bargain City. Go back to the Dairee Freeze. Better yet, fly out and visit your aunt and uncle in Arizona. Drop this silly crime-solving notion and let the police do their jobs. Trust me, Tressa. For your own sake, walk away."

There it was again. That trust thing. Could I trust Townsend? I noted the firm set of his jaw. The heat of his gaze. Could I trust him? Could I trust myself to make the right choice?

My heart wanted to say yes, but years of being Gilligan and never the skipper, of being greeted with titters and snickers, or, worse, years of being ignored altogether, made me want to say screw it.

Trust a gorgeous guy who happened to be seeing the spouse of a dead lawyer I'd found in a trunk?

Fat chance.

Chapter 17

I woke very early with no firm plans in mind. I was scheduled to clock in at Bargain City at two. I also needed to touch base with Stan the man so he could see I really was trying to earn my pay. I wondered if he would be impressed with what I'd learned. I hoped so. I was going to try to get him to cover the citations Deputy Samuels had issued me the night before.

I jumped in the shower, then donned a white tank top, light blue running shorts and a pair of running shoes that hadn't seen a lot of wear. I grabbed a water bottle from the fridge, and headed to town. I parked in the driveway of the vacant house next door, and swigged my water while I waited for activity from the Hamilton home.

Thirty minutes and a good twelve ounces of water later, Hamilton emerged from his residence wearing a navy tank top and gray running shorts. He entered the garage, got into his vehicle, and pulled out onto the street. I followed, more at home with the appropriate following distances to be observed when tailing someone. He pulled into the parking lot by the high school track, the same track I'd regularly thrown up at after competing. He got out of his car, entered the gate, and began hoofing it around the cinder track at a pace I thought I could match.

I chugalugged more water, hitched my shorts up, did a few stretches to show I was a serious runner, and jogged toward the track. I timed my entrance on the running track to coincide with Hamilton's own trek. I didn't want to appear too anxious to engage him in conversation, but I knew I only had a finite amount of time before I was breathing too hard to talk at all. I let Hamilton pass me, then took off behind him, in an adjacent lane. After about a quarter mile, I picked up the pace and came abreast Hamilton.

"Nice morning for a run," I said, with a smile I suspected looked more like a grimace. "Do you run here often?"

"Do I know you?" Hamilton gave me a quick look. "You look familiar."

I didn't want to bring up the incident with the CDs at the electronics counter, so I just shrugged. "I have that kind of face," I remarked. "But you might've seen me around the square. I work at the *Gazette*." I kept a smile on my face despite the fact that my legs were beginning to feel like I was wearing waist-high waders full of water. "I'm a reporter."

He gave me another look, not one of interest, exactly. Maybe disbelief.

"So, what do you report?"

"News, of course. Local news. I have to make a confession here. I've been hoping to have the opportunity to speak with you concerning a story I'm working on."

"You wanted to speak with me? And you are?"

I held out my hand awkwardly. "Tressa Turner. Tressa Jayne Turner."

His eyes took on the look of a hunted man. Or maybe a guilty one. "I've heard of you."

I nodded. "I'm somewhat of a local icon," I admitted, my respiration more compromised with each step.

"I'm not sure how I can be of help to you."

I debated how to proceed. My earlier bombshell routine with this male had submarined big-time. And it was a safe bet I couldn't intellectually spar with him. Frankly, I was getting too tired to do much more than breathe in and breathe out.

"Here's how you can help, Mr. Hamilton. Your law partner didn't drown. He was murdered. I found his body. In the trunk of a Chysler Le Baron that looked an awful lot like a Plymouth Reliant in the dark. Anyway, a client you referred to your law partner was murdered. Lucky me. I found his body, too. That same ex-con threatened me, and demanded in a very unpleasant manner that I return an envelope of money I found when I found my first dead body. I'm having some difficulty getting local law enforcement to give my account of events the serious consideration it requires. So, what I need from you right now are answers. Answers that will help me figure out why Peyton Palmer is dead, and why I keep finding stiffs. Were you and Sheila Palmer lovers? What was Peyton Palmer so preoccupied with in the days leading up to his death? Why did you insist Palmer take on Mike Hill as a client? Did the two of you argue? Did you set Palmer up? Who did Mike Hill snitch for? What was the nature of his information? Did you have anything to do with Peyton Palmer having a hole in his head the size of a Ping-Pong ball? Did you take his boat out early Saturday morning and drop Peyton Palmer in the drink?"

Hamilton began to run. I mean really run. I kept even with him, stride for stride, although my hamstrings were so tight, you could pluck a tune on them.

"Who hated Peyton Palmer?" I huffed and puffed. "Who hated him enough to blow him away, then stuff him in the trunk of a 1987 Le Baron? Was it you, Mr. Hamilton?" I was beginning to see white spots. My sentences were short and choppy. "Did you kill Peyton Palmer?" Huff, puff.

"I remember you now!" Hamilton stopped running. I was so thankful I could have kissed him—if he hadn't been really sweaty, that is. Oh, and a murder suspect, of course. "You were the nosy store clerk at Bargain City the other day asking all those questions. You know something, young lady, you've got a problem!"

I was now bent double, sucking air into tortured lungs. "Tell me about it!" I managed. "I keep finding dead bodies!"

"You were out in front of my house, too, weren't you?"

I straightened. "Which time?" I said, before I could stop myself. I frowned, a wave of nausea assailing me. Chugalugging that bottled water had been a mistake. I doubled over and water streamed out of my mouth and onto Hamilton's expensive running shoes.

"What the hell are you doing?"

I straightened, and swiped a hand across my mouth. "Sorry about that," I said. "It's just water," I assured him. "Really."

He shook his head and took off faster than Butch and Sundance on bath day.

Being the intrepid reporter, I followed.

"What the hell are you doing?"

"I'm jogging, of course," I wheezed.

"This is harassment."

"How am I harassing you? I'm exercising. Now listen," I said. "We all make mistakes. You know. Lust after someone else's woman. Have a bit too much to drink from time to time. Gamble away money we can't afford. Compromise our futures by choosing the road of low expectations. Mistakes are made. But somewhere along the line one has to step up and take responsibility. Right the wrongs of the past. You are a member of an honorable profession. Shouldn't you do the honorable thing? If you know something about Peyton Palmer's death, please, please tell me."

Hamilton stopped again. He put a hand to his forehead and massaged it. I could almost see the internal battle the attorney was waging.

"Everything is in such a mess. Such a godawful mess," he said, a hand shielding his eyes. "This was not the way I wanted my life to turn out."

Hope filled me when the counselor's arrogant facade slowly crumbled, and tears filled his eyes. Seconds later, however, the vulnerable, anguished look left his face, and his eyes widened. His gaze shifted past me to the gravel parking lot beyond the high chain-link fence. I followed his gaze and was disturbed to see two police vehicles parked near the gate. A uniformed officer stood with his arms folded, watching us behind dark glasses.

Hamilton made a sharp turn, and took off toward the officer, while I continued to hoof it around the track. Actually, hoofing it is an exaggeration, but at least I was still ambulatory. I wiped the sweat from my eyes vowing the next time I ran (like, as in never again, I hoped), I'd get one of those stretchy headbands and color coordinate it with my outfit and look fine.

I entered the last turn, casting a quick glance at the men visiting outside the chain-link fence. Hamilton motioned in my direction. I recognized the cop now. Deputy Doug. I made a face. Great.

I struggled around the track until I decided, the heck with it. My feet were harder to lift than my head from the pillow for the early shift. I slowed my pace. I morphed into what I hoped resembled a cool-down maneuver rather than a if-I-run-another-step-I'll-puke-again death march. I swung my arms out in front of me in my best impression of those power walkers who just can't comprehend how ridiculous they look, or they would stop with the arm-swinging already.

A second patrol car joined the first, this one an SUV with the wide, gold stripe and the word SHERIFF in big, gold, block letters that spelled out I was in deep doo-doo again. I watched as the head honcho himself, Sheriff Thomason, pulled long, uniformed legs from the vehicle, and shook hands with Dennis Hamilton. As if choreographed, the three men turned in unison and nailed me with three pairs of enemy eyes. I felt like Winona Ryder with a shopping bag. Or Michael Moore at a Republican convention.

Deputy Doug and Dennis Hamilton got into their cars and drove away, leaving Sheriff Thomason leaning on the tailgate of his vehicle. That saying about living to fight another day entered my head and I decided a hasty retreat was in order. The sheriff intercepted me before I could make good on my getaway.

"You know, I've tried to be patient, Miss Turner," he began, "but I must concede, I'm reaching the end of that commodity with you. Deputy Samuels tells me you staked out Dennis Hamilton's home again last night, and here you are harassing him this morning. He's threatening to file charges."

"Charges? For what? Jogging? Parking? Asking questions? I'm a reporter, Sheriff Thomason, that's what I do."

He shifted his weight subtly, effectively preventing me from opening my car door. "You've been asking a lot of questions of a lot of folks, I understand."

"Yeah. So? Last I knew that was protected in the Bill of Rights or Constitution or something." I didn't like the way he tried to intimidate me by tapping his handcuff case.

"Do you want to report the news, Ms. Turner, or make it?" he asked. "There is no physical evidence to indicate Peyton Palmer was anywhere except on his pontoon Saturday morning. Evidence suggests that he became drunk and either jumped overboard or fell. What you hope to get out of perpetuating this ridiculous hoax is beyond me."

"Hoax?" I repeated. "*Hoax?* That wasn't any hoax Joe Townsend and I came across the other night at the marina. And it sure wasn't death by drowning. How do you explain Mike Hill's demise? Playing with a Python, perhaps?"

The sheriff gave a tight smile. "We haven't come to a conclusion yet on how Mr. Hill met his death. If you recall, however, your fingerprints are on the murder weapon, you were at the scene of the murder, and, as you just pointed out, you discovered the body, so I'd be walking a fine line here, Miss Freedom of the Press." He looked at me for a moment. "I wonder how much of your dumb blonde act is just that? An act?" he asked, almost as if he were thinking aloud.

I was taken aback. No one had ever sought to challenge a persona I wore as naturally as Big Bird wears that ten-gallon tie. Under normal circumstances, I would be whooping it up that I had finally given someone cause to doubt the dopey blonde caricature. Why then did I suddenly feel so strongly that convincing folks I was every bit the screwball they believed me to be was the safest place to be right now? Maybe because of the threats I'd had lobbed at me like tennis balls from an automatic ball tosser. Maybe it was the possibility of incarceration looming. Perhaps because if I transformed myself into a force to be reckoned with, I'd have to be reckoned with.

Regardless of what the sheriff believed, I knew there was a killer out there. A minimum wage, college dropout with a history of underachievement poking about asking questions wouldn't be much cause for concern. However, if I lost that reputation and was taken seriously for a change, what more might I lose? Ironic, wasn't it, that I had to act the twit (okay, so it wasn't really that big a stretch for me), in order to avoid the notice of a murderer. It was not a position I ever expected to be in.

"Congratulations, Sheriff." I grabbed his hand and pumped. "Finally, someone has seen the truth of it. That dumb blonde thing *is* all an act. Way to go, Sheriff! Do you suppose you might, uh, spread the word? You know, a word from you that I'm a legitimate newspaper woman who is only out to get at the truth and report it will open up vast new sources of information to me," I said. "With my reputation, folks are a bit, oh, uneasy spilling their guts. You could help me out lots." I smiled, and continued to pump his hand while I maneuvered myself into my car. "Oh, dear," I said, and put a hand up to the ignition.

"Is something wrong?" The sheriff tipped his head inside.

"My car keys. They're gone!"

"Isn't that your key ring in your other hand?"

I looked down and gave a little chuckle. "Oh, yes. Thank you, Sheriff." I started the car. It cooperated by belching and farting, then dying. I giggled. "I think I need a tune-up. Is that something I could do myself, do you think? I already know how to change my oil. Which reminds me." I popped the hood release. (I knew where that was from years of adding motor oil.) I jumped out, grabbed a bottle of 10W-30 from my back seat, and prepared to dump it in.

The sheriff stopped me. "That's for transmission fluid." He pointed to the oil-covered engine. "That's where the oil goes."

"I know that," I said, indignant. "I've changed my oil before." I dumped the plastic bottle of oil in the engine, swiped an oily hand across my mouth for effect, then jumped back in the car. It sputtered, then started. "See? Back in business," I announced. "Thank you, Sheriff," I said. "Thank you for seeing me for who I really am." I drove off, oily mustache and all, hoping he'd reassess his earlier lightbulb moment concerning my intelligence quotient. Ah, irony, sweet irony.

I made a stop by the newspaper office and closeted myself with Stan for a couple hours until we had a decent front page article featuring the unflattering mug shot of Mike Hill, and the report of his death at the marina. Stan would wrangle the pathology and forensics report from law enforcement authorities. We decided he had a better rapport with the cops than I did. Gee, I wonder why?

Stan also gave me my very own cell phone to carry with me. He said it was in case I needed to get a hold of him. I suspected it was so he could keep track of me. Either way, I was tickled to finally be among the coolest of the cool and carrying a cell phone. Stan tossed me a cord.

"Don't forget to plug it in to recharge the battery," he said. "It'll be useless as tits on a boar if the battery is low."

I nodded. "Okey-dokey. Now what?" I asked. "I have to be at Bargain City at two. I'm only working a six-hour shift today. You want me to surveil Hamilton some more? You know, I got the feeling he was about to give me something when the cops showed and he clammed up."

Stan blew a puff of cigar smoke in my direction. "Surveil?" He snorted. "Hell, no. You show up on his doorstep again and they'll haul your ass to jail."

"There's still Palmer's wife, Sheila and her—" I was about to say something about her very good friend and confidant, Ranger Rick Townsend, but for some bizarre reason my jaw hinges stuck and nothing else came out. I couldn't picture Ranger Rick killing Peyton Palmer in the heat of passion over Sheila Palmer, but it was certainly possible Sheila Palmer had killed her husband in the heat of passion over Ranger Rick. The thought of Townsend and Sheila together made me think of Townsend's derriere. Thinking of Townsend's derriere made me think of our little tattoo bet I wanted so much to win. But, dang, in order to win the bet and see Ranger Rick permanently disfigured with a small but tasteful raccoon tattoo, I needed to produce the corpus delicti; but the odds of Peyton Palmer being accommodating enough to bob up from the depths of Silver Stone Lake just to help me win a bet was unlikely.

I ran home to shower and change for work. My machine was blinking. I had two messages. The first was from Joe Townsend, telling Kato to give the Green Hornet a call, and that he had freshly baked carrot cake. I drooled at the carrot cake reference, then shook my head. Townsend Jr. would release his menagerie of reptiles into my bedroom if I came within one hundred yards of his grandfather. I played the second message five times before I could convince myself it was on the level.

"Yo, Barbie. This here's Manny from the other night. You know, the Thunder Rolls. I'm at the county jail, and I need someone to bail me out. Maybe we can work something out. You know, bail money for info. Ya hear what I'm saying? Bail's two hundred. They take credit cards. Later, Barbie."

I sat at the kitchen table, and put my head in my hands. How had I gone from dipping cones for preschoolers to posting bail for bikers? Yet the possibility that Manny might really have some good information was too tempting to resist.

My first impulse was to call Stan and see if he would be willing to spring the biker, but I decided against it. If the guy was just yanking my chain and didn't have any information to barter, Stan would be out the two hundred and I would lose what little credibility I'd bankrolled with my new boss. I threw on my work clothes, retrieved the lone credit card I still had, which I kept in a locked file cabinet in a file folder marked: USE ONLY IN CASE OF EMERGENCY!

Chances were I was being conned, but knowing my luck, if I blew Manny off, I'd come face to face with him after he'd just been through a body cavity search and released. This was one guy I'd rather owe me in a good way.

I parked outside the courthouse on the square. The county jail is located in the basement of the courthouse. It always gives me the willies to see those long, black bars on the windows when I walk by. I entered the sheriff's office with my head down. I wasn't ready to engage in conversation with Deputy Doug or his fearless leader at present. I smiled at the uniformed police person at a desk behind the counter.

"Hello. I'm here to see about posting bail for a friend of mine."

The lady deputy got up and came to the counter.

"The name?" she asked.

"Manny," I began, then realized I didn't even know his last name.

"Manning?"

I shook my head. "Manny. M-A-N-N-Y. First name. Manny. As in huge, bald, biker-type with arms as big as my thighs. Manny." I put my hands out as if measuring the breadth of Manny's Herculean shoulders.

"He's your friend, and you don't even know his last name?"

My smile withered a bit. "I just met him last night," I said, praying word of this never got out to Rev. Stone at the Open Bible Church.

"You just met this guy last night. He winds up in jail. And you're bailing him out? He must be something," she muttered.

My face turned warm as hot fudge. "Can I or can I not bail out my friend, officer?"

"You got cash?" she asked.

"Even better," I said. "American Express. Don't leave jail without it."

We were just finishing up the paperwork when a voice to my left startled me.

"Well, look who we have here. Calamity Jayne Turner. Finder of dead guys. Corrupter of old men. Stalker of prominent town leaders. What brings you here? Reporting another body in a trunk? On a boat? In a plane? In a box with a fox? Please, tell me. I need a good laugh."

I turned to face Deputy Doughboy. "Look in the mirror, then," I said. "That should give you a good chuckle."

He lost his jocularity. "What are you doing here?" he asked. "I thought I made myself clear the other night."

I said nothing.

"She's posting for a 'friend,'" the woman deputy supplied.

Deputy Doughboy's forehead wrinkled. Gee, what was it with these foreheads, anyway? "What friend?" He directed the question to me, but I just smiled.

"Manny Dishman," the deputy behind the counter replied. "The disorderly from Thunder Rolls last night."

That got Deputy Doug's attention. "How do you know Manny Dishman?" he asked.

I shrugged. The cops had kept me in the dark so long I'd developed night vision and the urge to hang upside-down. No way was I giving Officer Samuels anything but a cold shoulder, and a cone with a hole in the bottom on his next visit to the Dairee Freeze.

"Is there some problem with me bailing out a

friend?" I asked. "A rather large friend. A rather large friend who is very impatient to be released from your fine establishment?"

"I just finished the paperwork," the woman deputy told Deputy Doug. "Is there a problem?"

The deputy gave me a long, hard look. "Where Calamity Jayne here is concerned," he said, "there's always a problem. But go ahead and execute the release." He gave me another one of his stepped-in-cat-poop looks.

"Thank you, officers," I said with a flourish, "for your assistance. Tell Mr. uh, Dishman, I'll be waiting for him outside."

I walked to the glass door, then looked back at the female deputy. "Is that uniform for show or for real?"

"Let me step around the counter and I'll show you firsthand," she warned.

I backed out the door. "No, that's all right. I just wanted to make sure you weren't being discriminated against because you're a woman," I said, tiptoeing out the door into the warm sunshine. I gave myself a light slap. "Dummy. Fool. Idiot," I muttered.

"You muttering to yourself again, Tressa? People will begin to talk, you know."

I whirled around. It was Ranger Rick in full uniform, looking better than any two-timing, reptile-collecting, grandson-of-a-nosy-old-fart had a right to.

"They already talk," I observed. "Thanks to insensitive clods who always try to portray me in the worst light."

He ignored that. "What are you doing uptown? Don't you have to work today?"

"For your information, I am working."

He put a hand on the back of his neck and rubbed.

"You mean that part-time job as a poor imitation of Barbara Walters? Didn't you listen to anything I said last night?" Townsend asked.

"Oh, I listened," I replied with a snarl. "But I discounted it as coming from a womanizing, fork-tongued jackass with a twenty-year track record of messing with my mind."

Townsend was about to say something further, when his attention wandered. A heavy arm curled around my shoulders, and I fought to keep my knees from buckling. "Gee, thanks, Barbie, for bailing Manny's ass out of that hellhole. Last time I was in, I got scabies."

I saw the look of disbelief appear on Townsend's face at the same time his jaw did a trapdoor motion. I tried to make a reassuring smiley face. I'm almost certain I looked more like I'd just given birth to Rosemary's horned baby.

"Who's the stiff?" Manny asked.

"Stiff? Oh, Townsend! Uh, this is Officer Townsend. He works for the DNR," I said. "And he's on duty, so we mustn't take up any more of the good officer's time."

Rick put out a tanned hand. "Rick Townsend," he said. "You're a friend of Tressa's?"

"Tressa? Oh, you mean Barbie here. Naw, we're more like business associates—aren't we, Barbie?" He gave my shoulder a squeeze with one mammoth hand. My arm ached down to my pinky.

"Hardly business associates," I disputed. "More like acquaintances. Very slight acquaintances."

"You said Barbie—Tressa here—bailed you out of jail?" Townsend looked from me to Manny and back. "You bailed this guy out? What the hell are you thinking, Tressa, or are you thinking at all? Jeez, you gotta be the most foolish, stubborn, pigheaded excuse for a woman God ever made. Do you have any idea how reckless your behavior has become? How dangerous? Get a grip, Tressa. Get a grip before it's too late."

I felt my eyes begin to water, and I was very close to tears, tears I most certainly did not want to shed in front of the man who was causing them. I was saved from the embarrassing situation by Manny.

"Manny don't like Rick the Dick," he said, muscling me away with all the finesse of a secret service agent removing his protectee from a suspected threat. "Jail food sucks. Manny's hungry. Let's eat."

I didn't balk at being pulled away from Townsend. At the look on Rick's face, I figured I was safer with the biker.

But as I looked on while the gargantuan fellow tried to fold his bulk into the front seat of my Plymouth, I thought, or maybe not.

Chapter 18

"So, Manny, what kind of information does two hundred bucks buy these days?" I took a mammoth bite of my big, tasty burger, folded a french fry into my mouth and washed it down with a big sip from my super-sized diet drink. "It better be good. I was saving the credit on that card for some Sketchers and a new case of motor oil for my car." I wiped my mouth with a napkin, and looked across at my lunch companion, who took up an astonishing amount of his side of the booth.

"Don't think you'll have much cause to ask for your money back." Manny unwrapped his second quarter-pound burger and tore into it.

As if I'd have the courage to ask if I did.

"Manny heard some talk while I was in jail."

"Talk? What about?"

"You know. What we was talking about the other night. About Mikey. About who he might be snitchin' for."

My hand on the plastic cup tightened. "Did you find out?"

"All in good time. I did learn that Mikey knew he was gonna get busted the last time before he got busted."

I frowned. "I don't get it. How could he know he was going to be arrested beforehand? Was he psychic? Did he have a premonition?"

"It was bogus, man. That drug thing with the lawyer and all. Mikey was put in jail to set him up."

I shook my head. "I'm sorry. I'm not following. You mean Peyton Palmer really didn't smuggle drugs to Mike Hill? Hill set him up? Why?"

Manny's huge shoulders went up and down. "Dunno that. He was a problem for someone, is my guess. He needed to be neutralized. There's different ways of doing that. One way is to trash someone's rep. Make 'em seem dishonest. Even criminal. That kinda stuff ain't hard to do with a friggin' lawyer."

"And the other way to neutralize someone?" This was a dumb question. I knew the answer. I just wanted someone else to be the one to say it out loud.

"You off 'em. Take 'em out. Erase 'em."

"Shoot 'em and stuff 'em."

Manny nodded.

I sat for a moment trying to process what he'd told me. "If the jail drug thing was a set-up, and Peyton Palmer didn't take drugs into the jail, then someone else did." I didn't realize I'd said that aloud until Manny replied.

He shrugged. "Or maybe," he said, sitting back in his booth, "the drugs were already there."

"Wait. What do you mean?" I asked, not quite

grasping the point, but sure as heck not wanting to let it escape me altogether.

"Mikey knew what was gonna go down before he was arrested, Barbie. Someone arranged to get him into jail. Someone arranged for your dead lawyer to visit him in jail—"

"I know who! I know who!" I interrupted. "Palmer's law partner, Dennis Hamilton, asked Peyton Palmer to take Mike Hill as a client. And he was involved with Palmer's wife. There's your motive."

Manny eyebrows raised. "You have been busy," he said. "Did your source also tell you that the dude is a junkie?"

I blinked. "A junkie? Who? Hamilton?"

He nodded. "One of Mikey's best customers." He took a swig of his monstrous drink. " 'Course, I ain't no friggin' Einstein, Barbie, but seems to me this couldn't have been pulled off without somebody on the inside helping pull some strings."

"The cops?" I squeaked, my chest tighter than when I'd hoofed it after Hamilton. "But why?"

Manny gave me a long look. "Mikey dealt. He dealt a lot. But he got picked up on simple possession. There's only one way that could happen. Mikey was hands-off. Untouchable."

I shook my head. "Hands-off? The guy is dead. How is that untouchable?" I asked, hoping he would draw me a detailed blueprint.

"Mikey obviously became a big problem for someone. He was not what you call the patient type. He wanted something from you, he wanted it yesterday. I guess Mikey finally pushed the wrong person too far." He made a finger gun at his temple. "Boooom!"

I jumped in my seat. "Gee, Manny. Hold it down. You scared me."

Manny gave me a look I could've sworn was sympathy. Or pity. "Manny's thinkin' it's a good thing you're scared. The more scared you are, the more careful you'll be. Manny's thinking Barbie better be real careful."

"The cops think it's possible Hill shot himself accidentally."

Manny crunched a mouthful of ice. "Yeah, right. The cops think."

"So, you believe I may still be in danger?"

"You gonna give up trying to find out what happened to that dead lawyer?"

I shook my head. "I can't."

"Barbie got a Ken to protect her?" Manny asked.

I drew a blank. "Ken?"

"The fish guy?"

"Fish guy?"

"The conservation geek. Rick the Dick. He your Ken?"

I shook my head again. "He's my hemorrhoid."

Manny nodded. "Manny's got more good news. You remember Carver from last night?"

I nodded. "Skinny. Long, greasy black hair. Dirty fingernails. Potty mouth. What about him?"

"He got thrown in jail with Manny."

"And you just left him there? You didn't want me to bail him out, too?"

Manny shook his head. "Manny can't stand him. But Manny here figures that skinny SOB heard the same shit I heard in lock-up. Maybe he even let the cops know what's going around that cellblock. Since you bailed Manny out, the cops will figure Manny told you. And there ain't nothin' more dangerous than a crooked cop, Barbie."

My tasty lunch wasn't so tasty anymore. I took a long sip of cola to wet my dry mouth, had trouble swallowing, and ended up dribbling much of it down my vest front. I rubbed my forehead. I'd always expected the boys in blue to be true blue, to uphold the highest standards of behavior. As the keepers of the peace and enforcers of the law, I always assumed those charged with this task would operate within the guidelines themselves. That was naïve, I now knew. And possibly dangerous.

"Who was Hill snitching for, Manny?" I asked.

Manny gave me a long look. "He was there. At the courthouse when Manny was released."

I felt my legs begin to shake beneath the table. "He always did seem to be Johnny-on-the-spot," I said slowly. "Thanks, Manny. For everything. I'm beginning to think you're right. Barbie does need a Ken."

Manny drained the last of his soft drink and crushed the container. "Screw Ken. Barbie needs a freakin' GI Joe."

I sighed. This Barbie was stuck with one ancient Green Hornet wannabe.

I dropped Manny off back at the Thunder Rolls. The cops had allowed him to leave his Harley there rather than impound the bike. He gave me a bear hug, and I was certain I would require a chiropractic adjustment to get my spine realigned.

I took my place behind the electronics counter at Bargain City and worked my six hours with about the same amount of enthusiasm I reserved for a bikini wax. It's hard to be upbeat when you could be served up as Grandville's next corpse-of-the-day special. Hold the slow, painful death, please.

I was about to walk out the door when I was heralded by a cashier. "You got a phone message. Kari says to tell you you're trying on bridesmaid dresses after work."

"You? A bridesmaid?" Landon in customer service snickered. "Now, that I gotta see."

I raised an eyebrow. "Too bad, because you won't be invited to the wedding," I said, with real pleasure.

"Oh yeah? Well, Brian's a friend of mine, so guess who'll be there with bells on? Hope you don't mess up the bridesmaid gown like that Bargain City vest you got on." He gestured to my soiled top. "Better wash it before the boss sees."

I gave him the royal raspberry (real mature, I know), and left. I wasn't in the mood to try on dresses. Okay, so I'm never in the mood to try on dresses. Especially long, girlie dresses in various shades of pukey pastels. I sighed and drove to Kari's apartment behind the local car dealership where my brother Craig worked. I threw my red vest in the back of the car and hoofed it up the stairs.

"These dresses better not be putrid," I warned as I entered her apartment on the second floor. "And no ruffles or bows, remember," I added.

Kari had selected several gowns and charged them to her credit card. She would then return the losers in exchange for credit.

"Are we having another bad day?" she asked.

"More like a bad life," I said, and slumped into the nearest chair.

"Why do these things keep happening to you,

Tressa? I'm almost afraid to contemplate what might occur at the wedding."

I felt another twinge of hurt. What did she think I'd do? Set fire to myself with the unity candle? Trip the ringbearer? "What could happen?" I asked, defensiveness creeping into my voice.

"Remember what happened at Craig's wedding."

"That was Townsend's fault. He squeezed my butt when we filed out after the ceremony. I told Craig not to pair me with him!"

"What about the wedding pictures? You disappeared after the ceremony, and when they tracked you down for family pictures, you had a trail of barbecue sauce down the front of your dress. They had to hide you in back."

"I was hungry and those cocktail weenies looked so good."

Kari just shook her head.

"So, where are the frocks?" I asked, hoping to distract her from another lecture on responsibility. "I might as well get this over with." I rose and followed Kari to her room. "You do remember I have full, unconditional veto power. Right?" I asked, getting a glimpse of some godawful red velvet thing laid out on her bed.

"Sure. Right. Gotcha," Kari said.

I stripped down to my panties and bra and tried the red dress on while I had the strength. I walked to the mirror and frowned in disgust.

"I can't wear this," I said to Kari's reflection behind me. "I look like Santa's niece, Tressa Kringle."

Kari nodded. "Too elf-like. Gotcha. Try on the green one."

I did. I looked like my artificial Christmas tree.

"Don't think so." I shook my head.

"What about this one?" Kari held up a satiny maroon strapless. I looked askance at the low bodice and cups that looked way too big for my 34 B's to fill. "I don't know. I'm not that busty," I said. "I'd probably pop out."

"We'd have to get it fitted, of course. I just want to see if the style works for you."

I held the dress in front of me. "Can I wear a turtleneck under it?" I asked.

Kari put the discarded evergreen dress on a hanger and put it aside. "Just try it on. You want a pop?"

I looked at the dress, remembered the soda mishap of earlier and Landon's smart remark, and shook my head. "No!" I barked.

Kari gave me a *chill, girlfriend* look, shrugged, and left the bedroom. I put the dress over my head and pulled it down, straightening what there was of the top over what there were of my breasts. I shut my eyes for a moment before opening first one, then the other. I laughed out loud.

"Kari, you've got to see this," I said, exiting her bedroom. "Get a load of this fancy, schmancy dress with my sports bra." I looked down at my décolletage with a grin, and waltzed down the short hall and into the living room like a bad impression of Miss USA on her walk down the runway after being crowned.

"I'd rather get a load of it without the sports bra," a male voice interjected. I looked up and ran right into Ranger Rick.

"You!"

"Yep. Little ole Rick the Dick. Isn't that what your friend Manny called me this morning?"

I managed to look uncomfortable. "Manny isn't my friend. Like he said, he's my—"

"Business associate. Right," Rick finished for me. He reached for me and grasped my arms above my elbows. "What the hell are you up to, Tressa? What have you gotten yourself into now?"

To his credit, his concern seemed genuine enough. But what did I know? For a time I thought O.J. was innocent, Rosie really had a thing for Tom Cruise, and the guys in uniform were the good guys.

"What's going on between you and Sheila Palmer?" I turned the tables. If he answered my question, I'd consider answering his, depending on his response, of course.

His grip on my arms tightened. For a moment, I thought he was going to come clean, but then his fingers relaxed and he shook his head. "This isn't a game of tit for tat, Tressa," he said.

I shook his hands from my arms and stepped back. "You think I look at what's happening as some sort of game?" I asked. "People are dying, Townsend. That isn't exactly my idea of fun and games, despite what you may think of me." I rubbed my upper arms.

"That's not what I meant, Tressa. Look. I just think you're too close to this police investigation. Way too involved. And now with this damned newspaper job, you'll have your nose stuck even further into this case. We'll need the jaws of life to remove you. Or a body bag," he added.

I winced.

"Are you ready to tell me who this Manny is, and why you posted bond for him?" Townsend asked.

"Are you ready to tell me what the nature of your

relationship with Sheila Palmer is, and what she was doing on your boat the night Mike Hill was killed?" I countered. A quiver in his clenched jaw told me there would be no quid pro quo here.

"Hell," was all he said, and turned away.

"What are you doing here, anyway?" I asked. "Where's Kari?"

"I'm Brian's best man," he announced, and I paled. Please, God, not another wedding party from hell. "Kari told Brian to scram tonight, so he called me to go grab a bite. We finished and decided to check out the bridesmaid dresses."

"Since when have you been interested in bridesmaids' dresses?" I asked.

"Since I knew you were going to be modeling them," he said.

I felt a tightening in my chest. I hadn't expected such an admission. Then I remembered who was making the admission.

"Won't Sheila be jealous that you're watching other women parading around in skimpy dresses?" I commented.

"You call that skimpy? I'm still waiting for you to take off your bra."

I sneered. "Don't hold your breath, Ranger Rick," I said. "On the other hand," I added as a thought occurred to me, "I might just be willing to lose this bra here and now under the right conditions." I covered the distance between us with a slow, casual move, trailing one finger up his arm, over his shoulder, around his neck to rest on his cheek. I thought I saw his nostrils flare. I was hoping this was a good sign and not sinus problems. I linked my arms around his neck and moved suggestively against him, ill at ease with my bad girl role, but figuring since he'd already seen me without my swim top in high school and I hadn't developed much since then, what was the big deal? Besides, I reckoned I could maneuver the bra down over my breasts without revealing a great deal. Not that there was a great deal to reveal. I was about ready to give my Marilyn pout, remembered how that had tanked with Dennis Hamilton, and instead ran my tongue ever so slowly over my lips. "Interested?" I whispered.

"Is this blackmail?" Ranger Rick asked with a lifting brow and, I was pleased to note, a bit of huskiness to his voice.

I shook my head slowly, then moved in closer so the tips of my breasts were just making contact with his chest. God, that felt good, I thought, then chided myself for letting myself become distracted from the task at hand—a very pleasurable task, I might add.

"Blackmail? Of course not." I rubbed against him once more just to see if it felt as good. It did.

"And what are the right conditions?" Ranger Rick asked while one of his big, tanned hands traveled up my arm to snag a bra strap.

"Huh?" I asked, losing my focus.

"You said you would lose the bra under the right conditions. What conditions?" He drew one bra strap down while he was talking.

"Conditions? Oh, yes. Well, in the spirit of cooperation and, uh, trust, yes, trust, as a sort of, uh, symbol of that trust, I might be induced to shuck the bra."

He nodded, and pulled my other bra strap down. I licked my lips again—not for effect, but because my mouth was dry as Gramma's legs during the winter.

"I see. And you would require what gesture from me as a, what did you call it, symbol of trust?" he asked, and stuck a finger down the front of my falling bra.

"Oh, I don't know, maybe if you shared with me what you really know about Peyton Palmer's death, that would go a long way toward, establishing a level of trrruuusst." I ended on a shaky note as his finger moved over my nipple. My legs began to do a cha-cha beneath the floor-length gown.

Townsend's finger passed over the peak, which was by now standing at full attention. I couldn't stop myself from closing my eyes and leaning into that intimate caress. I felt Townsend's breath on my face. I parted my lips, waiting, wishing I'd had time for a breathmint earlier.

"I get it," Townsend said. His mouth rested on the swell of my left breast above the bunched bra, his tongue making erotic little circles on my skin. "You're talking tit for chat."

My eyes popped open and I grabbed a handful of his hair and pulled. "Why, you . . . you . . ."

"Watch it, Calamity, your bodice is slipping."

Too late I realized that, without the bra, there wasn't enough me to hold up the rest of the dress, and the gown had slipped almost to my belly button. I tugged the top back into place to the tune of Townsend's ringing laughter.

"Sophomoric ass," I mumbled, certain my face was as crimson as the dress I almost wore.

"I suppose in all fairness, since you did, in fact, give me a look at your perfectly delightful breasts, I should return the favor in some respect." Townsend was dead serious now, and I was intrigued.

"Are you going to drop your drawers?" I asked. "I could help you determine the best spot for your tattoo."

He shook his head. "Not what I had in mind," he said.

"I've seen you without your shirt. That's no big thrill for me." It was a bald-faced lie. Seeing Townsend shirtless had propelled my resting pulse rate into the red zone on more than one occasion.

It happened so quickly I didn't have time to wet my lips. One minute Townsend was standing across from me, a finger tapping his cheek, and the next I was bent backwards in an embrace worthy of the formal gown I wore. I was kissed as I'd never been kissed before. Lots of lip. Lots of tongue. Lots of heat.

Unfortunately, it was over way too soon, and I was brought back to earth before I'd had time to savor the blast-off. I rearranged my gown, keeping hold of it with one shaky hand.

"What was that?" I asked, pushing my hair out of my eyes.

"Quid pro quo," Ranger Rick said with a grin. "Quid pro quo."

CHAPTER 19

I left Kari's apartment around eight with the infamous red dress (*Take it home, try it on with a strapless padded bra,* Kari instructed), depressed as hell.

As sucky as my life was, I realized I wanted it back. All of it.

I wanted to go out my front door again without peeking through the shades first. I wanted to eat supper at my folks', and not worry that I was putting them in harm's way. I wanted to hit a country nightclub, put back a few beers and find a good-looking cowboy to stomp around the floor with. I wanted a good night's sleep, a whole day off, and a full tank of gas to drive on. And most of all, I wanted Peyton Palmer to stroll up to me with his too-big nostrils and stiff hair and say to me, "Tressa, the tales of my demise have been greatly exaggerated."

Tattoo bets and *I-told-you-sos* no longer held the appeal they once had. I realized I didn't need to prove anything to my folks, or my friends, or the entire population of Grandville, for that matter. I needed to prove something to myself, Tressa Turner. I needed to prove that regardless of years of mishaps and missteps, of selling myself short and daring too little, of hiding my light under a bush I'd planted, cultivated, and fertilized, that I was smarter than the average blonde.

I drove home, locked myself in my bedroom with Butch and Sundance, and fell into a sleep disturbed only by images of red dresses, bare chests (male variety) and kisses to die for. I woke with my arms clasped around a pillow and my mouth plastered against a drool-soaked pillowcase. I looked down at the pillow with disgust, then at the dogs who'd joined me in bed. I hoped that was human drool.

I showered, shaved (I hate razor stubble, don't you?) and lightly spackled, deciding to take great care with my appearance today. I wanted to look polished. Professional. In charge. I looked in my closet. Let's see . . . khaki, khaki or khaki. I began beating my head against the closet door. Once I was through with Bargain City, I would never wear khaki again, I vowed. I scrounged around and finally settled on a calf-length, belted denim skirt and a sleeveless red top. I thrust my feet into a pair of red suede sandals with two-inch heels. I re-did my nails with a quick-drying shade called Extrovert, grabbed my cell phone (I just love to say "my cell phone"), and headed for town.

I walked into the newspaper office determined to let my little light shine.

"I've been trying to get a hold of you." Stan blew cigar smoke in my direction. "I've been calling that damn cell phone for the last hour. Don't you have it turned on?"

I slapped my forehead with an open palm. "I forgot and left it in the car. Besides, you can't blame me—that battery lasts about as long as a bag of Doritos among a *Survivor* tribe," I told him. "I'll just run and get it now."

"Forget the damn phone. Get in here and tell me what the hell you've been up to."

What was it with everybody wanting to know what I was up to?

"I heard you bailed out some dirtbag biker-type from the county jail yesterday. What's with that?"

I explained to Stan about Manny, and what he'd heard down in the bowels of Knox County Courthouse.

"He says it was an inside job all the way. That means corrupt cops." I spelled it out for my boss, although I was certain he could come to the same conclusion without my pointing the way. "But why would they want to strongarm Peyton Palmer?"

"It's like a shot across the deck of a ship."

I gave him my clueless look.

"It's like a warning shot. 'Prepare to be boarded. Behave and you won't get hurt. Don't behave and we throw you over the side.' "

I gulped. "Fish food."

"The question is, what did Palmer know?"

"If the police are involved, that means he had something on them."

"Not necessarily. You don't know the drugs came from the cops. Someone outside could have smuggled the dope into the jail to Mike Hill, so Hill could accuse Palmer."

"Dennis Hamilton is up to his two hundred dollar ties in this," I said, "but I'm not convinced he's a killer."

Stan jumped to his feet. "Stay the hell away from Hamilton. You get yourself hurt, your dad will catapult me off that damned cherry picker into orbit. You tried to get a statement from Hamilton. He declined. Hell, he's called the cops on you at least twice. Give it a rest."

I shook my head. "Hamilton didn't call the cops on me," I said.

"What?"

"Technically, Hamilton never really called the cops. The first time an anonymous caller phoned in a suspicious vehicle tip. The second time, they just showed up."

I thought about that, and the more I thought about it, the more I realized that getting close to Dennis Hamilton was about as easy as painting your toenails in the dark. And let's face it, you know how it is when someone forbids you to do something. It's like a KEEP OFF, WET PAINT sign. Don't tell me you've never stuck a finger out to make sure that wet paint is really wet. And those YOU BREAK IT, YOU BOUGHT IT signs. That's like inviting you to pick up everything in the display. Or the flashing DON'T WALK traffic signs. Get real.

"Keep your distance from Hamilton, Turner. Back off, or you're history."

Uh-oh. Red flag waved in the face of a pissed-off bull.

"Yeah, right. Anything you say, Stan. You're the boss."

"I wish people around here would remember that," he whined.

"So, are we gonna go with the stuff I got from Manny?" I asked.

Stan blew a ring of smoke. Cool. I wish I could do that. If I smoked, that is.

"The guy's a biker thug. You think he's got any credibility? He's probably got a rap sheet longer than my wife's honey-do list. We'll hang on to it and wait for the coroner's report on Hill, then see if we can slip it in on a follow-up."

I nodded. "Okay. What do you want me to work on now since you won't let me stake out Hamilton? You did say you didn't want me to stake out Hamilton, didn't you?"

"Go home, Turner!" Stan's voice rose and his cigar puffing increased to smog-alert status. "Take the afternoon off. Spend some quality time with your family. Go swimming. Take a nap. Read a good book. Just get the hell out of here. And remember, stay away from Hamilton's house. Or don't bother coming back."

I struck a military pose. "Aye-aye, captain. Arrrr, maties!" I snarled, and beat a hasty retreat to the sounds of "smart ass."

I'd walked a block or so when I found my newly-polished piggies taking me in the direction of the little brick building that housed Palmer & Hamilton, Attorneys at Law. I had promised Stan I would keep my distance from Hamilton, and I would. I wouldn't stake out his home or follow him by car. But what was the harm in sitting across from him in broad daylight at his legal office?

My gut told me I hadn't imagined the haunted look in Hamilton's eyes at the running track, or the fear when the cops rolled up. The boys in blue clearly didn't want me getting close to Mr. Hamilton. And for that reason alone, I knew I had to talk to him. Now. Before my courage fled.

Chin high, I marched into the offices of Peyton & Hamilton. "I need to see Mr. Hamilton," I announced to Annette Felders, who still didn't have a hair out of place. She jumped to her feet.

"He's very busy today. Besides, you don't have an

appointment. So get the hell out of here, or I'm calling the cops," she said.

"I'm here to see Dennis Hamilton. You're welcome to try and stop me," I challenged. With my party girl shoes and her diminutive size, it was an obvious mismatch. I made my way down the hall, oblivious to the dwarf at my heels. I went directly to Hamilton's office door, turned the knob and walked in.

If staring out the window qualified as busy, Hamilton was busy. He looked up when I walked in.

"What the devil are you doing in here? What's going on, Annette?"

I sat down in a comfy-looking chair across from Hamilton. "Mr. Hamilton, let's cut to the chase here, all right? I am not here as a newspaper reporter. I'm not here as some poor, misunderstood, woe-is-me cowgirl looking for legitimacy, or her fifteen minutes of fame. I'm not here to threaten or intimidate. I'm here to ask you to please help me. Help me find justice for a man who can no longer seek it for himself. You're an attorney. You seek justice for people everyday, for strangers who just walk into your office. Does Peyton Palmer deserve less?"

I was on a roll, with no clue where I was heading, but my mouth was fully engaged.

"So you slept with his wife. You probably weren't the first and probably won't be the last. Maybe you have some skeletons in your closet that you'd rather not see the light of day. But if you know something about a murder and you don't step forward, then this honorable profession you've sworn an oath to is just a lie."

"Don't listen to her, Dennis," Annette said. "She's mental. Everyone knows it. Now, are you leaving or do I have to call the sheriff?" She held the door open for me.

"If Mr. Hamilton wants me to leave," I said, "I'll leave."

She looked over at Dennis Hamilton, who looked oddly deflated. He shook his head.

"I'm getting the police," she said, and ran out of the office.

I shrugged, and turned back to Hamilton. "Mr. Hamilton, you deal with folks at their worst. Divorce. Deaths and estate issues. Criminal cases. The stress must be incredible. Things happen. Humans make mistakes. Sometimes really bad ones. We're not perfect. But at some point each of us must acknowledge the wrongdoing in our lives. You can choose to do it now, or take a chance and wait, in which case it might be too late. I don't think Peyton Palmer expected last week to be his last on this earth, but that's what happened. Ditto for Mike Hill. No second chance to get it right. No rain check for the next time around. No, I'll catch the next train. Just 'the end.' Or whatever comes after the end." I was using bits and pieces I'd picked up from a televangelist Gramma watched, Judge Judy and Dr. Laura. I couldn't tell if I was getting through or confusing the hell out of him. As I sat there and watched him, I just didn't see a cold-blooded killer. An egomaniac? Probably. Immoral? That, too, no doubt. Criminal? Yep. But a murderer? I wasn't so sure. Whatever Hamilton's secrets, and they were probably dirty ones, I just couldn't picture the guy nailing Mike Hill with a Python or stuffing Palmer in a trunk.

I stood. "You and I can walk right out of here now, and walk just down the street to Stan Rodgers at the *Gazette*. You know Stan. You can trust Stan. He's a stand-up kinda guy. Come on, Mr. Hamilton. What do you say? Shall we take a walk?"

I heard the front door. Hamilton heard it, too.

"Mr. Hamilton?" I asked, and held out my hand.

A couple uniforms appeared in the doorway.

"Everything all right here, Mr. Hamilton?" a thick-necked officer asked. "You want us to take her in?

Dennis Hamilton stared at my hand, then shook his head.

"That won't be necessary, officer," he said. "Miss Turner was just leaving."

I let my hand drop to my side. "Time is running out, Mr. Hamilton. Please. Do the right thing."

I passed a couple uniforms in the hallway, but just kept walking. Tears were streaming down my cheeks, but I didn't know why. Maybe because I felt I'd failed, that my words hadn't been persuasive enough, that I hadn't been credible enough. Those same old doubts and insecurities I'd battled for so long were hard to vanquish overnight.

I sighed. I thought about the little speech I'd just given. When I'd first started out, it had been just so much spin. But now, thinking about it, I realized that what I'd said was true. No one knew what day would be their final one on the earth. It just made sense to live each day as if it were your very last.

I was going to go home, hug my critters, and tell my family how much they meant to me. Even Taylor. I winced. This was getting way too warm-and-fuzzy, touchy-feely. Maybe I'd tell the animals how much they meant to me and save the hugs for family members. Yeah. That would work.

I jumped in my car, remembered to plug in the cell phone and drove home. I hummed a little tune as I did.

I was going to forget my worries for the afternoon and pretend all was right with my world.

I spent the afternoon with a Mexican general. You know: Manual Labor. I cleaned out stalls, picked up poop in the horse lot, spread the poop per environmental guidelines, then passed time playing with the dogs. I saddled Joker up and put him through his paces, feeling happy in the saddle as I never was anywhere else. Well, with the exception of bed, of course. And the shopping mall with birthday money burning a hole in my pocket.

I rode along the fence row, careful to watch for ground-squirrel and mole holes. One minute I was cantering along, at one with nature and contemplating my next shoe purchase, when a sharp crack accompanied by a strange whizzing prefaced a sudden lurch of Joker as he faltered, then tumbled to his side. I had just enough warning to kick my feet out of the stirrups and dive out of the way, when I heard a second crack.

I registered Joker's labored breathing at about the same time I noticed the blood pouring out from around his withers, understanding the significance of the crack and the whizz immediately. Some psycho had shot my horse! I was so filled with anger and rage that I lifted my head to get up, then remembered there had been a second shot. Two shots. Not one.

I let my head fall back to the ground, as if I'd just passed out. Or died. I tried to keep as still as I could, terrified the shooter would come finish the job, but more terrified to move and be picked off like one of those revolving ducks at the shooting gallery carnival games.

I prayed as I'd never prayed before. "Please Lord, don't let me die," I prayed. "At least not until I track down the son-of-a-bitch who shot my horse. Amen."

I remained on the ground, still as death for a moment or two, knowing that with each minute that ticked off, more life's blood was pouring from Joker. I couldn't let that happen. I couldn't lie there like some spineless coward and let Joker die. No, pilgrim. Not today. Today I was a true crime-fighter. Today I was Catwoman gone straight!

I crawled to Joker and cradled his head in my lap.

"Hold on, boy. Hold on and I'll be back with the good guys." I kissed his head, jumped up, and took off across the field, my boots barely touching the ground.

Just let me run into the lowdown polecat who shot my horse, I thought as I raced for the house and help. Just let me. I suddenly remembered little details like gunshots and blood. Okay, such a meeting could wait for another time, I decided. Like when I was wearing a Kevlar vest and was packing more than love handles around my waist.

"How is he, doc?" I asked. My mother, father and I looked on, stern-faced, as the vet examined Joker.

"He's lost a great deal of blood, but the good news is the round went straight through the withers." The veterinarian patted my arm. "Don't worry, Tressa. I won't let your horse die."

"Thank you, God!" I said.

"Hey, I may be a pretty good healer, but I'm not that good," Doc Davis teased. "I'll give him a painkiller, then we'll get him back on his feet, load him in the trailer and take him to the barn. I'll stitch him up there. He'll need daily antibiotic injections."

I nodded, my stomach still in a knot. "Done."

Between the four of us, we managed to get Joker up and loaded onto the trailer. I rode in the trailer with him and reassured him all would be well. Once Joker was unloaded, cleaned up, sutured, and given his first dose of antibiotic, Doc Davis prepared to leave.

"I'll have to report this incident to the county sheriff's office, you know," he said. "Being as how Joker was shot."

"I've already reported it, Ben." My dad shook his hand. "Thanks. Thanks for everything."

The vet drove away, and my vision blurred. I sniffled. My father took me in his arms and held me tight against him in the kind of hug only a dad can give.

"I'm so sorry about Joker, kid," he said. "I can't imagine how scary that must have been. Are you sure you're okay?"

I sniffed, and nodded against his shoulder. "I'm fine, Dad."

My mom put an arm around me and we stood there, a tight little group of three, grieving for the needless pain of our loved one, yet filled with the knowledge that it could have been so much worse.

At the sound of tires on gravel, I looked up to see a patrol car pull into the drive. Deputy Samuels stepped from the vehicle. My heart began to slam against my chest. My vision went red, as in Joker's blood red. Deputy Samuels had never taken me seriously. He'd scoffed and laughed at me at every opportunity. He'd dismissed me as sideshow entertainment. He'd written me tickets and practically accused me of being an attention-seeking psycho. He hadn't protected, and he hadn't served. And now my horse and I had been live target practice for some psycho, and I was pretty sure Deputy Dickhead was involved.

I broke free from my folks and ran full-bore at the deputy, knocking him to the ground.

"You son of a bitch!" I screamed. "You goddamned son of a bitch! My horse almost died, you fat bastard, because you can't or won't do your goddamned job!" I was out of control. I admit it. The previous week had all but robbed me of any good sense I had to start with. I couldn't seem to stop myself. "Tell me who is behind this!" I said. "You know. You know a lot more than you're letting on. You worked Mike Hill as a snitch. You put him in jail to set Palmer up. You supplied the drugs, didn't you? Why? What did Palmer know that he had to die for? What?"

The accusations, fueled by pent-up rage and fear, spilled over onto the unsuspecting Samuels. If my father hadn't dragged me off the officer, I don't know what might've happened.

"For God's sake, Tressa." My father pulled me a safe distance away. "What has gotten into you? Deputy Samuels is here to take the report on Joker. What are you talking about, snitches and drugs? You're distraught, honey. You're not making any sense."

In the meantime, Deputy Samuels had gotten to his feet and was brushing his uniform off. "I could file charges against you for assaulting a police officer," he said.

I gave the deputy my best make-my-day stare. "Go ahead," I responded. "I'll retain Dennis Hamilton as counsel," I said.

"Now hold on, Deputy." My father planted himself between his middle child and the law enforcement officer. "Tressa has been through a very scary time. Her horse was wounded. She was almost shot. Cut her some slack, for god's sake. Instead of threatening my daughter with criminal charges, shouldn't you be out there looking for the person who almost killed her?"

"That would require actual police work, Dad. The kind that doesn't involve donuts."

"Tressa! Quiet!" My mother shushed me.

The deputy and I had a staredown. I'm happy to report I won. He opened his car door and brought out a black notebook. "I'll need to see the animal," he said. "And the scene."

"You can't miss it," I hissed. "Take the path along the fence row, and when you come to a gallon of blood, then you've found the crime scene." I gave the cop a narrow glare.

"Tressa," my dad warned. "This way, Officer."

"Miss Turner?" Deputy Samuels motioned for me to precede him. Probably he thought I might attack him from behind. Probably he had reason to think just that.

The deputy had just finished up his report and was preparing to leave when a phone began to ring.

"Your car's ringing," my mom exclaimed to me. "Why is your car ringing?"

I ran to the Plymouth. "It's my cell phone," I explained, and reached inside.

"She drives a car that's falling apart, but she has a cell phone." My father shook his head.

"Hello?"

"Is this Tressa Turner?"

"Yeah. Who's this?" I asked.

"Are you alone?"

"If this is some sick obscene phone caller, let me just warn you that I've had a very bad day. And if you say one perverted thing like what color is your bra or are you wearing underwear, I'll hunt you down and stomp your gonads into fertilizer."

"This is Dennis Hamilton."

"Oh," I said, lowering my voice and moving away from the others. "How did you get this number?"

"That doesn't matter," he said. "We need to talk. You were right earlier."

I put my mind on rewind and tried desperately to remember what I'd said to him that morning during my infomercial for honesty, values and American jurisprudence. "Which part?" I finally asked.

"About owning up to your mistakes. Acknowledging wrongdoing and in doing so cleansing the soul of all the accumulated filth and grime. To take responsibility. To do the right thing."

Geez, had I been that eloquent?

"I see." I paused. "Just how were you planning to, uh, own up to your misdeeds? Are we talking about turning yourself in?"

Hamilton exhaled a loud breath. "I can't do that. Not yet. It's complicated. I can't trust the police."

I turned my back on my folks and Deputy Samuels, and put more distance between us. "I can take you to Stan Rodgers."

"Can't take that chance," he said. "But I can lead you in the right direction. Tell you where to look and what to look for."

I paused, unsure how to respond.

"Like you said," Hamilton said, "time is running out."

I heard someone agreeing, and couldn't believe it was me. "Okay. When? Where?"

"The observation tower at the lake. Ten P.M. sharp. I'll meet you at the top. Come alone."

"Just a minute. Wait!"

The line went dead. I punched up the number, hit

send, but the phone just kept ringing. I looked to the west at the darkening sky. A storm was moving in. And I was smack-dab in the eye of it.

Man, oh, man.

CHAPTER 20

It was past six when Deputy Samuels finally left. I got the impression he was stalling. When my mother asked who was on the phone, I could tell the deputy was more than casually interested in the answer.

"That was Stan," I told my mother. "He wants me to pick up the camera tomorrow and cover the skate park fundraiser."

My mother nodded. "I hear they're getting close to reaching their goal." She frowned. "I hope you're not thinking of trying any of those skateboarding tricks," she added.

I shrugged, then sent a benign smile to Deputy Samuels, who was listening to our exchange as closely as Gramma listens to the numbers being called at bingo. I'd bet my newest pair of shoes I'd have company once I left home that night. I had to find a way to lose the tail. And by now, my Plymouth was about as infamous as a certain white Bronco in an equally infamous low-speed chase. I sighed. I'd have to find some way to switch vehicles. And I certainly couldn't go alone. No way was I that foolish. Okay, so maybe once upon a time I might have been that dense, but not any longer. Not since finding two dead bodies and getting shot at. I'd learned a lesson from all this: date a merc.

My vehicle dilemma was solved rather unexpectedly by Gramma. Once the law enforcement officer left the premises (although I was certain he was sitting down the road a piece pretending to do paperwork), I showered, changed into jeans and a gray Hawkeyes T-shirt, and ran next door. My grandma was primping in the living room, gussied up way more than a night of bingo at the senior center merited. I sniffed her.

"Is that Evening in Paris I smell?"

"Tonight it's eau-de-get-lucky!" She winked and put her arms around me. "I'm so sorry about Joker, honey. Your mother tells me he'll be just fine, but that has to hurt. And you're okay?"

I sniffed again. Every time I thought of Joker, I got emotional. "I'm fine, Gramma. Just a bit bruised and sore. I was lucky."

"See, my eau-de-get-lucky is working!" She kissed my cheek. My grandma used to be as tall as me. She had the best posture until osteoporosis messed with her bones. She's lost several inches in height, but makes up for it by wearing two-inch heels. My mother has a fit. She says Gramma will fall off her shoes one day and break another bone. I say, let the woman have her heels.

"Are you planning to win the jackpot tonight, Gram?" I asked. "If you do, don't forget your poor, destitute granddaughter who has her eye on a gorgeous pair of Indian pink and turquoise Tony Lama boots."

Grandma took a tissue out and wiped the lipstick from my cheek. "I'm not going to bingo tonight," she said.

"Did someone else die I should know about?"

"No, dear. I'm going on a date."

This was the last thing I expected. "A date? With who?"

Color provided a natural blush to Gramma's cheeks. "I'm going out to eat with Joe Townsend."

I swallowed. Egads. "Do Mom and Dad know about this?" I asked.

Gramma moved to her favorite chair and sat down. She took out her compact and repaired her lipstick. "I'm a grown woman, Tressa. I don't need permission."

I sat on an ottoman near Gramma. "Of course you don't, Gramma. Is Joe picking you up?" I asked, thinking this gave me the ideal opportunity to slip away unnoticed. I could jump in the back seat of Joe's car, lie on the floor and no one would be the wiser. Except Joe and Gramma, of course.

"Yes, he should be here any time."

"What's he driving now?" I asked Gramma, certain with my luck, he probably drove some outrageous red two-seater.

"He drives a Buick, of course. Like your grandfather did."

I nodded. "Do you think I could catch a ride to town with you?" *And maybe borrow your date's car around ten?*

"You got car trouble again, sweetie?"

"In a manner of speaking," I said.

"I'm sure Joe wouldn't mind if you hitched a ride. He's rather fond of you, you know."

"He's not bad for an old coot, either."

I jogged back out to get my purse from the house, and the cell phone from my car. I felt safer just knowing I could call for help if I needed to. Joe was just pulling into the folks' drive as I returned next door. "Hey, Joe. What do you know?" I'd always wanted to say that.

"Long time, no see," Joe replied. "What have you been up to?"

"Other than being shot at and having my horse hit? Not much. How're things with you?"

"Someone shot your horse?"

I nodded. "Some slimy, no-good bird turd shot my horse this afternoon."

"What are you going to do?"

"Get 'em," I said. "You in?"

"Does Jackie Chan kick ass?" We did a jivey little handshake followed by a high five. I proceeded to fill Joe in as best I could about my new friend, Manny, and what he'd picked up in the jail (the information, not the little bugs), my visit to Hamilton, Hamilton's earlier phone call, and the arranged meeting.

"I'll need your car," I said.

"What about a piece?"

I gave him a blank look. "Huh?"

"A piece. A firearm. Handgun. Revolver. Weapon."

"Oh, that kind of piece. I thought you were offering me another delicacy from old lady Winegardner. I don't think it would be wise to carry a gun. Not after what happened the last time. If you'll recall, someone ended up dead."

"Yes, but it wasn't you or me. Oh, and I'd appreciate it if you didn't mention Mrs. Winegardner to your grandma."

I rolled my eyes. "Don't the cops still have your

Colt?" I asked. "You don't have other unregistered firearms just lying around the house, do you?"

"Of course not. They're all locked up."

I rubbed my eyes. Maybe involving Joe wasn't such a good idea, after all. Still, I couldn't very well undertake such a dangerous meeting on my own, gun or no gun. I needed back-up. Reliable back-up. Someone more substantial than the scrawny, bow-legged fellow cracking his knuckles next to me. I sighed, coming to a conclusion that was bound to give me acid reflux later on.

Trust me, Townsend had said. I sighed. I really didn't have much choice. I needed help on this one, someone who wouldn't let me injure or maim myself too badly. And with any luck, he'd talk me out of the whole thing. Yep. Rick Townsend was the man for the job.

Rick Townsend also wasn't at home. I used my cell to phone him, but got no response other than his answering machine. I supposed I could leave a message. *"Hello, Rick, this is Tressa Turner. I'm planning on meeting a murder suspect on the top of the observation tower at the lake tonight at ten. I'd love to have you join us. See you there. Bye!"* Yeah, that would work, all right. I sighed. What was I going to do now?

It was seven-thirty when Joe, Gramma and I pulled out of our driveway onto the gravel road.

"Whatever you do," I told Joe, "don't break any traffic laws. Stop at every stop sign. Don't speed. In other words, drive like the gramps you are for once."

"I resent that," Joe said, but he made a flawless stop at the first stop sign. I was sandwiched between the back of the front seat and the back bench seat admiring a very clean carpet.

"Tell me again why Tressa is hiding on the floor in the back?" Gramma said.

"Because she doesn't want that deputy sheriff to know she's back there."

"Oh."

I waited.

"Why?"

"Because she thinks that deputy may have shot her horse and might want her dead. Lots of deputies carry high-powered rifles, you know."

I hadn't. Loud swallow.

"Why would a police officer want to shoot Tressa and her horse?"

"To keep her from sticking her nose in places she shouldn't be sticking it. To silence her. To eradicate her. To exterminate, eliminate."

"I think she gets the idea, Joe," I spoke up. "Just drive the car."

The car stopped. "What would you like, Hannah?"

"Tacos sound good. And those little potato things."

"Tell me you're not going through the drive-up window!" I pleaded.

"We have to eat, don't we?" Joe hissed back. "We can't very well go out and eat now, can we? Besides, we have plans to make. Details to work out. Assignments to hand out."

"You are to keep your narrow butt home. That's your assignment," I said. "Besides, I'm arranging for back-up."

"Yes, hi, we need that taco special. The one with the soft and hard shells and all those potatoes. Yes, that's right. Thank you."

I drooled at the mere thought of tacos and realized I'd skipped lunch and supper altogether.

"Who's taking my place?" Joe said, and tried to get my food-derailed thoughts back on line.

"What? Oh. My back-up. I'm, uh, going to ask your, uh, grandson to ride along on this one."

"I knew it! I just knew it! You hear that, Hannah? Tressa and Rick are a couple."

"A couple of what?" Gramma asked.

"They're going undercover!"

"They're having sex!"

"Not yet, but it's a start," Joe said. "It's a start."

I wanted to do a Jeannie blink and open my eyes to find myself on board a luxury cruise ship with Kathi Lee and the *Love Boat* crew.

I tried Townsend's home number again and got the same leave-a-message-at-the-beep. Joe drove around and picked up the grub.

"Hey, is that crunching I hear?" I asked, moments later. "You're not eating all the tacos are you? Pass me one back, would you?"

"No way. You'll get it all over my car."

"Gramma, you're not eating all the tacos, are you?"

"Don't be ridiculous, Tressa. We're saving most of the hard-shell ones for you. With these new dentures, I can't bite into them the way I used to."

I nodded, reassured. Trust a grandmother to look out for her granddaughter.

Joe pulled into his garage. "Stay down until the door closes," he said, then helped my grandma out and into the house. I followed with the food bags, inhaling the aroma like some drug-sniffing mutt.

We polished off the Mexican feast at Joe's dining room table in record time. Joe poured us each a nice, cold glass of milk. "Nothing better with Mexican than milk."

I wiped a milk mustache and had to agree as Joe brought out a plate of sugar-sprinkled, peanut butter cookies with a yummy chocolate kiss pressed in the middle for dessert.

"Chocolate!" I exclaimed, and took a big bite. "My undying gratitude to Mrs. Winegardner, the Julia Child of Dakota Drive," I said.

I noticed Joe's violent head-shaking too late to call back the incriminating words. I prayed Gramma hadn't heard.

"Winegardner? Abigail Winegardner? Is that old bat still alive?"

"Gramma!"

"I suppose she's trying to get in your shorts via your stomach, old man?" She shook her head. "I always did say men let their stomachs rule their lives. That and their winkies."

"Gramma!"

"She likes to bake!" Joe was flustered. "She shares with the neighborhood. Cookies, candy, cakes, pie. Last week I sampled her sticky buns. She has the sweetest buns." He made a strangling sound and shot me a for-God's-sake, throw-me-a-life-preserver look. I had to smile.

"Gramma, I think I can assure you that Joe's only interest in Mrs. Winegardner is regarding her skills in the kitchen, not the boudoir."

"Oh, well, that's all right, then. I hate to bake. But give me a Crock-Pot and I take no prisoners."

I nodded. Gramma and I both had serious, long-term relationships with our microwaves and slow-cookers. And China Wall takeout.

"You gonna try the boy again?" Joe asked, watching me pace his living room. It was getting close to nine, and I was facing the likelihood that I would either have to go it alone or take Bonnie and Clyde here as back-up. Not a pleasant thought. "You know, he's missed out on a lot of sleep on account of you lately."

I looked at the old man. "Well, I certainly didn't ask—"

"That night your gramma's Buick got destroyed, the boy sat outside your house most of the night."

I blinked.

"And you think he just happened to appear at that law office, and at the courthouse by magic? He's been looking out for you, girlie." Joe gave my arm a squeeze. "Oh, and he looks good in tights."

"Tights?" I asked, thrown off by the fact that Rick Townsend had cared enough to play bodyguard for me.

"You know," Joe said. "He's your musketeer."

I smiled at Joe, nodded, and dialed Townsend's number and left an abbreviated version of the earlier, silly message I'd composed in jest.

I grabbed the backpack I'd brought with me, the same one I'd used on my first stakeout, oh-so long ago. I pulled out the flashlight I'd pilfered from Dad, and put in fresh batteries. I checked my billfold and noticed the card Manny gave me the night at the bowling alley. His pager and cell phone numbers were printed on the card. I looked at the numbers and rubbed my chin. Manny owed me for bailing his butt out of jail, and he did say to call if I got in a jam. Manny, who loooked like the Incredible Hulk without the green color and split pants. Manny, who could snap twenty lawyers in two on a good day without breaking a sweat. Manny. He would have to be my back-up. I grabbed my cell phone.

I tried his number, but no one answered. I left a

message. If he was on his Harley, he wouldn't be able to hear the phone, but he might feel the vibration. I also left my cell number on his pager. Sure enough, ten minutes later, I got a call.

"Yo, who the hell's this?"

"Manny? This is Tressa. Tressa Turner. The Tressa Turner who posted bond for you in Knox County. The Tressa Turner who almost got shot this afternoon. The Tressa Turner who is ready to kick ass big time. That Tressa Turner."

A pause. Then, "Oh. Barbie."

"Yeah. Barbie. I need your help. Now. Tonight." I filled him in on the latest developments since we'd parted company the day before.

"Observation tower? Why the hell he want to meet there? Don't sound good, Barbie."

"I know. That's why I need your help. All I've got backing me up is one Geriatric Joe with Green Hornet fantasies and Hannah Hellion, a woman who is jealous of sticky buns."

"Huh?"

"Please come." I was not above pleading. "Please."

"Yeah. All right. Manny owes you. I'm probably sixty minutes north of you, babe. But Manny'll get started that way. How about the hemorrhoid?"

"Huh?" My train of thought was low on coal.

"The conservation hemorrhoid. You try him?"

"He wasn't home."

Manny grunted. "Keep your head down, Barbie doll."

"Roger that," I said, and ended the call. I looked at the clock. Nine-thirty. Time to get the show on the road.

I helped Joe clean up, then drilled him and Gramma one more time: "Now, if you don't hear from me by ten-ten, what are you going to do again?"

"We're to call your father, Craig, the fire department, the rescue unit, the state highway patrol, the Army Corp of Engineers, your uncle Frank, and Mary at the convenience store on First."

I nodded. "Well, this is it," I said. "Time to go."

"I can't stand to watch you leave," Gramma said, and gave me a hug and kiss on the cheek. "I just can't." She entered the screened porch to the rear of Joe's garage.

"I'll be back," I told Joe, feeling very un-Terminator-like, and shook his hand—"shook" being a key word.

"I'm gonna go console your grandmother," the old man said with a wink. "You better use the john before you go. You have lipstick on your face. You don't want to have lipstick on when you go out looking for a murderer, do you?"

I shook my head and headed to the bathroom. I needed to go anyway.

While I conducted my business, I looked at the cabinet doors below Joe's bathroom sink. I wondered if Joe had any bladder control pads. As I backed Joe's car out of his garage a few minutes later, I wished I'd checked. I was thinking there was a very good chance that tonight, I just might need them.

Chapter 21

I pulled into the parking lot below the one hundred and six foot converted water tower-turned-observation tower at nine-forty-five P.M. I spotted Dennis Hamilton's silver Lincoln in the lot. His was the only other car. Dang. I'd hoped for people milling about. Probably most people were home with a bowl of ice cream preparing to watch the late news, or to roll over and fall asleep after a quickie. Probably I should be, too.

I'd already decided this interview would be a quickie, too. The gates closed at ten P.M., and the weather looked like one of Snoopy's dark and stormy nights. Definitely not the type of night to be meeting potential murder suspects at the top of a lake observation tower. What was I saying? No night was the night to be meeting potential murder suspects. I parked the car and grabbed my flashlight with sweaty palms. I grimaced and wiped them on my jeans.

"Brrruuub."

I stopped at the sound. Thunder? "Brrruuupp." An unpleasant smell reached my nasal passages. I turned my flashlight on, and pointed it into the back seat. I let out a yell when the light reflected off two sets of tri-focals.

"Gramma! Joe! What in God's name are you two doing down here?" They were hunkered down like they were conducting WWII trench warfare. "Besides cutting the cheese, of course."

"We couldn't let you face the enemy alone, honey." Gramma unfolded herself from the floor. I winced, hoping she wouldn't snap a bone or something. "We stowed away. Felt good, too."

"What? The farting or the stowing?" I asked, then shook my head. "Gramma, you can't stay here. I don't want to have to worry about you two."

"We can take care of ourselves," Gramma said, and pulled a gun from her purse. "This was your great-grandfather's service revolver when he was Grandville's Chief of Police. I knew Joe was interested in firearms, and I thought he'd like to see Daddy's gun, so I brought it along on our date tonight. I've shot this thing more times than I can recall. I'm quite the sharpshooter, if I do say so myself."

"I can't believe this. My grammy is packing heat!"

"I'm packin', too," Joe said and showed me a dark gray automatic. "It's a Glock," he announced, as if that told me anything.

"A Glock? What's a Glock?"

"It's a gun. A way cool gun. Everyone carries a Glock in the mystery books."

I put my head on the steering wheel. "Listen," I said after a minute or two of therapeutic head-banging. "I'm going to go up those stairs to tell Hamilton that tonight is not a good time for me, and we'll have to reschedule." Like, when hell sported an ice skating rink. Or Britney Spears didn't show her belly button. Or Al Gore was no longer boring. "You two stay here. And unload those guns before you shoot each other."

"Please, take it, Tressa." Gramma handed my great-grandpa's gun to me with reverence. "Papa would want you to carry this with you. Just aim and pull the trigger, dear," she announced as calmly as if she were instructing me on how to use a disposable camera.

I shook my head. Some families passed down artwork, antique furniture, quilts, farmland and family Bibles. My relatives passed down heirloom weaponry.

I took the gun from her, figuring it was safer with me than with Laverne and Shirley in the back seat. "Okay, Gramma. I'll take it. Thanks." I promptly slid it under the front seat.

I gave my cell phone to Joe and told him if I wasn't back on ground level within ten minutes, he was to call out the cavalry.

"Let's synchronize watches," he said, pushing his IndiGlo nightlight.

"Just watch the time, Joe. Ten minutes from now, if I'm not down, make those calls."

He nodded. "Yes, Herr Commandant!"

Against my better judgment, I stepped out of the car on legs that felt like I'd been walking a balance beam from one rim of the Grand Canyon to the other. I deposited my fifty cents in the place provided and slipped through the turnstile. I gazed up at the winding staircase, all one hundred seventy steps, with the same eagerness I show when I reconcile my bank statement. I put my foot on the first step. Only one hundred sixty nine to go. Halfway up, I stopped for a breath. Hey, I already told you I wasn't in the best shape. So sue me.

"Mr. Hamilton?" I called out to warn him I was on my way, as if the heavy footsteps and even heavier breathing weren't sufficient warning. I was beginning to get a not-so-good feeling about this major journalistic scoop. Like, if rather than snagging a by-line, I would end up with a bye-bye line. "Yoohoo? Mr. Hamilton, Tressa Turner here. I'm coming up." A hint of wussiness made its way into my voice. I actually found myself thankful for the golden oldie gun enthusiasts below. There was something comforting about having a card-carrying NRA member with Jackie Chan fantasies and his blue-haired associate backing you up on a murder investigation.

I resumed my climb. "Mr. Hamilton, this just isn't working for me. I'm thinking another time would be best." Yeah, like when the Minnesota Vikings brought home a Super Bowl ring. Or Double-Stuf Oreos actually helped you lose weight. "Besides, there's thunder and lightning and it isn't safe to be up in this tower during a thunderstorm. Mr. Hamilton?" A feeling like the one you get when you receive an unexpected letter from the bank hit me. I peeked up the darkened staircase. "Mr. Hamilton?"

I took the final turn and could see the last stair. "Thank God," I wheezed when I'd planted both feet on the floor, my legs feeling like slinkies. Lightning lit up the sky to the west, and a crack of thunder provided accompaniment for the light show. The top of the tower had three benches. I expect they thought folks needed a place to fall when they reached the top. I expect they were right. There was enough lighting to see that only one bench was occupied. I started toward the figure on the bench.

"Mr. Hamilton, we really need to go. It's going to rain buckets here any time now." I poked him on the shoulder. "Mr. Hamilton?" I poked him again harder. This time he fell over onto the bench. "Mr. Hamilton, are you all right?" I grabbed my flashlight and turned it on. The beam hit Hamilton in the crotch area. I winced. I started to avert my eyes when I noticed the large dark spot on the front of the khaki slacks. I made a gag-me face, hoping against hope Dennis Hamilton was merely incontinent and hadn't, uh, entertained himself before I arrived.

"Mr. Hamilton. Mr. Hamilton, wake up. Do you need a hand getting up?" I aimed my flashlight toward his face. A muffled scream escaped me. No, Dennis Hamilton didn't need a hand, at all. He needed a face.

Reconstituted taco meat burned the back of my throat. No way. Couldn't be. No one could find three dead bodies in the span of one week. As if on cue in some action-adventure flick, the earth shook, lightning crackled and the heavens opened up. I did a number across the floor of the tower toward the staircase like Disney on Ice (Goofy or, maybe Dopey). I proceeded to haul my ass down those stairs with one thought in mind. A vacation. I was taking a long vacation.

I lost my footing on the slippery stairs about two turns from the bottom. My feet went out from under me and I remember counting each stair as my butt bounced off it. I stopped counting when I hit the heavy pole at the bottom, and everything went your basic black.

In my dream, I was cradled in strong, protective arms. My wet hair was brushed away from my face with a whisper-soft touch. Hushed words of tender devotion and humble adoration were spoken ever so low against my ear, sending thrills and chills rippling throughout my inert body. I sighed and snuggled closer to the essence of my dream world. "Tell me again how you feel about me," I sighed, and arched my back.

"I think you're a total nitwit, devoid of any legitimate claim to rational thought processes, and not even on a nodding acquaintance with common sense or sound judgment." Ranger Rick's fire-breathing dragon breath singed my cheeks. "What the hell do you have to say for yourself, Tressa Jayne Turner?"

I gave a weak smile. "Your grandfather made me do it?" I tried.

"Are you in much pain?" Rick asked, and I wondered how badly I was hurt.

"I'll live," I said, pretty sure Dennis Hamilton wouldn't. It was hard to survive in the world without a face. "How did you know I was here?"

"I got your insane message, checked the number, and when I didn't recognize it, I called. Imagine my surprise when my grandfather answered."

I started to sit up, but Rick put a restraining hand on my shoulder. "Just take it easy, Calamity," he said. "An ambulance is on its way."

"Ambulance?" That got my attention, big time. Thoughts of doctor bills, seven-dollar aspirins, and *Overdue* stamped on all my mail made my head hurt even more.

"No." I managed to get myself to a sitting position. "No ambulance. No doctors. No hospital. No money," I added, by means of clarification. "I'm fine. Really. I've taken harder knocks to this noggin, believe me. And isn't this the same head you've been known to say is hard enough to pound deck nails?"

"You were unconscious when I found you, Tressa. You need to be checked out."

I tried to shake my head. It wasn't easy. "I wasn't *unconscious* unconscious. I just sort of passed out for a teensy while. There's nothing wrong with me that plain-label, over-the-counter painkillers and a nice, long nap won't cure."

"You could have a concussion. A hemotoma. A skull fracture."

I gave him a nasty look. "Aren't we just little Mary Sunshine?" I said. "No doctors," I reiterated. "No kidding."

Ranger Rick mumbled something about self-destructive women and the men who tolerated them, and helped me to my feet. I swayed a little before I regained my balance.

"Yeah, you're fine, all right," Townsend observed, "for someone who should have her head examined."

I stuck my middle finger up. "How many fingers am I holding up, Ranger Rick?" I asked.

He chuckled. "Actually, I'm kind of hoping the blow to your cranium knocked some sense into you for a change. Or a case of amnesia would be nice. That way you'd forget all about this crime-solving compulsion."

"When I feel better, I'll expect an apology from all three of you." I turned and almost stuck my nose into a silver shield. I read the nametag with a frown. "What's *he* doing here?" I asked no one in particular. "What are *you* doing here?" I glared at the deputy who was about as welcome right now as a big ugly zit on picture day at school.

"I believe it's within law enforcement purview to investigate suicides." Deputy Doug gave me a stern look.

I caught the suicide thing right away. I'm getting quicker on the uptake. "Suicide? What are you talking about?" I faced Townsend. "What's he talking about?"

Townsend took my arm and led me to the exit. "Looks like Hamilton stuck the gun to his own head. At least, the evidence suggests that."

"Suicide? No way. Hamilton had something for me. Information he wanted to pass along."

"To you?" Deputy Dickhead inserted. "Why you?"

"Because he didn't trust the police, that's why!" I shouted, rain hitting my face and dripping down my nose. "He was going to finger a killer here tonight."

I saw the deputy's eyes lift to a point behind me. He and Townsend were probably ready to exchange eye rolls. Or put their fingers to their temples and make a *she's cuckoo* finger motion.

"Did you touch the dead guy?" Samuels gestured to the stairs. I nodded, and he sighed. "We've already got more than enough sets of your fingerprints for comparison purposes than we'll hopefully ever need, but we'll need a statement."

"She needs to sit for a bit first," Townsend said. "At least until she only sees two of me."

"Thank you," I said, loath to turn my back on Deputy Doug even for the half-minute it took to leave the observation tower and head to Joe's car. I faltered. Joe's car. Townsend's grandad. My ass. My knees began to go south and I was grateful for Townsend's arm at my waist. I pointed to a Harley motorcycle in the lot. "Isn't that Manny's bike?"

"Your biker buddy? Yeah. He had a little accident."

"An accident?"

"My grandfather thought he was one of the bad guys and maced him."

"Mace? Your grandfather carries mace?" Why that should surprise me, I didn't know. My mind raced with images of biker paybacks. "Is Manny okay?"

"Yeah. The rain helped."

Rick led me to his pickup and helped me up. "You need anything?" he asked. "A glass of water? A cold rag? A CAT scan?"

I shook my head, wanting nothing more than to just sit and be very, very still. "Maybe later. After my MRI."

I looked on as activity picked up. I recognized the DCI agent who had sat in at one of my two police interviews. I shuddered at the prospect of a third. Why did this keep happening to me? Even as that thought filtered in and out, my brain was already composing attention-getting headlines and opening paragraphs for the next news article. I closed my eyes and rested my head on the back of the car seat. I sure hoped Joe remembered to hide his Glock.

Two days later I sat across from Stan with a bottle of water and a handful of extra-strength painkillers in front of me. I popped a couple tablets and washed them down with a long swig. I had a knot on my head the size of Sadie Tucker's goiter, a softball-sized bruise on my left buttock, and one on my right thigh that, interestingly enough, resembled Horton the elephant with two trunks. With my collection of cuts and scrapes, I looked like I'd gone several rounds with Muhammad Ali's daughter. I wasn't complaining. At least I still had a face. Not so for Dennis Hamilton.

The police had everything wrapped up in one nice,

neat little Knox County Special Delivery package: Peyton Palmer's disappearance, Mike Hill's murder, and Dennis Hamilton's apparent suicide. I was skeptical, but glad not to have to look over my shoulder anymore.

A search of Hamilton's home had turned up evidence of those "misdeeds" Hamilton had referred to. Records on Hamilton's home computer and a subsequent search of his office files showed years of embezzlement by Hamilton from estate and trust accounts. Drugs confiscated from the home, along with financial records, indicated Hamilton had a very expensive drug habit to feed. That was where Mike Hill, drug dealer and general all-around do-anything-for-a-buck lowlife came in.

Hill, according to the police, was Hamilton's drug supplier. When Peyton Palmer had begun looking into the accounting practices of his partner, which had ultimately led to Hamilton's exposure as a big-time embezzler and dope-user, Palmer had to be dealt with. The drug setup was to shut down Palmer's investigation. Discredit him. Scare him off. It had been the proverbial shot across the bow Stan had suggested. When that hadn't worked, Peyton Palmer had to walk the plank, matey.

Hill had been hired to carry out the hit on Palmer. Only something went very wrong, presumably a bad tire and electrical problems. Hill, an amateur in the kill-for-hire role and not the brightest hitman around, had left the car in the Bargain City lot, and of course, you know the rest of the story. Enter Tressa Turner, aka Ms. Monkey Wrench. I threw everything into chaos when I took the wrong car. Hill or Hamilton or both, followed me, and retrieved the body when I bolted. Searches were being conducted on both Hamilton and Hill's vehicles, and authorities were confident they would find forensic evidence linking the men to Palmer.

Once Palmer was disposed of, Hill realized he'd hadn't received his payment in full (i.e. the envelope of money), and had assumed I had taken it. Where that money was also remained a mystery, but certain I had it, Hill began his little campaign of cruelty to convince me to return the money. The vandalism, the notes, the threats. It was fortunate, the police said, that I didn't have the money, because as soon as I handed it over, I would have joined Peyton in the hereafter.

When I didn't cough up the dough, Hill went to Hamilton seeking recompense. Hamilton refused, probably because he had snorted away most of his money, or rather his clients' money, and didn't have it to give. When Hill tried to blackmail him, it was bye-bye Cobra Man. Police speculated Hill had followed me to the marina, called Hamilton in to assist him taking out one annoying blonde, they'd argued, and Hill got a head full of lead. Joe and I had unexpectedly returned to the pontoon before the killer could dump the body.

Police figured once I'd confronted Hamilton at his office, I had to be dealt with, hence the unsuccessful attempt on my life with the rifle. Perhaps Hamilton had lured me to the observation tower with his story of coming clean only to finish the job, or perhaps, to come clean and unburden his soul. Either way, it was obvious that somewhere along the line he'd changed his mind. Maybe he'd felt the noose tightening. Maybe he'd just decided to take the coward's way out. Maybe he was just a sick bastard who'd wanted the dumb blonde who'd unwittingly foiled his perfectly good crime, to find his grisly remains—as if Peyton Palmer's and Mike Hill's weren't enough.

Everything the cops said seemed so plausible. Yet, because it was the cops saying it, I was hesitant to accept it as gospel. Maybe because I was unwilling to believe a John Tesh fan could be a multiple murderer. Or because Peyton Palmer's body was still out there, somewhere. Unfinished business.

Stan and I worked on the article for several hours. I provided eyewitness testimony. Stan refused to print any graphic details of the suicide scene. Bummer. I had come up with some really terrific descriptive phrases.

"Too sensational," he said. "We're not a tabloid."

Stan and I shared the byline. Staring at my name alongside his on a story that made state headlines gave me a lump in my throat.

" 'Tressa J. Turner,' " I read. "Unbelievable." I stared at my name. Tressa Jayne Turner, not Calamity Jayne Turner. I smiled. I'd done it. I'd actually done it. I'd put Calamity Jayne to bed along with the *Gazette*. It felt good. Damn good.

"Something's been bugging me," I said as Stan and I were wrapping up. "I never thought to ask, how *did* Hamilton get my cell phone number? I never gave it to him. It had to be you."

"He came in looking for you yesterday, and one of the girls gave him the number. Sorry, kid. They didn't know."

"What time was this?" I asked, suddenly on alert.

"Don't know. You'll have to ask Shirley. I think she was the one who spoke with him."

I left Stan to proof the article one more time and found Shirley.

She dug around and came up with a steno pad. "Around two-thirty," she said, adding that he'd seemed very anxious to speak to me, but she'd never suspected he meant me harm.

I frowned. That was very close to the time Joker was shot. Why would a lawyer, of all people, waltz into his prospective victim's workplace, and ask how to get in touch with her if he was planning to cap her that very afternoon? It was possible Hamilton believed the horse-shooting would be considered an accident, especially with the local yokels on the case. Still, I wasn't so sure the police hadn't forced some of the puzzle pieces into the wrong places in the interest of expediency.

My head started to hurt again. I needed donuts. Lots of them. Or maybe one of those frisbee-sized cinnamon rolls from Hazel's Hometown Café. I walked the two blocks south from the town square to the small, ugly yellow building that housed a Grandville institution: Hazel's had been in town in one form or another for over fifty years. I made my way through a room smokier than most Country-Western hangouts I occasionally frequented. I eased myself onto a stool at the counter, oblivious to the chatter erupting around my arrival and ordered a cinnamon roll and coffee. The cinnamon roll would go straight to my thighs, but the last thing I was concerned with at the moment was how I looked in a bikini.

I ate my roll in silence, sipping black coffee and mulling over the events of the last week in a head that was still too sore to be contemplating anything more complex than what movie I'd rent on my next day off.

I'd played a major role in bringing down a multiple murderer. So why did I feel such a letdown? Apart from the bummer of finding three dead guys, of course.

I sighed and took a bite of my roll and winced. It even hurt to chew. I let the spit soften the roll in my mouth and considered what would come next. Selecting a tasteful but appropriate tattoo for Ranger Rick was something to look forward to.

"I wonder if he'll let me watch?" I said aloud.

"Watch what?"

I jumped, and coffee erupted from my cup and over the sides. I mopped the counter with a napkin and turned to the man at my right. "Why, watch you get your tattoo, of course. Have you scouted a good location?"

"So, you want to watch, huh?"

I shrugged. "I want to make sure the tattoo is up to spec. Nothing tacky," I said.

"Come see me in seven years and it's a date."

"What?" My mouth flew open. "Seven years! Why seven years?"

"Because if Peyton Palmer's body doesn't show up, it takes seven years to have him declared dead."

"Why you . . . you welcher! You'd make me wait seven years to win our bet?"

"Hey, it's not me. It's the law."

I shook my head. "You aren't ever going to give me the satisfaction of admitting I was right about Peyton Palmer, are you? You're going to make me wait seven frigging years! Well, screw you, Townsend!" I threw my money on the counter, got up, and walked out as fast as my aching muscles would allow. He caught up to me before I'd reached the Kut and Kurl next door.

"Can we call a truce, Tressa?" Townsend grabbed my hand. I wished I could hold on to my outrage, but, without my cinnamon roll, I wasn't up to fighting weight.

"Only until I feel better," I said. "Then I'm gonna hound you until you make good on that bet."

He laughed. "Thanks for the warning."

We walked in companionable silence back to my car. A first for us.

"How is your grandfather?" I broke the silence.

"Spending way too much time with Hellion Hannah," he said. "And your grandmother?"

"She's cool."

"What about you?"

"Me?"

"How are you?"

I gave him a smile. "I'm cool, too."

"You look like hell," he said. "Shouldn't you be taking some time off?"

"I can't afford to. Besides, I look worse than I am. Can I ask you something, Townsend?"

"Is it about the damned tattoo again?"

I shook my head. "It's about this case. Hamilton's suicide. The murders. Do you believe everything happened just like the police are saying?" I asked. "Are you convinced that Dennis Hamilton is the only bad guy here?"

Townsend's smile disappeared, and he seemed suddenly more alert. "What are you saying, Tressa? Did Hamilton tell you more than you've let on?"

"No, not really," I said, hesitant to open a whole new can of worms based on nothing more than feelings I couldn't account for. "It's just he seemed so scared. Really scared. If he was the murderer, then what would he have to be afraid of?"

"Did he say—give any hint who he feared?"

I shook my head. "He said he couldn't trust the cops. But maybe that was just to get me to the tower." I rubbed my eyes. "I don't know. Maybe I'm trying to over-analyze everything."

"You? Over-analyze? That'll be the day."

"People change, Townsend," I said. "Or maybe they weren't what other people thought they were all along."

• Townsend considered for a moment. "Are you working tomorrow night?" he asked, and my heart rate increased with the possibility that Rick Townsend was really going to ask me, Tressa Turner, on a date.

I cocked an eyebrow and tried to appear casual. "Why do you ask? Have you reconsidered and want to go tattoo shopping?"

"Not hardly. My grandfather wants to take us all out to eat. You, me, your grandmother, Manny."

"Manny!"

"Granddad wants to make amends for macing him."

"And he figures a supper at the steakhouse will make up for a face full of mace?"

Townsend shrugged. "So, what should I tell Joe?"

"Uh, I'd really like to join you," I said, bummed that the dinner appeared to be all Joe's idea, "but I promised Uncle Frank I'd close the Dairee Freeze for him so he could take in a classic car show in Des Moines. Tell Joe thanks and maybe some other time." I didn't want Townsend to catch whiff of my disappointment. "I'm really feeling tired, so I think I'll head home. I work the seven-to-three shift tomorrow, and then go straight to the Dairee Freeze, so it will be a long day. See ya, Townsend," I said, and backed out, drove home, did chores, undressed and went straight to bed.

I dreamed I was in a dense forest wearing my red Bargain City vest, a huge bull's-eye on the front and back. I was running as rifle fire ricocheted off trees and hit the ground by my feet. I tried to run faster, but my legs were heavy and aching, each step more painful than the one before. I kept moving, but every direction I went, I ended up tripping over Joker on the ground, blood flowing from his neck. When I could run no longer, I leaned back against a tree trunk. In my dream I watched as the barrel of a gun moved closer and closer. I strained to make out a face in the dark, but all I could see was a silhouette. Just as the face began to take shape, a scream woke me. It was only after I'd picked myself up off the floor that I realized the scream was my own.

Chapter 22

I was unprepared for the reception I received when I walked into Bargain City in my cola- and coffee-stained vest the next morning. I shook more hands than a politician in a tough re-election bid. There were reporters from several television and radio outlets, and a reporter from the state's largest circulation daily newspaper. He handed me a copy of his paper, headline reading, CALAMITY JAYNE SOLVES HOMETOWN WHODUNIT, complete with my high school graduation picture. I made a sour-milk face at the grainy portrait and way-big hair.

"How does it feel to help hunt down a killer?" "Is it true you were shot at?" "How did you get those bruises?" "Are you planning to write a book?" "You're known around Grandville as Calamity Jayne. Do you think this incident reinforces that image or dispels it?" "What do your parents think of all this?" "How did local law enforcement react to your involvement?" I noticed Sheriff Steve and his faithful companion, Deputy Doug, arms crossed, observing from a discreet distance.

"You'd have to ask Sheriff Thomason that question." I pointed out the sheriff, and took advantage of the moment to flee. This notoriety was all well and good, but I was holding out for Matt Lauer or Stone Phillips.

I hurried to the restroom and took a look at myself in the mirror while I washed my hands. It was hard to believe the battered and bruised face that stared back at me was now a celebrity. The country girl who provided more entertainment than Saturday Night Live, and gave the old-timers regular chuckles over their morning coffee and biscuits and gravy, was now the hometown sweetheart-turned P.I. who had solved a murder whodunit. It was the stuff dreams were made of. I thought of the reporter's question. A book? Movie deals?

Earth to Tressa. Earth to Tressa. I brought myself back down to the third rock from the sun with a castor oil dose of reality. Until those movie rights proceeds came rolling in, I still had bills to pay.

I really got very little actual work done at Bargain City, however, and felt a touch guilty, but I figured my just being there increased sales considerably. My boss must've done the same math because he actually appeared to smile at me several times during my shift. Of course, it might have been gas. I can't be sure.

As a result of my sudden popularity (everyone wanted to buy their CDs from a bona-fide newsmaker) I almost forgot I'd promised to lock up the Dairee Freeze for Uncle Frank that evening. I flew out of Bargain City, my red vest flapping as I ran. With a dark western sky, it looked like it might be a slow night. People generally don't like to go out in storms for a Nutty Bar.

I skipped to my car, thinking I really did need to do something about my transportation. It just didn't fit my image any longer. Besides, every time I looked at it, I remembered Peyton Palmer's body in the lookalike car. I needed something flashy, more in keeping with my reputation as an up-and-coming reporter (okay, so far part-time reporter) with an eye for adventure. Something small and red and fast that didn't require a can of oil a day. And I'd get a vanity plate. One of those plates that lets everyone know who you are. Like: HWKFAN, ITEACH, CEO2B. On impulse, I decided to pull good, old Whitie through the car wash. The manager was off-duty.

I parked at the back of the Dairee Freeze lot, near a storage shed that Uncle Frank has. For some reason, Rick Townsend popped into my mind. I wondered if he was still seeing Sheila Palmer, and if he ever thought about the kisses we'd shared. I shook myself, got out of the car, locked it (I do learn, eventually) and jogged to the kitchen entrance.

"I'm here. I'm here. Don't call out the National Guard. I just stopped off to wash my car."

Uncle Frank stepped into the kitchen, and wiped his hands on a towel.

"You washed your car?" He crossed the room and put his hand on my forehead. "Are you sure you're feeling okay, Kojak?"

I laughed. "Just coming to my senses, I hope. Besides, I'd like a slow night here, so I figured: wash the car and it's sure to rain. Is there anything I need to know?" I asked.

Uncle Frank shook his head. "Bernie is on the grill until eleven. You'll have Teri 'til eight. If it's slow, let Bernie go home and close up early."

"Sounds good," I said.

"I don't like to complain," Uncle Frank said, "but do you think you could quit advertising for Bargain City while you're working for me?"

I gave him my best, *huh?* look.

"Your vest. Think you could wear one of our aprons and actually promote *my* business?"

I looked down at the vest I'd forgotten to remove again. Oh well, it needed to be washed. I'd toss it in Uncle Frank's tiny stackable with the aprons and towels.

"Don't even think about mixing that red vest with my white aprons and work clothes." Uncle Frank waggled his finger at me. "I don't want to return to pink aprons and pink shirts. You put it in with my navy slacks. Okay?"

"Okay, okay. Give me credit. I do know something about doing laundry, you know," I said. "And what's wrong with pink, anyway?"

After two *tell-that-uncle-of-yours-to-shake-a-leg* phone calls from Aunt Reggie; four *make-sure-you-turn-off-the-grill-and fryers*; and seven (or was that eight?) *don't-forget-to-lock-ups*, Uncle Frank finally left the Dairee Freeze for the last time. Good thing. I was starving.

"What's quick and easy?" I yelled back at Bernie, making myself an M&M Cool Blast.

"Tacos, beef burgers, nachos . . ."

"I'll take a burger with the works," I said. "Oh, and toss some rings on, would you?"

The distant rumble of thunder got my attention. I

hate the windows on the front of the Dairee Freeze. You can't see out. Uncle Frank put these humongous food-special posters on the windows. If you want to see out, you have to go out the kitchen door, or stick your head through the drive-up window. I feel like I'm in a shoebox.

I got tired of listening to sounds of the fifties and sixties, so I changed the radio to my country channel just in time to hear about a heartache looking for a place to happen, which made me think about Townsend again.

I sniffed, blew my nose, then had to go and wash my hands.

I had completely lost my appetite, but forced myself to eat. At seven-thirty, I took over the drive-up headphones and sent Teri home. The wind was beginning to whip up and the sky to the west was an ominous shade of gray.

The rain started around eight-thirty, great sheets that the storm drains couldn't keep up with. Water collected in the streets. Drivers slowed, and folks ran to and from vehicles. At ten-thirty, it was still a downpour.

"Why don't you take off?" I told Bernie. "I don't think we're going to get much more business tonight. Most folks are home in front of their TV with a big bowl of buttered popcorn, watching a new-release DVD. Why don't you do the same?"

Bernie pulled his white apron over his head. "You sure?" he asked, and tossed his apron in the open top of the tiny washer.

"Positive. Uncle Frank told me it would be okay if it was slow."

"Okay, then. You're opening up tomorrow, right?"

I nodded.

"See you in the morning, then."

He ran out the kitchen door into the wet night. Feeling tired, yet knowing I wouldn't be able to sleep with a heart heavy as the fat in our fries, I decided to go ahead and do a load of Uncle Frank's work slacks, and throw my vest in at the same time, then clean the grill while the laundry was going. I put the CLOSED sign up and locked the front doors, then went back into the tiny supply room where Uncle Frank housed the cute little compact washer/dryer unit.

I started the water, tossed in one of those dissolvable detergent tablets that never dissolve, and grabbed the bag of dirty clothes. I sorted through it for Uncle Frank's navy pants and Aunt Jeanie's navy smocks. I checked the pockets, found one dollar and twenty-seven cents in change, and threw the dark clothes in. I remembered my soiled Bargain City vest and hurried to retrieve it from the coat tree out in front. Deciding to see if I could raise my laundry collections from a dollar twenty-seven, I checked the pockets of my vest. Two quarters, one dime and a penny in one pocket. I reached into the other pocket wondering how large the windfall would be and pulled out a thick manila envelope.

My hand shook. Like someone receiving a one hundred and fifty-million dollar lottery check. Or preparing to testify before a Congressional Committee. All I could do was stare at the envelope in my hand, an item that had monopolized my thoughts so often the past week. An item I'd rejoiced over, wondered over, fretted over, agonized over. An item that had been the cause of threats, vile acts, and attempted murder. An envelope that could just maybe condemn a killer.

With fingers I couldn't manage to get to work right, I opened the envelope and pulled out the stack of bills. I fingered through the money. I found what I was looking for at the very back of the envelope. I pulled out a hard, plastic card. I turned it over.

"Oh, my God!" I stared at the face on the driver's license. I checked the name. "Oh, my God!" I said again, and felt the burger ingredients I had eaten earlier churn in my gut. I stared at the phony driver's license.

The faintest of sounds from the kitchen snapped my head up. I held my breath. The kitchen door. I hadn't locked the kitchen door!

"Who's there?" I called out. "Bernie, is that you?" I bit my tongue, wanting to take back my blatant stupidity. I was doing exactly what got me yelling at the dumb bimbos (usually blonde) on the big screen for doing when they were being stalked. "Oh, that's right!" I would yell. "Just broadcast to the stalker that you are all alone by calling out for someone who has already left, and who the stalker knows already left, because, of course, he's a stalker. That's what they do. They stalk." I stuffed the envelope back into the pocket of my vest.

My eyes flew to the keys by the order window to the kitchen. They seemed an eternity away. Could I bust through the front doors? Get real. Uncle Frank had this place fortified like Fort Knox. The glass had to be three inches thick.

Another sound from the kitchen reached my ears, desperately trying to pick up the slightest whisper. Could I make it to the customer restroom? Were there even door locks that worked? My instinct told me that the paper-thin lavatory door would be so weak, Joe Townsend could kick it in.

I straightened. If I could just get to my keys. I turned and saw the red CLOSED sign illuminated. I reached out and hit the switch to read OPEN. Then I slowly put the red vest back on the coat tree and made my way around the long front counter toward the order window looking into the kitchen. I took a deep breath and reached out to snag my keys when a hand popped through the order window and grabbed my arm. I screamed, and tried to free my hand.

I remembered what Joe had mentioned in one of his Jackie Chan moments. Find where the thumb and fingers meet, then snap your arm in a twisting motion in that direction. I tried it and was able to free myself. I backed up against the drive-through window and saw the shadow of a figure emerge from the kitchen.

"Good evening, Tressa. It's not a fit night out for man nor beast." The killer shook water from his dark work-issued raincoat. Water dripped onto Uncle Frank's shiny floor. He'd be pissed.

"Yeah, it's a wet one for sure," I said, trying to keep the quiver of fear out of my voice. "I was just going to give the folks a call. They like me to check in, ever since, well, what happened and all." I reached a hand toward the wall phone. The killer smiled.

I picked up the receiver. The line was dead. The killer came toward me, took the phone, put it to his ear and shook his head.

"Must be the storm," he said with another smile, and hung the phone back up. "You closed early," he said. "Business slow tonight because of the rain?"

I shrugged and took a step back. "Sometimes we get more business when it's rainy. Folks come in to get out of the weather and sit and enjoy a dip cone, or an, uh, Cool Blast, or, uh, Goo Goo Bar, or a, uh . . ."

"Slurpee?"

"Huh?"

"A Slurpee. I had a craving for a tropical punch Slurpee. I was disappointed when I saw the closed sign."

"You want a Slurpee? Now?"

"Tropical punch. If it isn't too much trouble, that is."

Like the Tin Man from Oz, I walked stiffly to the machine that served up Slurpees and went to take a cup. I hated cat-and-mouse games. Especially when I was in the role of mouse. Unless it was Mighty Mouse.

"I forgot to ask. What size?" I managed to get out.

"Oh, make it a small. It's close to bedtime and I don't want to be up all night."

I nodded, filled the small cup with ice, squirted three squirts of tropical punch flavor in, then stuck it all under the mixer. I put a lid on when it was done, retrieved a straw and spoon, and prayed the entire time he didn't notice how much my hand was shaking.

"Will that be all?" I set the Slurpee on the counter.

"Not quite, Tressa," he said.

"I'm sorry. If you want something from the kitchen, I shut it down. I might have taco beef I could warm up for you if you'd like a taco."

"No, no belly burners for me tonight."

"Would you like some frozen Dairee Pops to take home? Let's see, we have cherry, chocolate, oh, and the butterscotch is really tasty. They're six for four dollars on special now. You can even mix and match. Would you like for me to wrap up a half dozen for you?"

I'd done it now. I was babbling, and I could tell from the look on his face that he knew I was scared. And he knew what that meant. It took all the courage

I could muster to stand there and stare him in the eye without making a run for the back door screaming.

"No, I don't care for Dairee Pops," the killer said. "They rank right up there with ditzy blondes who take off in cars that don't belong to them, team up with frail old men and play Keystone Kops, who think they're the next Woodward and Bernstein, and won't keep their nose out of things that don't concern them."

"Sorry. No problem. I don't like Dairee Pops either. And the butterscotch one"—I put my finger on my tongue and made a gagging sound—"isn't really all that good. Maybe some other time. If there's nothing else I can get for you . . ." I made an exaggerated yawn. "I think I'll just finish up and head home."

"Aren't you going to charge me for the Slurpee?"

I waved him off. "Professional discount. Uncle Frank always gives drinks on the house to folks in uniform. Thinks it's the least he can do when they put their lives on the line day in, day out."

"Now, that *is* nice of Uncle Frank, isn't it? Tell me, Tressa, do you share your uncle's admiration for men in uniform?" The killer took a long, noisy drink of his Slurpee. I felt the noose tighten.

"Uh, yeah, sure. My grandma's father was the Chief of Police here in Grandville for years. But, of course, you knew that."

The killer nodded. "Of course."

"I can let you out the front door." My stride was jerky and marionette-like as I made my way back to the short-order window. "I'll just grab my key."

"That really won't be necessary, Tressa."

"Oh, it's no trouble at all."

I had almost reached the key ring, when it was snatched up by the Slurpee-sipping psycho.

"Don't forget your laundry," he said.

My mind drew a blank. No surprise, considering it was operating while under the influence of terror.

"Laundry?"

"In the back room. The machine is filled. Looks like you were just getting ready to add something else, maybe?"

I shook my head. "I guess I just forgot to put the lid down."

"Really." He took the keys and put them in his raincoat pocket. Although he wasn't in uniform, I was under no illusions that he hadn't come armed and dangerous.

"You sure you didn't want to add, oh, maybe this Bargain City vest in with the laundry? That's a pretty bad stain there." He'd moved beside the coat tree and my chest felt tighter than when I'd tried to pull on last year's one-piece swimsuit.

"Can you put reds in with dark blues?" I asked, falling back on good old ditz to save my skin. "They won't bleed, will they?" If I could have managed to kick myself, I would have.

My tormentor raised a brow and smiled. "So, you're worried about bleeding?"

"Uncle Frank would kill me," I squeaked. Hell. I'd done it again.

"Somehow, I don't think you're going to have to worry about that, Tressa."

The killer, my killer, reached into his pocket and pulled out these godawful, dark purple gloves like the ones my gynecologist wore the last time I had my yearly exam. I backed against the drive-up window wondering if it would break if I flung myself out it. Unfortunately, it didn't look big enough for me to fit through.

The killer put a hand in the pocket of my Bargain City vest and pulled out the manila envelope now as infamous to me as a certain black glove in a high profile double murder case which shall remain nameless.

"You know, I've thought and thought about where this envelope could be. You sure seemed convincing when you said you didn't have it, so at first I wasn't certain. After Dennis died, I thought I could put this all to rest and move on, but the thought of that damned or, rather, damning envelope being out there somewhere, just kept eating at me. And the more I thought about it, the more I had to find it. So I went back to that first night and replayed everything in my head, and when I saw you wearing the red vest earlier today, that's when I remembered. You were wearing the red vest the night you found poor Peyton Palmer. So, I waited for an opportunity to get you and the red vest alone, and here we are." He put the envelope in his coat pocket along with my keys. "And now, Tressa, it's time to conclude this rather unpleasant business. Once and for all."

I pressed against the drive-up window and began to beat on it, screaming for help as I pounded. With steady rain still coming down, there wasn't a car on the street. It never failed. The one time I actually wanted a customer at the Dairee Freeze drive-up, everyone was either staying home or eating at Mickey D's.

"Listen," I tried to reason with someone who, I feared, had lost all reason. "You're sworn to protect life, not take it!"

He laughed. "I am protecting life. Mine." He

reached in his pocket and pulled out a rather wicked-looking knife, similar to the ones Uncle Frank uses to slice and dice. "Let's take a walk, Tressa."

"I'd rather not. You see, I don't have my new walking shoes on."

I was about to do something incredibly brave and daring, like dive head-first through the drive-up window when the drive-up buzzer sounded. I jumped a city block. It was then I realized that I was still wearing the space cadet remote headphone paraphernalia designed so I could hear the drive-up customer and he could hear me, but the restaurant clientele wasn't treated to the static, crackling, and popping of the mechanism.

I stole a look at my knife-wielding assailant. He appeared not to have heard. "You won't have far to walk," he said.

I took a deep breath, knowing my life could very well depend on the words that came out of my mouth in the next few moments. Oh, brudder. In that case, pick out a tasteful headstone, Ma and Pa. Nothing gaudy. No more than two, maybe three angels, at most.

"Where do you want me to walk?" I said, enunciating every word.

"The back room will do fine."

"Do you really plan to kill me with that big long knife you're holding?"

"What's wrong with your voice? You sound funny."

"Fear, I guess. Terror transmitting itself into my voice. After all, you've admitted to murdering two people. We're locked in here together. You have a knife. You want me to go for a walk into the back room so you can use that knife on me." I hoped the doofus on the other end of the drive-up transmission wasn't busy making out with his girlfriend and had missed my SOS.

"Something's wrong."

The master of understatement.

His eyes narrowed, then flew to the contraption on the top of my head. He whipped his head around and saw the OPEN sign lit up.

"You sneaky little bitch." He yanked my high tech headdress from my head. "Let's go or I'll do you right here. I swear."

All I could think of was the mess Uncle Frank would walk in on when he returned from his classic car show.

"Why kill me? You've got the envelope with the money and the fake identification with your picture on it that proves you were involved in Peyton Palmer's murder. Without that, there's no evidence."

"There's your big mouth, Tressa."

"But I'm Calamity Jayne. Remember? No one listens to anything I say! I'm a joke. A ditz. A space cadet. Remember?"

He shook his head. "Once upon a time you may have been those things. But not anymore. Maybe you never were. Maybe you just took the path of least resistance. Until it became too lonely."

I stared at him, thinking he was either brilliant or dumber than a road bump. Either way, it spelled the end for me.

"Listen," I pleaded, "I won't tell a soul. I swear. I'll move! I'll move to London—or make that Edinburgh. I've always wanted to see Scotland." There went my big mouth again. "I'll take a vow of silence! Just don't kill me!"

The fiend grabbed hold of my arm. I grabbed hold

of the order window and hung on for dear life. My dear life.

"You're not making this any easier." The officer-turned-killer grunted with exertion as he tried to pry my fingers from the window frame.

"I hope you're not expecting an apology," I grunted back, trying to kick him where it hurt, instead hitting the toppings dispensers, sending M&M's, fun confetti, chocolate chips, crushed sandwich cookies (Uncle Frank is too cheap to use real Oreos, but don't tell anyone) and crunched-up candy bars (ditto) all over Uncle Frank's highly polished floor.

"Now, see what you made me do!" I screamed.

In response, he reached out and slashed the knuckles of my right hand with the knife.

I'd like to tell you I did a Rambo here and worked through the pain. I'd like to, but I can't. I screamed bloody murder, an appropriate response given the circumstances, and catapulted myself backwards right into my attacker, who lost his balance on the candy-coated crunchy floor. We both went sprawling.

I recovered first and began to crawl as fast as my bleeding hand and the M&M's would allow. I hadn't made it far when my ankle was grabbed and I was tugged back, losing what progress I had made. The pain in my hand was intense, but the thought of that pain being inflicted on other, more vital areas of my body, kept me fighting.

A wave of nausea overtook me. Everything swam. My assailant pulled me toward him. I picked up a handful of Cool Blast ingredients and tossed them in his face. He swore, but didn't let go.

He straddled me and pinned my good hand with one knee. I tried to bring my knee up between us, but he blocked it. I felt my strength begin to diminish. My struggles now were more for show than substance. He knew it.

He shook his head. "I didn't regret the others," he said. "But I regret having to kill you. But hey, a man can live with regret, can't he, Calamity?"

He raised his knife.

I willed myself to keep my eyes open. It would be my parting gift to him. He would have to look me in the eye and kill me. And replay this moment for the rest of his miserable life.

He pulled the knife back.

I bit through my lip.

An eardrum shattering crash rocked the wall of the Dairee Freeze. It sounded as if the whole world were exploding around me. Glass was flying everywhere. The roar was deafening. My first thought was that a tornado had dropped out of the sky, and was whipping through the building. The roar intensified. My attacker no longer had hold of me. I pulled myself up to my knees and peeked over the counter. I opened one eye. Then, the other. I couldn't believe what either one told me. Where Uncle Frank's three-inch thick, top-of-the-line, super security, intruder-proof door should have been, a candy apple red Chevy four-by-four pickup truck was now gunning its way into the Dairee Freeze, right up to the front counter!

Just like in the movies, its driver dove out of the vehicle and tackled the bad guy who was trying to make his escape, slipping and sliding on the goodies rolling about all over the floor. Before I could say, "Oooooo, Popeye!" my hero had Bluto disarmed and unconscious.

"Sheriff Steve, you have the right to remain silent,"

Townsend advised the prone killer, letting the sheriff's head fall hard against the linoleum floor.

Ranger Rick reached out and hauled me to my feet. He put his arms around me so tight I could hardly breathe. Please note: this is not a complaint.

Geez," I said, woozy-headed. "Uncle Frank is gonna be pissed."

"Tressa, you're in shock. You don't know what you're saying."

"What? You don't think Uncle Frank will fire me for a thing like this?"

"Don't worry," he said. "I've got life insurance."

I pulled back and looked at his face, which was fading in and fading out. "Don't you mean auto insurance?" I asked.

Ranger Rick shook his head. "Life insurance. And I'm going to need a hell of a lot of it if I spend much time around you." He bent and gave me a passionate kiss.

"Ohh!" I said. "I think I like the sound of that. But Uncle Frank's still gonna fire me, isn't he?"

"Does a bear crap in the woods?"

"Oooh, Popeye!" And then, Olive Oyl fainted.

CHAPTER 23

I sat on the beach and admired the view from a chaise lounge. Townsend and my brother Craig were fiddling with their toys—Jet Skis that neither one would let me within ten feet of.

"It's not right," I told my sister-in-law, Kimmie, beside me. "It's so unfair."

"Well, of course it is," she agreed. "It's grossly unfair. As we speak, I'm probably ovulating."

I sent her an *are-we-talking-about-the-same-thing?* look. "I could handle one of those Jet Skis with no problem."

"Your brother needs to grow up, and quit playing with toys."

"I'm perfectly capable of operating a Jet Ski. My hand is healing nicely."

"If I wait until your brother is ready, the quality of my eggs will begin to decline."

"If I can wrestle a killer, I sure as heck can handle a Jet Ski."

"He's ready when I tell him he's ready."

Kimmie and I eyed the males who were giving us fits. I wasn't exactly sure what was going on between Townsend and me, but since that day a week ago when he'd sent his truck through the front of the Dairee Freeze in rather dramatic fashion, we'd spent a significant amount of time together. Okay, so most of it was in the hospital and subsequent police interviews, but somehow we had negotiated and maintained a tentative truce. No. Truce wasn't right. It went beyond a truce. We'd established a connection. Of what sort, I didn't dare speculate. I did know that of all the bods on the beach, his was the hottest. At least, in my humble opinion.

The public was just now coming to terms with the reality of an elected official and law enforcer turned dope dealer and killer. Although the investigation continued, and Sheriff Thomason wasn't cooperating, authorities believed that the not-so-good sheriff had been in cahoots with Mike Hill for years. Using his drug connections, Hill had provided information to the sheriff on other drug activities in the area while managing to operate his own home business below the radar, splitting drug proceeds with his partner, Sheriff Thomason. Dennis Hamilton was a long-time paying customer of Hill's and had, indeed, been stealing from the trust accounts and estates of his clients. While investigating his law partner's activities, Peyton Palmer had discovered Hamilton's relationship with his supplier, Hill, and later, the connection between Hill and local law enforcement.

The drug smuggling set up by Hamilton, Hill and Thomason was designed to warn Palmer off, to damage his credibility. The charges would be dropped, they'd said, if he would just leave well enough alone.

But Palmer refused. Later, the sheriff would try to reason with Palmer, using money to try to secure Palmer's silence and participation. Whether it was because of his sister's fate from illegal drugs or some other reason, Peyton Palmer had refused to be bought off. He then had to die. Thomason or Hill shot Palmer and stuck him in the trunk of a vehicle Hill had stolen. The plan, police thought, was to drive the car into the lake, and that would be the end of Peyton Palmer's interference. If foul play was suspected, it would be directed at the law partner who had embezzled, the wife who reportedly was not so faithful, or a disgruntled client, which every attorney has.

However, Sheriff Thomason hadn't planned on vehicular problems or his oafish accomplice badly stashing the car in an area that would be dark and inconspicuous until they could return later and dispose of the vehicle and body when no one would likely be about.

That's where one ditzy blonde came in. I had been the rather pesky fly in the sheriff's ointment. I had driven off with the getaway car, the stiff and the envelope, and the sheriff had had to alter his plan. When Hill was commissioned to get the envelope back, his aggressiveness became a liability, and later Hamilton became the perfect fall guy. Once the body count started rising faster than Aunt Reggie's homemade coney buns, Hamilton probably saw the writing on the wall. Knowing he couldn't trust Sheriff Thomason, he had decided to tell his story to the press, or a reasonable facsimile of same.

When Sheriff Thomason failed to kill me and hit Joker instead, he had to alter his plan yet again. Staging Hamilton's suicide was a cinch for a veteran law enforcement officer who knew exactly what to do to make the scene believable—all the way down to the powder residue on the hands, the bullet trajectory and wound analysis. It would have been easy for the big man to chloroform the much-smaller Hamilton, place the gun in his hand and into his mouth and pull the trigger. With all the evidence of Hamilton's wrongdoing collected at his home and office, his suicide would be consistent, even understandable, given the circumstances.

Except for that pesky blonde fly again—that annoying little ladybug who didn't buy Hamilton's suicide and just wouldn't keep quiet about her misgivings. The same pest who had carried around clear and compelling evidence of the true identity of the murderer in a pop-stained, red work vest for a week without knowing it.

I sighed. Okay, so my dazzling police work wasn't so much dazzling as accidental. I was still a star.

This "star" looked over at her hero and sighed again. He hadn't been what he appeared to be either. All the time he'd let me believe he was seeing Sheila Palmer socially, he'd actually been working with Sheila to try and find out what was going on with her husband. And working with Deputy Doug Samuels, of all people! The chief deputy had harbored suspicions about his boss for some time, like how he could afford many of the items he was able to buy on a county sheriff's salary, and how it always seemed Mike Hill was tipped off before an impending drug bust went down. Deputy Samuels and Townsend were working together to discover the truth. When Sheila Palmer spoke to her friend Rick about her husband's work troubles, after he'd disappeared, she'd joined forces with the men to get to the truth about her husband.

I let out a long, hot blast of air. I suppose I owed her an apology for thinking she killed her husband, or that she'd had him killed so she could be with Townsend. While I was at it, I probably owed Townsend an apology for thinking he would ever be with someone who offed her husband.

What really bothered me, and I was sure it bothered Sheila Palmer even more, was what had happened to Peyton Palmer after he was removed from the white Chrysler on that dark, gravel country road. The sheriff wasn't talking—not surprising, since much of the evidence was circumstancial, except for the attack on me and the discovery of the envelope. But without a body, the sheriff's attorney would argue that there was no proof beyond the testimony of one ditzy blonde that Peyton Palmer was even dead.

And you know what that meant—no raccoon tattoo for Ranger Rick. Dang.

My eyes sought a suitable place beneath the ranger's baggy trunks where such a tattoo might be placed, when I noticed a brunette had joined the men.

I drew a little figure in the sand with pointy horns and a pitchfork and labeled it Annette. What was she trying to do—wheedle her way back into Townsend's life again? Steal Craig from Kimmie? Not on my watch, girlie, I thought, and bounded to my feet, my flip-flops obliterating my work of art in the sand.

I stomped up to the threesome with my arms crossed in front of my black one-piece. "Annette." I planted one foot right next to Townsend's. "You find a new job yet?" I asked. "With both your bosses dead, you'll have the devil's time getting a good recommendation, won't you?"

She gave me a sucking-a-lemondrop look. "Actually, I'm taking some time off before I look again. This has all been very upsetting to me—as you can probably imagine, having gone through so much trauma yourself in the last several weeks."

"I could ask Stan at the paper if we have any openings for newspaper carriers, if you want." I gave her back my own eat-worms smile.

"No, that's okay." She smiled at Townsend and then over at Craig. "I think I'm dealing with some post-traumatic stress issues that I need to work through first."

"Having two bosses murdered would tend to be stressful," I said, trying to alert the two men that the she-devil in short shorts in front of them was hazardous to their health.

"As is finding *three* dead bodies, I'm sure," Annette countered. "Well, four if you count that cat."

I stared at Annette. "My grandma's cat? Hermione?"

"That's right. That madman Hill hung the poor little thing, didn't he?"

I felt my eyelid begin to vibrate. My ears started to burn. I stared at the woman in the leopard swimsuit top as if seeing her for the first time. All those loose fragments of who, what, where, when and how coalesced into picture-perfect clarity. Scary, I know.

"What did you say?" I asked, just to make sure I wasn't hearing things.

"Discovering your grandma's cat hanging in the doorway like a piñata must have been awful."

I nodded. "The kind of act perpetrated by a bottom-dweller, for sure," I said.

She nodded. "Most certainly."

"So, tell me," I said, planting myself directly in front of the busty brunette. "How is the weather down there with all the other scum-sucking, slime-covered bottom-feeders, Annette? Strung up any other kitties, lately?"

The stunned look in the dark beauty's eyes came and went so fast I wondered if I'd seen it in the first place.

"What absurd notion are you trying to peddle now, Turner?" she said, with a quick look at the men to see if they were paying attention to the conversation or her rather spectacular cleavage.

"How did you know Hermione was hung in the barn?" I asked.

She shook her brunette head, her hair neatly entrapped in a French braid. "I must have heard it around town. Or from one of the cops."

I poked her overly-abundant chest with my finger. "Wrong answer, Ms. Bottom-dweller. You see, the cops never knew how I found Hermione. No one knew, not even Gramma, because I never told a soul. So, the only way you could have known the cat was strung up was if you found out from the person who hung the cat, or you did it yourself. Either way"—I gave her shoulder a nudge—"you're screwed." I shoved her again. Harder. It felt good. Damn good.

Annette's eyes grew wide and doe-like. I wasn't buying it for a moment. She knew it. She took a step back.

"You were in on it the whole time, weren't you?" I said. "Who better to keep tabs on both Peyton Palmer and Dennis Hamilton without arousing suspicion than their own secretary? You could easily plant evidence without risk of discovery. It was you who took Palmer's boat out on Saturday, wasn't it? You did it to make it seem I hadn't really seen Palmer's body in that trunk, after all, to buy you and your new boyfriend, the sheriff, some time to rethink your plans. You probably cozied up to Dennis Hamilton in order to keep him in line, too. When that didn't work, you had to take him out, but you had to make sure there was enough damning evidence found in his home to justify a suicide scenario." I shook my head. "God, you're good, Annette. You fooled an awful lot of people. Funny, though—you never fooled me."

If I thought Annette Felders was going to take this particular newsflash lying down, I was dead wrong. I put out a hand to grab her, and she raked acrylic nails across the back of my injured hand, held together by thirty-plus stitches. I screamed in pain and watched her push Craig away from his Jet Ski, power up and take off.

My reactions at this point, you understand, were pure reflex. I gave Townsend a hard shove that sent him backwards into the water. I hopped onto his Jet Ski and took off in hot pursuit. We bounced over the top of water, made choppy by numerous water skiers crisscrossing the lake. I gained on Annette, determined to bring the cat killer (oh, and people, too!) to justice. I pulled up alongside Annette and screamed at her to give up. Her response was to ram my Jet Ski. Or rather, Townsend's Jet Ski. I cringed. Townsend was going to string *me* up. I shrugged. The damage was probably already done, so I rammed her back.

Up ahead, I spotted an oncoming speedboat, followed by a clearly novice water skier, a look of sheer panic on his face. Not wanting to risk injuring an innocent person by the madcap chase, I veered off at the last minute, permitting Annette to pull away. Annette looked back and raised a fist in the air in triumph. By the time she refocused her attention on maneuvering the Jet Ski, she had lost precious time and misjudged the distance between her and the skier. Too late, she attempted to take evasive action. She hit the tow rope in classic clothesline style. The Jet Ski kept going. The pond scum didn't.

I circled the perimeter until Annette was hauled safely out of the water and onto Townsend's boat, then discreetly headed back to shore.

It was a somber, overcast morning when a small group lined the shores of Silver Stone Lake. I stood with a group that included Deputy Doug, now acting-sheriff, whom I felt compelled to address with a certain amount of respect since he had turned out to be one of the good guys, after all; Ranger Rick Townsend, and his grandfather, Joltin' Joe; my grandmother, Hellion Hannah; Sheila Palmer; my now full-time boss, Stan the man; and me, Calamity Jayne.

I felt my nose sting and my eyes water at the sight of the flowers tossed into the water as a floating memorial to Peyton Palmer.

"How's the hand?" Sheila Palmer stepped beside me and asked.

"Doc restitched it. It'll be good as new," I said, trying not to cry.

"Thanks, Tressa," Sheila said.

"For what?" I asked. "For suspecting you of killing your husband?"

"For helping me find my husband's murderer. If you hadn't fingered Annette Felders as Sheriff Thomason's accomplice, we might never have known what really happened. So, thank you."

I wiped my eyes with a bandaged hand. Faced with conspiracy to commit murder charges, Annette had talked faster than an obscure Oscar recipient with a forty-five second time allotment for an acceptance speech. She'd just done what Sheriff Thomason had told her to do, she said, because she was afraid not to. In exchange for a lesser charge, Annette had led law enforcement to the location where, together, they had weighted Palmer down and dumped his body in the lake. It was unknown whether his body would ever be discovered.

Annette had agreed to testify against Sheriff Thomason at trial. Sheriff Thomason had reacted with predictable rage, vowing revenge on backstabbing bitches and Buttinsky blondes.

"I wish I had known your husband, Mrs. Palmer," I found myself saying. "I wish we had met. Spoken. Because of everything that has happened, I feel a connection to him somehow."

Sheila Palmer studied me for a moment. "You probably wouldn't have liked him much, Tressa," she finally said. "He could be a real son of a bitch. He didn't want to take down the sheriff for the greater good, you know. I suspect he knew that exposing the sheriff would make him a shoe-in for the next judgeship. He was ambitious, Tressa. Very ambitious. That ambition was his undoing." She put a tissue to her nose. "I'm sorry, Tressa. I wish I could tell you otherwise, but you deserve to know the truth."

I stared at her. All the noble, upstanding, good guy-versus-bad guy attributes I had gifted Peyton Palmer with eroded in a cloud of disillusionment. I felt cheated. Bitter. Empty.

I sat on a hill overlooking the lake trying to make sense of what would probably never make sense at all. People were complex. Hard to read. Like one of those

Gump chocolates. You never knew what was on the inside by judging what you saw on the outside. Which made life a hell of a crapshoot.

Townsend sat down beside me, and stretched out his long legs. "You look miles away. What's going on inside that ace cub reporter brain of yours?"

"Is anyone really who they seem to be, do you think?" I asked. "Or is everyone just wearing a cyborg-type mask that performs suitable facial expressions and appropriate responses for all occasions?"

"What are you trying to say, Tressa?" Townsend shifted his weight subtly.

"I guess what I'm wondering is where can I find one honest man?"

Townsend cleared his throat, and gently took my injured hand in his. "You're looking at one, Calamity. I'm a man of my word."

I gave him a *yeah, right* look.

"Aren't you the same guy who was working undercover with a certain deputy on this case all along, but chose to keep that from me? And aren't you the same person who made everyone believe you were performing under-the-covers moves with a certain widow? Sorry, but I need proof you are who you claim to be."

A dark eyebrow across from me went north. "Proof, huh?" he said, rubbing his chin.

I nodded.

Townsend suddenly reached out and pulled me into his arms, and gave me a long, searching, lingering kiss. He pulled away and looked into my face. "Does that help my case?" he asked.

I sighed, mostly because of the kiss, but also because I still wasn't sure of anything where this man was concerned.

"I need tangible proof," I said. "Proof that can be seen, felt, and touched. You know. Verifiable."

Townsend looked at me. "You're sounding more and more like a journalist every day," he said and stood. "Well, how's this for tangible, Ms. Ace Cub Reporter?"

Before I could respond, Ranger Rick Townsend had dropped his drawers. On one perfectly sculpted cheek was a dainty but tasteful raccoon tattoo. He grinned down at me. "I believe you wanted proof that could be seen, felt, and touched," he said with a wicked gleam in his eye. "Go ahead. Touch it!"

I stared at the tattoo and then at the audacious fellow sporting it. I screamed, jumped to my feet and ran for the hills—but not before making very certain, beyond all reasonable doubt, that the good ranger had, indeed, picked the perfect spot.

Hey, my mama didn't raise no fools.

BAYPORT-BLUE POINT PUBLIC LIBRARY
3 0613 00173 4833